EMPTY HEAVEN

Also by Freddie Kölsch

Now, Conjurers

EMPTY HEAVEN

FREDDIE KÖLSCH

UNION
SQUARE
& CO.

NEW YORK

UNION SQUARE & CO.

NEW YORK

UNION SQUARE & CO. and the distinctive Union Square & Co. logo
are trademarks of Sterling Publishing Co., Inc.

Union Square & Co., LLC, is a subsidiary of Sterling Publishing Co., Inc.

ISBN 978-1-4549-5162-9 (hardcover)
ISBN 978-1-4549-5164-3 (ebook)
ISBN 978-1-4549-5163-6 (paperback)

Library of Congress Control Number: 2024042015

For information about custom editions, special sales, and premium purchases,
please contact specialsales@unionsquareandco.com.

Printed in China

2   4   6   8   10   9   7   5   3   1

unionsquareandco.com

Cover design by Liam Donnelly
Interior design by Kevin Ullrich

For the girl who died on Christmas Day—
I love you more than words can say.

PART ONE

THE BANQUET OF THE NEEDLE

CHAPTER ONE

Sunday, August 27—Saturday, October 28, 2000

If you picture it like a diorama, or one of those scale-model villages, we were just two girls in the center of a tiny town surrounded by sunflower fields. The road where we met was Good Earth Way, the main artery of the little Massachusetts village where I spent my summers. Beyond the village and the sunflower fields were the woods, and—if you zoomed far out enough on the diorama—one particularly large body of water. The sky was dotted with high-up clouds like falling feathers.

The school year (senior, finally) beckoned from the beginning of September. I'd already been given my traditional end-of-vacation send-off by my three best friends the night before, because Senovak was a hideously early riser, but KJ had asked me to stop by K-Family Pizza when we drove out.

It was too early for her by a long mile, but she had been waiting outside her family's pizza place to say goodbye to me one more time under the pretext of giving me a mix CD. She could've given it to me the previous evening when we'd all stayed up late out in the orchards that surrounded Jasper's house, but she had held off until it was just the two of us.

I remember this part with the clarity that memories take on before a huge disaster: KJ seeing me. Stubbing out her cigarette with the economy of motion that always made her seem graceful and a little showy when she actually *did* something. Standing in the early sunlight with the little wispy clouds way up above her. When I reached her, she'd taken my left hand like she was going to hold it, and that was an unusual enough move on her part that my heart had started pounding. But instead of putting her hand in mine, she pressed on my fingers until they opened. With her other hand, she pulled out the promised CD, ensconced in a clear plastic case, from one of the cargo pockets on her stupid khaki skirt.

"This one is incredible, I promise," KJ said, her tone imbued with her usual airy bravado. "Possibly the greatest CD ever mixed by human hands. You're totally going to love it."

Her hands shook slightly when she placed the CD into mine. Her sunglasses were hiding her eyes, making her expression unreadable as usual, and after she handed off my gift she leaned against one of the flower boxes like she was the chillest person who ever lived. But I could see that she was nervous.

"I doubt I'm going to *love* it," I said, falling back on my habit of giving her shit even as I wrapped my fingers around the CD case. My pulse was ticking along quickly, and my face was hot, but I thought I seemed relaxed. Normal. We made each other mix CDs regularly, and when I got home I always listened to the songs she picked for me on endless repeat, looking for hidden meanings. "Not if it has Alice in Chains on it again."

"God. You put *one* song about Vietnam on a mix for a girl and she never lets you forget it." KJ was smiling, but her tone told me things her words didn't. There was a thread of uncertainty in it.

The case was light in my hand, light for something that felt so important to me. On the CD itself, in green Sharpie, she'd written *for the loneliest girl in new york city*, all lowercase in her messy cursive. There was a smudge mark on the end of *city*. Underneath that, she'd drawn the tiniest little heart.

"I really doubt you're actually the loneliest person in New York," KJ said, and did the thing she sometimes does when she's nervous or embarrassed where she scrubs at the back of her neck with one hand. "I was trying to be funny, because of how you have this, like, Heideggerian parlance going on, where you say we're all going to *ultimately die alone*, which seems like a bold assertion for someone who's never died or seen another person die, but then it felt stupid and I tried to wipe it off. But it was too late—"

"It's really more of a broad pessimism, like Schopenhauer or something," I said, which pulled an actual laugh out of KJ. I imagined she was rolling her eyes behind her sunglasses.

I didn't say *I actually have seen someone die*, because it felt like that would derail our conversation. And also because nobody knew that. The few people who were aware of my Bad Day back in 1996 all thought I'd found that person dead to begin with.

"Great. Another philosopher to learn about. I didn't even know who the fuck Heidegger was until Jasper told me," KJ said, putting her hand on top of my hand, still holding the CD case. I didn't even laugh. Didn't smile. All of my thoughts were concentrated on her fingers brushing the back of mine.

"Uh. So. I'm going to miss you, Darian," KJ said, calling me by my full name instead of D, which was a departure for her. It made what she said sound serious.

Then she pushed her sunglasses up on her head (another departure for her), revealing the entirety of her face. Dark eyes and dilated pupils. The eye contact was so surprising that I almost forgot about the hand thing.

"Yeah. I hate leaving," I said. "I mean all of you. But you the most."

I seemed flat, so flat. If it sounds like I'm not a person who gives a lot away, well, I'm really not. I had kept myself safe from these feelings for so long that I felt more like an alien than a normal person with a crush.

This was me *trying*, desperately—with the person I cared about more than anything—to push past my awkwardness and make it sound as real as it felt. But I sucked at it, honestly. I think a less confident person or less perceptive person would have been discouraged. But KJ, nervous as she was, had this bottomless, confident wellspring of *her*-ness that she could always tap into. She kept going.

"It gets harder every year. I was thinking next summer we could . . . do something," KJ said.

"Like what?"

"See a movie?" KJ asked, as if we hadn't seen a hundred movies together. But I knew what she meant, the essential difference of what she meant.

I nodded. "Yeah. *Yes*. Do I sound weird? I'd really like that, that . . . sounds good. Fun."

"You always sound weird," KJ said. But her smile widened, reached up to her dark eyes with the heavy lashes, crinkling them up. "But I know what you feel. I see you."

"Oh," I said, faintly. I could hear my heartbeat in my ears. "Good."

For a second it seemed like KJ was leaning toward me, and I couldn't look away from her.

Then Senovak rolled down the window on the Lincoln and said something like *We can leave any day now, Darian,* and whatever KJ had been about to do next was lost. He'd probably seen that we were about to kiss—his eagle eyes missed nothing—and interrupted at that exact moment on purpose.

I was so quiet on the drive back to the city that Senovak got worried about me, and stopped off to get us milkshakes at a place in Connecticut called The Wagon Wheel. But I wasn't just quiet because I was sad about leaving. I didn't even think to be mad at him for messing up my moment with KJ. All I could think of as I turned in the car—as I waved goodbye and she waved back and I watched her long, lean silhouette getting smaller and smaller in the back window, and for all the hours after as we drove home— was that I wanted to go back. I was finally ready to try and do this.

I was desperate to know what would have happened next, if I was different. More inviting. Less reserved. What would have happened next if we'd had a minute more. At home in Manhattan, I listened to her CD. Touched the green inscription, complete with one smudge on the second *y* from where she'd put her fingers on it before it dried.

to the loneliest girl in new york city
♥

I thought about KJ while the ghost of Dexter watched me from outside my bedroom doorway, in shadow except for the glint of his teeth and the shine on his glasses. I thought about her when I woke up from nightmares of Christmastime in New York. I thought about how long I'd felt this way. Basically the entirety of my adolescence. Our years of looks, our exchanges of music, our long conversations at night when Alex and even Jasper had crapped out for the evening. Always waiting to see her again. Talking close. Sitting out on the town common while the sky got lighter and the ancient stars vanished into the dawn. The gestures that never quite translated to touching.

It was that final exchange—the forward sway of her body, the things she didn't fully say—that drove me to plan my surprise visit. And so, two months later, after begging my dad and taking time off from school and getting Senovak to ferry me all the way back up to Massachusetts, I returned to my summer home, unannounced (not even a whisper of warning over AIM), to spend my very first Harvest Hallow there. I had never visited Kesuquosh during the school year before. When we rolled into the little town center the sky was white-gray with cloud cover and the leaves on the trees were brilliant sunset colors, and I saw KJ standing in almost the exact same spot where I'd left her back at the end of August.

Perfect. Like kismet or a nice turn of the karmic wheel, both things I didn't believe in. But I believed in KJ, as stupid as that sounds. I did. And when I got out of the car, I thought we would be a couple by the end of the weekend. I thought my life was going to be more than just hanging on to normalcy by my fingernails. Something romantic. Something *good*.

Hope held me upright, hope made my throat tight, hope wrapped around my neck like a windblown scarf. The only worries in my mind were about how I would navigate this new thing between us.

I had never understood what was wrong with Kesuquosh, you see. The place had a way of making you look past all of that, making you incurious about the strangeness. I didn't know what was hidden in the sunflower fields and in the hearts of the people around me. I didn't know to be afraid of what was coming.

By midnight the KJ I loved would be gone. Obliterated by a monster in service of a false utopia. I had eight hours left with her on that October afternoon. Eight hours before she vanished into a swirl of darkness, and of redness, and was reborn as something . . . new.

CHAPTER TWO

Saturday, October 28, 2000

On the day of my surprise return, when I saw KJ outside K-Family Pizza, she was alone. I was excited to see Jasper and Alex, too, but I was glad they weren't there at that exact second. It made it feel as if all the time that had passed since our goodbye had just been a quick pause of reality. KJ was cleaning off the tables outside the restaurant with her headphones and sunglasses on and her mouth in the half smile it always seemed to settle into when she wasn't talking. I was so excited to see her that I asked Senovak to stop the car and let me out right there.

"Will you go to the cottage without me? I'll walk over later," I said.

"Okay. You have your cell phone with you?" Senovak asked. Dan Senovak (my dad's driver, but also like . . . a nanny, a personal assistant, my other parent) tended toward being overprotective. And nosy. His voice had the tone of parental concern that I had heard from him since I was a little kid, but then again he was paid to care.

"Obviously," I said, and threw myself out of the dark green Lincoln Town Car (my father's signature car, because Edward Arden

10

was the kind of guy who had a signature car) in my excitement. Then I ran up behind KJ as stealthily as I could, and tapped her on the shoulder.

She rounded on me, and I was struck, like I usually was, by her lanky grace, her modelesque collection of attributes. By how attracted I was to all of the component things that made up this one person. KJ and her twin brother, Alex, favored their Japanese dad in terms of features—Ken Kobayashi was fairly modelesque himself—but they both had the same dark messy hair as their mom, Rita, who told me she was Greek. Alex always wore his hair long, and KJ was in the process of growing hers out. Her longest waves almost reached her upturned lips, and when she turned toward me I saw that she'd tucked her hair back behind her ears, probably to allow for the headphones she was wearing.

KJ usually had her sunglasses on, and so over the course of multiple summers I'd learned to watch her mouth. When she turned around at my touch, she looked a little annoyed, like she thought it was one of her siblings bugging her as she did her chores—and then she realized it was me, and she was shocked. I saw the shock jerk up the corners of her lip.

She knocked her sunglasses up onto her head, revealing her lovely dark-gray eyes, perpetually dilated pupils . . . and an expression that turned from surprise to horror.

Horror. *Horror.*

KJ looked at me like I'd walked into a funeral and set the coffin on fire. She pulled off her headphones with unsteady movements. I nearly recoiled from the awful look on her face. But she leaned over me. Put her hands on my upper arms—and KJ usually wasn't physical with me at all, which is why even the prospect of hand-holding

11

eight weeks earlier had been enough to get my heart pounding. Mostly she acted as if I had a force field around me, like her hands would glance off me if she even tried to touch. "D-Darian? D, what are you . . . why . . . you're here? Why are you here right now?" KJ asked, and her hands kind of reflexively gripped my arms. I almost felt like she was going to shake me or something.

"Um," I said, "I came for the Harvest Hallow? I wanted to—"

Surprise you, I was going to say. *I wanted to surprise you.*

But now I felt insane. I felt like I'd gravely misconstrued everything that came before. Maybe I'd misconstrued it so badly that even the friendship was in doubt. Why would a friend look at you like that when you surprised them? Like . . . like it made them sick? Like they were ill at the very idea of you being there?

"You came for the Harvest Hallow?" KJ repeated. Her hands clenched around my upper arms even harder.

"Yeah, I thought it would be fun," I said, wincing. I felt panicked, reflecting the inexplicable fear that KJ was directing at me. "KJ, you're hurting me."

"Oh," KJ said, and then I think what I'd said finally sunk in, because she dropped her hold on me as if she had been burned. She looked . . . like she'd just watched a bomb detonate. Stunned.

"Sorry," she said, taking a few steps back, until she bumped up against one of the flower boxes behind her.

"Um," I said, "what the hell is wrong?"

It wasn't just that she'd exploded all my fantasies about a romantic reunion. She actually seemed so *afraid*.

"Sorry," KJ said again. "Sorry, D. You just . . . surprised me. Are you okay? I didn't mean to—to *hurt* you, oh fuck—"

"I'm fine. Should I not have come?" I asked, in a brisk tone that I hoped covered up my real feelings. What I actually wanted to say was *Why aren't you happy to see me?* in the most pathetic way possible. And then maybe curl up into a ball and cry.

KJ looked at me for a second, eyes tracking up and down my face like there were answers to be had. Then she seemed to physically compose herself, put together all the nonchalant pieces that made her KJ, like she was building a wall. Her shoulders relaxed. Her easy smile came back.

"Nah. It will be fine," KJ said, and the residual discomfort around her vanished. She was chill-to-the-bone again. Positively refrigerated. "Should be fine. You just surprised me, is all."

"No way," I said. "That wasn't only surprise, KJ—"

"Darian!" someone called, from a little way off. "Oh man, what are you doing here?"

Alex's voice. I looked away from KJ for a second and saw her twin brother coming around the side of the pizza place, followed by Jasper.

Actually, I saw Jasper's purple mohawk first. Then his plaid pants—the chains on them caught the cloudy light like a prism—and then Alex, resplendent in a hideous all-tie-dyed outfit. Alex was eating a slice of pepperoni off a gray recycled-material plate, and Jasper was eating . . . a can of Sprite, which was basically the only vegan option at K-Family Pizza besides plain chopped iceberg lettuce and French fries. Alex looked absolutely delighted to see me, in the unfeigned, sincere way that he always had about him. His narrow face split into a grin, and he jogged over to me with his long hair flying behind him.

And Jasper looked . . . almost as freaked-out as KJ. He recovered fast—but not so quickly that I didn't see him flinch. He definitely flinched. Then he kind of shook his head, and set his Sprite can down on the edge of a planter filled with red chrysanthemums.

"Darian, where the fuck did *you* manifest from?" he asked.

His tone was belligerent, but that actually didn't raise any more alarms for me. Jasper's tone was always belligerent.

"Ed let me take a long weekend off from school. I begged him. I said that the Harvest Hallow festival was culturally relevant to me, since my mom's family was from here," I said, feeling decidedly insecure and awkward and uncomfortable and like my visit was the shittiest idea in a lifetime of shitty ideas. But I tried to sound normal.

"The *Great* Harvest Hallow," Jasper corrected automatically. "You . . . *wanted* to come to this?"

"Yes," I said. My voice sounded very small. "I . . . thought it would be cool?"

"Oh, man. This is awesome. I'm so glad to see you," Alex said, and held his arms out to be hugged.

"Thanks," I said, giving him a squeeze. Behind him, I saw Jasper and KJ exchange some kind of loaded look before KJ put her sunglasses back on.

"You like my tie-dye?" Alex asked, utterly unaware of how awkward everything was.

"Yeah. Wow. Tie-dyed sweatshirt *and* tie-dyed sweatpants?" I said. "Rock on, earth child."

"So dope, right? I did them myself," Alex said, looking down at his modified Phish sweatshirt with some pride. "I'm not as good as Aunt Judy yet, but like . . . she knows all the advanced folding techniques."

KJ, who basically had the exact fashion sense of Fred Durst (if Fred Durst were into floor-length khaki cargo *skirts* instead of *almost* floor-length khaki cargo *shorts*, colorblind, and had a trademark bucket hat), had the audacity to snort. She seemed to have recovered from her earlier shock. She touched me on the shoulder.

"Darian. Don't encourage the tie-dye shit. He's sooooo pleased with himself for a person who looks like—like a walking Grateful Dead concert," KJ said.

"You do look like you smell bad, Al," Jasper said. He sounded normal, too.

"Hey!" Alex said. "I smell excellent!"

"That's subject to debate," Jasper said.

"You do *not*," KJ said, and made a gagging face at her brother. "You smell like patchouli mixed with armpits."

"My hygiene is actually really good," Alex said. "It's definitely better than yours." Alex was bad at teasing. He was bad at being anything other than painfully sincere, which made him slightly at odds with basically every other teenager alive.

I, as a qualified person who put tasteful dabs of Ralph Lauren Romance on my pulse points every morning, stepped in to defend him. I still felt a little bit like this whole conversation was happening underwater, but I spoke casually enough. "You smell nice, Al. Like the woods."

"Oh shit, I didn't know you'd gone tragically noseblind," Jasper said, raising one eyebrow at me like the world's shortest, punkest Mr. Spock.

"Interesting. In that vein, I didn't know you'd tragically become a fucking bitch," I said.

Then we smirked at each other, and held the expression for point-five seconds before we both laughed. Jasper didn't do hugging, but we bumped fists . . . and just like that, things were okay again. I almost could have convinced myself that I was imagining the earlier weirdness. Except that I could still feel the place on my upper arms where KJ had grabbed me.

"So what have you guys been doing since the last time I was here?" I asked, and Alex started telling me about songs that Army of Dolly (the band the three of them had formed, named after Dolly the cloned sheep) had been working on while I'd been gone.

I wondered, then, if all their anxiousness and awkwardness had something to do with the Harvest Hallow.

Not Halloween, even though it culminated on the same day. The Harvest Hallow was something totally different. Because Kesuquosh was . . . unusual.

The annual Harvest Hallow, which was a legendary bit of New England weirdness—and Good Arcturus, the scarecrow deity and symbol of plenty that Kesuquoshians celebrated during the Hallow—was a thing I would have been fascinated by even if I had never stepped foot in Kesuquosh. Good Arcturus was as firmly lodged into the folklore of the towns around the massive Quabbin Reservoir as the legends of the specter that granted wishes in Stepwood Cemetery, or the Weary Travelers, or Sad Sam, the Quabbin's own Bigfoot. More, even, because he was kept alive and relevant by the inhabitants of this one specific town.

Like, their town hall literally had a big art piece in the main entranceway, done in classic North American folk art style, of

Junie Apostle-Root and Good Arcturus marching through a blocky, dollhouse-looking version of Kesuquosh in the 1700s. The prophet and the god of the religion, respectively. Basically it was a gigantic ugly oil painting, with the perspective all screwy in classic folk art tradition, of a woman walking in front of a scarecrow. But it was antique, framed in gold, and treated like absolutely factual historical documentation by everyone in town. Alex had shown it to me once like I was going to be really reverent. I was very nice about it, even though it was weird. But the strangeness of a whole town taking the scarecrow story seriously enough to commission a painting for the *town hall* in the late 1800s and then keep it on the wall for more than a century was so insane, I loved it.

That extremely odd belief system (and the town that believed it) typically got a full chapter in any book on New England folklore. The whole situation was considered charming, cool, spooky . . . and ultimately benign.

I loved the weirdness and I *did* think it was benign. My mom's family was from Kesuquosh, even though she had died when I was too little to really remember her. Per family tradition, I'd been spending summers at my family's cottage in town since I was born.

But it wasn't until the vacation between eighth and ninth grade that I actually made friends with my trio of townie kids.

After the first summer I spent hanging out with Jasper and KJ and Alex, I realized that for the first time since everything happened, I hadn't seen Dexter *anywhere*.

Not in the back of a crowd. Not seated in the corner of a restaurant. And not by the foot of my bed at night, with nothing but his glasses glinting in the dark, like the eyes of a nocturnal animal.

And I think that I was pretty self-aware, for an almost fourteen year old. I understood that the psychological implications of not seeing Dexter when I spent my first summer with the three Kesuquoshian kids were *good* implications.

In Jasper and Alex and KJ, I had found the best friends I didn't know I was lonely for. I traced the edges of their flaws eagerly, after years of trying and failing to measure up to the rich and beautiful geniuses who populated my exclusive Manhattan private-school world.

And it was good. It was the only time I really felt like myself. Felt okay.

Every August I would go home to New York, Pelham Academy, and what I thought of (unhappily) as the *real world*, where Dexter watched me from every crowd and every night-lit window of every skyscraper. My friendships in Kesuquosh survived the school year on a diet of AIM conversations, the demented contents of care packages constructed by demented minds, and long-distance phone calls. But I knew when their big holiday took place, although I'd never attended it myself.

At some point Alex had stopped talking, and KJ had started. I tuned back in as she was describing her latest (dubious) triumph of entrepreneurship.

"—so then I buy pot from this woman in Rabbitville, right? And then I pad it out a little with oregano from the restaurant. It's total skunk weed, so the stink when it burns covers up the smell of the herb. Of the *kitchen* herb. And then I mark it up and sell it to the rich kids at Cold Falls."

KJ had spent the last year making extra money by getting irresponsible (or just plain gullible) adults to buy her cartons of cigarettes at the Citgo on Route 202 and then driving down to Rabbitville or up to Cold Falls Prep or North Dana to sell smokes to other high schoolers at extreme markups. Now, evidently—in the, like, eight weeks since I'd last been in Kesuquosh—she'd graduated to selling weed.

"Hmm," I said. "That doesn't sound like it would . . . work."

"It works," KJ said, putting a hand to her heart like I had wounded her. Now that she was discussing one of her grifts, she seemed so in her element that it was even easier for me to tell myself she hadn't been afraid a few minutes earlier. I ignored the phantom feeling of her fingers on my arms. "I've never had a single complaint about my product. The lack of faith in you, D. When you of all people should know that rich kids"—here she looked me up and down pointedly—"have no idea what good marijuana looks like."

"That may be true out here," I countered. "But in the city they definitely know. This con only works on hicks."

"Yeah, you're a dumbass who sells to dumbasses, KJ," Jasper said. He dug a pack of cloves (Djarum Black, as always) out of the ultra-tight back pocket of his plaid pants and lit one with a flourish. "An ouroboros of idiot capitalism."

"*Ouroboros*," Alex said through a mouthful of pizza. "I love that word."

"I made four hundred dollars profit this month!" KJ said.

"Incredible. Who's the rich kid now?" I asked.

Did KJ need extra money? No. Like everyone else in Kesuquosh, her folks were financially comfortable. I kind of thought that KJ grifted for the sheer *love* of it.

She did not take after anybody else in her family. I knew them all, and KJ was like some changeling, the daughter of an amoral used-car salesman who had been dumped on the Kobayashi-Jenetopolous household. She liked to, um, embellish. I guessed that at least the part about the oregano was a lie, if not the whole operation.

I know these are legitimate behavioral issues that I am describing, so it might seem strange when I say that all of the grifting and lying was part of why I liked her so much. I . . . it was . . . she was complex. Interesting. Even more interesting than she was beautiful, and she was *really* beautiful.

"You made that money, sure," Alex said. "But, like . . . you're not factoring in the cost of gas. Don't you have to fill up the PDA every third time you do that drive?" PDA was not, in this case, short for *Public Display of Affection.* Instead it meant *Pizza Delivery Automobile,* which was what the Kobayashi twins called their family's Chevy Tahoe. It had a little light-up car topper with a pizza slice on it and everything.

"My own flesh betraying me, too? So uncool how nobody appreciates my motivation," KJ said.

"Because you're a dumbass, like I said," Jasper told her, and then turned to me. "*You* need to listen to our new set. I want constructive feedback."

Jasper actually wrote zero of the music for Army of Dolly, but, like every lead singer everywhere, he thought he was in charge.

"Lead on, maestro," I said, and he crushed his Sprite can and stuffed it into the recycling bin before heading down the road. Alex ditched his pizza remnants, KJ put her cleaning stuff back inside, and we all followed Jasper, who always walked like he had a really urgent appointment. I caught the sweet smell of his clove cigarette as it streamed past me in the crisp air. It was a perfect fall smell.

Alex managed to catch up with him, and I watched the two of them as they walked. They were opposites, visually. Jasper was short and "teen heartthrob" looking and had an angelic face . . . qualities that his DIY punk look and surly expression couldn't totally hide. Whenever he and the twins went anywhere together (which was all the time), they kind of looked like two unmuscular bodyguards working for a very alternative teen idol. Or two wiry mooks following around a diminutive crime boss.

As we marched down Good Earth Way toward the Kobayashi's "art studio," which was really an embellished shed behind their house where the family members pursued their various hobbies, I looked sideways at KJ, studying her for further signs of unease. I couldn't see anything out of the ordinary in the way that she was acting now.

"We're really going to blow you away with the new stuff," KJ said, inclining her head sideways at me and then grinning her wide grin. "I promise."

"I'll believe that when I hear it," I said, smiling in return. No way to read her eyes. I felt like we were miles away from finishing our *going to a movie together* conversation now, and I tried to push back my sadness about that.

"*Pfft.* You're a snob, such a huge snob," KJ said.

"Or I just know more about music than you."

"Yeahhh . . . ," KJ allowed. "But I know how much I don't know. Which is the foundation of wisdom. So who really knows the most here?"

"Still me, obviously," I said, laughing when KJ huffed and threw her hands up dramatically.

I once had—before everything that happened with Dexter—a bright future in music.

I was a skilled piano player, and I'm not trying to brag. It was the one thing I was actually *really* honestly good at. I'd composed my own songs from like age eight onward. I'd been the kind of kid adults paid attention to, a kid with a decent shot at going to Juilliard or Berklee College of Music. I had written compositions to express my feelings the way other kids wrote angsty poetry.

I always had an ear for music. And I recognized a similar skill level in Jasper. He had a depth of talent that reminded me of my own (never-to-be-realized) potential.

Jasper couldn't even read music. But his *voice*. It was astonishing. He had perfect pitch. He could project like a megaphone. And his voice wasn't characterless, either, like so many people who could sing exceptionally well. It was always kind of . . . Jasper-like. A cathedral bell, but sarcastic-sounding.

Not that he wanted to use it for anything but guttural screaming. He might have sung in a church choir (if the hypothetical church didn't spontaneously burst into flames when he stepped into it), but Kesuquosh was pointedly devoid of any houses of worship, except for one crumbling church foundation from more than two hundred years ago, out at the edge of a field between the Quabbin and the sprawling acreage of Plum Farms.

So Jasper took all his musical energy and screamed it into their band. Army of Dolly was kind of a hilarious mash of influences. Jasper liked punk, Alex was into jam bands, and KJ . . . KJ liked alt rock and grunge. A lot. Her AIM screen name was xXMellonCollieGuitaristXx.

So what they had was a three-person band with a lead singer who couldn't read music but knew how to play the bass (poorly) and used his golden voice for shouting; a hippie drummer-slash-percussion player; and a guitarist who was obsessed with the vocal stylings of Billy Corgan.

And . . . it actually worked. It was even pretty excellent. But sometimes their songs needed a little massaging, and I spent time listening to their stuff and giving them notes for improvements. For a while, back in the beginning of high school, Jasper had been bugging me about actually *joining* the band. But eventually KJ made him stop. It was like she could sense that there was more to my refusal to play music than I was giving away.

In the Kobayashi-Jenetopolous family studio, I sat on the yellow velvet love seat adjacent to the easel where the oldest Jenetopolous sibling, Isabella, did her watercolors, and directly across from the long wooden table where their mom did her crafts (Rita did everything from using the table saw to felting, making dollhouses and dolls—she was artistically multitalented), while red and orange leaves blew in through the open doors on little gusts of wind. On the makeshift stage in the far corner Jasper screamed and Alex noodled and KJ made guitar playing look about as cool as humanly possible.

Jasper had exaggerated when he said they had a whole new set—it was only four songs—but I enjoyed it anyway.

"Rank them," Jasper commanded when they were done.

"Um, the best one was 'Vivid Oblivion.' You need to fix the bridge, it's way too long, *Alex*. But the whole thing was really good," I said.

"YES," Alex said. "I knew it was solid. I did write that one, how could you tell?"

"Because the bridge was way too long," I said.

"Oh, right," Alex said, not looking too upset about it.

"And also because it's about taking mushrooms," I added.

"Which Alex has never done," KJ said, putting down her guitar to light a Newport 100 with a book of Citgo matches. (She had definitely fallen into the trap of sampling her own merchandise with her cigarette-reselling scheme.)

"Never done *yet*," Alex said mellowly. "My experience of time and space flows like a river. I wade in and wade out and draw inspiration from past and future."

"You are the world's *worst person*," KJ said. "Rancid as fuck!"

"Guys?"

Our conversation was cut short by Rita Jenetopolous, Alex and KJ's mom, coming in through the open double doors of the studio. She brought the smell of pizza with her and looked pretty as usual, always seeming slightly too young to have kids as old as she did, her curly hair tied back and a smudge of flour on her cheek.

"What's up, Ma," KJ said, crushing out her cigarette on the unfinished floor.

"Are you smoking in here? Oh my god. I told you not to smoke in here. The neighbors just got here, guys. It's time to start getting ready—Darian! I didn't know you were here!"

"Hey, Rita," I said, getting up from the love seat.

"I already *told* you she was visiting," KJ said.

"No you didn't," Alex clarified. "She's lying, Mom. Darian surprised us. She's coming to the Banquet tonight."

"Kahie, why do you just make things up like that—"

"I don't, Ma," KJ said. (This was an insane lie, the biggest lie known to humankind.) "And don't call me Kahie. It's KJ."

"You keep on lying," Jasper said, giving KJ a double thumbs-up. "Gotta stay true to yourself. Maintain a clear head. Especially now."

"You got it, boss," KJ said, thumbing-up back at him.

Rita sighed, visibly gave up, and came over to hug me. "Your dad knows you're here, right?"

"Yes, ma'am. I got permission from my school."

"That's *wonderful*," Rita said. Her face was open and happy, her dark eyes (with dilated pupils, of course) luminous. "It's such an important holiday for us. This year, especially. I am so glad you're coming. The family connection—well. It will be so nice to have you here."

I let myself be held in Rita's comforting arms (Senovak and my dad were not big on hugging) and glanced over her floury shoulder just long enough to see Jasper look . . . concerned.

Jasper's eyes never did the neat trick of everyone else's in Kesuquosh—his irises contracted and expanded like normal, turning his pupils to pinpricks in bright light—and right now his baby-blue gaze darted around with distinct unhappiness.

"It's because he can't hear the Lord of the Field," KJ told me once, when I commented on it. "He fell out of the trapdoor of his parents' attic as a kid, got a concussion and probably, like, a brain injury or something. And he never could hear the voice of Good Arcturus after that."

I believed that about as much as I believed every other obvious lie that KJ told (not one iota) and kind of dismissed the whole thing. I had never, for example, felt bold enough to ask Rita or any of the other adults in town, *Why are your eyes so strange? Is it something in the water?* and so it became a charmingly weird mystery, like so many other charmingly weird things about Kesuquosh.

There were a lot of strange things I didn't think about too closely when it came to Kesuquosh, a village full of people who never seemed to argue, driving cars that never honked at each other in the streets. A village full of people who didn't ever fight over politics or get impatient waiting in line.

And I didn't notice myself *not questioning* those things, not until later.

"You don't *have* to come to the Hallow, though," Jasper said abruptly. "Even though your aunt . . . was from here. It will be boring."

"I'm dying to go," I said truthfully. I wasn't sure why he'd mentioned my aunt Blanche, who had died when she was a child, when actually my mom's whole side of the family had been Kesuquoshians. But I disregarded it. I wanted to get up close and personal with the weirdness.

"Wonderful. Why don't you go home and change, sweetheart," Rita said. "Wear something red, if you can. You meet us back here before we start the Banquet at about quarter of nine. Okay?"

"Okay," I said, kind of baffled by my dismissal from our hangout. But I knew that Kesuquoshians were bizarre about their religion. "See you guys later."

"Bye, D," KJ said, and Alex waved. Jasper didn't answer.

It was almost five. I picked my way down the street to my family's summer cottage as the sun fell below the rim of the horizon, admiring the round lanterns and the dried bundles of sunflowers and calico corn and the red-painted scarecrows that decorated Good Earth Way: none of it precisely *Halloween* decorations, but all of it cooler and more evocative than any plastic skeletons or foam board gravestones ever could be.

A cool breeze moved the leaves on the street. The sides of the road were jammed with cars, like everyone from Kesuquosh had come home for the weekend. It was even busier than during the height of summer, when rich people used the village as a scenic getaway. The Fieldstone Inn's parking lot was overflowing. Windows glowed with orange light against the darkening sky. The flat clouds of the day were breaking up as night crawled in, and the moon cast a thin smile down over everything.

I saw car doors flung open and the little old houses that lined the street opening in turn, heard music and laughter coming from inside of warm homes.

I was already forgetting . . . *actively* forgetting. Reinterpreting my initial encounter with KJ. Her fear. How powerful her fear had been, before she put it away.

I decided that the frozen anxiety I thought I had seen in KJ . . . and Jasper . . . was just garden-variety surprise.

In case you can't tell, I am extremely adept at bullshitting myself.

Everything is good was the bullshit I was selling to my own brain in those initial hours after I surprised them. It was good for me, because I got melancholy in the fall, when the days grew shorter and darker, to be in my favorite place with my favorite people. And it was normal. There was no weirdness.

It was a smart move to come here, I thought. Here, with KJ and Alex and Jasper, far away from my dad's high-profile existence and the pressures of acting out a Well-Adjusted Girl With No Problems life, I felt like myself—my *truest* self—all the time.

I should have heeded the unspoken warning in the actions of the only girl I'd ever loved.

I *should* have. But I wanted to belong there, to be accepted, to be a part of it. To escape my life. I wanted it more than anything. So I ignored the little voice in the back of my mind, whispering concerns.

I carried on walking home, feeling good enough, after a few minutes, to whistle a piece I had been working on in my mind. Not on paper. I never actually wrote down my compositions anymore. But this one was fully in my head, and so I whistled it through the chilly streets as the Banquet of the Needle drew closer.

CHAPTER THREE

Saturday, October 28, 2000

By the time I was born, my mom's family had basically already ceased to exist. Blake Sabine's parents died when she was barely eighteen, and her older sister, Blanche, had died when she was eight and Blake was only five.

Blake had been on the verge of a pretty promising career in modeling, supposedly—but instead she married Edward and had a daughter (Darian Sabine Arden, a.k.a. me, born on Christmas Day 1983), and stopped working because she wanted to stay home with her baby.

Blake fell and/or jumped in front of a subway train on October 31, 1985—when I wasn't even two years old—and nobody could ever really determine whether it was a suicide or not. Edward had been using Senovak as a proxy to overprotect my every move ever since. With limited success.

I didn't remember my mom. I tried not to think about her too much—not to let myself be haunted by the ambiguity of her death. I *tried* . . . but I looked for her sometimes, sifting through hieroglyphic old stories and photos. Bits of my dad's love for her hung around like museum artifacts, and the biggest one was the house in Kesuquosh.

It was Number 19: an old white house with gingerbread trim. Blake had grown up there. She held on to it, even after her move to NYC to "make it big," and it had become our vacation home. The back half of the house was mostly porch, glassed in for all seasons, jutting out over the river that flowed away from the Quabbin Reservoir. The New England view from that porch was so picturesque, you could choke on it.

With little more than four hours to go until the Harvest Hallow, I blew in through the door in a swirl of gold birch leaves, threw my bag down on the old floral sofa in the living room, and switched the six-disc CD player from Crosby, Stills, Nash & Young to Poe. "Angry Johnny" thrummed through the house, and I hummed along.

"Hey! I was listening to that!" Senovak called from the kitchen.

"You shouldn't admit things like that!" I called back. Through the shelves that separated the living room from the kitchen, I could see Senovak shaking his head. He was faced away from me over the stove, definitely making lackluster pasta.

"I can't do this 'Johnny' song again, it has to stop," Senovak muttered, loud enough for me to hear. I laughed and sang along dramatically, just to be annoying.

Senovak had a fire going in the living room fireplace, and it gave the space a cheerful glow. I unzipped my suitcase by firelight and contemplated the contents, looking for red clothing.

"I thought we'd do dinner together before they start up the little pagan festival thing," Senovak said.

"Sounds good . . . It's not a pagan festival, though. They made it up, like, a few centuries ago. The town, I mean. Townsfolk or whatever."

I didn't have a large selection of clothing packed—I'm a big believer in having a few really nice designer pieces, which I *know* sounds snobby but whatever—and what I did have was mostly plaid and green and blue and gray, what KJ called "Hollywood Schoolgirl."

I pulled a majority-red plaid skirt out of my suitcase. A red sweatshirt that I'd brought as part of my pajamas was literally my only color-coded shirt option.

"Pagan doesn't mean 'ancient,'" Senovak said. "It means something *niche*, religious beliefs besides the main world religions."

"Oh. Okay, then it's *definitely* pagan," I conceded. I dumped my selected outfit on the back of a chair and went into the kitchen.

"Did you have a nice time with your friends?"

"Life-alteringly good," I said, taking a seat. "Amazing. Perfect. Grand."

"Are they well? Enjoying senior year? How were the boys? How was the girl?" Senovak asked. His usually neutral voice got all bitchy and icy when he said "the girl." He didn't like KJ, because she was a slimy slippery liar, and had lied to Senovak (truly an almost idiotic act of bravado) about multiple inconsequential things, including her age, her birthday, the fact that she and Alex were twins, and the *name* of her family's business. Which he could literally drive down the road and check.

He *did* acknowledge the fact that she was a girl, which was a thing some other, lesser grown-ups would have failed at. But he disliked her anyway.

"Yeah, that's what I asked them," I said. "I asked them, *Are you well, kiddos? Are you enjoying senior year?* I went full Grandpa with my conversation."

"Fabulous," Senovak said, ignoring my sarcasm. "And how is my dear Professor Plum?"

Senovak actually liked Jasper a lot, making him possibly the only adult who ever had. "I was an angry adolescent trapped in a small town once, too," Senovak said, when I asked him once why he was being so (suspiciously) nice. "His little musical lectures are tedious, though. I swear to god that teenagers think they invented the Ramones. You're not the first people to ever be young, you know."

Senovak seemed generally okay with Alex, too, even though he called him "the pothead" and asked me if I was stoned, like, every other time I came back from the Kobayashis' house. It was only KJ who pissed him off. You couldn't win them all, and I was aware that KJ was kind of a hard sell when it came to adult approval.

"Jas is good. They're all doing fine, actually," I said. And then, thinking of the fear on KJ's face, and the tension Jasper had exuded when I surprised them, I rubbed my upper arms and asked, "Have you ever been to one of these Harvest Hallow things?"

"Oh yes," Senovak said, surprising me.

"Yeah?"

"I went with your parents the first year I worked for them. Your mother used to come back each year for it." Senovak spooned limp ziti and jar sauce into two bowls. "Your old man told me I wouldn't want to miss it . . . and he was right."

"Why?" I asked.

"Because it was weird as hell. I felt like I was in *The Wicker Man* or something," Senovak said. He picked up a cup of tea that had been steeping, reconsidered, dug through the cabinets, and came up with a dusty bottle of gin and a dusty jar of honey, made the world's grossest-looking hot toddy, and sat down across from me at the table. "They call this first night the Banquet, if I remember correctly. So they all wear red sacks and have a big parade to the center of town where they've got baskets of offerings all arranged."

"Offerings?" I said. "That's creepy."

"Not like dead goats or anything. It's all the crops they grow here. They sing over the vegetables and then have another parade where they carry the baskets down through the fields past that abandoned church—it's a mile walk or so. At the end there's a great big bonfire where they toss in all their offerings. To, uh, Mr. Arcularis the scarecrow."

"Good Arcturus," I said. "That sounds fun."

"It is if you're drinking. That was the major reason I enjoyed attending, I think, not that I'd go again. And then only if you're *old* enough to drink," Senovak said, raising his mug. "Which you are not. And you'd better not."

"Oh my *god*," I said. But I felt reassured by the fact that Senovak was being so chill. If he said the Harvest Hallow was no big deal, then it was no big deal.

After dinner I left in my cobbled-together red outfit and walked fifteen minutes back to the center of town. The slim fingernail of a moon shone down from a sky so blue that it was almost violet. The air was cold, and despite my layering I wished I'd brought a coat. But then I got to Good Earth Way, and I forgot the cold and watched everything with fascination.

A crowd was moving down the main street. Everyone I could see was cloaked in red—not *sacks*, like Senovak had said, but actual *cloaks*—long red velvet cloaks that had ornate embroidery on them. A kid about my age passed by with a nod and a smile, holding a ceramic pitcher of something that he was pouring out onto the street at odd intervals. It looked like piss, and for a second I was grossed out. But then a sweet smell wafted up from the street and I realized it was apple cider.

I crossed the road and headed to the Kobayashi-Jenetopolous house, passing a group of six red-robed figures, each one holding a large copper-colored censer that wafted out thick clouds of cinnamon-scented incense. In the backyard, the art studio door was thrown open to the chilly night, and I could hear Jasper talking as I approached.

"It's *so* fucking irresponsible, it's literally *fucked* that you guys would even consider letting her participate," Jasper said, and I stopped short. He sounded angry . . . and scared. Angry was pretty standard for Jasper. Scared, not so much.

"It's a beautiful experience," someone else protested. Alex. "I'm so excited to get to see a Great Hallow. Everyone should—"

"I don't have time to listen to your brainwashed bullshit right now, Al," Jasper snapped. "This is about our friend being involved in a thing that she doesn't *need* to be involved in—"

"He isn't going to pick her, boss," KJ said. I took another step, trying to hear better without giving myself away.

"Are you sure about that?" Jasper asked. "You'd better be sure about that. Because we didn't do a very good job of discouraging her from coming."

KJ sounded firm and totally confident when she answered him. "He wouldn't pick an outsider. You know that. And . . . to fix it, we'll just make sure she doesn't have any of the cake."

"But her *aunt*—"

"Guys," I said, stepping into the doorway. "What the hell is going on right now?"

KJ and Jasper froze. Looking wide-eyed and freaked-out, just like earlier that day.

"They're worried that Good Arcturus is going to pick you to be His next Incorporation," Alex said, smiling. His red cloak had a bunch of sunflowers embroidered on it in yellow.

"No, I'm not," KJ said. An unlit cigarette dangled from her mouth, and while she talked, it threatened to fly off her lower lip in a sloppy way that I thought looked stupid and awesomely roguish at the same time. "You weren't born here and you don't live here. I mean, not all the time. You're just going to be an observer."

"We *hope*," Jasper said, and he seemed so disturbed at the idea that I did the polite thing and acted concerned in response. But I wasn't concerned—now that the cause of the weird energy KJ and Jasper had given off earlier was made clear, I actually felt relieved.

I knew that my friends believed in Good Arcturus. Even Jasper. Even my *mom* had believed it, if what my dad and Senovak said was true.

I had always known that the people in Kesuquosh thought their strange earthbound deity was legit. And . . . as much as a reasonable person could . . . I tried to respect that belief, like how I respected my classmates at Pelham Academy who really believed in the healing power of crystals or the inherent truth in tarot cards or astrology. Or a God.

"I'm not scared of being called on by Good Arcturus," I said, touching KJ's shoulder.

KJ looked at me nakedly (no sunglasses now), and inquiringly.

"Are you sure? You gotta be *sure*, D," KJ said seriously. She reached one hand out, like she was going to touch my face, but stopped short.

"I am *sure*," I said, and flicked the unlit cigarette out of her mouth.

"Hey! You are *such* a bitch!"

"Oh my god, what happened to your Newport?" I asked, all wide-eyed concern, and KJ lightly shoved me. I went with it, falling dramatically onto the yellow couch. There was a moment of sustained eye contact between us that made my heart race.

"Hi," I said, looking up into KJ's dilated eyes.

"Hey," KJ said, leaning down over me. Her cheeks were slightly red. There was a small triumphant voice in my head that said *Oh, she totally does still like you. Look at that face.*

But anything I could've said in response was interrupted by the arrival of Rita, who brought along her husband, Ken, and their eldest and youngest daughters, and a swarm of neighbors, and a ton of twine-wrapped sage. Then everyone was hustled out into the street.

"This one is for you," Rita said, handing me a long bundle of sage, which KJ then lit with her Citgo matches. We all stepped into the road holding smoldering sage sticks.

Jasper was very quiet. He had on one of the red robes, embroidered with stone fruits of some kind (I assumed they were plums, for his family name), but it was undone and fell open over his regular punk wear. His face was paler than normal, the angry tinge of his cheeks faded into nothing. He tapped my shoulder and spoke into my ear.

"Darian," Jasper said.

"Yeah?"

"I know you don't really believe us," Jasper whispered urgently. "I know you never have. He keeps outsiders from believing in him, no matter what they see. But I am telling you, as one reasonably intelligent individual to another, that Good Arcturus is *real*—"

"Jasper," someone called, a woman with a formal-sounding voice that cut through the night. Definitely Mrs. Plum.

"Fuck," Jasper said, looking over his shoulder. Then he turned away completely. "Yes, Mom?"

Jasper's parents, who always seemed stern and too old, appeared a little distance behind the Kobayashi family. Jasper gave me one last searching look, then fell back in line with his folks.

There were literally hundreds of people in the street now, all moving in the direction of the town common, and Good Earth Way had become a riot of smells—cider, smoke, sage, cinnamon—and of voices. About halfway down the street the voices started to unify into one harmonious sound, and a song came from ahead and behind us. I strained to make out individual words:

> *Oh, Lord of the Straw who protects all we love*
> *For health and for happiness outside and in*
> *For cleansing our vaunted good village of sin*
> *We give you another new shield from above*

It was Jasper's voice, audible even from some distance behind our group, that helped me to hear the words best. I was surprised he was participating at all, but his voice was a good guidepost.

"Funky, huh?" KJ asked. In deference to the cold, KJ had swapped out her favorite bucket hat for a purple beanie in the exact same shade as Jasper's hair, with a hand-stitched Soundgarden patch on it, which looked as incongruous with the red velvet cloak as anything possibly could.

"Very *Something Wicked This Way Comes*. You're all the spooky Autumn People," I said.

KJ whistled. "High praise? You've always said you *hated* Ray Bradbury."

"I do," I said, feeling a little queasy about bringing it up at all. It wasn't like anything that had happened was Bradbury's fault. "But . . . he used to be my favorite."

"You gonna tell me about it someday?" KJ asked.

"Sure. Someday," I said. At that moment, in the firelit dark of the October street, I had no intention of *ever* telling KJ about Dexter.

Our group approached the town common, which was a long rectangular area of grass lined with trees and topped off with a big old stone gazebo. I had spent tons of summer afternoons there before, listening to music on KJ's boom box or eating K-Family pizza on a blanket. But tonight as we came through the trees I saw a place that had been totally transformed.

Torches hung with braided calico corn ringed the whole common, just beyond the wall of trees, making the space glow and flicker. Big smoldering cauldrons lined the green, and as we passed everyone dropped their burning sage sticks and incense into the pots, adding to the diffused smell.

Long tables—the cheap particleboard kind used at school functions—were arranged in a sort of squarish spiral that covered the whole area, starting with a huge central table loaded down with local crops. (There was a big old painted sign right on the village line that said KESUQUOSH—HOME OF SQUASH! and they definitely lived up to their slogan: pumpkins were arranged artfully all over the common area.) Decor had clearly been contributed by a lot of the townspeople—I saw a few of the ornate dollhouses that Rita made and sold (mostly to summer tourists) among the pumpkins, tea lights inside their little rooms turning the houses into lanterns.

But the thing that drew my eye was a cake that stretched the entire length of the centermost table. It looked like it was meant to feed more than a thousand people. It was a red velvet cake with white icing drizzled over the top and dripping down the sides, tiered like a wedding cake—but so long that it looked like a scale reproduction of the White House, or something. The other tables were bare of food and covered with thin lace tablecloths. Red taper candles burned in candelabras on each tabletop, dripping wax onto the lace.

"This is *so* cool," I said, taking in the homespun grandeur of it all. People had fallen into a long line and were finding their seats in a deliberate way, first walking left around the feasting table, past the gazebo.

There was something in the gazebo.

I had been so drawn in that I hadn't even looked over there. The gazebo squatted to the left of the banquet table, interrupting the flow of the space, and was covered in sunflowers. The steps were paved with bunches of sunflowers cut at the moment of their fullest bloom. Bundles of hay were piled inside of it . . . with something crouched behind them, dominating the back of the structure. A shape.

I couldn't make out anything more. The sunflowers were stuck into the earth around the gazebo, obscuring the view through the empty windows. People stopped at the gazebo one by one and mounted the stone steps, crushing sunflowers underfoot and stepping inside. Disappearing for a moment and then coming back down the stairs to find their seats.

"Okay, this is great, I'm so excited. This is the best night ever. I'm so happy," KJ said, pushing at her beanie. She reached out and squeezed my hand pretty hard, which was weird. Like I said, she was never touchy with me.

For a minute I was so surprised by the hand-holding that I didn't process the urgency of the gesture. Then my brain caught up, and I realized KJ's hand was clammy. Panic-sweaty. And then I realized something else.

KJ was lying.

KJ, who struggled with the truth on her best days, was not having her *best* day. She was telling herself a string of lies. But . . . it wasn't her normal style of lying. That type of lying was usually casually impulsive and stupid enough that I suspected it was pathological. *This* had purpose and import. There was a reason for it.

"Why are you lying?" I asked.

"Gotta keep a clear head," KJ said, and smiled tightly at me. She kept her hold on my hand. "Feel my real feelings."

"Okayy . . . ," I said, and squeezed her hand back, which drew a slightly less tight smile from her. "If lying is how you feel your feelings, I guess I won't stop you."

"I knew you'd understand," KJ said. I did not understand at all.

"Sure," I said, feeling uneasy.

"This is the best part. I've been waiting my whole life to do this. I'm so glad you're here," KJ said.

More lies. Her hand squeezed mine again, hard enough to be uncomfortable. I wanted to be insulted by the fact that KJ was lying about being happy that I was there, but I was not that thick. KJ was unhappy about me being there *because* she cared about me.

We were rounding the banquet table now, in a long, slow line, and Alex was just ahead of us. A good chunk of the crowd was still singing, but there was a cacophony of other sounds: chairs moving, kids yelling, people talking.

"I'm so excited," Alex called over the din. Torchlight highlighted the curtain of his long dark hair. His lean face was split by a sweet smile.

Alex definitely wasn't lying.

The majority of people around us seemed happy. Almost everyone was having fun . . . though I caught a few glimpses of townies who looked a little flat, like they'd rather be somewhere else, or like they were trying to remember something. Maybe if they'd left the stove on at home. But nobody looked *miserable*.

Except, of course, for Jasper. I turned back and saw him, flanked by his parents. His face was closed off, his eyes totally downcast.

Rita dropped back a little, touching my shoulder. "When you go up to greet Good Arcturus, you can introduce yourself, and ask for something, if you have something you need. I know He'll be happy to meet you, since you're a Sabine by blood. I'm so happy you're here, honey. It's nice to be a part of something, isn't it?"

"Um. Good Arcturus is in the gazebo?" I asked, believing that about as much as I believed that God Himself was hanging out inside of the Cathedral of Saint John the Divine.

"Yes, of course," Rita said, and moved forward to rejoin her husband. The two of them disappeared inside the darkness of the gazebo, coming out a few moments later. Ken had tears in his eyes and Rita was smiling, saying something to him as they went to take a seat.

Alex turned around, threw up a peace sign with both hands, then ran lightly up the steps.

"It's like an effigy, right?" I asked KJ.

"I don't know," KJ said. Now she was telling the truth. Her voice was strained. "I've never been to a Great Harvest Hallow before."

"But you said you came to these every year!"

"I come to the *Harvest Hallow* every year. It's different—like, we do a big one every thirty-five years. When His shield wears thin."

"Okay, KJ," I said. "What the hell does that mean?"

"Your turn," Alex said, coming down the stairs as lightly as he'd gone up. It had been maybe two minutes since he'd gone in.

"What did you—" I started to ask, but Alex was gone, and KJ was stepping up the stairs.

"You can still leave right now," KJ said, out of the side of her mouth. She wasn't looking at me. And I, despite all my skepticism, was getting pretty nervous about Good Arcturus. For a second I considered backing out. But something inside me refused.

"I have to see him," I said.

And it was true. I hadn't come all the way here and dealt with my friends freaking out just to back out seconds from *doing* the thing.

I went up the stairs with KJ, sunflowers under my feet, and looked into the darkness.

CHAPTER FOUR

Saturday, October 28, 2000

KJ climbed the steps half in front of me, her body language more eloquent than any speech could have been. I nudged her over.

"Stop being a human shield," I said, which was a sentence I would think about often, later. But KJ's eyes were fixed on the shape far back in the shadows of the gazebo.

"Greetings, my Lord," KJ muttered, and then knelt down on the flowery gazebo floor without hesitation. "It's an honor to be here. I ask for the continued prosperity of my . . . of the Kobayashi family. We love and keep You every day."

I didn't kneel, even though KJ clearly wanted me to. She tried to pull me down via our connected hands until I dropped my hold. I was staring at the still and silent shape in the dark. *I have to know*, I thought, and took a step forward. Under my sweatshirt, my arms broke out in goose bumps.

I took another step.

"Darian, wait—" KJ said.

One more. The thing in the darkness was very tall. It waited behind massive bouquets of sunflowers like it was hiding. But it was too large to hide. It brushed the ceiling of the gazebo.

"Hello," I said. I tried to make my voice normal, but it broke a little as I spoke. I took one more step forward, waiting for the thing to move, and suddenly the shape in the darkness resolved into an object that made sense.

"Oh," I said, and a little nervous laugh came out of my mouth without my permission. "I see you."

It was a scarecrow. Of *course* it was, I thought—but KJ and Jasper had seemed so intense about the whole thing that for a minute I'd actually been expecting some living god/monster to be waiting for me.

Good Arcturus was huge, yes, and creepy in the inherent way of scarecrows and other things that live in the uncanny valley of almost-but-not-quite-human, but he was just a scarecrow. Like you might see in any field.

It was hard to see colors in the dimness, but I thought the scarecrow's straw body was painted red underneath all the cloth that it was shrouded in, which was some lighter color. The cloth reached to the ground, hung drapelike over twisted stick arms that spanned the entire space of the gazebo, and wrapped around the scarecrow's head entirely, so that it stood hooded and faceless.

"You're not real," I whispered. "Obviously."

I reached out my right hand, about to touch him. But however bold I was when asserting myself as a realist, I couldn't *quite* bring myself to touch the yards and yards of torn and leathery-looking fabric around the scarecrow.

"Are we good?" I asked KJ, taking a step backward without turning around. I didn't want to take my eyes off Good Arcturus. He'd been oddly placed . . . like he was bracing himself to leap forward.

"We're good," KJ said. This time when she offered her hand, I pulled her up. KJ wiped her hands on her robe, staring at the no-faced effigy in the sunflowers.

"Thank you, my Lord, for your love," KJ said. "I am so honored to be here with You, so grateful to be held by You, so glad that Darian got to meet You. Gotta go now, but it was incredible."

Together we backed out of the gazebo. Good Arcturus stayed motionless, like a scarecrow was supposed to.

"Not so bad, huh?" KJ asked, when we got down the stairs.

Whatever fear had been plaguing KJ all day was gone. She looked *actually* relaxed now.

Did you really think Good Arcturus was going to be alive? You did, didn't you? I thought. I was too polite to say it. But I was relieved to see that KJ was relieved.

We walked away, leaving the next person to ascend toward the scarecrow. The rest of the Kobayashi-Jenetopolous family met us at one of the tables in the square spiral of seating that meandered around the green.

"Kahie?" Rita asked. "How was seeing Him?"

"It was great, Ma," KJ said. "We both loved it. It's KJ, though, remember?"

"I'm sorry, baby, I just forget sometimes," Rita said. "Darian, did you enjoy meeting Him?"

"An experience for sure," I said.

"I'm so glad," Rita said, and pulled out a chair. "You girls sit down."

I took a seat. The red lace tablecloth brushed my thighs, and KJ slumped into the chair next to me, every inch of her long body communicating relief.

"Why were you nervous before?" I asked KJ, when the crowd of milling people got loud enough for us to talk without being overheard.

"I don't know," KJ said. "I didn't have any reason to feel nervous. Not that I can think of right now, anyway."

A bunch of people—I was pretty sure they were part of the family who ran the local garden center—sat down at the next table. A kid around our age leaned across the space to say something to KJ, and Alex looked over and smiled at me, guileless and glad.

"I'm grateful to be here with you, Dare," he said.

"Likewise," I said, and patted his shoulder.

And it was true. I *was* really glad to be there, even though KJ had gotten me all freaked-out to meet the scarecrow. I had nobody to tell me that the harmless evenings Senovak and my mom and dad had spent in Kesuquosh on Harvest Hallows of the past were *not* what I was getting into. That the *Great* Harvest Hallow—which happened every thirty-five years and just so happened to fall on the year I had chosen to visit—was really something else altogether.

A group of red-robed kids started winding through the angular spiral of tables, filling everyone's cups with something gold. I handed over my water glass for one of them to pour the drink into, and looked at KJ, who was chugging hers.

"Is it cider?"

"Nope," KJ said. "Sunflower-honey mead. It's made here. I personally think it's nasty as hell, but it is *highly* alcoholic."

I examined my cup, and thought with amusement about how disapproving Senovak would be if he knew.

"I have to drink this out of respect for your religious observances, right?" I asked.

"Absolutely," KJ said. "It would be majorly insulting if you didn't."

I drank half of the mead in two enormous gulps. It was nutty and flowery and almost sickly sweet. You couldn't taste the alcohol so much as feel it in your throat. KJ polished off her glass. Alex grinned at us and followed suit, drinking quickly.

"Guys!" Rita chastised from the end of the table. "Save some for the toast!"

"Sorry, Ma," KJ said, not looking sorry at all. I felt a pleasant buzz starting—a buzz that eased the remainder of the slimy unease I'd felt from seeing Good Arcturus in the flesh. Or the straw.

At a table closer to the center of the green, Jasper and his family took their seats.

Jasper's angelic face (Alex said Jasper looked like Leonardo DiCaprio in *Romeo + Juliet*, but I thought he was much cuter and I *knew* he was much shorter) was, as always, incongruous with his expression. He was glaring blankly at his place setting while the festivities went on around him, his mead untouched, for all the world looking like the only Grinch in Whoville.

Then, at some signal that I missed, a sound of flutes and pan-pipes came from the far left of the green. People were playing a tune that matched the one they'd been singing in the streets before, and the great seated crowd of Kesuquoshians grew quieter as the music got louder. There was a grisly, ear-bending moment of feedback from a microphone, and then the amplified voice of a woman came from near the table that held the monstrous cake.

"Good evening, my friends," said the voice. I caught a glimpse of the speaker, highlighted by torchlight: a petite woman of late middle age, with short gray hair. The First Selectwoman of

Kesuquosh, a.k.a. Birdie Plum, a.k.a. Jasper's aunt, who always looked nicer than she was. Kesuquosh was maybe *slightly* more diverse than the wealthy, isolated, super-homogenized Massachusetts towns around it, but there were still a great deal of early-fifties, upper-middle-class, well-dressed white ladies around. And Birdie was a part of the multitude. But she had . . . something to her, beyond a small familial resemblance to Jasper. A kind of charisma that separated her from other people. Her face was pretty, her red robe thrown across one shoulder in a jaunty way, her smile accentuated by bold red lipstick. But Jasper had always claimed that underneath her sweet exterior (the same sweet and guileless exterior that seemed to be the default in Kesuquosh) she was *highly* unpleasant.

"After thirty-five years, we're here again, for another Great Harvest Hallow," Birdie said, and she was met with a great swell of applause from the gathered crowd. The musicians played on, their pipes and flutes not drowning her out, but adding a perfectly surreal backing to the surreal scene.

"In this lonely and frightening world, spinning through a vast and unknowable cosmos," Birdie said, "nothing is guaranteed. People die alone. People die in poverty. People live—and die—in fear and misery. But . . . in all of this fear and emptiness, there is one place—one enclave—where you can have *exactly* what you need."

"To Kesuquosh!" someone shouted from closer to the center of the green. There was a little bit of whooping. Scattered laughter. Birdie Plum allowed herself a small smile.

"And you all know why," Birdie said. She turned toward the sunflower-enshrouded gazebo and the dark shape within. "Because we live by His grace. On His good earth. *His voice in our thoughts—*"

"His voice in our thoughts," said the assembled crowd. The speech was turning into a call-and-response.

"His heart in our skin," Birdie said.

"His heart in our skin," everyone echoed.

"In our weakness and smallness and loneliness and nothingness, He loves us still," Birdie said, her sweet voice taking on added volume and import. "He has loved us since that October twenty-eighth two hundred and forty-five years ago, when He first came to Kesuquosh."

Birdie gestured to her left, and an old and wizened-looking man sitting with the other members of the town council got up and took the mic from her hand. He cleared his throat and then started speaking in a measured grandpa voice.

"In Kesuquosh, back in those early days, adherence to religion still very much shaped the values of the town," Old Council Guy said. "The townspeople valued godliness and conformity, things that were valued by a people who could not see the values of *true* love and peace. A people who, sixty years before, had been executing blameless women accused of witchcraft. A people who lived on stolen land and understood only domination and suspicion and false piety. A people who decried the ethics and intellect of all those not like them."

This might sound like a surprisingly liberal sentiment, coming from an old man in a tiny town in the middle of nowhere. But it was par for the course when it came to Kesuquosh. Part of the reason that it *was* slightly more diverse than the towns around it. Part of why someone like KJ could be herself relatively safely, when the rest of the world was scary as fuck. Part of the reason I'd often fantasized about the prospect of living there full-time.

"And when people could not or would not conform, they were driven away. So it was with the mother of Junie Apostle-Root."

I had heard of this originating myth of the local religion before, but never so concisely or in a setting with such an awesome atmosphere. That didn't stop KJ from being bored out of her mind. She swirled the dregs of her mead and stared into the distance with the look of a person who had been told this story a thousand times.

Councilman Grandpa made an all-encompassing gesture with his arms, nearly flinging the mic away in the process.

"Elisabel Apostle-Root was different from the other people in town. She was a strange girl and a strange young woman, and she seemed to disdain the church. She had a voice, it was said, that could call animals and bend the wills of men. She had little tricks for building things, fixing things—bodies, gardens, sick livestock—that, a few decades earlier, would have likely gotten her murdered. These people called themselves Congregationalists instead of Puritans, but they still carried many of their old prejudices. The narrow-minded villagers whispered that she was a *witch*. And she was forced to live in the woods, in a small black house on the edge of town, shunned by the villagers until they needed something.

"Though it seemed that not *all* of the villagers shunned her. Elisabel fell pregnant. She was with child, but whoever had fathered the child would not come forward . . . and Elisabel was too honorable to name him. She carried her daughter in solitude, with no one to help her or care for her, birthed her alone, raised her alone.

"And her daughter, Junie, was even more talented than her mother at working within the wild and forgotten rules of the world. Elisabel taught her the secret ways of hands that could do more than ordinary hands, and the unknown paths through the pathless forests. Junie's education was rich and strange.

"But Junie was always *lonely*, with no one to keep her company but her mother. She was fascinated by the Kesuquoshians. She grew up watching them, wishing to be accepted by them. To be one with the many hearts of the village. Always terribly lonely."

KJ looked over at me and mouthed "terribly lonely" with a big exaggerated expression of sorrow. But most people were *hooked*. Enraptured. Rita was misty-eyed.

"And then, when Junie was a young woman, her mother became ill. So ill that none of the secret remedies could help her. And Junie was afraid. For her whole life her mother had been her only companion, the only soul who acknowledged her existence. Desperate to save her, Junie went into the village and beseeched the people of Kesuquosh, begged for mercy, for aid.

"But the villagers cared not for Junie, or for her mother's suffering. To them, the Apostle-Root women were barely human beings. The town's minister himself, along with several of the men, drove her off, sent her back to the black house outside of town. And then, one cold October morning," Old Council Guy continued, "Elisabel Apostle-Root died."

"Definitely died of syphilis," KJ whispered into my ear. I covered my mouth so that nobody could see me laughing. KJ's older sister, Isabella, who always seemed like she was weighed down by the burden of seriousness that gets put on eldest daughters, glared at us from across the table.

"Show some respect," she hissed at KJ.

"Shhhhh," KJ said, holding a finger to her lips, which made Isabella glare at her even harder.

I was actually kind of invested in the story at this point. *It would have sucked to live in the 1700s* was my main takeaway.

"And Junie was finally and truly alone. Alone, she buried her mother. Alone, she went to the woods that grew thick around the Swift River. Alone, she sat down on the mossy bank and wept. She did not believe in the god of her people, but she prayed to the beautiful world and the secret things within it for a companion in her loneliness. And then, as she sat there in sorrow, she saw a shimmer. A crack in the very air around her. A flash of brighter green in a world of autumn colors."

Everyone was quiet, even KJ. I had this sharp mental image in my mind of the painting in the town hall. The woman and the scarecrow. And a thought about my mom, dying.

Councilman Grandpa had us all in the iron grip of his story. He lowered his voice.

"And she was unafraid. She called out to ask who had followed her into the woods. And Good Arcturus—who has no mouth— replied in her mind.

"'I am a traveler,' He said. 'I have torn my traveling cloak and lost my way. The doors between the worlds are closed to me. I am a stranger in a strange land. Can you help me, little one?'"

Even Jasper was listening now. I could make him out at his family's table, his body language intent and focused.

"Junie went to Him, and when she saw that He was not a human being, she told Him: 'I don't know how to help you, strange traveler.' But she saw that His beautiful green cloak was torn in three pieces. So she brought Him to the black house, took a needle and thread, and tried to sew His cloak together. But the material was not of our world. It was scarcely a cloak as much as it was a *door*. A way to walk through worlds. Junie's needle bent and her thread frayed to nothing. And she looked upon the traveler with despair. *'I want to help you,'* she told Him. *'But in my smallness, and my nothingness, I cannot.'*

"*'Your kindness has helped already,'* Good Arcturus said. *'I am much restored. But tell me, little one—why were you crying all alone, far from the others of your kind?'*

"*'Because they despise me,'* Junie said. *'For being different from them.'*

"Good Arcturus could not understand. In the place that He had come from, differences were prized. But that sentiment was as alien to Junie Apostle-Root as Good Arcturus Himself.

"*'Show me the place of your people, little one,'* Good Arcturus said. *'Perhaps we can find help there.'*

"So Junie walked, with Good Arcturus tall behind her, into the village of Kesuquosh. She knew that she would be met with derision and hatred, but she braved those things to help the lost traveler. She had no idea, however, how afraid the villagers would be when they saw *Him*.

"When they got into the village, people screamed at the sight of the creature behind Junie. She raised her hands and tried to explain that He was a kind soul, lost, and with His traveling cloak torn in three pieces. But there was a great panic. Everybody thought that the devil had come to Kesuquosh. And the men grabbed their rifles and muskets and whatever weapons they could lay hands upon. In the center of town they waited in a line, too afraid to approach Him. And when Junie and Good Arcturus met the men of the town there, one of them—the minister himself—raised his rifle, screaming for his God to help him, and shot at the strange visitor.

"Junie threw herself bodily in front of Good Arcturus, who did not understand that they were being threatened. And the rifle shot meant for Him struck her instead, and killed her where she stood. Right there," Old Council Guy said, gesturing to the gazebo. "In that very spot."

There was a collective sigh from everyone around me.

"It took Good Arcturus a few moments to understand what had happened—that His only friend in this new world had been killed. Human beings were still very much a mystery to Him. But as He stood over her body, caressing her face with His many sinews—"

"His many *sinews*?" I asked KJ. She shrugged.

"—He felt a great sorrow overtake him. And a great wrath. And He spoke to every last villager within their minds: *What makes you cruel?* He asked them. *What makes you afraid?*

"And they could not answer Him, of course. But He saw in their hearts and minds the idea of their god. Their pitiless god. Their fear of hellfire and damnation. The beliefs that harmed them. He saw that, within each of them, they had the ability to be as kind and loving as Junie Apostle-Root. But they were constrained by the prejudices of their beliefs. And do you know what He did next?"

"He tore the church down!" someone yelled, and Old Guy nodded.

I traded a glance with KJ, smiling. She smiled back, although I don't think she knew what I was so delighted by. This was normal to her, but to me it was so *strange*. I loved this story. The savior-slash-monster from another world. The insane Kesuquoshian attitude toward Abrahamic faiths. The subversiveness of it, cloaked in normalcy. I was absolutely all in.

"He tore the church to its foundations," he agreed. "He reached into the mind of every last human being in Kesuquosh and made them *see*. See the love and harmony and goodness of which they were capable. The ways to exist *with* the natural world, instead of against it. To care for the earth as it cared for them. That their lives could be different.

"The villagers were changed by His love. They finally understood.

"But this world was not *His* world. Good Arcturus could not survive for long without His traveling cloak. He was weakened by the act of changing everyone. And He was lost. Unable to return to His home and heal. Even as He transformed this place, He was dying.

"So the minister of Kesuquosh stepped forward. '*I am sorry for my cruelty,*' he told Good Arcturus. '*For hurting a good woman. I wish to repay your kindness. With my very heart.*'

"Then he reached forward and embraced Good Arcturus.

"'*I will keep you warm,*' the minister said. '*If you cannot have a cloak, then you shall have a shield. We two shall be Incorporated into one being. And when I can shield you no more, I will stand beside you, as your right hand, and help you take away the cruelties of our kind.*'

"Good Arcturus, healed by the love around Him, returned it in equal measure.

"'*And I will never leave you,*' He said. '*You will have peace and prosperity until the very end of this world. You are safe, my children.*

You are loved. You are one with the good earth. This harvest season is now a hallowed time, a time to remember our love for each other. And I will live in the black house out in the fields, always, and watch over you, always.'

"And He has. And when the minister's time as His shield was done, a new Incorporation was selected, and the old Incorporation joined our Lord in the black house beyond the fields.

"Together, they—and the five Incorporations who have served since—take the sin of this town, which is not *Biblical* sin, but cruelty and prejudice and tyranny and hate, and transform it into love and goodness.

"And, like Junie, we *all* became His Apostles. And the fields grew lushly and well from His presence. And Kesuquosh was always prosperous, and always safe, even when the other towns of the Swift River Valley were flooded to make the Reservoir. We will be safe in our love forever."

I felt like clapping, but everyone else was silent.

"That was *great*," I told KJ, who shrugged with the noncommittal boredom that familiarity brings. She couldn't see the excellence of the legend. But Rita smiled at me when I said it, her sweet face communicating joy.

"Our town is founded on something wonderful," Rita said. "True acceptance. For always."

I nodded, trying to look serious. Rita didn't understand that I was approaching all of this like . . . like it was really good genre fiction. A story. A movie.

Old Council Guy put the mic back on its stand and sat down. For a moment there was an almost reverent silence from everyone assembled. Then Birdie Plum stood back up.

"Now. If you'll join me in a toast," Birdie said.

There was a clamor as more than a thousand people got to their feet. The torchlight gleamed off hundreds of different kinds of glasses.

"To the Great Harvest Hallow, culmination of three and a half decades of prosperity. Of safety. Of love. Of the rhythms that make up our lives, and the abiding connections to our fellow townspeople. To Kesuquosh."

"To Kesuquosh," the crowd echoed.

Jasper was the only person who hadn't gotten to his feet. I had a clear view of him from where I stood: Mr. Plum was grabbing him by the upper arm, like he was trying to forcibly lift Jasper out of his seat.

Jasper shrugged off his father's grasp with force, and said something in response. I didn't know *what* he said, but his stubborn expression was clear. Mr. Plum gave him a last look, full of a kind of withering dislike that I didn't think a parent should ever direct at a child. Then he and Mrs. Plum proceeded to completely ignore their son, who kept his seat, defiantly, in the face of all the earnestness around him.

I was torn. I saw Jasper's pain and frustration, and I wanted to empathize with him . . . but I couldn't determine the *cause*. All of this seemed . . . so . . . harmless. A little creepy, but essentially harmless. I was secure in my enjoyment, especially after having seen Good Arcturus. Just a scarecrow, nothing more.

I was so focused on Jasper that I missed most of Birdie's toast. I caught the end:

"—so we honor each other. We censure all that is cruel and evil. And we honor our Lord of the Field."

"To the Lord of the Field!" a few people near the front shouted, prompting a small round of cheers.

"Tonight we gift Him with a new shield to adore for decades hence!" Birdie Plum said. "Tonight we set the last thirty-five years to rest and begin anew. A toast to Good Arcturus, and to Kesuquosh, our heaven on earth!"

CHAPTER FIVE

Saturday, October 28, 2000

The air of solemnity was broken. People raised their glasses, the musicians took up their flutes again, and the First Selectwoman started issuing orders through her microphone:

"We're going to start at the centermost table and move out! This year we've tried to simplify the cake-cutting process . . . I don't know how many of you remember 1965, but there was a long wait as they organized. We've got numbers on your tables and we're going to call you up a few at a time . . ."

"You said you thought it was great?" KJ asked.

I had been so engrossed in the story and spectacle that I kind of felt like I was surfacing from somewhere deep down in my brain. Like Bradbury, but untainted. Something about the woods and the magic of the world had really hooked me. I fumbled for some kind of coherent answer under her gaze—which always felt intense to me, even when it wasn't.

"Yes. I wasn't kidding. These council people should be stage actors. It was so well done—I think it's all very charming," I said, and then cringed inwardly at how condescending that sounded. I hoped KJ wouldn't call me on it—but KJ *always* called me on stuff like that.

"Oh yeah? You think our wittle bitty customs are charming, D?" KJ teased. "You feel happy about coming to the tiny town and seeing us do our *silly stuff*?"

"Shut up," I said. "I just meant that it was interesting, like a good movie or something. Or not a movie, but a play—"

"Oooohhh, I like watching them cavort on the stage of their belief," KJ said, making her voice all breathy and high-pitched in a (kind of) passable imitation of me. "I'm Darian, fresh from Manhattan. Yes, these *are* real pearl earrings, and I loooove seeing the simple countryfolk practice their darling Harvest Hallow—"

"You are profoundly annoying, do you know that?" I asked.

"In the face of patrician derision, I can only defend my common brethren from unduly harsh judgment," KJ said. "Elitist."

"No, you're right, you're right," I said. One of the red-robed kids refilled my mead glass, and I sipped it, feeling a little drunk and a little giddy. "I should be careful of my tone. I know how you sad backwoods people make, like, *feuds* out of things. Don't run back to your shack and get your shotgun."

"If you piss me off you never know how far I might take it," KJ said. "The Kobayashi-Arden feud will be the new Hatfield-McCoy conflict."

"I don't really know what the Hatfield-McCoy conflict is," I admitted.

"Me either," KJ said. "Probably something to do with Heidegger and Schoopenhoer."

"*Schopenhauer*," I said, but I felt all fluttery inside because she was picking up our conversation from August. Like she'd thought about it as much as I had.

"Oh rocks, all my apologies to the littlest future philosophy major," KJ said, doing a fake hat-tip without touching her actual beanie.

"Apology accepted," I said, and laughed. Then she laughed, too.

For a beat we *looked* at each other. I couldn't entirely keep the smile off my face.

"So you're happy you came?" KJ said. She looked down, rubbing the back of her neck with one hand, definitely embarrassed by the sincerity of her own question.

It was like she had forgotten her reaction when I'd shown up. I had a flash of it—the horror on her face—and put it aside. I wanted to be here. I wanted to be happy. I wanted to forget the strangeness of my arrival.

"Seriously? I'm *really* happy," I said. "Compared to Jasper, I'm ecstatic."

"Yeah, he's not too thrilled about this whole thing," KJ said, sparing a glance at the Plum family's table. "But you like it?"

I nodded. "It's atmospheric. Plus there's free booze. I'm having a good time."

"That's cool," KJ said. Her voice was soft, pitched only for me to hear. "All joking aside, I want you to like it."

"You do?" I asked. I felt nervous all over again. But this time it wasn't from the threat of existential scarecrows—it was from the seriousness of KJ's voice.

"Yeah. I think I have the . . . I think I can say this right now," KJ said, and took a giant sip of her mead.

"Say . . . this?" I asked. KJ was blushing, I could see it even in the torchlight. My heart sped up.

"Yeah. This. Remember in August? When I gave you the—"

"The CD," I said quickly, doing a pretty bad job of pretending that I hadn't been obsessing about it for months. "I remember that, um, very well."

"I want you to like it here. Even with this religious stuff. I want you to *like* it. Because . . . I think about you. I mean, about what you think about us—about our snow globe."

"What?" I asked, baffled by her weird turn of phrase.

"Our *town*, I mean. I'm having a hard time . . . what I mean is, I—I don't want you to—" KJ broke off and looked directly at me. She seemed to be struggling for words. After a second, she gave up, shrugged in her trademark *I could care less* move, and touched my left hand with her right, under the table.

Nobody was paying attention to the two of us at that moment. In the loudness of the crowd and the dimness of the light, we might have been the only two people in the world.

KJ took my hand under the red lacy tablecloth, and it felt significant. Not like she was freaked-out. Just significant.

"Darian," KJ said, her voice low and her eyes impossible to look away from.

"Yes?" I asked, trying to keep my voice steady.

"Our turn!" Ken Kobayashi said, leaning over us, and I jerked back, pulling my hand away from KJ's in one quick move. "Time to get your cake! Bring your plates up with you, guys."

KJ's dad hadn't noticed us holding hands. Ken never seemed to notice much. He was a tall man with John Lennon glasses and a kindly, absent smile.

KJ stood up abruptly. I followed behind her all the way through the spiral of tables.

The wind carried over a waft of cigarette smoke as we waited in line, and KJ transferred her plate to one hand and with the other, dug her Newport 100s out of the depths of her red robe at the smell of *other* people smoking. Rita whirled around like she had eyes in the back of her head.

"If you smoke a cigarette over the sacred cake . . . ," Rita said warningly.

"Relax, Ma, I'm not," KJ said, stowing her smokes. Alex laughed from behind us.

"Shut up," KJ said, reaching over me to shove her brother.

"Hey, no *pushing* near the *sacred cake*," Alex said, still laughing.

"How about you don't be a little bitch near the sacred cake," KJ said, quietly enough that Rita couldn't hear.

"I said I'm not fucking *eating* it, so why does it matter which piece I take?"

Alex and KJ both looked around at the sound of Jasper's voice. I looked too, until I finally located his Manic Panic hair. Jasper was up ahead of us in line—his family sat slightly closer to the center of the spiral—and he was almost yelling. Mr. and Mrs. Plum were standing next to him, flanked by two other men in red robes, and Birdie Plum right in front.

"Jasper," Birdie Plum said, "this is a necessary part of the Banquet. You have to take a piece in the same order as everybody else. It's to keep it fair. You can't be *claiming* your own piece, trying to affect the *outcome*. All of us citizens share an equal chance of—"

I moved up with KJ, as close as I could get without cutting the other people who were lined up for their piece of cake, trying to hear the argument clearly. Alex was right behind us, craning forward.

"And you *will* be eating it," Jasper's mom told him. "That's part of the ritual, too, so—"

"I'M NOT *EATING* IT! I'M A FUCKING *VEGAN*!" Jasper shouted. He could get really loud, with his golden voice, and now he got *catastrophically* loud. All the adults surrounding him jumped back at the same time, like in a cartoon. "I'M TAKING *THAT* PIECE, RIGHT THERE BY THE FUCKING SIDE, AND IF I DON'T GET THAT ONE I'M NOT TAKING ONE *AT ALL*! AND FUCK THE CONSEQUENCES! I'LL STOMP THIS FUCKING CAKE INTO THE GROUND—"

Jasper was pulled sharply to the side by his mother and father. The two older guys in red robes leaned over him along with them.

"Stop making a scene and take your piece," Mr. Plum snapped. He had a tight grip on Jasper's shoulder. I watched as Jasper attempted to shrug his dad's hand off, like he had during the toast. This time he failed. Seeing all those adults surrounding him made me feel a twist of very real anxiety, and that prompted me to speak before I really thought about it.

"Why don't you leave him alone?" I said. All of the adults turned to look at me. "He's vegan. He doesn't eat any animal by-products. He doesn't want any cake. Why don't you leave him alone?" I repeated, refusing to wilt under the weight of all those strange stares.

"It's okay, Dare," Alex said. "It's for his own, like, well-being."

"Fuck you, Alex," Jasper snapped, and Alex looked honestly wounded for a second, before his expression melted back into blank tranquility.

"It doesn't *seem* like it's for his well-being," I said.

"And who is *this*?" Birdie Plum asked, looking me up and down with her lips pursed. We had actually met before, but I don't think we'd ever really been introduced. She definitely knew I wasn't a full-time Kesuquoshian.

"Birdie, this is Darian *Sabine* Arden," Rita cut in. "Blake Sabine's daughter. She came to celebrate the Great Hallow with us, isn't that beautiful?"

"I see," Birdie said. "Very beautiful."

Then Rita pushed past all of us and went to Jasper. Alex and KJ's older sister, Isabella, rolled her eyes.

"Why does he always have to make a scene?" Isabella asked.

"Why do you always have to be an uncool asshole?" KJ said, sticking her hands into the pockets of her robe with supreme slouchiness. "It's just *in your nature*."

I watched Rita talk to Jasper. He stared at her obstinately, with his arms crossed. But as she spoke, the obstinate look faded.

"—just to make certain you're safe," Rita said, holding Jasper's shoulders. That seemed to be the end of the argument, and Jasper sighed. He nodded, once.

"I get it," he said. "But. I want the piece *I* want. I'm not taking any other piece than that—"

"Rocks *around* us, you are such a little bastard," Birdie said. She looked at her nephew with an expression of absolute dislike. Jasper returned it in equal measure.

For a few seconds, the two of them were locked in an unblinking battle of wills. I held my breath. I had no idea *why* this was such a big deal, but I was rooting for Jasper to win.

"Birdie, just let him," Rita said. "It won't break anything."

Then Birdie deflated. "Fine," she said through her teeth. "I don't care. Take it and get out of my sight."

"I *will*," Jasper said, and took the long silver knife. He sliced himself a piece of cake far away from all the others, a curved piece right on an edge that protruded out from the body of the monstrous cake.

"Good, honey," Rita said, and turned back to Mr. and Mrs. Plum. There was a slight coolness in her expression as she looked at them, and I thought (not for the first time) that Rita wouldn't have been too upset if she was told to adopt Jasper and raise him as her own.

Jasper went off to his table, and I watched as each of his parents got a piece of cake. It was a truly bizarre process, not like how Jasper had picked and cut his own slice: Birdie Plum took the knife and used it to carve a largish square piece from the highest tier of the baked monstrosity. It was clear that the cake was being cut in a specific order, and that Jasper had gone off-script by forging a new location with his selection.

Then Mr. Plum stepped back, holding out his plate.

Birdie plunged a metal cake server into the mass like she was knighting someone. She levered out the piece of cake—the red velvet hole it left behind looked like a wound—and deposited it on Mr. Plum's plate with a ridiculous First Selectwoman solemnity.

Then Mrs. Plum repeated the process, taking her cake from her sister-in-law with the utmost seriousness.

These people are insane, I thought. I remembered my earlier fear, before KJ and I had "met" Good Arcturus, and felt stupid for even having momentary anxiety. What could the Kesuquoshians possibly do to anyone? They acted like getting one cranky teenage vegan to take some communal cake was the most important thing they'd ever done. They were all ridiculous.

"The cake looks really good. Hunter's mom and like six other people who are the 'best bakers in town' made it from some secret recipe that's been passed down. I bet it's gonna blow your mind," KJ said.

"The banana pudding tarte at Don & Lea's didn't move me, so I don't have huge hopes for this," I said.

"Is that some yuppie New York reference, D?" KJ asked.

"Only the greatest restaurant in Brooklyn," I said.

"Rancid, you're *so* rank," KJ said.

"Extremely harsh," I said. "And here I was, thinking you liked me."

"I do like you," KJ said. Her expression made the comment seem loaded, suddenly.

"I like you too," I said softly.

"I *know*," KJ said, and I knew she was aiming to be teasing, but her voice was still so serious that it made her words . . . important.

"Your turn, wad," Isabella said, elbowing KJ in the side, making both of us jump. The moment was broken.

KJ walked around the side of the cake with her brow furrowed, Birdie Plum did her fancy cake-server move, and KJ waved me over with her free hand.

"You're up next, D," KJ said.

I started to walk up to where Birdie Plum waited, holding my plate out kind of formally, like the other people had. But then, from nowhere, I felt a strong hand grip my wrist.

It was Jasper, who'd come back up unnoticed.

"You forgetting something, KJ?" Jasper asked.

KJ's expression clouded. She stood between me and the impatient-looking First Selectwoman, and looked at Jasper with her brows knitted together. "Huh?"

"We agreed on this earlier. *Darian* doesn't need to take a piece, remember?" Jasper said.

"Oh, shit, you're right," KJ said, looking almost—almost *horrified*. She brought one hand up to her mouth. "I totally spaced on it, boss. I can't—"

"It's fine, I get it," Jasper said, with an actual real hint of sympathy in his voice. "He's right there."

I watched this baffling exchange like it was a tennis match, turning my head back and forth each time one of them spoke.

"Uh . . . guys . . . what?" I asked.

"Can we move this along?" Birdie Plum asked impatiently.

"Yeah. Sorry, ma'am," KJ muttered, and stepped away from the table.

"Darian? You *can* have some cake if you want," Alex offered nicely.

"Shut up," Jasper said to Alex, and then to me: "You're not eating the cake." He kept his grip on my wrist and basically started *dragging* me away from the table. I shrugged at Alex, and he passed us to go get his slice.

"I kind of want the cake," I said to Jasper.

"Too bad," Jasper snapped, and he sounded *shaken*, shaken and shaky, from the top of his purple head to the steel toes of his secondhand Doc Martens.

"Okay, okay," I said, taking in the tightness of Jasper's mouth and the miserable line of his hunched shoulders. "I won't eat it if you really don't want me to."

"Of *course* I don't want you to!" Jasper said, speed-walking me toward the table where the Kobayashi family had been seated. His voice was staccato with fear. "KJ doesn't want you to participate either, only she's so fucking zonked right now that she can't lie. She's lost the plot, man. Because of that . . . *thing* in the gazebo. Honestly she held out longer than I . . . whatever, it doesn't matter. But if she *could* think, then she'd tell you to sit the fuck down and not participate."

It freaked me out to see Jasper *this* frantic. It was so unlike him that I found myself trying to be comforting, without knowing exactly why.

"It's okay, I'm not going to do it," I said. "Thank you . . . for caring about me. You're a good friend."

"I'm a *great* friend," Jasper said. "I'm your *best* friend. You showed up for this shit show. You're lucky I can improvise."

We reached the table, and I took the moment of privacy to lean in. "I know you thought it—the scarecrow—was real," I said. "But . . ." I paused, trying to navigate Jasper's beliefs without being offensive or patronizing.

"Yeah?" Jasper said.

"But you *saw* it," I said. "I know it's like ten feet tall and creepy as fuck, but . . . it's just a dried-up old scarecrow in torn fabric. So what are you so worried about?"

Jasper nodded—pale and tense, but reasonable. "I know. I think it might just be . . . hibernating. Sleeping. I'm worried about what comes next."

"What comes next?" I asked, not believing him . . . but also really not digging the whole "hibernating" angle for the massive scarecrow that waited at the back of the gazebo like it was poised to leap forward.

"I'm . . . not sure," Jasper said.

"Well, you're making it sound pretty *bad*, Jasper—"

"You're fine," Jasper said, and looked over his shoulder at his parents. "You didn't take the cake."

Then he walked away, and the Kobayashi family came back, their plates full of luxuriously colored slices of red velvet. I stared at KJ with my eyebrows raised until she sat down.

"What's *up* with you guys?" I asked KJ.

"Huh?" KJ said.

"This whole drama over whether I can eat cake or not," I said, "is truly bizarre. What are you so worried about?"

"Nothing," KJ said, avoiding my eyes. "Just, like, erring on the side of caution."

Finally, after a decent stretch of time, everyone was seated. The cake was gone from the central table, cut into more than a thousand pieces and distributed evenly across more than a thousand plates.

The music stopped. Even the kids who had been pouring water and mead were sitting quietly with their families.

"Now! My beloved ones!" Birdie Plum yelled. A gust of wind dropped dead leaves over her central table as she spoke. "YOU MAY BEGIN!"

Everyone except for me took a fork in hand. A thousand people moved in sync, stabbing their utensils deep into the red hearts of their sacred cake slices.

There was the soft sound of rhythmic chewing coming from the people surrounding me. It was, somehow, a *gross* sound. Forks squeaked along plates. I looked over at Jasper. He was stabbing his cake with a look of total terror in his eyes. He flattened every last crumb onto his plate, like he was searching for something, then dragged his fingers through the pancake he'd made out of his slice.

He looked up at me, his face showing abject confusion. He mouthed something to me, but I couldn't make it out.

What? I mouthed back.

"*Hhhhh*haaaaaoucch," KJ said from next to me. It was a hiss of surprised pain that morphed into speech, and I glanced over sharply.

For a second, I couldn't understand what I was seeing, because it was so incongruous with everything else. KJ's mouth was suddenly oozing red, from her lips or tongue: not the deep satiny red of the cake, but the brighter red of fresh blood. And then I realized that KJ had bitten down on something gleaming and metallic.

It was a large sewing needle. So large, in fact, that I had no idea how KJ hadn't noticed it when she was forking cake into her mouth.

"KJ? How the hell did that get in the cake?" I asked. "Are you okay?"

KJ pulled the needle out from between her teeth with a grimace. "Ouch," she said, and then turned it around in her hand.

Across from us, Isabella's eyes had gone huge. Rita noticed too, and put one hand to her mouth in an expression of surprise. The whole table was staring at the glinting needle that KJ held. It was tipped with one very small pearl of blood.

"Whoa, go, KJ," said a burly dude at the next table. Rita stood up and gestured at KJ, who got slowly to her feet, still holding the needle. The Kobayashi-Jenetopolous family walked as a group, with KJ in the center, toward the central table, next to the crumbs of the giant cake, where Birdie Plum and a number of town council people sat.

I stayed seated, staring. But I felt a visceral stab of anxiety as KJ got farther away from me. What the hell was *this* now? Was this . . . part of the Banquet, somehow? Hadn't Birdie called it "the Banquet of the *Needle*"?

Then Birdie took the microphone.

"Fellow Apostles," she said, her pretty voice piercing the night, "Good Arcturus has made His selection." She took KJ's hand—the one not holding the needle—in her own, raising their fists together in the air."Our new Incorporation is—Kaherdin Jude Kobayashi! May He live joyously within them!"

At the table to my right, a bearded guy with a Red Sox sweatshirt peeking out from under his red robe whistled and clapped. Other people followed suit. The crowd broke out into riotous, deafening, ear-bending applause.

"KJ! KJ! KJ!"

A bunch of kids from the parochial school were cheering for her. I saw Hunter Warren, the guy KJ had been "kind of dating" during the first half of junior year, clapping wildly and grinning his handsome grin from over at his table.

People smashed their mead glasses on the ground. The musicians, who had taken a pause to eat the sacred cake, immediately reassembled near the heart of the green, and reedy music mixed in with the applause.

"Would you like to say something, my dear?" Birdie Plum asked. She sounded much nicer than when she'd been talking to Jasper.

KJ took the microphone hesitantly. She held up the needle—invisible from this distance, except that it caught and threw back one single spangle of light from the torches—and cleared her throat.

"I just gotta say that He has great taste," KJ said. "It's an honor!"

This simple declaration was met with uproarious laughter, like *way* more laughter than was appropriate for the occasion. The excitement of the crowd almost seemed . . . manic. Again anxiety jabbed at my brain, my lungs. I didn't like what was happening.

"Now we will make our pilgrimage," Birdie Plum said. "To His house!"

Everyone stood up, pushing their chairs backward. An old woman from the central table took KJ's Soundgarden beanie off her head and replaced it with a crown of sunflowers. It ringed her dark hair like a halo.

I stood up. I looked over at Jasper, to confirm that I was following suit in the correct way, and saw him on his feet between his parents. Jasper's face was bone white. His pale blue eyes were enormous. He looked like someone had just died in front of him. And the expression of horror on his face was so profound that it made my own unease gallop straight into fear.

What the fuck, I mouthed at him. But Jasper didn't see me, didn't look away from KJ.

"To Kaherdin Jude!" Birdie Plum said again, before she set the microphone down. "Our newest Incorporation!"

The mass of people paused. Like they were waiting for something. I tried to catch Jasper's eye. *What happens now?* I thought.

Then Jasper's frightened eyes moved away from KJ. Now he was looking past me. I turned, following the general direction of his gaze. My eyes drifted past the gazebo, toward the streets beyond. And then my breath caught in my throat. I forgot about KJ's new status as the star of the party. I forgot about Jasper's look of terror. For a second, I forgot about *everything*.

Dexter was there. Waiting for me. He was at the edge of the green, forever thirty years old, wrapped up against the cold in his retro jacket. Blood across his mouth. Standing right where the torchlight melted into darkness. He was entirely shadowed, except for the gleam of his glasses and the knife-white slice of his smile.

Kesuquosh was no longer a safe haven: Dexter was here now, too. He had invaded my last and greatest sanctuary during the Great Harvest Hallow.

One hand, dark with moss and livid with the discoloration of death, beckoned to me. His mouth moved.

I wasn't close enough to hear what he was saying, but I knew that he was whispering something in the scratchy voice of the grave. If I got close to him, I would be able to hear him singing one of the songs he'd written for me. I couldn't tell which. Maybe "Later, Adrian," or "Oh Phantom Mine." Those were the two that you could most often catch on the radio. "Please go away," I said. My voice was lost in the sound of the crowd.

Then there was a break in the noise. Dexter stopped singing and glanced over at the gazebo. His smile glinted again in the dark, and he looked straight at me, gesturing toward that dark and flowery space. *Look*, his hands said. *Look at this new surprise.*

Inside the darkness where the scarecrow had stood, braced to leap forward, there was a sound of rustling. Like something long asleep—something *disguised* as an effigy—was stirring, stretching. Waking.

I heard the creak of old branches in the wind without any wind. The shadows shifted in the torchlight. The thing inside the gazebo began to move.

CHAPTER SIX

Saturday, October 28, 2000

It was moving.

The faceless scarecrow, enormous and swathed in faded leathery fabric, walked down the steps of the gazebo. Or—it didn't have *feet*, exactly, and I couldn't see how it was moving. Slithering. Gliding.

Someone is carrying that thing, I thought. *There are people lifting it and carrying it and it's just that I can't see it because I'm at a weird angle and I—*

The gazebo was cutting off part of my view of the scarecrow. Yes, it *seemed* to move on its own, but it was definitely being *carried*. There was no way it wasn't being carried.

The whole crowd had been very still for a moment. And then the cheering redoubled. People were screaming, shrieking. A lady in L.L.Bean overalls twisted the edge of her cloak between two hands with a rapturous expression, an enormous smile distorting her face.

Good Arcturus—and whatever hidden people *had* to be carrying him—melted into the darkness at the far end of the green. I whipped my head back to where Dexter had been, and he was gone. Vanished.

"Come, my dear ones!" Birdie said. She, the other adults she'd been sitting with, and the whole Kobayashi family all started to follow after Good Arcturus. KJ was in the center of them, easy to spot with her golden crown of sunflowers. She looked like a coin that was being pushed along by a bloodred river. There was something small and . . . helpless-seeming about the way she moved in the throng. Then everyone was walking in the same direction. The crowd headed to the far end of the green. Senovak had mentioned this part. I figured that this was the mile-long parade that led past the crumbling church foundation and out to a big bonfire. But none of the rest of this . . . *choosing* someone stuff had been discussed. Nothing about seeing someone crowned as some kind of *shield* or *Incorporation*, which I was still unclear on the meaning of. Nothing about a needle. Or a banquet. Not even a single word about a sacred cake.

Because this is Great *Harvest Hallow*, I thought. *And it's not the same. They've been telling you that all night.*

"Jasper?" I said as the Plum family passed close by me. "Did you see—"

I was going to ask *Did you see the scarecrow move?* but Jasper cut me off.

"I'll take care of this," he said. His face was drawn and pale. "You go home. I'll come get you later."

"Wait, Jas," I said, and tried to grab his sleeve, but Mrs. Plum turned and gave me a *look* that made me drop my hand.

"Go *home*, child," Mrs. Plum said. Her hooded face looked hollow and ancient, like a recently unburied skull.

There was absolutely no way I was going to go home. I was too frightened by the appearance of movement from the scarecrow, too worried about what exactly was happening to KJ. I waited until almost every last one of the villagers was in front of me, a great train of red-cloaked bodies moving into the shadows. Then I pulled out my cell phone, opened up my list of contacts, and scrolled down to *Dan S.* My finger hovered over the green Send button. I really, *really* wanted Senovak to be here to back me up. The sudden creepiness of everything was making me feel paranoid.

But I couldn't think of what I would *tell* Senovak if I did call him. *Can you come hang with me? I got scared because KJ ate the special cake piece.* Or, better yet, *I'm exactly as drunk as you told me not to be and I think I saw the scarecrow move by itself and it freaked me out!*

I couldn't tell him about seeing Dexter. I thought Senovak might be the only one who suspected the truth of what had happened with Dexter, and I didn't want him asking a lot of prying questions about why I was haunted by Dexter's ghost.

I kept my phone out with Senovak's number pulled up, and followed the crowd, trying not to think about Shirley Jackson's short story *The Lottery*, and what happened to the person in *that* small town who was lucky enough to "win."

The eastern side of Good Earth Way turned into Deep River Road, and from there the pavement and the houses gave way to an old cobblestone street that led deeper into the woods, heavy with moss. The moss-covered road crumbled into a dirt track (which had once been Church Street, presumably so long ago that it was before the religion of Good Arcturus had come to Kesuquosh). I and the few stragglers behind me passed the church that had been "torn to the foundations" in the story the old councilman told: the place that the locals—or at least Jasper, KJ, and Alex—called Empty Heaven.

A nickname that had made me profoundly uncomfortable the first time I'd heard it. Now I was somewhat inured. At least I didn't flinch when they said it anymore.

Of course they would come up with that nickname because of the song "Empty Heaven," which was pretty popular, maybe his third biggest single, at least if you were into alternative rock or regularly tuned in to college radio. And of course all three of them liked him. They couldn't all agree on Ian Curtis or Kurt Cobain, but they could agree on *him*.

I tried to pull my thoughts away from Dexter. I almost expected to see him sitting inside the crumbling foundation of the church as we passed it. But of course there was nothing.

All that remained of that former house of worship was, as I said, the old stone rectangle . . . and one perfectly preserved doorframe. The door still hung within it. It was a deep green, or once had been, before time had cracked and peeled the paint. There was really no reason for the door to still be a *door* when the rest of the building had long ago succumbed to ruin. And yet . . . it was preserved in a way that suggested that somehow it was younger than the rest of the ruins, as if the door hovered there in stasis while the bulk of the church had been subjected to time.

We passed the green door that swung outward forever—or inward forever, depending on your perspective—toward a church which was no longer there, and headed deeper into the woods. There was a downslope, a brief and dark stretch of true forest, enormous pines and younger deciduous trees, and a path that crunched with dead leaves under every step. Normally I felt a level of peace in these woods that I couldn't feel in the city *ever*. But tonight I felt lonely and watched, although I was surrounded by other people. Smiling, happy people who should not have made me feel so nervous. But they were all strangers, or vague faces I'd seen around town, and I was dressed differently from all of them, sans cloak. And the rest of the Kobayashi family were so far ahead that I'd lost sight of them.

Where the fuck was KJ? I couldn't see her. *Where is she*, I wondered, *and what's happening to her?*

I didn't know if it was reasonable to feel scared for her like I did. But I wished I could just get a glimpse of her. It would make me feel better about literally everything that was going on.

I kept my eye on Jasper's distant back and the occasional glimpse of his purple hair in the light of someone's flashlight or the flicker of one of the many torches that people carried.

Then, after what seemed like an eternally long time, we came to a place where the line of trees was abruptly cut off, and the path moved directly into one of the many sunflower fields that surrounded the town of Kesuquosh.

I could see a guy maybe twenty feet in front of me holding a torch. Because the sunflowers were so tall—even though a great deal of them were dead or dying in this late part of the year—the guy carrying the torch had to hoist it up well over his head, holding it near the very bottom to keep it from catching the dried-out field on fire.

The torchlight falling down from above and the flashlights cutting through the darkness of the field below made an odd interplay of light and darkness, like one of those fun houses at a carnival where the entire point is to disorient you.

One by one, the people ahead of me as well as the few people behind me stopped singing and talking and laughing. I didn't even notice them falling silent at first. It just seemed like the night sounds overtook the sounds of human voices until all at once there was nothing except for the wind and the bodies moving through the sunflowers.

It was in this quiet that I started to feel a creeping certainty that I and all the townies and everyone in the Great Harvest Hallow parade were being watched by something deep within the sunflowers.

I imagined countless eyes following the progression of this long ribbon of human beings as it wound through the October fields. Flat eyes, like doll's eyes (or nocturnal animal eyes, like Dexter's eyes) gazing out from deep within the darkness afforded to them by the sunflowers.

And then just as the thoughts of eyes and watchers were becoming too persistent for me to dismiss any longer, the sunflowers fell away, and we walked out into a massive clearing. The packed dirt of the ground was strewn with hay, like a farmer's fallow field. But in the center of that explicable clearing, nonsensical as a nightmare, stood a house.

In no way was it a regular farmhouse. Sitting as it did, old-fashioned and dark, on a perfectly round patch of grass, it looked like it had been plucked straight out of an illustrated *Grimm's Fairy Tales*. It was such a bizarre sight in the middle of a field that for a second I thought it was a mirage, or a hallucination.

The house was clearly older than anything else in Kesuquosh, older even than the remains of the church that we'd passed by not long before. Intermittent flashlights and flickering torchlight glanced off the exterior, tracing peaked grooves and wooden siding, revealing it to be painted black. Narrow and many-paned windows caught the light and threw it back.

And hunched over, because his great height did not allow for him to stand fully upright inside the short doorframe of the old house, was the scarecrow.

Now that I could see Good Arcturus fully and in slightly better light, it was obvious that it had been carried there. I felt like a moron—an idiot who had been caught up in the frightening imagery of the evening—for thinking that the thing had ever moved on its own. It didn't even have *feet*. Its body terminated somewhere under the tattered folds of the cloak it wore, and I guessed that the bottom of the scarecrow was made out of a single wooden pole. It probably had movable limbs—the arms certainly seemed to have been rearranged for it to stand in this doorway instead of the gazebo—and was not a real scarecrow for a field at all. The likeliest explanation was that it was a prop that the citizens of Kesuquosh dragged out once every thirty-five years to make their Great Harvest Hallow *really* immersive.

Not that it made me feel any less uncomfortable with this whole display, or any more inclined to move my finger away from where it hovered over the green Send button, should I need to call Senovak.

Beyond the mass of villagers, who were beginning to gather around the antique house, was KJ. She was standing very straight, and was encircled by Birdie Plum and the other people from Birdie's table back at the green. She looked luminous in her golden crown of flowers. And as solemn as I had ever seen her.

Then Rita moved through the circle of people around KJ to hug her daughter tightly. She paused for a second a few feet away, talking to Birdie, their heads close together, before she rejoined the rest of the Kobayashi-Jenetopolous clan.

I hovered on the periphery of the clearing, watching as the same kids who had been pouring mead and water earlier assembled a bonfire from kindling and logs, under the direction of some older teenagers.

I don't like the look of that, I thought. *Not at all.*

I had a terrible vision of KJ, lashed to a pyre in the middle of a blazing bonfire, about to be burned alive like a modern-day Joan of Arc. KJ meeting death with her lovely narrow face turned up toward the moon.

You're being ridiculous, I told myself. *There's no need for you to be ruining what should be a bit of spooky fun on a vacation that you* begged *to have by deciding that everything is some kind of horror story.*

"Darian, come over and stand with us," Rita said, and I turned toward the spot where the Kobayashi family now gathered in a loose knot.

"Rita? What's going on?" I asked.

"You don't need to look so scared, honey," Rita said. "I know our beliefs are unfamiliar to people who grew up outside Kesuquosh. But I promise you that everything is okay. You don't have to stay for the ceremony if you don't want to. Nobody will mind. It should be a straight walk back through the fields."

Rita's honest attempt to comfort me made me feel kind of stupid. For quite a while, I had been torn between fear and the feeling I was blowing something rather innocent out of proportion. I leaned back toward *I'm blowing something out of proportion* now.

Still. "But what *is* the ceremony?" I asked. I couldn't relax until someone gave me a clear answer.

"Well, Kahie will present the needle to Good Arcturus," Rita said. "She puts it in his eye. And then she becomes His new Incorporation. And then we all go drink beer and eat pumpkin soup and apple bread at Holly Garland's farmstand. She has it all decked out for the party."

"That . . . doesn't sound so bad," I admitted.

"It's not bad," Rita said. "It's lovely. There's nothing better than being part of a community, how we all work our magic together, you know? I wish your mom could be here, too. She would think you were such a great person. I think you're a great person."

Rita seemed like she was around my mom's age. Maybe a bit younger. And she'd always spoken to me about Blake's quiet sweetness, her gentle approach to interpersonal relationships, her beauty. I didn't think it meant that they'd been particularly close—Rita was nice like that about everyone. But it was always meaningful to me when she brought up my mom specifically. And she always acted like the fact of my mom's goodness somehow reflected on me. I knew that people who died young were always described as *the kind of person who lit up a room* after they were dead. But I believed that my mom had actually been an angel. Maybe a doormat, to marry Ed, but an angel nonetheless. Nothing like me. I felt like I was all broken edges, no matter how sweet Rita thought I was.

"Thanks, Rita," I said, not knowing how to respond to so much affection at once. Rita's love always felt like something I didn't deserve. "It means a lot to me."

"Of course. Are you still feeling nervous?"

I was just feeling stupid. I hoped that this thing could wrap up pretty soon so I could be hanging out with Alex and Jasper and KJ and eating apple bread and forgetting my horrible paranoia. Maybe KJ and I could finish our interrupted conversation.

"I'm fine," I said, "but thank you. For looking out for me. I'm not trying to be a baby or . . . or anything."

"I don't think you're being a baby, honey," Rita said. She ruffled my hair and pulled me into a side-hug that left us both still able to see KJ clearly.

Okay, I knew that I was far too old to be so completely taken in by ruffled hair, that it was embarrassing how much I wanted to let Rita reassure me. But I . . . I closed my eyes for a minute anyway, and leaned my head against her shoulder, imagining that Rita was my mom.

Finally it seemed like everyone was there. A thousand people filled the space, making the massive clearing feel small. In the flickering light, I didn't have a good view of everybody—except for KJ, who was obviously the star of this odd spectacle. I couldn't see Jasper, or any member of the Plum family besides Birdie.

The bonfire was lit. The flashlights were turned off. The torches—the ones that still burned—were stuck into the dusty ground. All of the townspeople began to hum. I couldn't hear Jasper's distinctive voice rising above the others. Maybe he wasn't singing.

The Kesuquoshians clasped each other by the shoulders, swaying. They sang with such sweetness, and with such happiness, that for the second time that night I thought of the Whos in Whoville from that old cartoon.

Whenever Good Arcturus comes to town,
Because his current shield is wearing thin
We sweep our streets with cider and with smoke
From frost to falls, to rid our hearts of sin

I wondered when the hell they'd learned all these songs. Were these, like, the *nursery rhymes* that they were taught? The songs that rocked them to sleep as babies?

"It is time for the new Incorporation to present the needle to the Lord of the Field," Birdie Plum said. "Kaherdin Jude, Apostle of Good Arcturus, do you accept your destiny with open arms, an open mind, and a heart full of gladness?"

"It's, uh, KJ," KJ said. "And yeah, I do." She paused and squinted at the assembled crowd when her response drew a round of laughter and cheers. Then she looked back at Birdie. "Uh . . . ma'am?" KJ asked, in what was clearly supposed to be a whisper but came out a bit loud and awkward. "What do I . . . do now?"

Another round of laughter from the crowd, and even Birdie Plum cracked a smile. "It's simple enough, *KJ*," she said, and touched one hand to KJ's shoulder. She gestured with her other hand toward the doorway directly behind them.

"You'll approach our Lord, and press the needle into His face," Birdie said, "through the shroud around him, and directly into one of his eyes. It doesn't matter which eye."

"Okayyyyy," KJ said, "but . . . um . . . He doesn't have eyes?"

"Just try to approximate it," Birdie said.

"Yeah. Okay. No problem," KJ said, nodding. Then she turned, with one hand wrapped around the needle that had been in her cake, and marched across the old slate walkway that led to the house, putting one foot after the other with a level of deliberation I'd never seen from her before.

The musicians were playing again, haunting music in a melodic minor key that echoed the strange hymns they'd sung on their walk out here. Between that sound and the crack of the flames from the bonfire, it took me a minute to hear the murmuring of the people around me. It was a low and barely audible buzz, at first. But after a minute I realized that they were all whispering in unison.

You are safe, my child. You are loved, my child. You are one with the good earth.

KJ made it up to the faceless scarecrow. It leaned down over her from the doorway of the secret house, making her seem quite small, for once.

The needle glinted in her hand, and just as she was about to stab it up into one of Good Arcturus's empty sockets, a voice cut through the sound of the music and the chanting and the crackle of the flames.

"Wait! *WAIT!* Stop—don't *do* this!"

It was Jasper, and he was screaming. He fought his way through the crowd, circled the bonfire, and shouldered past his aunt, running along the slate path until he could touch KJ's back.

"You don't have to do this," he said. "KJ. Remember my plan? It's up to you now. Try to focus. We're in the snow globe, right? You hate it, don't you? Tell me one thing that isn't true."

"I've had just about enough of you, little man," Birdie said. "Thomas, Hunter, Lake, come here and hold him still and silent. Now." ·

"No! No, you fucking *zombies*," Jasper said, and he grabbed KJ's arm, but she shook him off with one shrug, her hand still held aloft.

"I want to do this, boss," KJ said.

"How can you *want* to do this? You don't even *know* what you're *doing*! Stop listening to whatever bullshit it tells you—"

Hunter and Thomas got Jasper by the shoulders. They were both much bigger than him, and held him pretty easily. Lake, the last and tallest of the boys, put one large hand over Jasper's mouth and then quickly withdrew it, eyes wide.

"He *bit* me," Lake said, shaking his hand.

"Oh, for the love of the world," Birdie Plum said. "Jasper, I cannot tolerate—or, frankly, *believe*—this level of melodrama. Even from you. Since you will not be compliant while we try to complete our ceremonial rites, which are participated in *willingly* by *all here*, you are going to be escorted into the field for the duration. Hunter, Thomas, Lake. Please take Jasper away. I want him out of sight and out of earshot if possible."

"KJ! THIS IS OUR ONLY CHANCE! Oh, you fucking shitholes, leave her *alone*!" Jasper shouted. He was fighting so hard that Thomas and Hunter had to actually carry him away from the firelight while his legs kicked out dangerously in the air. It would have been comical . . . if not for how utterly serious he was.

I didn't look over to Rita for reassurance as they took Jasper into the sunflowers. I didn't need to go for another round of people telling me how harmless everything that was happening was, or how much Jasper was overreacting. I listened to my gut. I pressed the green Send button on my cell phone, dialing Senovak.

KJ looked around one more time, gave the crowd a thumbs-up with her free hand (which provoked another round of cheering), and plunged the long needle into the place where—if he *had* eyes— Good Arcturus's left eye would have been.

I brought the phone to my ear.

For a second I was afraid that out here I wouldn't get service. There was generally pretty bad cell phone service around the Quabbin. But the phone was ringing. Static was crackling on the line, but it was ringing, and I listened to it ring with relief.

Up in the doorframe of the old black house with the peaked roofs and the crooked chimney, the needle sank through the leathery pink fabric that swathed Good Arcturus's blank face and disappeared into the body beneath. KJ held up both her hands, triumphant. The crowd went absolutely wild now: cheering, screaming, chanting, yelling, bursting into snatches of song, musicians playing at full bore, people dancing, slapping each other on the back, hugging each other, kissing each other.

Then, as KJ turned, smiling, and started making her way back down toward the crowd along the walkway of paving stones, I doubted myself again. Even as the phone rang in my ear, I thought that maybe this was all there was to the ceremony. Now KJ would become the new . . . shield or Incorporation or whatever, until the next time they had this party. Maybe, just maybe, it really *was* harmless.

Someone picked up on the other end of the line.

"Hello?" I said.

I could hear something, maybe somebody talking, but it was difficult to pick out individual words over the cacophony that everyone was making. I turned my face away from the crowd and took two steps closer to the edge of the clearing. "Hello?" I said again, "Dan? It's really loud, sorry—"

Then I heard the voice on the other end. There was a strong background crackle, like the caller was coming from very far away. And he was singing one of the songs he'd made just for me, the one that used an anagram of my name. *Adrian* for *Darian*.

> *Oh, Adrian, your hands brush mine*
> *Oh, Adrian, oh, aren't you sweet?*
> *Oh, Adrian, my light divine*
> *My southern cross, my empty street*

I dropped the phone at the sound of Dexter's voice. When I picked it back up, I could still hear him.

"Dariannn," the thing in the static crooned. "Baby. *Baby.* You promised to come with meeee—"

I pressed the End button on my cell phone with shaking hands, and the call was terminated.

KJ had reached the bonfire. Her eyes looked out over the crowd. She was still smiling, her face bright and open under her crown of sunflowers, and her eyes found mine.

Not safe, I wanted to tell her. *You're not safe, KJ. There's something wrong.*

Then KJ broke our shared look. She glanced downward, in obvious puzzlement, at something invisible near her foot. She raised her feet one at a time, and shook them the way someone might if they had walked through a particularly large spiderweb and wanted to get the strands off their body.

The crowd was absolutely uncontained. Their volume, their overt partying, kept them from noticing exactly what was happening to KJ . . . except for Birdie Plum. I saw that Birdie was watching the scene avidly.

KJ moved her arm up and down as if something—again I thought of a spiderweb—had wrapped around her wrist. She waved her hand, looking confused, and then turned back toward the doorway where Good Arcturus waited.

And that, like a dam breaking, signaled a flood. But not of water. Thin, sinewy red strands—like hay, or thread, or very delicate veins—started to push their way out of the body of Good Arcturus.

Lines of red slithered out of the pale shroud he was wrapped in.

"What . . . ?" I said out loud. But no one answered me.

Each one of the thin red threads moved through the air with an eerie sentience, finding KJ's body and spinning around some part of it: her arms, her legs, her torso, her ears and fingers, her mouth. KJ looked down, obviously bewildered.

The strands kept coming, by the dozens; and then, it seemed, by the hundreds, and as more and more of them sprung out of Good Arcturus to entwine themselves with KJ, the scarecrow started to . . . *deflate*, almost. As if it were a skein of yarn that someone was quickly unspooling. The body under that tattered pink fabric began to fall in on itself.

The crowd actually got quiet. Most of them seemed—at first anyway—to be frightened by this turn of events. Disturbed.

For a second, I saw a look of absolute horror on Ken Kobayashi's face. But by the time Ken had taken two steps forward—as if he were going to extricate his daughter from the web of red string that was rapidly cocooning her—his features had already smoothed back out into a benign excitement. He started to clap.

Other people joined in with clapping. KJ was clearly realizing that something was not right. But *slowly*, like someone who has woken up from a deep sleep and finds their house on fire. She was struggling a little, moving her shoulders to keep the red strings from holding her completely still.

"WHAT IS HAPPENING TO HER?" I shouted. "What is going on? What—"

I looked for some spark of human emotion in the people around me. I took two running steps forward, slammed into Alex's back, and spun him around by the arms.

"Are you okay, Darian?" Alex asked in the exact same gentle, even, pleasant tone that he always used for everything. He looked mildly concerned.

I didn't answer him. I suddenly didn't believe that he was really there, that any of them were really there. I was in a field watching something terrible happen to KJ, and the only other witnesses might as well have been mannequins.

I shoved my way to the front of the crowd, almost falling into the bonfire—which had become enormous, a conflagration that seemed like it could devour someone whole—and then I ran wide around it.

"Darian, *wait!*" I heard someone yell. Rita. I ignored her. I stopped in front of KJ.

She was almost entirely held in place by red strings. She looked like—my first thought was like a fly caught in a web—but no, it was more extreme than that. She looked like she was being mummified. Only her eyes were visible.

"KJ!" I said, and reached for her.

Lines of deep red sinew twisted across her mouth and nose, and I realized that she probably couldn't breathe. I tore with all of my strength at the strands around her face. My hands pushed through a mist of red strings that moved with their own sentience, sliding around my fingers, unbearable as they brushed against my arms. I could hear a muffled sound: KJ trying to scream.

The strands moved away as I touched them, like living things. They were slimy and cold, the undersides of rocks that hadn't seen daylight for a very long time. My fingers went numb where they grazed my skin.

I could hear my own voice, like someone outside of me was running my mouth, saying total nonsense in a high-pitched stream: "KJ. You're okay, you're gonna be okay, okay? Okay, just hold still. Just *get off her*! *Get off of her*, oh god. Oh god, please no, oh *stop*, oh stop, oh god, please no—"

Then, more panicked than I had ever been, I tried to push KJ—who could barely walk because she was so bound up—toward the edge of the clearing, thinking, nonsensically, that she would some-how be safer if she was hidden by the dead sunflowers.

Red thread unraveled what had been Good Arcturus's body faster and faster, surrounding us in a sinewy mist. And no matter how much I tried to bat it back, no matter how much KJ struggled, it was inexorable. The last of Good Arcturus flew out toward us. The leathery and faded cloth that had once covered the scarecrow fell to the ground with a soft *whooshing* sound.

I was crying, at some point I had started crying, but I didn't have time to wipe my tears away. KJ was *disappearing* into the red string. Again I tried to drag her away from the thread, but I wasn't strong enough.

The end of the thread was attached to a needle. The needle that KJ had found in her sacred cake.

KJ was trying to say something, but when she did manage to open her mouth, the threads immediately covered it again. At the last second she swung her shoulder out and shoved as hard as she could at me, making me stumble back. She made a gesture, a wordless and stifled gesture with her shoulder. It said clearly: *Get away, go away from here.*

But I couldn't leave her.

The needle moved through the air like a birch leaf caught on a gust of wind. It spun, sinuously, toward the rest of its red thready body. And then it paused, hovering over KJ's face like a wasp about to sting.

"No no no *NO!*"

I was screaming. I understood what was coming. I actually jumped up and tried to grab at the needle. It evaded me like it was being moved by an expert puppeteer.

Then Birdie Plum was there, holding me by the wrist as I watched the needle move toward KJ.

"Do *not* interfere," she hissed. "I don't care if you *are* a Sabine. Touch Him again and I'll bury you out here."

I ripped my hand away from Birdie's grip. Her nails left welts on my skin, but I could barely process it. I took a stumbling step toward KJ, and the needle that had been poised above her face struck downward, in a sudden, incredibly quick movement.

"DON'T, *OH GOD!*" I shouted. The needle pierced KJ's left eye, and despite the gag around her face, I could hear her shriek of agony. And it didn't stop—no, the needle went in farther and farther, leaving a single bloody tear in its wake, until it had disappeared entirely inside KJ's body.

The string started to unspool as quickly as it had wound her up. Now I could see that it was all one connected mass—one string—topped off at the end by the long stinger of the needle. All of the thread followed the needle into KJ's eye. Slithering, disappearing inside her body, although it seemed as though there was too much string to ever fit inside one single human being.

I got close enough to try to grab one of the ends of the thread and pull it back out by force, but then KJ—whose mouth was fully uncovered now—let out a cry of such immense agony that I dropped my hold.

"AHHHAhahhhhhhhha . . . ahhh . . . ," KJ moaned. Her voice trailed off into a gurgling whisper. It was like she was drowning.

The thread moved exponentially faster, gliding so quickly into KJ's eye that it was almost blurred. The last of it disappeared, and KJ shuddered. Her eyes closed. She started to fall backward.

"KJ!" I screamed, and tried to catch her, hold her. But she never hit the ground. KJ's body was lifted up entirely in the air. She floated, lying on her back like someone asleep, bloodred tears dripping from her left eye. And then, after a second, her body jerked as if invisible hands were pulling it through the air on an invisible wire. KJ's body flew toward the doors of the old black house and shot inside. The doors slammed shut with a sound so enormous and final that it shook the very clearing where we stood. The people of Kesuquosh cheered throughout all of this, like they were watching a sporting match where their favorite team was winning.

I wasn't thinking. I bolted toward the old double doors, stepping over the worn leather shroud that had covered Good Arcturus, and grabbed at the iron handles, trying to open them.

"Stop screaming, girl, or I'll give you something to scream about," Birdie Plum said. She came and stood right next to me as I tore at the doors, willing them to open, pounding on them.

"Please," I said. "Oh, please, please give her back! Oh god. Oh god, let me in, let me in, *please*—"

Birdie bent over and picked up the leathery length of fabric. She held it up by—by what would be its shoulders—for the crowd to see, and I felt a new horror consume me. I realized that the cloth didn't look like cloth anymore.

It bore a remarkable resemblance to the shape of a person's body. To a corpse, in fact. A dried and husked-out corpse. A little one, like a child, so small and dry and mummified that Birdie could lift it with no effort.

"To our new Incorporation," Birdie cried out, holding the little withered body aloft. "And to our last shield—to all that remains of Blanche Sabine!"

The crowd cheered for the woman holding the sad and shriveled body of a dead girl. Of my *aunt*, supposedly. Birdie, in one gesture, threw the husk of a person onto the bonfire, where it was immediately engulfed by roaring flames.

I ran, then. I ran as fast as my shaking legs would carry me, away from that terrible place. I ran into the darkness while the crowd went wild with applause.

INTERLUDE

2001

CHAPTER SEVEN

Wednesday, September 12, 2001

Eleven months after I lost KJ to the black house, 9/11 happened. And my dad sent me and Senovak away from Manhattan, where I'd been doing nothing at all with the gap year I'd taken after graduation. He sent us back to our summer house in the town where the monster lived. The town full of mannequins.

The trip back to Kesuquosh from New York—even on the day after the Twin Towers fell, when getting out of the city was hard and the world felt like it was actively ending—was too fast. It hadn't taken us long enough. Not even *close* to long enough for me to get used to the idea of going back to the village that had once been my favorite place on earth. By midafternoon on September 12, we had already made it to Rabbitville.

And I was scared. Rabbitville was southeast of Kesuquosh, each town standing alongside the Quabbin Reservoir like silent sentinels. But since the Quabbin was so huge (it was still called the *lost valley* by some locals, in homage to the four towns that had been abandoned when the reservoir was made), I figured we were twenty-five minutes away by car. If Kesuquosh still existed, that was. For all the contact I'd had with it, in the almost-year since I (and Jasper and Alex) had tried to save KJ, the little village might have been swallowed up by the earth.

But I knew that it hadn't. Even now, when it seemed like we were on the brink of World War III, I knew that Kesuquosh was lovely and safe and quaint and untouched. Glowing windows on a firefly-filled night. Gently rocking swings on dim porches. A monster in the sunflower fields, yeah, but *otherwise*, the place was still perfect. Perfect.

Good Arcturus could not let it be any other way. Good Arcturus always provided for his people.

In Rabbitville, we ate lunch at a restaurant called The Tributary that looked like it catered exclusively to people over seventy. The place was empty except for me and Senovak—and a waitress who was also the hostess, and one cook. Senovak and I sat in a tiny booth by the kitchen doors. Once we got our soup and salad, the cook rolled a TV on a cart into the dining room, and he and the waitress sat with us in silence and watched the ongoing news coverage about the attack on the World Trade Center and the Pentagon. I couldn't really bring myself to eat anything.

The whole world felt abandoned, like people were hunkered down waiting for it to end. We left Rabbitville behind. The minutes ran through my fingers like water. Closer and closer and closer. By the time we hit the Citgo on Route 202, my fear at the thought of going back to Kesuquosh was uncontrollable.

The gas station—like almost everything else I'd seen on the day after the planes flew into the Twin Towers—was quiet. A guy in a sedan was at the pump ahead of us. A painted van with a bumper sticker that said *War Is Not Healthy for Children and Other Living Things* pulled out of the lot when we pulled in.

"Go put twenty dollars on pump three, please?" Senovak said, and I went into the Citgo with two tens, hoping that it was Aunt Judy working the counter. Aunt Judy knew about Kesuquosh, about what we'd all been through. Seeing her would be really good . . . it might even make me less afraid.

For a second I didn't see anyone inside the Citgo—and then I did actually spot Aunt Judy, rolling around the side of the counter in her blue wheelchair, clad in familiar stoner-wear. She looked distressed before she even saw me, and when she saw me she looked *more* distressed. And surprised.

"Darian, I didn't know *you'd* come back, too," Aunt Judy said, her familiar scratchy old-lady-voice like a balm.

"Dad made me leave New York," I said. Then I bent down and hugged her, putting my arms around her narrow shoulders. She hugged me back tightly.

"I was worried about you, cupcake," she said when I stood up. "Being in Manhattan and everything. I've been worried about you since last year, actually."

"Did Alex come and see you? After . . . after Halloween?" I asked. Did she know what had happened? She must know enough to know things went really *bad*, anyway.

"Yes," Aunt Judy said. "Just the once. Then not again until today. And he just left between customers, before I could really talk to him. But after I found out what happened to Jasper—"

"Alex came and saw you *today*?" I asked.

"He isn't with you? He was just in here," Aunt Judy said.

The bells tinkled, and Senovak walked in. "Darian?"

"I'm paying, I'm paying," I said.

"No," Senovak said. "Look outside. It's the pothead."

I handed the money back to Senovak when he reached me.

"I'll call you tonight," I told Aunt Judy. "You're in the phone book, right?"

"Yes, but you should be careful—" Aunt Judy started to say something more, but I didn't look back, only ran around Senovak and out the door to the parking lot.

Alex *was* there. Standing right next to the car, probably right where Senovak had told him to wait, with a SoBe in his hand and a beaten-up drawstring backpack over his shoulder, staring at the ground with a blank expression.

"Al!" I said, and ran over to him. He smiled when he saw me.

"Oh man, Darian, I'm so glad you're here," Alex said. He grabbed me and held on to my shoulders. It was less like the hug Aunt Judy had given me and more like the grasp of a drowning man. And then I actually *looked* at him.

Alex had shaved his head. He'd gone from wiry to gaunt. His cheeks were hollow. The sleeves of his hoodie were pushed up to his elbows, revealing arms that had healed-over track marks. I'd seen track marks before, on random junkies and recovering addicts and, most of all, on Dexter. But my understanding of Alex made the idea of him doing heroin . . . very weird. He was a weed-and-psychedelics kind of guy if he was anything.

"I know I look bad," Alex said, pushing down his sleeves. He said it kind of sheepishly, like he was sorry I had to look at him, and it made me feel so awful for him that it felt like a phys-ical thing in my stomach. A stone of sadness for my fucked-up friend.

"You look fine," I said, which was a lie. I didn't mean it literally. I meant something closer to *you'll be fine*, which was probably also a lie.

"Why are you back here?" Alex asked, before I could ask him the same question.

"My dad made us come," I said. "He basically sent us away and stayed behind, like in some wartime drama."

"When I heard about the planes, that it was in Manhattan, I was so freaked. Would've called you . . . a long time ago, probably, once I got my brain together a little, but I never memorized your cell phone number. Jasper and KJ always knew it by heart."

"It wouldn't have made a difference," I said. "At least not if you tried today. All the cell phone service in the city is down. Everything's fucked. It took literal hours to even get out of New York. Ed sent us away at like four in the morning and we just got here now."

"I can't believe Dan would agree to be, like, *sent away*, during a national emergency," Alex said. "Even if your dad *is* his boss."

"I mean, he didn't need to be convinced to leave," I said. "Honestly the only thing he was pissed about was that Ed wasn't coming with us right away. It's . . . it's really scary there right now. There are . . . there are bodies. In the streets. Everyone is getting out. Like an exodus." I knew I was rambling, but I wanted to paint him an accurate picture of how much it felt like the apocalypse had come to New York. "There's all this dust. It's hard to see. Ed knows a lot of people who work in those buildings. A *lot*. There are rescue crews searching now, but I don't think they're going to find many people alive. And Dan says he doesn't know what's going to happen with the army. He's an officer and he never resigned his commission when he 'retired,' so maybe he can be recalled? Or something?"

I tried to sound nonchalant when I said that. But Alex wasn't fooled.

"If Dan has to go to war," he said, raising his eyebrows, "you will freak out."

"I would freak out worse than if my dad was literally exploded by another plane tomorrow," I agreed.

"Heh. Yeah. But it sounds really scary there," Alex said.

"It is. But like . . . I would rather be there right now than on my way to Kesuquosh," I admitted.

Alex nodded. "I don't want to go back either."

"Why are you?" I asked.

"I . . . I haven't seen my family in a year, or even talked to any of them," Alex said, crossing his arms over his chest like he was cold, despite the warm September sun. "I wouldn't even be going home . . . except . . . well, this shit that happened yesterday . . . it kinda makes it feel like life as we know it is over."

"Yeah," I agreed, "it does."

"And I felt like I had to check on them. Last night I decided to come back. Just for a few days," Alex said. "I hitched rides from Allston. The last people were a really nice hippie couple in a van, they brought me all the way from that mall in Wickford."

He looked at me squarely then, and I saw thin lines of pain around his mouth. "I hate my family, you know," Alex said. "For what they went along with. I—I understand why Jasper hated *me*—"

"He did *not* hate you," I said. "Alex. He loved you. He knew you were being controlled. And so are they."

Then I noticed that his pupils were pinpricks in the sunlight.

"Your eyes," I said, and Alex put one hand to his temple. "They still look normal. Are you . . . can you hear him—or *it*, I guess—talking right now?" I asked. The skin on my arms prickled at the thought of that disembodied voice whispering in his brain.

"No. I've been freaking out about it all day," he said. "But I don't think so, at all."

"Would you be able to tell?" I asked.

"Yeah," Alex said. "It's really distinct. Like . . . have you ever read anything by William Faulkner?"

"Oh god," I said. Alex and Rita were the big readers in his family, word-lovers, the kind of people who did the Sunday crossword puzzle together in pen. "Only a short story, and only because I had to for school."

"Well, he wrote a lot of his narratives in stream of consciousness, it was all kind of weird and fluid, like the way thoughts really are in your head. But then there's the voice of Kesuquosh, and it's, like, solid. Relentless." Alex's voice took on an eerie low rasp. "*You are safe, my child. You are loved, my child. You are one with the good earth.* It's not a *stream* of consciousness. It's like a hammer and a nail. But I can't . . . it's not working on me right now."

"Are you worried it might . . . um . . . ."

"Brainwash me again?" Alex asked. He smiled, but it was strained. "It's all I've been worrying about since I decided to come. I'm scared that if I spend too much time in Kesuquosh, I'll forget why I wanted to leave in the first place."

"Are you sure you want to go back?" I asked. I hadn't fought against this return trip to Kesuquosh as hard as I could have. There had been tons of chances, even after we left the city, for me to protest. Ask Senovak to go somewhere else. Anywhere else. I was pretty sure Ed had offices in Boston. We weren't exactly in a position where staying in a hotel was a financial concern. And even if he refused, well—I had my own credit card. I was a high school graduate who was turning eighteen in December. I could have gotten out of going back, if I'd really tried.

I hadn't really tried. As terrified as I was, some part of me wanted to know what had happened, *since*. But wanting to know was less important than Alex. He was still here, alive and himself, and I needed to keep him that way. But I'd obviously come in at the end of a long internal debate. Alex's nod was firm.

"I have to check on them. I still love them, you know, even though I hate them. How can I love them after what they were complicit in?"

"What were they complicit in?" Senovak asked, and I turned around to see him standing there, deceptively unimposing, with his head tilted and his gaze narrowed. He was so quiet when he wanted to eavesdrop (which was always, basically).

"Ugh!" I said. "Can you not do that? This is a private conversation!"

I decided long ago that what had happened in Kesuquosh was too unbelievable and too dangerous to let him in on. Like what had happened with Dexter, it was necessary for me to keep Senovak in the dark about last Halloween. For my sanity and his.

"I'm *so* sorry, Darian, but I have to stand here to pump the gas. Alex, I don't see anything here that looks like it could be a vehicle of yours."

"I hitchhiked," Alex said.

"Mm-hmm," Senovak said, in a way that managed to convey disapproval for the entire practice of hitchhiking. "Do you need a ride?"

"That'd be great, thanks, Dan," Alex said.

I got in the back seat of the Lincoln so I could be next to Alex. He followed me in and set his battered backpack down between us on the seat. But he kept one hand on it.

Senovak finished pumping gas and drove the car out of the parking lot. "So where were you, that you had to hitchhike home?" Senovak asked.

"Boston," Alex said. "I'm homeless and to stay inside at night I started sleeping with this rich BU freshman who has her own apartment. Bianca."

That was pretty direct. I watched in the rearview mirror as Senovak's eyebrows climbed up toward his hairline.

"That's not the best situation," Senovak said. "For you *or* Bianca. Why haven't Ken and Rita been helping you?"

"They didn't know where I was," Alex said. Between his honesty and Senovak's insane nosiness we might be in for an interesting car ride.

"You chose not to inform them of where you were?" Senovak asked.

"Yeah," Alex said. I wondered how much he would tell Senovak. Hopefully not so much that he thought Alex had lost his mind. I inched my hand closer to the middle seat, to squeeze his arm if he started saying anything that was *too* honest. But Alex just dragged his backpack onto his lap and held it protectively.

"Why?" Senovak said. "Are you in some kind of danger?"

Senovak had asked me loaded stuff like that several times in the almost-year since I'd left Kesuquosh. Especially after I refused to go there for my summer vacation. I didn't know what he *thought* had happened. Obviously not what had actually happened.

"Not exactly," Alex said. "Not from my *parents*, anyway. Unless we . . . unless I really cross the line. We didn't part on the best of terms."

Understatement of the millennium.

Then we were at the town line. It had happened without me noticing it. There had been a sharp turn off 202 onto a tiny road. Once you were on it, the heavy woods around the Quabbin melted into a line of trees that guarded enormous expanses of sunflower fields, holding the little town like a secret. We were a quarter mile down the road now, in view of the town sign. And that book-shaped official sign said:

KESUQUOSH VILLAGE INC. 1743

Just a bit beyond that was the hand-painted sign, about billboard height but much smaller than a billboard, that read KESU-QUOSH: HOME OF SQUASH! in a cheerful font. Senovak cruised past both signs, his eyes in the rearview. "Do you want me to drop you off at your house, Alex?" he asked.

"Um," Alex said. We traded hesitant glances.

"I don't know," I said quietly. "Like you said, we didn't exactly leave things—"

"Yeah, but. They're not gonna be violent," Alex whispered.

Senovak was *alive* with interest. I could see him visibly straining to hear us.

"Can you actually drop me off here?" Alex asked. "Right here. I'm going to walk."

"I'll come with you," I said immediately.

"No, I'm good," Alex said.

I didn't know why he wanted to go off on his own, but I wasn't going to let him. I had a lot of guilt about letting him leave after what had happened last Halloween. At the end of everything we did and didn't do, he had wanted to be alone so that he could destroy himself. I saw that now, looking at how fucked-up he'd gotten.

But this was another chance. I could help him this time. Curb his destructive impulses. It wasn't like I didn't get it. I had lost a lot. Almost more than I could stand thinking about. But Alex had lost *everything* in the span of a few days.

And something about how he was acting put me on edge. "I need to have a big reunion," I said blithely. "With KJ and Jas. It'll be *great*."

Alex looked over at me. Senovak braked on Good Earth Way.

"I didn't know they even still lived here," Senovak said mildly. But his glance in the rearview was penetrating. "Considering the fact that you never speak to them anymore."

"It's going to be great," I repeated. I swung myself out of the car after Alex, who was up and trying to walk away quickly. "Home by midnight, I promise!"

"Be careful," Senovak told me. "Make good choices. You have your cell phone on you?"

"I will, I will, I do," I said. "Just like, so excited to see them, you know?"

"Right," Senovak said.

I slammed the door. Senovak did *not* look convinced. He kept the car idling until he saw me catch up with Alex.

"What *gives*?" I asked, almost running to keep pace with him. "I thought you wouldn't want to be separated. After everything that happened."

Alex shook his head, not looking at me. He was holding his backpack in two hands in front of him, with his half-finished SoBe in his back pocket.

"Seriously, Al." I got in front of him so that he was forced to stop power-walking down the road. "You already walked away from me once. Don't you care? I thought we were in it together."

Alex's set expression kind of faltered. "I love you, Dare," he said. "But I can't, like . . . I can't *involve* you in this."

"In what?" I asked. I was already as involved as it was possible to be, and he knew it.

Alex looked around: at the flower-filled window boxes and planters. At the bustling street with the bikes and the cars and the pedestrians all moving in harmony. Nobody had recognized him yet, but it was only a matter of time. The village was not a huge place.

"In this," Alex said, and opened his bag between our bodies.

Just for a second. But it was long enough for me to see the gun.

"What are you *doing*?" I asked, glancing left and right as Alex closed the bag back up. "Why the fuck do you *have* that?! What the HELL, Alex—"

"Because," Alex said, and started walking down the street again. Straight toward the town hall building.

"Because?" I asked, jogging next to him to keep up.

Alex looked down at me. His eyes were tired, but calm. His mouth was set in a straight line.

"Because I'm going to kill her," he said.

PART TWO

THE FROST AND THE FALLS

CHAPTER EIGHT

Saturday, October 28 & Sunday, October 29, 2000

After KJ was consumed by the thing the villagers called Good Arcturus, adrenaline made me run from the black house in a blind panic. I was crying as I fled the clearing and ran through the dying sunflowers, soundlessly crying, and it wasn't long until I couldn't sustain a sprint. I would jog for a few minutes and then run for a few more. Spiderwebs broke across my face and body but I hardly felt them. I wiped my hands on my red sweatshirt over and over again, trying to get rid of the horrible cold feeling from where the red threads had touched me.

I was only thinking about KJ and escape, KJ and escape. Those two things alternated in my head like flashing lights.

But then I thought about Jasper and Alex. I pictured Alex's blank expression of acceptance, his undisturbed happiness. I didn't know if I could persuade him to leave . . . or if he even thought that anything bad had happened at all.

But Jasper knew. Jasper had been dragged away into the field by Lake and Thomas and Hunter Warren. Jasper could be in danger. I slowed down, wondering if I could get back to him. Get to him and get him to leave with me. *He doesn't belong here. He doesn't belong here and I don't belong here, oh god, I never belonged here*, I thought. I'd never really known anything about Kesuquosh, despite Jasper's warnings.

I kept moving, walking on semi-autopilot. In my mind images played on a loop: KJ shoving me away with her shoulder in a last effort to keep me from harm as the red strings mummified her, KJ standing in front of me when we walked up the stairs of the gazebo, Birdie Plum's expression of fascination as she watched that *thing* inhabit KJ, and the body.

The dry corpse of a little girl being immolated.

Your aunt Blanche died when your mother was just a small child, my dad had told me.

In 1965. At the last *Great* Harvest Hallow.

I started to laugh as I walked, and covered my face with one hand, giggling helplessly and breathlessly. They fed one person to the scarecrow every thirty-five years? Is *that* what was happening here? And every time that someone was all respectful because I "was a Sabine," they were just honoring the tiny victim of this monster?

My little aunt. Just a kid. It wore her skin like a jacket, I thought. That made me laugh harder, even though it wasn't funny at all. My head felt like it was wayyyyy above my body. Unreality washed over me. It was how I'd felt after Dexter died . . . like nothing existed. Like I didn't exist.

Then the field ended, spitting me out onto the remains of Church Street, which led past the ruins of the old church and toward town. There were no villagers on the path—they were all still partying out in the secret clearing by the black house.

I thought of Rita cheerfully telling me that after the ceremony was over everyone was going to go have pumpkin soup and apple bread at the Garlands' farmstand, and I felt a wave of nausea sweep over me. I gagged, and then started laughing again.

"You don't need to run. They're not coming after us." The speaker was to my left, and I spun to the side, ready to sprint again. But it was Jasper. He looked pale, and had a smudge of dirt over his left eyebrow, but he seemed otherwise unscathed.

"Oh god, Jasper," I said, and laughed harder. "I—what—*what was that*?"

"The Great Harvest Hallow," Jasper said. He turned his face up toward the crescent moon for a second, looking exhausted, and I saw tear tracks on his cheeks. He'd been crying. "I didn't want you to come, Darian. You didn't deserve to see all that shit. Fuck. I—she wasn't supposed to get picked. That was completely fucking wrong, that fucking asshole *lied* to me—"

"We need to go get Dan," I said. "You can come with me. He'll listen to me. We can get away and call the cops." I held out my phone. "I can't hear—I keep hearing other voices when I dial it—but *you* can call them—"

"The only pigs in Kesuquosh are the Sumners, and they're out in the field right now with all the other zombies," Jasper said.

It was true. And the Sumners were only constables, a father-and-son team that felt like they belonged in *Twin Peaks*. There was no crime in Kesuquosh, except when tourists got up to petty shit.

"But we could call the cops in Rabbitville, or Amherst," I said.

"We could," Jasper said. "I called them a *bunch* when I was a kid, after I had my accident and realized that everyone else in town was fucking brainwashed. I called CPS. When I started to put shit together I even reported your aunt as a missing person once, thinking that might actually make them investigate something."

He started walking down the path toward town, and gestured at me to keep pace with him. "Do you know what happened?"

"What?" I asked, dreading his answer. My scalp prickled.

"Abso-fucking-lutely nothing," Jasper said. "Good Arcturus doesn't *let* anything happen. Nobody will believe you, even if you stuff the proof right down their fucking throats. They'll forget. It will disappear. Did *you* ever believe it?"

"No. But Dan will believe us. Or he'll at least listen."

Jasper thought about this for a second. "Maybe. I don't know. This wasn't the plan. Not KJ. It was supposed to be me. We had the PDA ready and everything."

"What do you mean? You *wanted* to have it . . . possess you or something? I—I don't even know what happened," I said.

"Uh. I don't actually know where to start." Jasper lit a Djarum with a pack of Citgo matches.

"You could start by telling me what Good Arcturus is," I said. I wiped off my hands on my sweatshirt again.

"It's a parasite," Jasper said. "I think."

He looked sideways at me—his blue eyes shadowed in the darkness, clove held tilted inward between his thumb and three bent fingers like a private eye in an old movie—and in his face I saw the thing that made us kindred spirits since the first time we'd met, back when we were barely even teenagers yet.

I had never understood what it was. Why, as different as we were, we were somehow the *same*. But now I could finally see it.

Jasper carried Good Arcturus around with him the way I carried Dexter. He was alone with the monster in a world full of people who didn't understand.

Like me.

Jasper was never big on touching—but then, when he looked at me so lost and vulnerable and unable to find the words to describe the prison he'd been living in—I reached for him and put my hand on his shoulder. And he let me do it.

"I get why it's hard to talk about. And how alone you've been," I said.

Jasper nodded slowly. "You do, don't you," he said, half to himself.

"Tell me about Good Arcturus," I said. "You can tell me while we walk over to the cottage, okay?"

We passed the ruins of Empty Heaven, and the oddly preserved green door, and Jasper looked sideways at me again. "I guess I should start with my accident," he said. "When I fell out of the attic."

"Okay," I said. The wind picked up, and clove smoke streamed past me in a banner and vanished into the blue-black night over our heads.

"I've never told anybody this," Jasper said. "I remember what it was like to be one of those zombie fucks, because I *was* one of them. I was one of them until I was nine."

"What happened when you were nine?" I asked.

"So in the attic at my parents' house, there's this old, like *really* old, bed with a brass frame, and all this antique clothing and shit. And we used to play up there. Me and Alex, especially, because we did everything together. You follow?"

"I follow," I said.

"We'd hang out there and color in our coloring books, or play with my Matchbox cars, or Pogs. Or imagination games, with the old stuff as props. Sometimes we'd pretend to be married. I wanted to marry Alex when we grew up. I thought if we just acted like a married couple it would make it come true. So I'd cover his head in like a piece of lace and then we'd pretend we were having a wedding ceremony, like the ones they do out in the sunflower fields. Then one day I fell out of the trapdoor in the attic. It was just dumb shit, we were playing with a Nerf ball, and I slipped. I slipped and fell out eight feet into the third floor hallway, and I didn't shield my head because I was a stupid fucking child.

"And then . . . they had to take me to the *real* hospital, not that little brick building in town that has a pediatrician and a family doctor and a tiny obstetrics office. I remember throwing up like eight times and the world being all blurry and far away. And in Amherst the doc said I had a concussion. I stayed overnight in the ICU. But then I came back home . . . and he was gone."

We'd passed from Church Street to Deep River Road back out onto Good Earth Way. The town was completely empty and silent. Nothing moved on the green. The ruins of the Banquet gaped up at us from the disarrayed tables. Some of the houses up and down the sides of the town green had lit windows, but where before I had found the glowing light from within comforting and festive, it now felt flat and ominous. Empty eyes gazing into an empty place.

"He was gone? Good Arcturus?" I asked, when Jasper was quiet for a solid thirty seconds. He nodded, his eyes on the ground as he walked.

"Yeah. I got home and the voice didn't come back. It shouldn't have gone silent when we were only as far away as Amherst *anyway*, but I was a kid and I didn't think of that. And then I was totally alone in my head. And like I know most people are alone in their heads, right, but I *never had been* since I was born. *You are loved, my child. You are one with the good earth. We are as solid as the rocks around us. We are facing a star. We are together in the cosmos.* Blah blah fucking blah. The words were meaningless, it was what they *did* to me that mattered. I was suddenly alone in this quiet world. And I thought I was gonna get in trouble, you know, for not being able to hear him. So I didn't tell anyone and I just waited for it to come back."

"But it didn't come back," I said.

"But it didn't come back. And then I started noticing other things. How everyone had to give birth in town. How we didn't do all these things I saw on TV or read about, like . . . like how we don't celebrate any holidays except for birthdays and the Hallow, how nobody practices any religions. And alllllll these feelings I'd never felt before started to creep in."

I tried, unsuccessfully, to imagine feeling an entire spectrum of emotions I'd never felt before. It was an alien thought, desolate and horrible. "Like what feelings?" I asked.

"When I got angry, it wouldn't go right away like it always had. Ditto when I got scared, or sad, or jealous. And then I started fighting with my parents sometimes, about stuff I didn't want to do, and they had, like, no idea what to do about that. I'd never been in trouble before, because I'd never been disobedient before."

"I've never seen you be anything *but* disobedient," I said.

"Yeah," Jasper said, nodding, "and Alex . . ."

Jasper stopped talking again. He was quiet as we passed K-Family Pizza, where all the windows were dark and only the neon sign threw off light.

"Alex," I said, after a lengthy pause.

"Alex wasn't Alex anymore," Jasper said, in a rush that made it clear he'd been thinking about this for a long time, much, much longer than our conversation. "Or I wasn't me. He wasn't my best friend. My best friend and my . . . I thought we were like, soul mates, you know. I didn't have the words as a little kid. But I had the idea."

If I hadn't already experienced so much shock that I was numb, this admittance by Jasper would've been the shock of *all* shocks. It went well beyond pretending to be married as a little kid . . . into an implication of how Jasper felt now.

I knew Jasper was gay, of course. Everyone knew Jasper was gay, and if you didn't know, he'd quickly inform you in the most confrontational way possible.

But he'd never shown interest in any specific guy, except for once telling me that he "regularly jerked off to *Fight Club*," and I'm (pretty) sure that was a joke.

And he'd definitely never shown interest in Alex. Not in front of me, anyway.

In fact, Jasper sometimes treated Alex with the same barely-concealed wrath that he showed to the adults of the village: like his parents, for example, or Birdie Plum. Not Rita, not for the most part, but she was a special case.

It had always bothered me. But I never said anything, because it never seemed to bother Alex. And because I assumed that KJ would have said something if her twin was *really* being persecuted.

I didn't interrupt Jasper, though, and when he looked at me like he was waiting for a comment, I rolled my hand in a *keep talking* gesture.

"He still . . . we've, like, made out and stuff," Jasper said. He kept his face turned away from me while he said it, and it sounded like it hurt him to force the words out. "I can't have sex with him, though, you know? No matter what I want, or what he says he wants. It would be wrong, because . . . he isn't really there. He can't really understand love, you get what I mean? You can't love if you'll do whatever someone else says. They don't give you *Nineteen Eighty-Four* at the fucking school in *our* town, but I gave it to him anyway. I thought he would get something out of it, maybe it would reach him or something. And he read it in like two days. But you know what he said after? You know what he fucking said?"

"I don't know if I want to know," I said.

"He said that weren't we *so lucky* we didn't live in a totalitarian state! The FUCKING MORON," Jasper said, and his golden voice echoed through the empty street, "said that with a *fucking mouth* that the *fucking Thought Police* were speaking *right* through! That's what he *is*, you know, Good Arcturus, he's the Thought Police, and he's so much better at it than anything else could be, because he's *inside* you—"

He paused for a minute, shaking his head.

"I'm sorry, Jas," I said. "I'm sorry I didn't believe you."

"It's not your fault," Jasper said. "I was complicit. I hid it from you. On purpose. Like, until you showed up here today. Yesterday. Whatever the fuck time it is." He avoided my gaze, turning his face away. Shame all over him, making him seem more vulnerable than he ever had. "You had no *idea*, Darian. And I wanted . . . I wanted you to keep coming back. To stay ignorant. You're my best friend and I didn't want you to run away. You weren't in any danger, so I figured—why try to tell you?"

I was thinking about all of the odd things I had never thought too deeply about. Senovak had never mentioned the myriad oddities of Kesuquosh either, and he noticed *everything.* "Even if you had told me I'm betting I wouldn't have been able to take it seriously, right?"

"Right," Jasper said.

"So stop punishing yourself, okay?"

"I should've still tried," Jasper said. "Instead of being selfish."

"I wouldn't have run away," I said, meaning it. "I could have tried to help you."

"He won't let anyone help me. There was nobody who could help me . . . except KJ. That's why I thought we could beat him together. I had a plan."

"KJ," I said, and the pain and horror of what had happened to her rolled over me again, almost made my voice break when I said her name.

"I think I can still save her," Jasper said.

"*How?*" I asked.

Jasper shook his head. "Not sure yet."

We rounded the corner of the road and there was Number 19, with its back hanging out over the Styx-black river water.

"Why would KJ be able to help you if everyone in town is controlled by the Thought Police?" I asked.

"Because she had a way to get around it, sometimes," Jasper said, and then he stopped and nudged me, pointing.

Senovak was standing in the doorway, his form silhouetted by the light that spilled out from inside. When I saw him I started to jog up the driveway, tugging Jasper along.

"Dan!" I said with palpable relief at the sight of him. I had no idea how to tell him what had happened. Or if I even should. But I wanted to, right then. If *anyone* could help us—

"Darian," Senovak said, and I slowed down as I approached him. Something was wrong. The way he stood was all off: instead of his shoulders being thrown back ramrod-straight, Senovak leaned against the door like someone had sucker-punched him.

"What's wrong?" I asked, stopping in front of him.

And Senovak *hugged* me. He was about as big on hugging as Jasper was. It was so weird that I hugged him back without thinking—he squeezed me really tight for a second and then dropped his hold and nodded at Jasper.

"Professor Plum," he said, but without any trace of his normal humorous formality.

"Dan, *what's wrong?*" I asked.

"I . . . I just . . . I had a call. You remember my friend Linus?" Senovak produced his cell phone from a pocket, like I needed a visual aid to understand how a person got a phone call. Or maybe he was just really out of it.

"Yeah, of course I remember Linus," I said, with a sinking feeling. "Why?"

"He's dead," Senovak said.

"Oh no," I said, and Senovak almost absently sat down on the front steps.

"He was at the Minneapolis Field Office," Senovak said, kind of slowly. Thoughtfully. "They were prepping for a . . . it doesn't matter. They think he had an . . . a thoracoabdominal aneurysm."

So Linus, the guy who Senovak was talking about, was U.S. Secret Service Special Agent Linus A. Hekekia, and Senovak had known him forever and ever, since they were in the military together.

Senovak called Linus his best friend, which was a super-weird thing for Senovak to call someone. (He was not a "This is my best friend!" kind of guy.) They both had jobs that occupied, like, all of their lives, but they spent their limited free time together . . . including vacations, when those lined up. I'd even met Linus, though I don't think my dad ever had.

The upshot was that I was about 99.9 percent certain that Linus and Senovak were a long-term couple . . . or whatever the equivalent was for extremely intense (ex) military guys with Serious Jobs who weren't able to come out of the closet. The expression on Senovak's face just then pushed me from 99.9 percent right over into 100. I thought I couldn't feel any more distress than I was already feeling . . . but the way Senovak looked made my stomach flip over. He looked so *lost*.

"He's only forty-four," Senovak said, in that same eerily calm tone. "He was supposed to be in DC right now. He must've gone to Minnesota at the last minute."

"Are they sure he's dead?" I asked—stupid question, I know. Senovak nodded.

"I'm so sorry, Dan," I said. "I'm really sorry. I—"

"Do you have a cigarette on you?" Senovak asked Jasper.

"I've got cloves," Jasper said.

"Eugh, no," Senovak said. Then he seemed to come back to himself a little. He stood up and dusted off his pants, even though there wasn't a speck of dirt on them.

"I don't want to ruin your vacation," Senovak said. "But I'm listed as his next of kin, you see. I have to go make arrangements for the—the burial. I've spoken to your father. He's comfortable with you staying on your own in the cottage for a few days, provided that you tell Rita and Ken what's going on. I'll be taking the car but I can leave you cash, and you have your credit cards . . ."

"That sounds great!" I said, looking at Jasper again. No way we could tell Senovak what had happened right now. He wouldn't believe it, which I'd already expected, but also . . . he couldn't handle it. I couldn't burden him with this when he had to bury his boyfriend.

Jasper nodded, slowly, clearly understanding my plan to stay.

As out of it as he was, Senovak must have heard something in my voice—my tone of false cheerfulness tripped some internal alarm of his—and he looked at me more closely. "If you actually *want* to stay, that is," he said. "You don't have to."

"I want to stay," I said. An enormous, massive lie. Senovak couldn't stay, so logic suggested that if I started telling him something seemingly insane, he would simply force me to come with him. No way he would let me stay there alone if I said the town was populated by brain-controlled monster-worshippers doing ritual sacrifice. But I couldn't leave my friends. Jasper said he thought he could save KJ. And I knew, though he seemed reluctant to say it, that he needed my help.

The lie was enough to convince Senovak. He nodded distractedly and gestured for us to come inside.

"We'll be right in," Jasper said. After Senovak disappeared inside the house, Jasper lit another clove and sat down next to me on the steps.

"Linus?" he asked.

"It's his . . . Linus *was* his boyfriend," I said. "I think."

"Pegged him for a homo," Jasper said, nodding.

"You did not," I said.

"Did too," Jasper said with a wan smile. "You don't have to stay. I don't even know if you should."

"*You* don't have to stay," I said. "Dan will take us both away from here right now."

But Jasper shook his head. "Can't," he said, and blew out a massive cloud of smoke. "I think I might still be able to . . . do something about this."

"What do you want to do?" I asked.

"Kill Good Arcturus," Jasper said. "Whatever kind of thing it is, it can't survive long without a human being to live inside. That's what all of this is about, you know?"

"You were trying to get the needle," I said, picturing Jasper's tantrum about which *specific* piece of the sacred cake he was going to have.

"Yup," Jasper said. "KJ even flirted with Hunter again, like hinted that they might get back together, because Hunter was the one who was gonna get blindfolded and insert the needle into the finished cake this year. He was supposed to peek for us, but obviously he didn't. Fucking liar."

"Ugh, Hunter," I said, though when it came to my would-be relationship with KJ, Hunter Warren was now the least of my problems.

"She doesn't like Hunter," Jasper said pointedly.

"She can't like anything anymore, can she? Can she?" I asked.

Jasper shook his head slowly from side to side. "I don't know," he said. "It's all fucking shrouded in mystery. Is he an alien? Did he convince Junie Apostle-Root he was good, like, Good with a capital *G*, get her to lead him to the village, and then destroy the town? Why? Why did he take over the minister's body? Why did we get assimilated? And I talked to Aunt Judy about it when I was making this plan—"

"The gas station lady?" I asked. "The one who tie-dyes with Alex?"

"Yeah," Jasper said. "She wasn't born here but she *knows* stuff. And the conclusion I ended up coming to is that *he needs a body.* The whole thing where he keeps us happy and healthy, gives us stuff, makes our lives *easy*, it's like some fucked-up Faustian bargain. He can't live without a human host."

"What *is* he?" I asked, and Jasper shook his head.

"No clue," he said. "He *does* something to the people he takes over, like. Uses them up or some sick fucking thing. And then it gets to this point where he needs a new 'shield' body, and every thirty-five years we have a Great Harvest Hallow and he gets a new victim."

I shook my head. Internally I was recontextualizing their founding myth. I had thought it was a story about belonging and community. Now Junie Apostle-Root changed from a brave martyr to a misguided one. She died to protect something she didn't know was a monster. And then it laid waste to the community she'd yearned to be a part of, destroying the free will of everyone.

"But how would *you* getting chosen make any difference?" I asked.

"Because he doesn't have me all fucking indoctrinated," Jasper said. "I wouldn't just go willingly to the black house. I didn't know what happened next—what horrible thing was gonna happen— but I knew I was going to *run*, and that it would have to chase me. There's some kind of obligatory dark magicky metaphysical shit with the passing of the needle so, like, if the needle 'picked' me, then I'd *have* to be the next Incorporation. He would be locked in, tied to me. And I figured that if I *ran*, and I could keep ahead of him for the rest of the Hallow, I could maybe kill him when the old Incorporation—your aunt, in this case—was too worn out to sustain him."

"The Incorporation body dies," I said, "and Good Arcturus ends up like a snail with no shell?"

"Yup. At least that's what I was hoping. I had the PDA filled with gas. KJ was going to be my getaway driver and we were just going to drive south and west as far and fucking fast as we could. Drag out his transitional period. Weaken him."

"I have questions," I said, but then Senovak came out through the front door holding his suitcase, and we both got quiet.

"I'm going to head out," he said in that same distracted voice. "Darian. I will be back on the thirty-first. Maybe earlier. You be safe, please. No drinking. No drugs. Make good choices."

"I will make the best choices possible," I said, seriously enough that Senovak seemed appeased. He put his luggage in the trunk of the car. Then he got into the green Lincoln and drove away, raising one hand in a motionless goodbye.

I watched the taillights turn down the dark road and disappear. When I couldn't see Senovak anymore, I exhaled and stood up.

"Inside," I said to Jasper, feeling *watched* by all the silent trees and the crescent moon overhead.

"I'm not done smoking," Jasper said.

"You can smoke inside, I'll open a window or something," I said.

"Already not making those *good choices*," Jasper said, and followed me in. I gave him a chipped *Garfield* mug to ash into and cracked the window over the sink. We sat at the table in the kitchen and drank some cans of Diet Coke that I'd forgotten to put in the fridge earlier, pouring them into cups filled with mostly-solidified ice.

"You had questions," Jasper said, pushing a lock of purple hair away from his eyes. He looked very tired now.

"Yeah," I said, and went to the closet to get out a quilt for the couch, figuring he would crash soon. And that he wouldn't want to go home. I checked to make sure the fire in the fireplace was properly banked, and switched the CD player from Poe to *from the choirgirl hotel*, skipping through the first couple of tracks until I got to "Black Dove." Then I double-checked that the front door was locked.

"First question," I said, returning to my seat at the kitchen table. "You said that KJ was going to help you. How could she help you if she has the Thought Police living in her head?"

"Because she's different from everyone else here," Jasper said, pouring more soda over his glass of ice. He didn't even complain about Tori Amos playing in the background, which was a serious testament to his mental state.

"But not like you, right? She can still hear him," I asked, thinking of KJ's perpetually dilated eyes.

"Yup," Jasper said. "But she's also . . . I think she's a compulsive liar. She's always made shit up, since she was old enough to talk. Good Arcturus couldn't take that quality away from her, it's like innate or something."

I knew all this about KJ. Frankly, it was impossible *not* to know this about KJ, if you'd ever spent more than ten minutes with her. "I get that," I said. "But how does it—"

"I don't know how, or why," Jasper said, "but something about her lying gives her these . . . little moments of respite from his voice. She can think for herself, then."

I remembered Jasper giving KJ a double thumbs-up earlier that night. It seemed like it had been weeks ago, rather than hours.

You keep on lying. Gotta stay true to yourself. Maintain a clear head. Especially now, he'd said.

"So she would tell even *more* lies? Not just compulsive lies, like on-purpose lies?"

"When she needed to," Jasper said. "Everybody else here doesn't lie, I don't think he lets them. It's even more disgusting when you think about it, that they all *believe* what they're saying. But KJ's lying is like her X-Man power. She's so much less complacent than the rest of them. And I could get through to her enough for her to know it was important to help me. But tonight she kind of lost all her willpower when she saw him."

"Okay. Next question," I said, thinking about how KJ had shoved me away with her shoulder at the very last moment before she was taken into the black house. She'd been aware that something terrible was happening to her then, at least. Which made it even worse.

"I'll try to answer it," Jasper said, "if I can."

"Why didn't you ever just run?" I asked. "Skip town. I know you wouldn't *want* to leave KJ and Alex. But, like, why take such a huge risk attending the Banquet at all?"

"Oh. Right." Jasper let out a clipped little laugh. "You don't know about the most fucked-up part."

"I'm kind of dreading what the *most* fucked-up part could be," I said.

"Every single person born in Kesuquosh has to come back for every Harvest Hallow—and I mean every one. If you don't come back, you'll die," Jasper said. "If you don't participate, you'll die. That's what Rita was reminding me about when I bluffed and said I wouldn't have the cake unless I got my special piece."

"He kills you?" I asked. "That can't actually be true, can it?"

"You won't be murdered," Jasper said. "Well, not in any way that could be proven. You just die, and nobody who isn't from Kesuquosh will realize why. It happens right after midnight turns October thirtieth into October thirty-first. It's the price you pay for refusing to come home and honor him. Or, if it's a *Great* Harvest Hallow, for refusing to come home and take your chances like everybody else."

I thought about my mom dying in the subway in New York, all those years ago on Halloween, and felt goose bumps stand up all over the back of my neck.

"Jas," I said, "my mom—"

"I know," Jasper said. "She was one of them, at least according to Rita. Every year we close out the Hallow by laying out flowers for the dead—or the soon-to-be-dead—the ones who didn't come home."

"I don't understand. Why wouldn't she come back? If she was going to die?" I asked, feeling something twist inside my stomach. The mental image of my mother's death that I had involuntarily constructed, shifting.

"There are always a few who don't come back," Jasper said. "It's tempting to leave, because the blessing of Good Arcturus means that Kesuquoshians will be successful in whatever they choose to do. But out in the real world, supposedly his voice gets smaller and smaller until it's eventually inaudible. I think that most people still end up coming back, because they have loved ones here to, like, encourage them to return. But some people can . . . I think some people realize they're being controlled. I think some people would rather die than be controlled."

"It's a trap that lasts forever then, isn't it?" I asked. "For your whole life. Whether you know it or not." My throat felt tight.

"Everything that happens here is a trap," Jasper said. "That's why it wasn't enough for me to just, like, leave. I wanted to . . ."

"Set everyone free," I said, when he trailed off.

"Yeah," Jasper said, rattling ice around in his cup. "Pretty stupid. I wanted to save them from him. All of them. Except for my horrible bitch of an aunt."

I exhaled slowly. "This is a lot to take in."

"I know. I kept you in the dark on purpose, like I said. I hoped I could handle it and then when you came back next summer it would be *over*. I didn't want to tell you. I always feel like you have . . . your own shit going on," Jasper said.

"I don't have anything like *this* going on," I said. "I don't think anybody has anything like this going on."

"Heh. Yeah," Jasper said.

"One more question," I said as Jasper stifled a yawn.

"Fire away," Jasper said.

"So you say like nobody in town can *get mad* or *lie*," I said. "Because of Good Arcturus."

"Yeah," Jasper said.

"But your parents are pretty much always mad at you. And Birdie, too. And Hunter lied about where he put the needle in the sacred cake."

"That confused me for a long time," Jasper said. "In a place where nobody ever fights or . . . or is dishonest or cheats on their spouse or even parks in a parking space they shouldn't, why did I get to be the special whipping boy?"

"Yeah," I said. "Why?"

"The conclusion I've come to is that Good Arcturus lets people feel hate and contempt and be dishonest *only* in service of him. Like because I pose a constant threat to the brainwashy sanctity of this shithole, everyone hates me. He lets them all stand in opposition to me. And Birdie is just always a bitch, but I think it's more than her personality. It's like she's on the lookout for . . . threats, or something."

Something about that built-in clause of "your subjects being allowed to hate only those who defy you" extra creeped me out. It felt so gross and small. So petty. So *human*, in some way. But it also made sense—if you were trying to keep a whole bunch of people under your control—that you would have them kind of police themselves.

"So the next thing that happens—again, the *Great* Harvest Hallow hasn't happened since 1965, but—the next two nights are the 'Nights of Love.' During normal years it's just a big party. The week where all the engaged couples get married, or try to conceive a child, or both. First dates and flower exchanges. Mom and Dad host these stupid fucking candlelight hayrides through the apple orchards for couples who get engaged."

"That happens for the next two nights?" I asked.

"Yeah," Jasper said.

"And what happens on Halloween?" I asked.

"They say that All Hallows' Eve is when Good Arcturus is reborn," Jasper said.

"Reborn?" I asked. "He wasn't reborn tonight?"

I suddenly felt hopeful, and I saw hope reflected back at me in Jasper's face.

"Exactly," Jasper said. "If he isn't done gestating or whatever until Halloween, then—"

"That's how you think we can save KJ," I said. "Stop whatever's happening."

"Yup," Jasper said. "At least I hope so."

"Did you ever see him? Before?" I asked.

"Good Arcturus? Never," Jasper said. "Some people go to visit him at the black house and ask him for favors and shit. Or *say* they do. Rita says she's been to see him. But I've walked the eastern fields an assload of times and tonight was the first night I ever saw that clearing at all."

"If we can't find the house," I said, "how will we find KJ?"

"I don't fucking know," Jasper said. "I guess I'm going to go look for it again tomorrow." He stubbed the butt-end of a clove out into the *Garfield* mug and yawned again, which made me yawn, too. I thought I was too scared to sleep, but now that the adrenaline rush had worn off I felt like I was going to black out for ten hours.

"*We're* going to go look for it tomorrow," I said.

Jasper looked like he might tell me I shouldn't come with him. I saw the reluctance on his face, but he nodded. "I could use your help," he muttered. "I know I could use your help. I just feel really shitty about it."

"Stop," I said. "I'm not just doing it for you, though I definitely would. I'm doing it for KJ. And Alex, too."

Jasper collapsed on the couch and pulled the blanket over himself. I went into my little bedroom, which had one window and a twin bed, and construction-paper drawings I'd made when I was nine taped to the walls. And one construction-paper music piece I had composed around the same time. The notes were clumsily drawn and the music itself was very obviously a rip-off of the opening arpeggio of Debussy's Arabesque No. 1, but I was willing to forgive my child-self for the lack of originality. I'd been obsessed with an Aldo Ciccolini recording of the two arabesques for an entire summer.

That was before Dexter. I shouldn't have thought about him right when I was trying to go to sleep. I slit my eyes open in the dark of my tiny bedroom, feeling paranoid, but the room was empty.

Then I rolled over and looked out the window, and Dexter was there, standing on the grass just before it sloped down into the riverbank. Watching me from outside in the dark. There was no ambient light to reflect off his glasses, but they were shining anyway. He smiled at me through bloodstained teeth.

I startled, even though I had gotten pretty good at training myself not to jump when I saw him, in case someone noticed. Then I took my comforter and backed out of the room, keeping my eyes on him until I could shut the bedroom door.

Jasper stirred a little on the couch, and then pulled off his spiked collar with a grimace and chucked it onto the floor.

"I'm gonna stay out here," I said.

"Okay," he mumbled, and retracted his legs so that I could climb onto the couch.

I slept facing the glass doors that led out to the porch, and whenever I opened my eyes I scanned them to make sure that nothing and nobody was out there. But Jasper's presence kept Dexter at bay for the time being.

Finally I managed to get some sleep. For a long time I floated in nothingness. And then I heard a voice, from way above me:

"—get the *fuck* up!" Sleep trickled away like water down a drain and I woke up to full sunlight. I was totally confused. And Jasper was shaking me by the shoulders, his eyes wide and his hair sticking up crazily.

"Uhhhhhhmmmwhat?" I said, trying to orient myself to reality.

"Get. The. Fuck. Up," Jasper said through his teeth. He pulled me, rolling me off the couch until I had to catch myself by standing.

"What is happening?" I asked, now fully awake and panicking.

Jasper turned me toward the glass doors that opened onto the back porch, which hung out over the river. Nobody should have been able to get onto that porch without walking through the cottage first.

"*Look*," Jasper said, pointing one shaky index finger at the doors.

It was KJ. She was standing there motionless, gazing in at us, with both palms pressed flat against the glass. Her robe was immaculate. Her crown of sunflowers was perfect. And her eyes were as flat and red as a dying sun.

CHAPTER NINE

Sunday, October 29, 2000

"What do we do?" I asked, unable to tear my eyes away from KJ.

"I have no idea!" Jasper said. His face was white and drawn. "I—I thought we'd have to go and drag her out of the black house, not that she was going to show up all fucking possessed!"

"GUYS? YOU OKAY? WANT TO OPEN THE DOOR?" KJ said, and she looked like herself, but she didn't *sound* like herself. Her voice was doubled, like two KJs were speaking at the same time. But her intonations and her words were normal.

However, her red eyes were *not* normal. They were pupilless, featureless, like glowing coals.

I took a step toward the glass doors, Jasper right beside me.

"KJ?" I said cautiously. "Uh . . . how are you doing?"

"WE ARE OKAY," KJ said, raising her voice to be heard through the glass, and, yeah, her voice was definitely doubled.

"*We?*" Jasper asked. "You and who?"

"Us," KJ said. "HEY, BOSS . . . WE TRIED TO DO WHAT YOU SAID. WE KIND OF LOST OUR FOCUS. BUT WE FIGURED WE SHOULD COME MEET YOU. AND YOU WERE NOT AT YOUR HOUSE, SO WE THOUGHT MAYBE YOU WERE AT DARIAN'S."

She clearly didn't notice how she was calling herself *we*. But she looked freaked-out, and confused, and it made my chest hurt in a weird combination of horror and relief.

"You know I hate it when you call me boss. It makes me sound like a fucking 1920s gangster and it makes you sound like my stupid gangster goon," Jasper said. He was just kind of talking to talk, edging closer to the sliding doors.

"IT IS NOT BECAUSE YOU ARE THE *BOSS*," KJ said, and cracked a smile, which looked terrifyingly incongruous with her dully glowing red eyes. "IT IS BECAUSE YOU ARE A BOSSY LITTLE BITCH."

"Right," Jasper said, still looking her up and down. His hand kind of hovered out like he was going to turn the lock on the door, but he didn't actually touch it. "You said you went to my parents' house?"

"YES. THEY SEEMED PRETTY SURPRISED TO SEE US," KJ said.

"I fucking bet," Jasper said.

"If we let you in, are you going to kill us? Absorb us into your red threads or cocoon us or whatever?" I asked. Jasper looked at me with his eyebrows raised, and I shrugged. "Figured we might as well ask," I said.

"*KILL* YOU?" KJ asked in her echoing voice. "D, WHAT THE HELL? WE WOULD NEVER HURT YOU, WE LO—" She stopped, shutting her mouth in the middle of a sentence. Then she started talking again: "WE WOULD NEVER HURT YOU. DO YOU GUYS . . . WHY ARE WE SAYING *WE*?"

"Because you were—" Jasper raised his voice to be heard through the glass, then paused. "Do you remember anything about last night?"

"Maybe?" KJ said. "Our eye really fucking hurts and we feel like we have bugs under our skin."

"Good Arcturus isn't a vampire, right? Like he doesn't need our permission to . . . come inside?" I asked Jasper, while KJ rubbed her face with an expression of discomfort.

"I don't know. Probably not the right time for a 'coming inside' joke, huh?" Jasper said.

"Gross," I responded, and then I unlocked the door. I wasn't being brave—I just thought that if whatever was inside KJ wanted to hurt us, a sliding glass door wasn't going to keep it out.

"Thank you," KJ said, and walked in, bringing the smell of ozone and a weird staticky quality that spread outward from her body and suffused the air. I tensed, bracing myself for her to do something scary. But she just took a few unsteady steps over to the squashy floral sofa and slumped onto it, scratching her head under the sunflower crown.

"We feel like garbage," KJ said. "What the hell happened?"

"Do you remember anything?" I asked.

"Do you remember being chosen by the needle?" Jasper asked. He was white-faced and looked terrified to go any closer to her. But his voice was steady.

"No, it was supposed to be you!" KJ said, shaking her head emphatically. But then her expression clouded—or at least, I *thought* it did. Her red eyes made it hard to read her emotions. "We were . . . going to get away in the PDA . . ."

"It was supposed to be me," Jasper said. "But your disgusting fucking bootlicking ex-boyfriend lied to us. Or else Good Arcturus fucked with the outcome, I don't know. *You* got the needle."

"Good Arcturus went . . . he like *slithered* his threads into your eyeball and pulled you into the black house," I said. "It was really bad." That was an understatement.

KJ shook her head again, her face screwed up with thought.

"OH . . . OH? OH, FUCKING ROCKS AROUND US, *FUCK,*" KJ said. She looked horrified now. She got to her feet really fast, making me and Jasper both jump back, and ran into the bathroom. I followed her cautiously, stopping at the open door.

"KJ?" I asked. She was staring at her own face in the mirror, pulling her eyelids open, touching her cheeks.

"Yeah, he's definitely in there with you," Jasper said. He still seemed afraid, but he also sounded as astonished as I'd ever heard him. "I can't . . . I can't believe you're up and walking around. You ought to be fully fucking possessed."

"WE . . . WE *DID* WAKE UP IN THE BLACK HOUSE," KJ said. "WE DID. WE WERE SLEEPING IN HER WOODS. IN HER LITTLE WORLD. HOLY SHIT—WE JUST—WE GUESS WE GOT UP AND WALKED OUT?"

"*Her* woods? A world *in* the black house?" I asked.

"UHHHHHHHH," KJ said, and put her forearms on the edge of the sink, bent almost in half, her head hanging down. "WE DO NOT . . . DO NOT WANT THIS TO BE HAPPENING," she whispered. Her whispering doubled back in on itself and made the bathroom into an echo chamber.

I took a step into the bathroom. Immediately the staticky buzz in the air and the smell of ozone intensified, but I ignored the fear-feeling those things gave me and carefully rested my hand on her left shoulder.

"KJ?" I said, expecting my hand to be grasped, at any second, by the red tendrils that I'd seen the night before. I looked at my own manicured nails, where my hand touched the fabric of her cloak, and waited. But nothing happened—except that KJ straightened up and turned around at my touch.

"DARIAN," she said. I had to look up to make eye contact, and her fathomless red eyes felt like they were boring into my brain. But she sounded sad and scared when she spoke.

"JUST FORGET WHATEVER WE SAID LAST NIGHT ABOUT HOW WE WANTED YOU TO BE HAPPY HERE," KJ said. "WE WERE WRONG, OKAY? THIS FUCKING SUCKS. THIS TOWN SUCKS. WE ARE WITH JASPER ON IT NOW. WE DO NOT EVEN HAVE TO TELL A LIE TO KNOW WHAT WE FEEL ABOUT IT."

"You don't?" Jasper asked. He was still standing in the doorway, his face and voice guarded. "You mean . . . you mean you can't hear him telling you what to feel anymore?"

"HEAR HIM?" KJ asked, turning to Jasper. "WE DO NOT NEED TO HEAR HIM. WE ARE—"

Then she broke off, touching her forehead. "WE'RE BOTH IN HERE," she said.

"Right. I'm getting that," Jasper said. "But who's running the show?"

"WE DO NOT KNOW. WE . . . WE MIGHT . . . WE REALLY DO NOT THINK WE WERE A GOOD CHOICE FOR THE INCORPORATION," KJ said. "BOSS, WE HAVE NO IDEA WHAT IS GOING ON."

"I don't either," Jasper said.

KJ looked so miserable and scared that it was almost possible for me not to be terrified of the fact that she was harboring some kind of evil monster underneath her skin. "Maybe we can still kill him," I said, and grabbed her hand. It wasn't meant to be a big thing—more like an *I am not scared to touch you* gesture, a show of confidence, a mirror of how she'd held my hand last night. But when I wrapped my fingers around her hand, KJ actually blushed. Her cheeks got almost as red as her eyes. She shook her head, though.

"WE DO NOT WANT THAT, D. WE WANT TO SURVIVE. *BOTH* OF US."

"Is he listening to me?" I asked, feeling trepidation about saying something so flagrant. What if Good Arcturus got pissed-off at me and killed me for saying we should kill him?

But KJ nodded, not looking murderous whatsoever. "WE ARE BOTH LISTENING."

"Okay, so maybe not *kill* him," Jasper said, giving me a look behind KJ that undercut the sentiment. He was definitely still planning for us to kill Good Arcturus if we needed to. Which would be a tricky thing to plan with him listening in via KJ. "But . . . remove him. Somehow. I don't know how it works. Maybe we have until Halloween, when he's 'reborn.' KJ, can you feel him, like, gestating inside you?"

"HOW THE HELL ARE WE SUPPOSED TO KNOW IF WE CAN FEEL SOMETHING *GESTATING*?" KJ said. She was looking down at our still-joined hands.

"The constant referring to yourself as *we* might be a little clue," I said, and squeezed her hand. "Come sit down, okay?"

I started to tug KJ back toward the sofa.

"I wish we knew more about what was fucking going on," Jasper said. He sounded more normal, but he was still keeping his distance as KJ walked past him. "Every time I try to get clarity I get some dipshit answers from my fucking family like *ohooooo, it's all so beautiful!*" Jasper said. "But like, what is *actually* happening right now?" He paced around us as KJ sat down. "They all talk in these stupid fucking euphemisms."

"Maybe we can ask Alex," KJ said. "He might know things about the Great Harvest Hallow that we were never entirely privy to. And he's doing whatever we tell him to do right now."

"You saw Alex?" Jasper asked.

"Uh, yeah, we made him drive us over here," KJ said. "He is waiting in the car. because we told him to."

"What the fuck, KJ, is he okay?" Jasper asked.

What *I* was wondering was how Alex—or anyone else in town—could be privy to things about the Harvest Hallow that *Good Arcturus* was not privy to. That seemed really weird.

"Why would he not be okay?" KJ asked, but Jasper was already up and running through the front door. I followed him.

The PDA was parked out front, and Alex was sitting in the driver's seat. He looked over slowly when Jasper pulled the car door open, and then broke into a beautiful smile.

"Hi, Jasper," Alex said. "Hi, Darian. I looked for you guys at the Garlands' farmstand last night, but I couldn't find you—"

Jasper touched Alex's shoulders and pushed the waterfall of his hair aside, his eyes scanning up and down. Then he huffed a sigh and stepped back.

"You're fucking fine," he said contemptuously. "Just a stupid fucking zombie, per usual."

"Of course I'm fine," Alex said, looking confused. "I'm great. Actually, the most incredible thing happened—"

"Yeah, we've borne witness to the wonders," Jasper said.

KJ came out of the house. The world seemed to ripple around her as she walked. She strode over to us with her red robe blowing back behind her, and Alex stopped talking to us as she approached. All his attention was focused on her.

"My Lord," he said as she walked up. He had that rapturous expression on his face that all the Kesuquoshians had been wearing the night before. It was so *weird* to see it directed at KJ.

"WHAT SHOULD WE DO?" KJ asked, looking between me and Jasper.

"To get it out of you?" Jasper said. "I'm not sure. I think we should take you to Aunt Judy. She might have some ideas. Maybe a fucking exorcism."

"Is being separated something you both want?" I asked, feeling nervous. Jasper couldn't keep his murderous contempt at bay for even a second, and Good Arcturus probably didn't want to be exorcized.

KJ tilted her head, seeming to think about the question. "YES. WE WOULD LIKE TO BECOME OURSELVES AGAIN." She paused. "AND GO HOME."

"Okay, good, that's good," I said.

"If it's true," Jasper said.

"Right," I agreed, and then lowered my voice. Tried to whisper to Jasper, leaning in. "What if she's . . . if it's still dangerous? Should we be bringing it to an old lady?"

"I don't know," Jasper said. He still looked scared. But I saw him trying to force himself to get closer to KJ. To really *look* at her. "I'm trying to . . . I have to believe that KJ wouldn't show up here just to *trick* us. I don't even think we're enough of a threat to get Good Arcturus's attention. Right?"

"WE DID NOT COME TO DO HARM," KJ said. "AND NEVER TO YOU."

I had trouble trusting people after Dexter. But I trusted KJ. Even now, in this monstrous situation. I believed that at the very least *she* believed what she was saying was true.

"My Lord," Alex said, looking worried, "shouldn't you be, like, *resting*? In your house? I thought you needed these two days to make your transformation—"

"She's not going to make a *transformation*, idiot," Jasper said. "KJ, tell him."

"JUST DO WHAT WE SAY," KJ said to Alex, and he nodded, his face getting all tranquil again.

"We're going to go see Aunt Judy," Jasper said. "Right now."

"I—" I strongly wanted to protest leaving immediately. I was about as grungy as I ever got. "Can we leave in, like, fifteen minutes? I'm still in my pajamas," I said, gesturing at myself.

Jasper squinted at my sleepwear, then looked up at me with one eyebrow raised. "What is that logo that looks like a little planet?" he asked.

"Vivienne Westwood," I said, "but—"

"I think you'll be fine going out in your *Vivienne Westwood* pajamas," Jasper said. "Put a coat on."

"But my hair," I added, touching my fried blonde ends, knowing that I was going to get steamrolled.

"You look like a movie star. Like Alicia Silverstone with Courtney Love's hair," Jasper said. "In designer clothes. You'll be fine. Put it up in a ponytail."

"It's just really sticking up," I said, feeling like a princess even as the words came out of my mouth.

"So SORRY, D," KJ said. "IS OUR SITUATION NOT URGENT ENOUGH FOR YOU? IS THERE SOME OTHER ENTITY THAT WE SHOULD HAVE CRAWL UP OUR ASS BEFORE IT IS IMPERATIVE ENOUGH A SITUATION THAT WE JET OFF IMMEDIATE-LIKE?"

"Oh my god, fine," I said. I ran inside and got my house keys and my trusty checkered coat (it was Coach, but no way was I letting Jasper and KJ know that) and a pair of boots. Jasper followed me in, grabbed his battered-as-fuck Doc Martens (already secondhand and ancient when he acquired them—Jasper did not buy leather goods firsthand) and his spiked collar, and raced me back to the Chevy Blazer with his boots in his hand.

"Go to the Citgo on 202," KJ said, sliding onto the back seat.

"I'll sit next to her," Jasper said, like he was trying to protect me. But I shook my head.

"I'm good." I was less afraid than he was. I don't know why. It was terrifying. *She* was terrifying. But I hadn't been brought up with the idea of Good Arcturus. I could still see *KJ*.

I climbed into the back across from KJ. The smell of ozone seemed less sharp, now, and the air less staticky. Maybe I was just getting used to it. But it was still intense enough that the hair on my arms stood up at her proximity.

Alex took KJ's directive about the Citgo as a divine command, judging from the speed at which he got the car out of the driveway and onto the road. The music came on; something off *Mellon Collie and the Infinite Sadness*. KJ had definitely been the last one to use the CD player.

"Absolutely not," Jasper said. "I am not listening to 'Thru the Eyes of Ruby' again right now."

He stabbed the Eject button—but then, when the CD was in his hand, he turned it around carefully. Held it up for all of us to see. It was *At Fillmore East*—which was an Allman Brothers album (Alex would say it was *the* Allman Brothers album). Definitely not The Smashing Pumpkins.

"We all just heard Billy Corgan bitching and moaning, right?" Jasper asked.

I nodded. So did Alex.

"Okay," Jasper said. He switched the audio to FM radio. The music came on after a second. It was crackling with static, like most radio stations did within the boundaries of Kesuquosh, except for the teeny-tiny community station over on Haven Road. But then the sound sharpened, with a surprising clarity.

The radio was playing "Thru the Eyes of Ruby."

"What the fuck?" Jasper said, and hit the Scan button. Stations blipped by, the FM numbers cycling through, and each and every station was playing the same song.

"*Why we're forever frozen, forever beautiful, forever lost inside ourselves,*" Billy Corgan sang seamlessly as the radio went from station to station.

Jasper hit the AM button, but instead of talk radio he got more of the same. He turned around in the passenger's seat and glared at KJ. No matter how frightened he was of the thing inside her body, he still hated it when people fucked with the music.

"Are you perhaps doing this, *my Lord*?" Jasper asked.

"Not on purpose!" KJ said. "We just really wanted to hear it!"

"You should honor His desires," Alex said.

"Okay, Al, we'll honor his desire to listen to The Smashing Pumpkins, you utter dipshit," Jasper said.

"Great," Alex said, with a tinge of relief, like he really meant it. He turned onto Good Earth Way.

The daylight over the road revealed a changed scene: apparently the villagers had been redecorating. All the businesses were closed, but the town hall—which was a smallish stone building with twin stairs leading up to the entrance—had its doors thrown open. People emerged from the town hall in groups, carrying bunches of chrysanthemums. Petals littered the road, which was devoid of traffic and full of people. The PDA was immediately stuck behind a slow-moving group of adults who were adorning the hair of a woman in a knit sweater and jeans with flowers while a dude held her hand and smiled at her adoringly.

Something like this would have struck me as charming the day before. But now it was *gross*. These people were, like Jasper said, zombies. Trapped into enacting the will of an inhuman creature that could dominate them mentally.

And that creature was sitting next to me in KJ's body, humming along to The Smashing Pumpkins. I watched the Kesuquoshians coming and going while Alex crept the car along the road at like five miles an hour, waiting patiently for people to get the hell out of the way. His gentle smile, which I'd always considered an outward expression of who he really *was* as a person, unsettled me now. I wished that we could take it away, see the real Alex. I wasn't sure that I knew who that would even be. Maybe even he didn't know.

Jasper made an irritated sound at the slow-moving villagers. Then he rolled down the passenger's-side window and screamed into the street: "Hey, you brain-dead shit piles! GET OUT OF THE FUCKING ROAD!"

When this got him some vague looks of affront, but very little in the way of movement, Jasper leaned over and started tapping on the horn. Rapidly.

BeeBEEPeebeBEbeBEEPbeepBEEPBEEP went the horn, making the people in the street in front of us jump.

"Very rude!" some old dude said, waving an admonishing finger. "I'm surprised at you—"

"Suck my ass, Mr. Mulgrew!" Jasper said. People moved aside, and Alex started cruising down the road again.

"You're going to get disowned," I told Jasper as we exited the microscopic downtown of Kesuquosh and drove through the dying sunflower fields.

"That's fine. You're rich," Jasper said. "You can be my patron."

"You have to *do* something to have a patron," I said.

"You can be Army of Dolly's patron," Jasper said.

"You guys are probably gonna have a pretty weird first album," I said, looking over at KJ.

We crossed the Kesuquosh town line (with its two signs) and just like that, the radio stopped playing The Smashing Pumpkins and reverted to fuzzy classical on WJIN, a local station that I knew only because of how quickly it was always getting turned off.

"You can't control the radio out here?" I asked KJ, who shrugged.

"WE HAVE LIMITS TO OUR AWESOME POWERS," she said.

"Maybe your awesome powers end at the town line," Jasper said. "Darian. Maybe if we keep her out of Kesuquosh until Halloween she can beat him."

"Maybe," I said. "We could stay at a hotel—"

"WE HAVE NEVER STAYED AT A HOTEL," KJ said. Then she looked over at me and away. I think it was supposed to be stealthy, but it wasn't—she was being super obvious about watching me. Normally KJ was like 95 percent unreadable, especially with her sunglasses on. So I wondered if the lack of subtlety was a Good Arcturus thing.

KJ's (long-fingered, perfect, beautiful) hand moved out across the (fuzzy, red, pizza-smelling) back seat, until it touched mine.

"Um," I said, displaying my extreme eloquence in moments of interpersonal significance, "what are you—"

"You are very beautiful, Darian," KJ said, and lightly touched my wrist. "We have always thought so. We were going to tell you, but did not. For some reason. Jasper always says we like 'sad girls,' but the reality is that no other one of these tragic individuals would be adequate. We have only cared for you—"

"Hey, your Lord of Dipshittery? My BFF KJ—whose body you are squatting in—would not appreciate you giving the game away like this. Private things are *private*," Jasper said from the front seat. He had turned around, taking in the scene. And he gave me a look that held more than a little fear. "Don't let it touch you," he added. "I still don't trust it. No matter how much it seems like KJ."

"Umm—" I pulled my wrist away. My heart was racing. It was easy to be afraid of Good KJ, or whoever the hell this person was, as she leaned toward me smelling like ozone and talking like a baby's idea of a Tolkien elf. But I was also . . . well . . . It *was* her. I could see her still in there, that effortlessly charismatic mess of a person that I'd been attracted to for so long. My opposite in every way. I was small and contained and rigid. Never sharing. That was the only way I knew how to deal with the things that had happened to me.

But when KJ faced adversity she just . . . spread out like molasses, gentle enough but impossible to get rid of, implacably covering everything. Making it work. Her irrepressibility. Her stupid slouchy posture and her scrubby attitude and her lies, her there-and-gone wit, her perfect face. I wasn't surprised that she'd come up with a way to fight whatever was being done to her. I mean I *was*, I was quite literally near to being in shock from everything that had happened over the last day. But if there was someone who could fuck up an evil sacrifice cult that had been in place for centuries just by being themselves . . . it was KJ.

"WE ARE *NOT* 'GIVING THE GAME AWAY.' WE HAVE BEEN DISCUSSING THE PROSPECT OF A DATE ALREADY, UNBEKNOWNST TO YOU," KJ said. Then she leaned back nervously, ignoring Jasper's scoff, when I said literally nothing in response to her. "DARIAN. DID WE MAKE YOU UPSET?"

"She's just not buying what you're selling right now," Jasper said a little nastily. He was being a dick to cover how frightened he was, how much he hated being out of control. Protective of me. Protective of Alex. Protective of KJ even now that it was too late. But the part of KJ that was KJ was clearly upset by the prospect of upsetting *me*.

"Shut up, Jas," I said, rubbing my wrist where KJ had touched it. "KJ," I added, looking at her frowning face and red eyes. "I'm . . . it's not that I don't like you, um . . . I just . . . I think we should talk about this later? Like maybe after your possession crisis is over?"

"I *knew* you guys liked each other," Alex declared, turning into the Citgo. "That's so nice. You should be honored, Darian, because now she's the Incorporation of our Lord."

"You are a moron," Jasper said. "Darian. Under no circumstances should you trust her."

"I'm not a moron! I'm just being, like, zen and joyous and celebratory and respectful," Alex said.

"I really am not rejecting you," I said to KJ, trying to project my earnestness despite the hideous mortification I felt. "I mean, I'm not rejecting KJ. Or . . . whatever. It's just—"

"WE UNDERSTAND," KJ said, looking very serious. "WE HAVE ALSO BEEN HURT BY SOMEONE WHO WIELDS POWER OVER US."

I took that statement at face value, thinking about the towns-people and how they had betrayed KJ to their god. Not for a second did I think that it was Good Arcturus who was saying that.

In fact, I was so concerned with the idea that KJ had intuited something about me being "hurt by someone who wielded power over me" that I ignored everything else.

"I'm fine," I said with an awkward little laugh. "Really."

"Let's go," Jasper said. We'd parked in a shady spot near the side of the gas station, and he walked ahead of us, past the cob-webby overhang and the pumps, and into the little building where Aunt Judy worked. The Citgo was cozy, for a gas station—it smelled like just-brewed coffee, and the entrance was totally dominated by Halloween-themed snack displays. There were racks weighed down with Halloween Oreos, Hostess Scary Cakes (with "S'Cream Fill-ing!" and lurid slime-green font on the packaging), and Brach's Dem Bones sour candies.

The alternative station that Aunt Judy kept on religiously was playing "Porcelain" by Moby, a song that we had discussed and dis-sected over the summer: KJ liked it, Alex adored it despite its being a far cry from jam-bandness, and Jasper hated it.

I wanted to like it. It was pretty, and driving, with the four-chord progression and the melancholy piano and cello lines running through it like veins. It was mixed beautifully. But some-thing about the sentiment, if not the sound, made me think that Dexter would have loved it. He'd never given me his opinion on Moby. I thought his opinion might have been derisive. But this song would have . . . he would have been really into it. And—though it was impossible for me to deny that he'd influenced my taste in music—I felt revulsion at the thought of having any opinions in common with him. *Not anymore*, I thought, and looked behind me. Through the glass doors that led to the pumps I saw no other cars and no trace of Dexter.

KJ picked up a package of Scary Cakes and then shoved it into the pocket of her cloak, which actually made me feel relieved. KJ trying to steal (and Alex invariably ratting her out to Aunt Judy) was normal.

"Guys," Jasper said, and we joined him in the back, where the counter was. Aunt Judy presided over the Citgo from behind the register, the wall of cigarettes as her backdrop. She could have easily been one of the many Birdie Plum–esque women in this part of Massachusetts, but life (and a good personality) had taken her in a different direction. Her long white hair had a bluish tint. She was wearing a vintage Fleetwood Mac shirt and a bunch of beaded necklaces. Jasper had evidently told her something urgent, because she came around the counter in her blue wheelchair at top speed.

"What's so bad, huh?" she demanded, in her scratchy old-lady voice. "And what's that smell? Smells like lightning."

"Hey, Aunt J," Alex said.

"Nice work on that hoodie, cupcake," Aunt Judy said, which made Alex just about glow with pride. He looked down at his Phish sweatshirt like he was seeing it again for the first time.

"Speaking of cupcakes," I said, "KJ wanted to purchase some." I didn't trust Alex to sell out his god the way he normally sold out his sister.

"Speaking of KJ, that's our problem," Jasper said.

"Trying to shoplift, you little delinquent?" Aunt Judy said, and then she looked up at KJ and her mouth dropped open. Her hands went to the wheels of her chair like she was about to back away in shock.

"They had the Banquet of the Needle last night," I said, and Aunt Judy tore her eyes away from KJ and glanced over at me like she'd just realized I was visiting out-of-season.

"Were you there?" she asked incredulously. Then she narrowed her eyes at Jasper. "You invited her to go to that evil ceremony?"

"I didn't know she was coming!" Jasper said. "And then I figured since my plan was to just get the needle myself, she'd be safe—"

"What? Oh hell, you little imbecile," Aunt Judy said, putting one veiny hand to her cheek.

"But *obviously*," Jasper said, indicating KJ again, "that didn't work."

"WE ARE TOGETHER NOW," KJ said. Then she pulled the package of Scary Cakes out of her pocket, ripped it open, and bit into one.

"It's amazing, isn't it?" Alex said, looking on with admiration. "I can pay you for those."

"Good Arcturus *never* leaves Kesuquosh," Aunt Judy said. She clearly couldn't tear her eyes away from KJ. "Especially not when it's molting."

"She said she was *sleeping in her woods, in her little world*," I said, because that phrase had stuck curiously in my mind.

"WE AWOKE. WE AWOKE AND WE LEFT BECAUSE ... WE NEEDED TO FIND JASPER," KJ said. "TO EXECUTE THE PLAN."

"It was too late," Jasper said. "We already fucked up the plan. Or Good Arcturus did."

Aunt Judy wheeled a little closer to KJ, and looked up into her eyes. "You in there, cupcake?" she asked.

"WE ARE *BOTH* IN HERE," KJ said.

"Maybe . . ." Aunt Judy squinted like she was deep in thought. "Maybe we can do something about this. I'll have to ask the Freys. You all need to stay out of your village. If your people catch a whiff of what's going on, I don't know what they'll do."

"OUR PEOPLE?" KJ asked, tilting her head.

"Yes. Your villagers. The ones who worship you," Aunt Judy said. The bell tinkled on the door as someone came in. They must have pulled in after I checked the parking lot in my paranoia.

"I WILL SENSE THEM IF THEY COME NEAR," KJ said.

"That can't possibly be true," I said, because the person coming in was *Rita*. Rita stood in the doorway, her eyes wide and freaked-out, looking at all of us.

"Guys?" she said, stepping into the Citgo.

"Oh fuck," Jasper said.

CHAPTER TEN

Sunday, October 29, 2000

"What's going on?" Rita said as she got closer. "KJ, why are you outside of town?"

"You know why we wish to leave, Apostle," KJ said, which, like, no. Rita looked taken aback by that statement. She definitely could not understand why KJ would be anywhere but waiting for her obliteration back in Kesuquosh.

"Jasper?" Rita asked. She came closer to us, and I saw that her beautiful dark hair was woven through with red chrysanthemums. "Was this your idea, honey? She really should be home right now—"

"Of course it was my idea," Jasper said, his voice harsh, even as he looked completely frightened. He and I were standing almost shoulder to shoulder, and I could feel him shaking a little. But he stuck his chin out and glared at probably the only adult who loved him with an immovably wrathful expression.

"I understand that you're upset, okay? I know how everyone treats you. I know it hurts, honey. But revenge is never the right answer. And KJ needs to come back now," Rita said, fixing her dilated eyes on Jasper. Her normally smooth forehead creased with a line of worry. "The Incorporation and Good Arcturus undergo their transformation together during the Nights of Love. Without a shield, He will—"

"Fuck your fucking shield! Let him fucking die," Jasper said, raising his voice. "How can you not care if this happens to your fucking kid? Rita, come on. I know there's a real person inside of you somewhere fucking *screaming* about this!"

"WE DO NOT ACTUALLY WANT TO 'FUCKING DIE,'" KJ said from my other side.

"Come home with me," Rita said, approaching KJ like she was a particularly dangerous animal. "I don't want to get anyone else involved. Don't make me call the Sumners. Please listen to me, all right?"

I moved back as she stepped forward. We all did, except for Aunt Judy, who pulled the locking brake on her chair like she was expecting rough winds or a downward slope or something.

I'd never wanted to get away from Rita before in my life. But now just looking at her made my skin crawl. She seemed transformed, somehow, by my perception, like everyone else in Kesuquosh. Like there was nothing behind her eyes. Just a hungry void.

"She's not going anywhere with you," I said. My voice came out pathetic and small to my own ears, but Rita turned to look at me.

"Darian. You shouldn't have to be here," Rita said. "Dan should take you home."

"Oh yeah. And I come back next summer and pretend everything is normal?" I asked. "That sounds *great*."

"Guys, please." Rita reached out to Jasper, but when he backed away even more, she tucked her hands under her arms.

"Perhaps you *should* return home, my Lord," Alex said. "It will be better for you, while your transformation takes place." He stepped away from us, toward his mom.

"Don't you fucking *dare*, Alex," Jasper said.

"ALEX...," KJ said. When I looked at her, her apocalyptic red eyes seemed to be pointed at her brother.

"I'm calling the constables," Rita said, and took out her cell phone.

"Excuse me!" Aunt Judy said as Rita brought the phone to her ear. "I don't think anything has happened here to warrant you calling Barney Fife and son to this place of business in a different town. In fact, why don't you get the hell out and stop harassing these kids?"

"They're *my* kids, Judy," Rita said, looking terribly upset. "I don't know if you underst—yes, hello? This is Rita Jenetopolous. Do you know where the Incorporation is right now?"

Then there was a sound. A crackling, like the air was full of carbonated fizz, or sparklers. And a thrumming vibration underneath that. The smell of ozone got stronger.

"You will not call your dogs upon us," KJ said, and I turned my head and saw that she was walking toward her mom and brother, eyes aglow. It seemed like the whole gas station got darker as her eyes lit up. Her hair, and her cloak, and the sunflower petals on her crown all blew back in a wind I couldn't feel.

"You will not ensnare us again," KJ said.

"Kahie," Rita said, backing up, "I'm only trying to do what is best for you—"

"We alone decide what is best for us," KJ said. "Disconnect the call."

158

"But—"

"NO. YOU WILL CEASE THIS," KJ said, and then it seemed like the air grew hands and *moved* the cell phone from Rita's grasp, blowing it across the room and smashing it into the glass cooler, making the doors rattle. The phone was crushed into pieces on impact and scattered across the ground. Rita let out a little cry, holding her hands over her face, and then she was shoved to the side by that same air, forcibly moved away from where she blocked the door, stumbling back and slamming against the Halloween snack display. The wire shelves rattled, one coming loose from the force of Rita crashing into it, sending the Brach's Pumpkins tumbling down onto the shelf of Halloween Oreos and creating a landslide effect with the other items. Rita righted herself unsteadily in a sea of orange Oreos and Hostess Scary Cakes.

Even after all I'd seen, this sudden show of telekinesis (or whatever it was) shocked me. The room buzzed and my head buzzed. I could barely make out Aunt Judy shouting something over the static in the air.

"Are you okay, Mom?" Alex yelled.

"WE WILL TAKE OUR LEAVE," KJ said. "YOU *WILL NOT* FOLLOW US. YOU WILL NOT TOUCH THE WOMAN WHO WORKS HERE. YOU WILL RETURN TO YOUR HOME."

"Holy *shit*," Jasper said, his eyes all bugged out. He and Judy shared a look of astonishment.

"WE WILL GO NOW," KJ said. "JASPER. DARIAN. ALEX."

Then she started walking toward the door, kicking aside Scary Cakes as she went. The wind followed her.

"You should come with us!" Jasper said to Aunt Judy, but she said something quietly to him—I saw him leaning in—and then he nodded, and followed me and KJ. Alex remained where he was, looking hesitant.

"I think you really need to go home, my Lord," Alex said, standing shoulder to shoulder with Rita.

KJ stopped in the doorway, silhouetted by the light outside, and looked back at her twin. "THIS IS TEDIOUS," she said, and reached out. The static sound intensified, and for a moment I saw a few red tendrils—the cold threads from the night before—slip out from underneath her fingernails, waving in the air like under-water veins.

"YOU ARE CUT OFF FROM THE VOICE OF KESUQUOSH," KJ declared, and one of the red threads crossed the space and brushed lightly against Alex's left temple.

He gasped and clutched at his head. "Ahhhhh," Alex said, covering his eyes.

"Alex!" Jasper said—and then, to KJ—"Don't hurt him!"

"YOUR THOUGHTS ARE YOUR OWN," KJ said, with a note of finality in her voice.

Then the tendrils and the static and the wind were all gone. Rita seemed like she could move freely, but she wasn't approaching us yet. She looked *freaked*.

"GOODBYE," KJ said to Rita, and then walked out the door.

"Wait!" Rita cried. "Kahie, please—"

"Alex, come on." Jasper guided Alex outside, holding his elbow. I jogged after them, passing the Kobayashis' family sedan, which was parked outside at a hurried-looking angle.

KJ walked toward the PDA. The driver's-side door opened before she reached it.

"I guess her powers do extend beyond the town line," I said to Jasper, who nodded tersely as we climbed into the car. He waved me into the passenger's seat and helped Alex into the back.

"You okay?" he asked Alex from behind me.

"I'm fine . . . I think?" Alex said. He sounded a little blurry, but not tranquil. Not like usual.

"If you have *Carrie* powers then why couldn't you keep The Smashing Pumpkins on the radio?" I asked KJ.

"We have to expend much more effort outside of Kesu-quosh," KJ said. "But if we focus, we can alter things. Your . . . our world . . . is malleable."

I really looked at KJ then. I imagined that even in her new and horrible state of being, she would be upset about the confrontation with her mom.

But she didn't seem like she was thinking about Rita. She was sitting behind the steering wheel like she was winded. For a minute I could see movement under her skin. The sinews of Good Arcturus. And I realized that I wasn't afraid of her at all anymore. I was afraid *for* her.

Stop it, I wanted to scream, *leave her alone, please. Get out of her.*

"KJ," Jasper said, "if you're gonna go you need to do it now."

I glanced in the rearview and saw Rita emerge from the gas station.

"Okay, let us get the hell out of here," KJ said. She pulled out onto Route 202 like a crazy person, which was how KJ always drove. As we zipped along, she glanced to the side and smiled at me.

"We have never driven before," she said, going even faster. I was personally shocked that she'd had her license for a full year without getting a ticket or a suspension or something.

"You've definitely driven before, even if the circumstantial evidence points toward you not knowing how to drive *at all*," I said.

"Yes. We have driven before," KJ said, "but we have also never driven before. It is . . . fun."

"Great, I love the sound of that," Jasper said.

"We do not need your input," KJ said. "You are a virgin who cannot drive."

She was quoting *Clueless*. She quoted *Clueless* to me all the time, as a shorthand way of letting me know when I was being a princess. Which was annoying.

But it was nice to hear her say something so regular. When Jasper laughed, he sounded relieved, too. She seemed trustworthy, especially after how unerring she was in our confrontation with Rita. If Good Arcturus had sinister intentions toward us, he was doing a terrible job of acting on them.

"Fair," Jasper said, "though I did do mutual handies with Brooks Gould-Greenwood in September. So I'm only a technical virgin now. KJ, you should pull off at one of the gates for a while. The Sumners are probably going to be looking for us on 202."

"Brooks? The kid from the private school?" I asked, surprised. "You ranted at me on AIM about what a stuck-up asshole he was and how you only talked to him because of his record collection."

"All of those things are true," Jasper said, "but he is also hot."

Alex, who had been quiet for the past few minutes, suddenly spoke up. His voice sounded firm and clear, not blurry anymore—but not tranquil, either.

"You did what?" he said, and when I glanced into the rearview mirror, Alex's eyes were totally normal. No dilation. "Jasper. You did *what*?"

I could see Jasper looking over at Alex, too. He looked pretty surprised. Alex didn't normally sound that adamant when he talked.

"I said Brooks Gould-Greenwood was hot?" Jasper said. He turned it into a sarcastic question, by virtue of his voice, but he still seemed taken aback.

"You gave him a *hand job*?" Alex asked.

"I mean, we gave each other hand jobs, that's what mutual means," Jasper said. His face was actually getting kind of red. I didn't think I'd ever seen Jasper embarrassed before. It was amazing.

"I know what mutual means," Alex said. "When was this?"

"Last month? At the Falls senior back-to-school party?" Jasper said.

"When I was at the Phish show," Alex said. "Cool. Great."

Alex was being sarcastic when he said *Cool. Great*, which, again, would be normal for anyone else but was extremely weird for him.

"Alex?" I said, interrupting whatever emotional thing he and Jasper were getting into. "Are you okay? How do you feel?"

Alex tore his eyes away from Jasper and looked over. "I'm . . . I feel weird," he said. "I feel . . ."

"Angry? Pissed-off?" Jasper asked, clearly having the same realization that I was.

"I . . . guess?" Alex said. "But it's not going away, like it normally does."

"What are you mad about?" I asked, looking at Jasper. Jasper looked back at me. He was still flushed, but now he'd started to smile.

"I . . . I think it's about Jasper and that private-school guy," Alex said. "Brooks. Why would you want to fool around with Brooks when I'm right here?"

"OH, GROSS," KJ said, sounding close to normal for a second.

"KJ," I asked, "what did you do to him, again? I was distracted by the big fight we were having with your mom."

"HOLD ON," KJ said. Then she jerked the wheel and pulled the PDA off the road at a terrifying speed, whipping the car onto Gate Nine, one of the many little gravel roads that surrounded the Quabbin. These gates all led to walking paths that would take you into the woods around the water—woods dotted with the remnants of the four towns that had been flooded back in the 1930s to make Quabbin Reservoir. There were dozens of gates to the Quabbin, because the reservoir was so enormous, some well-hiked and busy and others really empty. Gate Nine was of the really empty variety, luckily.

KJ drove through a little overgrown parking lot and then pulled the PDA into the woods. We were surrounded by brightly-colored trees just on the verge of dropping the rest of their leaves. Route 202 was hidden from our vantage point. And we were hidden from anyone who might drive by, looking for a runaway god.

"I feel weird," Alex said from the back seat. "Really weird. I have to get some, like, fresh air, that might help, yeah?"

Then he opened the back door and climbed out. He took a few steps away from the PDA with his hands shoved into the big front pocket of his sweatshirt while the wind moved the red-gold-orange leaves.

"You cut him off from your voice," Jasper said, looking at KJ.

"FROM THE VOICE OF KESUQUOSH," KJ said. "WE COULD DO THAT FOR OUR TWIN, THOUGH IT PAINED US."

"It pained you," Jasper said. "Why, exactly? Because you want—because Good Arcturus wants to be controlling him?"

But KJ turned her face away, shaking her head. Her red eyes were downcast.

"She didn't say she cut him off from Good Arcturus's voice," I said. "She said that she cut him off from the voice of Kesuquosh."

That seemed like a really important distinction to me, for some reason.

"The voice of Kesuquosh *is* the voice of Good Arcturus," Jasper said. "Trust me, I've heard it." He leaned forward from the back seat, so that his face was between me and KJ. "Why did you set him free?"

"WE WANT HIM TO BE *HIMSELF*," KJ said, looking down at her hands, which were threaded together in her lap.

"Excellent," Jasper said, gesturing in Alex's direction. "Now do that for everyone else in town. Right now."

But KJ shook her head no. "WE CANNOT DO THAT."

"Why not?" Jasper said.

"IT IS BEYOND OUR CLOAKLESS POWERS," KJ said. "WE COULD BARELY DO IT FOR THIS ONE, AND ONLY BECAUSE HE IS SPECIAL. HE IS OUR TWIN. TO ATTEMPT IT IN DEFIANCE OF HER POWERS AGAIN WOULD . . . TEAR THIS BODY APART, WE FEAR."

"What does *that* mean?" Jasper asked. "What does *cloakless* mean?"

"*Tear this body apart?*" I asked, feeling frightened.

But KJ just shook her head. She swallowed, like she'd been forcibly prevented from speaking. Outside, Alex had wandered past the parking lot and down the path toward the Quabbin. I saw him walking almost aimlessly, back turned to us, with his hands still in his front pocket.

"Should we check on him?" I asked. Jasper followed my gaze and nodded. We got out of the car, just the two of us—KJ and her brain-passenger stayed in the driver's seat.

"Al!" I said, heading down the path. The sun that filtered through the trees was warm, but the air was crisp and chilly, full of the smell of dead and dying leaves. I rubbed my hands together and jogged to catch up to Alex, Jasper a little ways behind me.

"Al?" I said again, when I got closer. I tapped him on the shoulder.

Alex turned around, and he was crying.

Crying, and looking kind of bewildered while he did it. He pushed his long dark hair away from his face and covered his mouth with one hand.

"Hey, what's wrong?" I asked.

"I—I just—oh man, I, rocks around us, I feel so—"

Jasper touched Alex's back.

"Alex," he said. Alex turned to face him.

"Why do I feel so weird? Why can't I hear him?" Alex asked, almost frantic. I'd never seen Alex frantic.

"It's a good thing," Jasper said. He reached way up and put his hands on both sides of Alex's face, dragging his head and shoulders down so that they were just about eye to eye. Their normal pupils looked at each other.

"I feel really bad," Alex said.

"It's okay," Jasper said. "It's okay to feel bad."

"It's awful. I feel so gross, I feel so mad, I hate that Brooks guy, I'm . . . I think I'm jealous, and I . . . I don't know why everyone let KJ get turned into the Incorporation, why would they do that? Why would *I* do that? Why?" Alex moved his head between Jasper's palms, shaking with the intensity of his emotion.

"You had no choice," Jasper said. "It's okay."

"I hate this, I don't want it," Alex said with tears in his voice. "I hate it, Jas. I want to go back to normal. I don't want this—"

"Don't you fucking dare," Jasper said. He was still holding Alex's head so their faces were almost pressed together, nose to nose. "Don't you dare say you love Big Brother."

Alex blinked, his long eyelashes brushing the skin underneath his eyes, then looked back at Jasper with a focused intensity.

"Like *Nineteen Eighty-Four*?" Alex asked.

"Yeah, exactly," Jasper said. "No more Big Brother. No more Thought Police."

"No more Thought Police," Alex said. He sucked in a breath and let it out slowly. "Right. No more Thought Police."

"We hate Big Brother," Jasper said. Then he dropped his hands from Alex's face and wrapped his arms around him.

Alex looked down at Jasper like he was totally baffled. But then something in his expression kind of melted into softness. He hugged Jasper back, and they stood there like that in the speckled golden sunlight with the breeze moving around them.

I turned away to let them have their moment and walked back toward the car. A day before, I'd been in the dark about this furtive romantic undercurrent to their relationship. I was surprised at how right the idea of them together was—a puzzle piece I had been missing since I was thirteen, neatly slotted into place.

I slid into the PDA's passenger side and looked over at KJ. "They're inches away from making out over there, thanks to you," I told her.

"THAT IS VERY UNFORTUNATE," KJ said. "OUR TWIN IS NOT FIT TO MAKE OUT WITH ANYONE. JASPER IS PERHAPS EVEN LESS FIT TO MAKE OUT WITH PEOPLE."

"Tell that to them," I said, laughing. "They seem pretty into each other."

"PERHAPS THEIR MUTUAL GROTESQUENESS AND WORTHLESSNESS IS ALLURING," KJ said.

I almost laughed again. "Are you using the mouth of the god inside you to craft these Ren Faire–ass insults?" I asked. "Because they are hilarious. Or they would be, under better circumstances."

"WE ARE *BOTH* USING OUR MOUTH FOR INSULTS," KJ said, and suddenly I thought of something.

"KJ?" I asked. "You have Good Arcturus inside of you. Right?"

"WE HAVE ESTABLISHED THAT, D," KJ said.

"So how could your mom be doing something you didn't want her to?" I asked. "Like calling the cops, telling on us. How can her eyes still be all dilated and brainwash-y? How can she act against your will, if she can always hear the voice of Good Arcturus?"

But KJ didn't answer. She just stared at me, and then looked down at her hands again.

"She *was* acting against your will, right?" I pressed. "Or are you fighting against what Good Arcturus wants? Using his power against him, or something?"

"No," KJ said immediately. "WE ARE ALIGNED. WE ARE ONE."

She had been firm on that all day.

"Okayyy," I said, not knowing what to believe. It seemed to me like things weren't totally adding up.

Then Jasper and Alex opened the back doors of the PDA. Jasper looked kind of starry-eyed, which was cute and also very strange. Alex was a little teary, but he seemed much less stressed.

"Let's fucking goooooo," Jasper said. "I think they've probably passed this gate by now, if the Sumners *are* looking for us. KJ, take us to Aunt Judy's. She's going to hide us for the night."

"I've never been there," I said. Aunt Judy had invited me to join her and Alex for a day of tie-dyeing last summer, but there had always been something more interesting going on. Tie-dye was pretty low on my list of "best recreational summer activities."

"You're going to love it," Alex said.

"No you are not," Jasper said. "It's a fucking nightmare place. It has seventies flower linoleum."

"I like vintage linoleum!" Alex said.

"You're a dipshit," Jasper said.

When I glanced into the rearview, I could see that the two of them were holding hands across the back seat.

Then we rolled back out onto Route 202, and for a little bit I forgot all about my questions, my feeling that there was some innate contradiction in what we had learned, in everything we had seen.

Which was a mistake.

CHAPTER ELEVEN

Sunday, October 29, 2000

If Kesuquosh was "the perfect New England town" (ha ha), then Cold Hollow was its larger, less perfect, but wayyyy artsier cousin. In the summers we would drive up there to visit Sonic Sanctuary, possibly my favorite record store in the world, and that was including my five favorite ones in New York.

At the edge of Cold Hollow was the Cold Falls Preparatory School. You may know that name—the Falls makes top ten lists for "best boarding schools in the United States" all the time. Most of the seven-hundred-plus students who went there would be bound for Ivy League schools. It was the kind of place that my peers attended—teenagers with parents as rich as my dad—if they could get in. That was where the notorious Brooks Gould-Greenwood went to school.

And even beyond that, out on the very fringes of forest that separated the town of Cold Hollow from the state-owned land around the Quabbin, was Aunt Judy's home.

To get to her place, we had to take the PDA down a patchy street, beyond a mostly overgrown trailer park, and then onto a narrow dirt road that arrowed through the woods (two mailboxes were mounted at the mouth of the road, making me feel like we were leaving the world as I knew it) for an extremely bumpy half mile—KJ barely lifted her lead foot, even when the pavement disappeared—before we were finally spit out into a spot surrounded by tall pines.

"This must be the place?" I asked.

"Overrated," Jasper said.

"That's the Talking Heads' best song!" Alex said.

"If you haven't ever listened to any of their other songs, sure, I could see why you might think that," Jasper said.

In the clearing, poised at opposite sides, were two tiny A-frame houses. Between them was a stream, a lush span of autumnal gardens, and a bunch of gnarled old apple trees. The A-frame that was farther away, closer to the woods, was painted midnight blue and had a line of woodsmoke curling up from its chimney. The one nearer to us was lavender and gold, with tie-dye shirts on the clothesline and a wheelchair ramp leading up to the front porch. The sliding glass door at the front of the purple house opened as we walked up the ramp, and a medium-sized black mutt came running out, tail up and wagging. A big orange cat with three legs hopped after it. Jasper, who was the first one to the porch, had the dog pawing gently at his legs and the cat rubbing wobbly at his ankles, until they both saw Alex and forgot Jasper existed.

"Hey, Midnight, hey, Orlac," Alex said, and sat down cross-legged on the porch to pet both of them at the same time. The dog—Midnight—sniffed his hair and licked his head, while Orlac immediately got into his lap.

"I'm coming!" came a man's voice, and then a short fat man with an absurdly strong jaw, like a cartoon drawing of a superhero, walked out and looked at us with his hands on his hips. He had a gray streak in his dark hair, and he was wearing big old-guy glasses, a (yes, tie-dyed) T-shirt with pink lettering on it that said *Creedence Clearwater Revisited—1995.*

"Darian, this is Surendra Karnik," Alex said, "Aunt Judy's significant other."

"Pleased to meet you," Surendra said, and shook my hand so vigorously that I had to take it back and make sure it was still attached.

KJ was behind me, still only halfway up the ramp. She looked . . . anxious, like she didn't want to bring her buzzy, godlike, ozone-smelling self over to freak out Surendra with. But he pushed past me and Jasper and walked down the ramp to meet her. When he got there, he stood on his tiptoes and looked into her eyes.

"Judith called me and told me what was going on," Surendra said. "I didn't know what to think, honestly. But you really have done it, haven't you? Absconded with the god of Kesuquosh?"

"WE HAVE ABSCONDED WITH EACH OTHER," KJ said.

"I didn't know this was possible," Surendra said. "Would never have thought of it, not in a million years."

"WE HAVE NOT DONE ANYTHING WRONG," KJ added.

"No, no, no, you haven't," Surendra said, and clucked his tongue like he was thinking really hard, or else pretending to be a chicken. "In fact, you've accomplished something amazing. Come in, darlings, come along. Shoes off in the house!"

While we took off our shoes I looked around. It *was* 1970s-looking—the linoleum floors were covered with an orange-white-yellow print of huge daisies. Next to the door was a silver walker with tennis balls capping all four of its feet. An orange kitchen table sat underneath a stained-glass lamp with drag-onflies on it—half of the table was covered in newspaper and pumpkin guts. Surendra had apparently been in the process of carving jack-o'-lanterns.

The walls of the A-frame were dark panel wood. Instead of a living room, there was a low, comfortable-looking bed in the room next to the kitchen, facing a fireplace. Several equally low bookshelves lined the space, all pushed against the walls, I guessed to make it easier for a wheelchair to get through. While I looked around, Surendra shuffled around in a pair of house slippers, making tea for us.

"Sit," he said, and waved at the orange table. We all obeyed him.

"Is this the lowest-income house you've ever been in?" Jasper asked me in an undertone as we sat down. "You look like you're walking through a museum. The Aging Hippie Museum of the Lower Middle Class."

"Shut up," I whispered back. "Why don't you go cry on Alex because he can *feel stuff* now."

"Bitch," Jasper said to me, clearly trying not to laugh.

"*You're* the bitch," I said, also trying not to laugh. KJ looked at us quizzically while Alex petted Orlac, who was still sitting in his lap. Midnight was by my feet, resting her head on my socks. I felt pretty honored, especially when she periodically gazed up at me with her intelligent brown eyes like we were already good buddies.

"Now, tell me everything that happened," Surendra said, pulling out a chair for himself after all the tea was distributed and some shortbread cookies had been produced. KJ looked at the cookies for a second and then ate like six in a row.

"THESE ARE GOOD," she said through a mouthful of crumbs.

"I need the story," Surendra said. "You have gotten yourselves into a strange situation, darlings."

So Jasper told him everything that had happened since yesterday, and Surendra listened without commenting. But he also didn't look too surprised.

"You know all about the Great Harvest Hallow," I said to Surendra, when Jasper was done talking. "You knew Good Arcturus was real?"

"I've lived around the Quabbin for my whole life," Surendra said. "And I pay attention. That's enough for me to believe in strange happenings. But—anyone want more tea?"

"Yes, please," Alex said.

"WE WOULD LIKE MORE LORNA DOONE COOKIES," KJ said. "PLEASE."

"You ate the whole box," Surendra said, opening the cabinets. He gave KJ a box of blueberry Pop-Tarts and put the kettle on again, bending over the low stovetop.

"In response to your observation, Darian," Surendra said, "my grandparents emigrated from Maharashtra when they were first married. They settled in Kesuquosh, which—especially back then—had a reputation for being a little kinder and more diverse than other places in New England."

"It's bullshit, though," Jasper said. "They're not kinder. They just don't discriminate because they want more victims to worship Good Arcturus."

"I am inclined to agree. But there is no proof one way or another about the intentions behind the acceptance. My mother was born in Kesuquosh. She also suffered from major depression."

"Oh. I'm sorry," I said.

"As am I," Surendra said. "However. Good Arcturus cannot cope with diversity of the mind, no, no, no, not at all. Jasper has told Judy about how KJ had moments of clarity while under his control. Possibly because she tells lies. My mother—at her darkest moments—also had clarity about Good Arcturus. What he was and what he meant for the town. She understood enough to make sure I was not born within the town lines. And to educate me on the dangers of the place."

"So there are more people who have those moments of clarity," I said. "It isn't just KJ."

Jasper and I looked at each other. He looked a little horrified. Maybe wondering how many other people were walking around pretending to be okay with everything all the time. I was thinking of the flickers of discomfort I had seen on some scattered faces during the Banquet of the Needle.

"Yes," Surendra said. He set tea down in front of Alex with a distant expression on his face.

"My mother killed herself, albeit passively," he added, "by refusing to return home for one Harvest Hallow. On October thirty-first, 1986, she tripped on the stairs in her house and fell. She was older and quite frail. Hit her head in just the right way to never wake up."

"God," I said, "that's horrible." My stomach was in knots. I couldn't shake the idea that my mom had done something similar, abstaining from the Hallow and dying for it.

"It was very sad," Surendra said. "But it was on her terms. Unlike the majority of the people who live there, forever under his spell, she was aware enough to make a conscious choice."

"An opt-out," Jasper said, and I looked over at him. I wondered if he had ever considered "opting out" during his years trapped with all the zombies.

"You better not even think about it," I said.

"No fucking way," Jasper shot back, pulling out a clove. "I want to live, bitch."

"Certain types of minds outside of what we would consider, albeit simplistically, the *standard*, make people harder to control," Surendra said. "I think."

"So you're saying that KJ managed to run away after becoming the Incorporation because she's a pathological liar?" I asked.

"The DSM–IV lists pathological lying as a symptom, not as a mental illness," Surendra said. "We don't know what we don't know, etcetera. I think there are nuances here that we cannot grasp. But we should ask KJ."

We all looked at KJ, who looked back at us with her mouth full of Pop-Tart.

"Well? How did you manage to escape?" Surendra asked gently.

But KJ shook her head. She almost looked like she was in pain. "To speak of it is beyond our cloakless powers," she said. Then, having demolished her Pop-Tarts, she pulled the other Scary Cake (with S'Cream filling) out of her cloak and started eating that.

"That shit again," Jasper said. "What does it *mean*?"

KJ looked over at him. "To speak of what it means is *also* beyond our cloakless powers," she said.

"Really great. Helpful. Two personalities sharing one brain, and they're both dipshits," Jasper said, and opened the door so he could smoke on the porch.

"If you can't talk about it, darling, then you can't talk about it," Surendra said, and squeezed KJ's hand in his little plump one. "We'll find a way to help you regardless."

"WE WOULD BE MOST GRATEFUL FOR YOUR ASSISTANCE," KJ said.

"We'll find a way," Alex said. "I'm not going to let him kill you, KJ."

When I looked over at him, Alex met my eyes. His mouth was set in a straight line. "I mean it," he said. "It's wrong. I can't believe I didn't see how wrong it was."

"Feels good to be out, doesn't it," Surendra said, studying Alex.

"Yeah. But it feels like a *lot*," Alex muttered.

"WE ARE SORRY," KJ said, reaching across the table to touch his arm. "MAYBE IT WAS SELFISH. IT DEFINITELY COST US. BUT WE MIGHT ONLY HAVE A FEW DAYS LEFT. AND WE WANTED TO BE WITH THE *REAL* YOU."

Alex looked at her hand, then her face. "I'm grateful for it, actually," he said. "I'd rather be upset to be myself than happy to be nobody."

I couldn't process his answer, though. I was caught on *we might only have a few days left.* Inside me there was a feeling of anxiety that threatened to become panic. *Not going to let that happen,* I vowed to myself.

Then Surendra showed us how to bake cinnamon-sugar pumpkin seeds while we waited for Judy to get out of work. When Aunt Judy's blue minivan pulled up, we all went outside to meet her. Jasper was talking at her before she even had time to transfer her wheelchair out of the seat and herself into it.

"Their mother met those constabulary morons out in the parking lot," Aunt Judy told him. "I don't know if they tailed you. Seems like they *tried* to—they went north."

Surendra told his—wife? I wasn't sure—what was up with Alex, and then Aunt Judy wheeled in, just in time for KJ to get up from where she was reading a copy of *Rolling Stone* with Blink-182 on the cover. **"WE ARE FAMISHED,"** KJ said.

I looked sideways at Jasper and Alex. The constant hunger thing was starting to put me a little bit on edge. But Aunt Judy seemed unphased. "You can all stay here," she told us. "You'll have to sleep in Surendra's office"—she pointed up toward the loft— "and you're going to need to go buy your own food. I cannot feed four teenagers and one peckish monster."

"I can buy us food," I said. "I have credit cards."

"Sweet, let's go," Jasper said.

"Do you guys need anything?" I asked Surendra and Judy.

"No, darling. We're going to smoke some marijuana and discuss what to do about your problem," Surendra said.

"Do you think anyone in your family will be looking for that car?" Aunt Judy asked.

"I mean, maybe, but they don't need it," Alex said. "All the businesses in Kesuquosh are closed until after October thirty-first."

Then Alex fought KJ for the driver's seat and won, which made me and Jasper both sigh in relief.

"You are the world's worst fucking driver," Jasper told KJ.

"WE ARE COMPETENT AND ENJOYING OURSELVES," KJ said, sliding into the back seat across from me.

On the way to the grocery store I started thinking about how KJ (and, weirdly, maybe Good Arcturus) had come on to me that morning. That ridiculous Ye Olde Beautiful and Tragic Womyn kind of talk that she'd been doing was not KJ at all. But the *feelings*, oh yeah. I believed in her feelings for me. I believed that we both felt the same way about each other.

Maybe I looked at her with something on my face that gave away how I was feeling, because KJ met my eyes with raised eyebrows. "ARE YOU ALL RIGHT, D?" she asked.

I'm terrified, I thought. *Of what might happen to you.*

I didn't want to say that. I looked out the window.

Outside, the town of Cold Hollow was settling into another October night. String lights glittered in shop windows. Prep-school juniors and seniors walked down the street in groups, breathing out puffs of foggy air. The tiny, indie Pleasant Street movie theater, which only had two screens and somehow fit into an old shoe store, had a line outside the ticket booth.

"I'm okay," I said. "Just kind of worried about you."

"PERHAPS IF WE KISSED YOU WOULD BE ASSURED THAT WE ARE DOING WELL," KJ said.

"Holy shit, is this the kind of game that Good Arcturus has?" Jasper asked. "Because it is *bad*. I bet no other demon creatures want to fuck him, ever. What are you going to do, annoy her into dating you, or something?"

"You're really embarrassing my sister, probably, so maybe stop," Alex said. He was addressing KJ . . . or the thing inside KJ. "I get if you think you're like, helping her, but—"

"WE ARE SIMPLY BEING OPEN WITH OUR FEELINGS!" KJ looked defiant, but also embarrassed. "WE DO NOT ENTIRELY REMEMBER THE REASON FOR—"

"—but KJ's playing the long game with Darian," Alex continued, "because Darian was like, sexually abused or raped or something horrible, we don't know what. So, like, she needs space and time?"

"Alex," Jasper said, and reached over and smacked him on the head, "shut the *fuck* up."

I felt like the bottom dropped out of my stomach. Or the car. "What . . . what did you say?" I asked.

"Nothing," Alex said, though he clearly knew denial was pointless.

"You—you guys," I said, "you knew? You guys have . . . all this time, and I was . . . and you were just talking about me—"

"It was *not* like that—" Jasper said, but I cut him off.

"—speculating about me, like trying to guess what terrible thing happened to make me so fucking pathetic?" I had started out trying to be calm, but now my voice sounded high and shrill to my own ears.

"Darian, it was *never like that*," Jasper said. "Alex, you fucking moron—"

"Were you making fun of me? Is it obvious?" I asked. I could feel my cheeks burning. I was horribly afraid that I might cry.

"We would never make fun of you for that, idiot!" Jasper said, looking extremely upset. "We just know you. We all know you. We didn't expect you to talk about anything you didn't want to—"

"I'm sorry, I'm new to the negative feelings stuff, I didn't mean to," Alex said, his face a mask of misery. He turned around to try to look at me, and managed to swerve the PDA over the yellow line.

Through the half-rolled-down window, I heard a car horn honk, and someone yell, "Nice driving, pizza douche!"

That made me laugh, right in the middle of my big emotional thing. When I started giggling, Jasper looked even more alarmed, like he thought I was having a nervous breakdown.

"NICE ... DRIVING ... PIZZA ... DOUCHE," KJ echoed, like she was just learning English. That made me laugh even harder. Kind of hysterically, I think.

"Are you even in there at *all*?" I asked KJ, through my laughter.

"OF COURSE, D," KJ replied immediately and with an ease that sounded like her *real* self. "JUST SHOWING OURSELVES AROUND. IT IS NOT SO BAD. EVEN IF WE ARE CURRENTLY DESTROYING OUR CHANCES WITH YOU, WHICH BLOWS EXTREME CHUNKS."

Alex pulled into the parking lot for Martin's Quality Market, parked the car, and turned around. He and Jasper were both staring at me.

"We aren't speculating," Jasper said. "We aren't making fun of you. We all have our vulnerable fucking bullshit. This stupid fucker was being mind-controlled by a scarecrow until like five hours ago. How's that for an experience most people can't relate to?"

"We love you, Darian," Alex said. "I—I'm really sorry for bringing it up. They told me not to bring it up, and it was easy to do that before. Bad things had a way of kind of . . . leaving my head. But now it's harder not to think about all the bad stuff."

"Welcome to being a person," Jasper said. But he didn't take his eyes off me. "Can you forgive us?"

"WE PERSONALLY DID NOT DO ANYTHING WRONG," KJ clarified from next to me.

"She's right. You haven't done anything wrong," I said. My heart was still racing. But I clamped down on it. Stilled my body. Control, control, control. I was good at that. "Sorry for freaking out. I was just kind of shocked."

"We wouldn't ever judge you," Jasper said. "Okay? Not for stuff that *happened* to you, stuff you can't help. Your taste in music is another whole thing. I do judge you for how bad that is."

"Right back at you on the music stuff," I said, which made Jasper smile. I glanced out the car windows then, but Dexter was nowhere in sight. Then I clocked Alex and Jasper seeing me look around, and I realized it wasn't the first time my friends had ever noticed me acting . . . odd. Obviously. I wondered how weird I seemed from the outside. Traumatized? Paranoid? Hunted?

"The other stuff I don't want to talk about," I added.

"No shit," Jasper said. "I'm not going to make you. I fucking hate talking about feelings."

"We love you," Alex said again. He tried to crawl over the armrest to give me a half hug, and ended up honking the car horn by accident.

"Rocks around us, you're so stupid," Jasper said, which was funny, because he never used any of the trademark Kesuquoshian slang. I guess all the emotions of the day were getting to him.

"You are a real bitch, huh?" Alex asked him, kind of speculatively, still flopped halfway over the armrest like a salmon. "It's kind of adorable."

I hadn't heard Alex use even a whisper of foul language in my life. It clearly flustered Jasper, who sputtered and failed to immediately come up with a retort.

"Okay. I think I'm good now. Let's get food," I said. I didn't want to think about how deeply I was *seen* by all of them anymore. It felt good. But also scary. Painful. Grossly vulnerable in a way I hated being.

KJ held the door open for me, and when I looked up at her I paused. "You have your sunglasses?" I asked.

"It's almost Halloween," Jasper said. "People will probably assume it's a costume."

But KJ did have her sunglasses. She pulled them out of her red robe, along with her Soundgarden beanie, and dropped the sunflower crown on the pavement.

"DO WE LOOK PASSABLY NORMAL?" she asked me, all serious.

"Yeah," I said.

As we were walking into Martin's Quality Market, my cell phone started ringing.

"It's Dan," I said. "Be there in a sec."

Then I picked it up. Wherever Senovak was, there was a lot of background noise.

"Darian?" he said.

"What's up?" I asked. I didn't think Senovak was able to tell anything from my voice, but with him it was better safe than sorry. The deeper I got into this, the more I felt like I couldn't tell him about it. Kesuquosh was dangerous. I needed him to stay away, to believe things were normal, to focus on his own grief without worrying about me. I channeled all the "casual relaxation" energy I could.

"Just checking in. How are you?"

"Fine. We're getting food in Cold Hollow," I said. "How's all the sad stuff going?"

"About as well as can be expected," Senovak said. He sounded very tired.

"I'm sorry," I said.

"Can't be helped," Senovak said. "I'll let you go eat. The services are tomorrow, so I'll be unavailable during the day. But I'll call you in the evening?"

"Sure," I said, but then before he could hang up, I thought about KJ's Citgo showdown with Rita. "Dan?"

"Mmm?"

"Do you think that someone can act in opposition to themselves?" I asked. I pictured KJ, the Incorporation of their god, literally *filled* with their god, telling her mom to leave us alone. And Rita not immediately doing so. Even though Good Arcturus had everyone in town brainwashed. "Like want one thing but also direct people to do another thing that . . . isn't what they actually want?"

"Of course they can," Senovak said. "People do that all the time. Saying they want one thing and doing another. Like saying you want to get well and then telling your therapist that nothing is wrong."

This was a flagrant jab at me and my alleged uncooperativeness with Dr. Schebecki's team after Dexter's death. I rolled my eyes so hard that I was sure Senovak could feel it through the phone. "That's *not* what I'm talking about. I mean, like, say someone has power over a situation. Absolute power. It's demonstrably proven. But then, suddenly, they can't do the things they've done before."

"Are you all right?" Senovak asked me suspiciously.

"Yes! I'm talking about the themes in a concept album," I lied. It worked, though. Nothing could make Senovak less interested more quickly.

"Maybe the creator of the concept album made a stupid oversight," Senovak said. "Breakdown in world logic. A mistake in continuity. Happens all the time with television and things."

"Not possible in this situation," I said. Considering the concept album was actually all of reality.

"Okay," Senovak said, "well. Then the answer to the supposed conundrum is obvious."

"Is it?"

"Yes," Senovak said. "You, as a teenager, should be painfully familiar with this. If someone purports to have power, but they can't enact their will . . ."

"Yeah?" I asked.

"Then they are either lying or mistaken. They do *not* have the power. Someone else has the power. Someone else is pulling the strings."

"I don't know how that's possible," I said.

"Well, listen to your album again," Senovak said. "Perhaps the answer will reveal itself. You go eat. Make good choices. I'll call you tomorrow."

"Okay," I said, and hung up.

I looked up at the darkening October sky and thought about what Senovak had said.

Someone else has the power. Someone else is pulling the strings.

"Who could that be?" I asked.

No answer suddenly popped into my head. Just that weird phrasing that KJ had used.

In her woods. In her little world.

It would be almost a year before I found out what that meant. I turned it over in my mind for another few seconds, then went inside to join my friends.

CHAPTER TWELVE

Monday, October 30, 2000

That night we slept on the floor in the shag-carpeted loft of the A-frame, which was also Surendra's office. It turned out he was a certified public accountant, a job so normal that I was shocked.

KJ stayed up late and got up before us. In the morning I found her sitting cross-legged against the far wall of the loft, standing out like red-cloaked Death against the dark panels, with Orlac cuddling her and a bunch of *Rolling Stone*s and three empty boxes of Little Debbie's Pumpkin Delights.

When I looked at KJ in the daylight, I could see thin, worm-like strands moving restlessly under her skin. It raised the hair on my arms.

"Good morning," I said to KJ. "Don't you sleep?"

"For the time being, we need less sleep than you," KJ said. "Instead we have been catching up on the general music scene." She gestured to the magazines.

"How's that looking?" I asked, getting up. I felt *so* grimy. Another day of wearing my pajamas loomed on the horizon like a punishment.

"IT IS LOOKING PRETTY SO-SO," KJ said. "WE ARE AFRAID THAT THE GOLDEN AGE OF GRUNGE IS OVER. MUSIC GENERALLY HAS SHIFTED TO A DIFFERENT SET OF AESTHETICS. THE HEAVY DISTORTION THAT GIVES THE ELECTRIC GUITARS THAT INCREDIBLE SLUDGY SOUND IS BEING REPLACED BY SOMETHING SOFTER AND MORE MELODIC."

"Yeah. Something pleasant to listen to, why on earth would the people want that," I said. This was a debate we'd had before. No amount of me playing Ravel or Chopin and reveling in the beauty of *beauty* could change her mind.

"WE HAVE NO IDEA!" KJ said, crushing a Pumpkin Delights box with her fist to emphasize her point. I laughed and met her big red eyes. They were still kind of beautiful, even like that. I toyed with the wild idea of bringing up the kissing thing she'd talked about last night. Maybe it would work like a fairy tale. Bring the real KJ back, or something. I could *hear* her in there, almost being herself.

Or even if it didn't bring her back, I'd like to kiss her, just once.

"You alive up there, darlings?"

"Noooooo," Jasper moaned from under a comforter.

"Yes," I said. Then Surendra half-ascended the narrow stairs and looked in at all of us.

"We went ahead and talked to our neighbors about this," Surendra said. "The Freys. They're coming over to meet with you. I think if anybody can help, it's them."

"Why can they help?" I asked.

"They can do things," Surendra said, a little mysteriously, and vanished down the stairs.

"I've always wanted to meet them, but they're usually busy," Alex said. "They call themselves *praecantrices*, each of them is a praecantrix. Like a witch, I think, or a sorceress."

"Excellent," Jasper said. He stood up, stretched, raked one hand through his hair, and put his spiked collar on. "If they can't help, there's a group of kids at the regional high school who can also supposedly 'do things.' Brooks knows one of the guys from track meets—"

"Oh man, Brooks just knows it all, huh?" Alex asked in a snarky tone that was totally new for him.

"—and if *they* can't help, we could always go to the closest Catholic diocese and ask for help," Jasper said. "Or consult a rabbi. Or maybe someone at a mosque, I think there's one in Boston. I don't really know anything about the Abrahamic religions, but it wouldn't hurt to try."

"I don't think any of those religions, like, *work*," I said. "At least not like *yours* works."

Jasper shrugged. "Who knows? Maybe everything is true. You want to weigh in on this, KJ?"

KJ also shrugged. "WE ARE STRANGERS IN A STRANGE LAND. WHAT YOU CALL *MAGIC* OR *RELIGION* IS WHAT WE MIGHT CALL *REALITY.*"

"Unhelpful," Jasper said. But I smiled at KJ as we all went down the stairs single-file.

"What's Good Arcturus's world like?" I asked. I wasn't sure if he was from another *world*, really, or even exactly what that would mean. But I was trying to get info. I didn't understand where the perimeters of what KJ could and could not talk about were.

"Beautiful," KJ said, with such a note of sorrow in her voice that I stopped on the linoleum and looked up at her as she came down the stairs.

"Not like here," she added. "We should not have wandered—"

It didn't seem like something that a conquering creature from another universe would say while gleefully possessing a whole town. It sounded *lost*. Full of regret.

Then she broke off, and looked down at the ground. "To speak of it is beyond our cloakless powers."

Aunt Judy was sitting in the kitchen, rolling up joints from a huge pile of finely ground weed.

"Morning. The Frey sisters are on their way over to speak with you. Be polite to Friday and Flora, please. I have to continue living a hundred yards from them after this is all over. *Jasper.* I'm talking to *you*, cupcake."

"I'll be polite!" Jasper said unconvincingly.

"Sure," Aunt Judy said as a knock sounded on the door. "One of you get that, please?"

I went to answer it while KJ pulled a box of Toaster Strudels out of the freezer.

The woman at the door was gorgeous. Very tall, Black, youngish—not in my age range but youngish. Her shoulder-length cornrows ended in glittery green beads, and a tote bag from the local bookstore was slung over one shoulder. She was wearing a green dress that reached down almost all the way to her feet. I felt like she was the most beautiful person I'd ever seen, like if we'd gone to Pelham together through some weird warping of space-time I would have been composing music about her, even though on the streets of New York I probably walked past a dozen actual models a day. I felt *very* much like I was in wrinkly pajamas and hadn't showered in way too long.

"Hiii," I said stupidly, and then backed away so she could get in the house.

"Hello," said the beautiful woman.

"Morning, Friday," Aunt Judy said, and handed her a joint, which she took and tucked into the front of her dress. Then another woman, who was holding a dark blue yoga mat under one arm, jogged up to the door and slipped into the kitchen.

"And this is Flora," Aunt Judy said as the second woman shut the door and looked at us.

Flora was very different from Friday in both looks and style: she didn't give off "witch" energy, she gave off *lesbian* energy. She was short, with a close-cropped Afro that tapered around her face and curls dusting her forehead. Wearing a flannel shirt and jeans. She didn't make my heart flutter like her sister did, but she seemed cool. She smiled at us and nodded.

"Flora," Aunt Judy said, and reached out to give her a joint, too. "Thank you for coming. That's Jasper, that's Darian, Alex, and the one with Good Arcturus in her head is KJ."

"Nice to meet you," Flora said. Her eyes swept to KJ, who was standing by the toaster oven while her strudels, like, toasted. Flora looked intent and surprised, like she hadn't expected whatever Judy had told them to actually be true.

"Hey, you two. You need space to work?" Surendra said, appearing from the direction of the bathroom in a flowered robe with a pink towel wrapped around his head. He gestured to the living room area, and Friday nodded.

"Let's see what was so urgent that we had to cancel on a day's worth of clients," Flora said.

"I can pay you for the missed work," I said, but the disapproving look I got from Flora made me feel like kind of a dipshit for offering.

"Getting rid of one of the dark things that plagues this part of the world will be payment enough," Flora said. "You're gonna try to kill a god, huh?"

"WE DO NOT WANT TO KILL US," KJ said quickly. The toaster oven dinged behind her. "JUST . . . WE *BOTH* WANT TO AVOID THE . . . CULMINATION."

Someone else has the power . . . someone else is pulling the strings, I thought. Just like Senovak said. I believed it now. Good Arcturus didn't want to be complicit in this.

"Okay," Flora said. "You. KJ. Come in here and lay down for me for a minute?"

KJ, who was apparently fine eating molten-hot pastry, looked at me mid strudel bite. At least I think she did. It's hard to tell where someone is looking when they have no visible pupils or irises. I nodded. *It's okay,* I wanted to convey. I didn't know if the Frey sisters actually had *magic powers,* but I trusted Judy's and Surendra's judgment. And we didn't have a lot of options, no matter what Jasper said about Catholic exorcisms.

"Will you light a fire, Surendra?" Friday asked.

"Of course, dear one, of course," Surendra said.

Friday went to the far side of the living space–slash–bedroom and pulled curtains over the big window wall, shrouding the room in the soft glow of the lamps. Flora unrolled her dark blue yoga mat while Surendra coaxed a fire to life.

"KJ, you lay here," Flora said, and Friday took the tote bag from her, rifled through it, and pulled out a long piece of sky-blue chalk. KJ lay on the mat, looking stiff and trepidatious, with her mostly-devoured plate of strudels next to her.

"Scoot down," Flora said, and KJ slid down until most of her legs hung off the end of the mat.

"Okay. I'm gonna touch your face," Flora said. KJ nodded, and Flora put one hand over her forehead and closed her own eyes. She took a deep breath. Her left hand drew shapes on the mat with the chalk in a halo around KJ's head, things I couldn't identify, like runic shorthand, little pictograms.

I looked over at Jasper and Alex while this was going on. Jasper looked pretty skeptical, but Alex seemed fascinated. Surendra, who had finished starting the fire and moved to sit cross-legged on the bed, looked fascinated too.

After a minute, Flora opened her eyes and exhaled, like she was surfacing from deep underwater.

"Fri," she said. Then Friday came over and knelt down, examining the pictograms.

"I don't . . ." She paused, tracing a series of lines that held absolutely no meaning for me, her fingertips smudging the chalk the way that KJ had smudged my *to the loneliest girl in new york* CD. She looked at Flora. "Are you sure?"

Flora nodded. "We need to be together. I'm not going back in alone just to *be sure*, if that's what you're asking. It's so cold in there that I thought I was gonna die."

"What did you see in her head?" I asked.

The sisters looked over at me.

"Is there someone else controlling him? Controlling Good Arcturus?" I asked. I was thinking about what Senovak had said on the phone.

Jasper and Alex gave me confused looks, but Flora just sighed. She looked worried, which made me even more worried. "I don't know if we can stop this from happening," she said. "But there are a few things we can try."

"There are a lot of cracks in reality around the Quabbin," Friday said. "Bad things. Good things. Thin spots. That mall in Wickford—"

"The lost cemetery in North Dana," Flora said. "The altar in Wickett, the islands in the water down by Rabbitville, the Prince of Spring—"

"She means whatever goes on at the school over there," Friday said, gesturing vaguely in what I thought was the direction of Cold Falls Prep, "not to mention the *underneath* of the Quabbin itself."

"Or the things that live in the woods around Route 202," Surendra said.

"What about Sad Sam? The reservoir Bigfoot?" Alex asked.

"He's not real," Flora said. Alex looked incredibly disappointed.

"But there's always been a cold wind blowing out of Kesuquosh," Friday said. "Catching people in its chill. Creating victims, like Surendra's mom. I don't know how tourists can stand it. It's like walking into a room full of mannequins."

I'd had that exact thought, about mannequins, the night that KJ was sacrificed to Good Arcturus.

"We don't go there," Flora said. "Not even for the awesome pizza."

"That's *our* pizza!" Alex said. "We're them! The . . . that's my family's pizza place, I mean."

"What I'm saying is, we want to help you," Flora said. "You don't deserve to be prisoners."

"Yeah," Alex said. "We're all being controlled by the Thought Police."

Out of the corner of my eye, I saw Jasper touch his fingertips to Alex's hand.

"Typically, I do the mindwork and Friday does the spellwork," Flora said.

"You're a psychic and she's a witch?" I asked. I tried to keep any hint of incredulity out of my voice.

"We don't put it like that," Friday said, dazzling me with her smile. "*Praecantrix* sounds so much more expensive. But yes, basically."

"What's the report?" Aunt Judy asked, appearing in the room. She used her silver walker to make her way over to the bed, then sat down carefully next to Surendra.

"So I can feel two consciousnesses inside this kid," Flora said. "They go allllll the way down. Very deep and very cold. You can sit up for a minute, KJ. And I need Friday to come with me, poke around inside her mind for a bit. But in a perfect world, I could send KJ out of her head while I did it, and have a little tête-à-tête with the *thing* in there."

"How are you going to send KJ out of her own brain?" Alex asked.

"Should be easy. She's barely using it on a good day," Jasper said.

"You know what would make it easier . . . ," Friday said. She and Flora exchanged a look, and then Flora turned back to us.

"I know these two aren't magic users," Flora said, gesturing to the bed, "but I don't suppose any of you have gifts? Premonition, intuition? Power of persuasion? A *gut feeling* about things?"

"I have good taste in music," Jasper said. "Does that count?"

"He doesn't really have good taste in music," I said.

"I'm just, like, kind of starting my journey of self-discovery," Alex said, "but I don't *feel* like a witch."

Then Flora raised an eyebrow at me and KJ.

"WE ARE CHARMING AND A WONDERFUL LIAR," KJ said. "BUT NOT, WE THINK, A PRACTITIONER OF MAGIC."

"A so-so liar," Jasper said.

"A bad liar," Alex said. "Like about the dumbest stuff."

"Not that it would matter right now for you, KJ. You're the one who needs to be magicked *at*," Flora said, and looked at me pointedly.

"I'm not a witch," I said. "I don't believe in anything. Except Good Arcturus. My aunt Blanche was the last shield or Incorporation or whatever, but I don't think that gives me a home field advantage?"

"We can test them," Friday said. "See which one of them will need to take KJ into their mind. Maybe get the rock out now?"

"Take KJ into their *mind*?" I asked.

Flora started digging around in the tote bag they'd brought.

"Oh, the rock!" Jasper said. "Now we get to stone you to death, KJ!"

"Speaking of getting stoned," Alex said, "KJ, what happened to all the weed you were selling? Is that what you were rolling up, Aunt Judy?"

"I would never buy that low-quality garbage," Aunt Judy said. "No offense, cupcake."

"None taken," KJ said. "We have a pound in our car. If we end up dying on Halloween, or whatever, you guys have to go to Mrs. Kersh's place on Church Street in Rabbitville and return it. That is the stash house."

"In the PDA?" I asked. "We've been driving around with a *pound* of pot?"

"Here we are," Flora said. She held up a gleaming chunk of amethyst. The purple facets of the rock caught flickers of firelight when she held it up.

We were doing freaking crystal magic. It made me think of the girls I knew at Pelham who were really into dumb New Age crap. I tried to look like I was taking it seriously.

"What's that for?" Jasper asked. He sounded incredulous, but restrained. Probably because Aunt Judy was right behind him, watching for any signs of rudeness.

Flora handed the rock off to Friday.

"This specific crystal has been imbued with a metric ton of magic, over a period of several years. We have a bunch like this at home. It can be used for many things," Friday said, and grabbed my hand. She lifted my arm and pushed down the sleeve of my coat, exposing the lines on my wrist where Birdie Plum's nails had scratched me at the culmination of the Great Harvest Hallow.

"For example," she said, and touched the rough points of the amethyst to my arm.

And then—before my very *eyes*—the marks healed. I could *feel* a light coolness on my skin, left behind from the stone, as the shallow scratches knitted themselves back together.

"Uh," Jasper said, staring. "What the fuck?"

Aunt Judy laughed from up on the bed.

"*Pfft.* That's barely a party trick," Flora said. "This rock can do lots of stuff."

"But it's best for traveling," Friday said. "While it is pretty unfortunate that none of you is gifted, I think we can work with you just the same."

"Traveling?" I asked.

"You'll all need to let Flora look at your minds, and see who is the most equipped to share their consciousness," Friday said.

"Can't you do it? Share your consciousness or whatever?" I asked, but Flora shook her head no. "I need my sister with me when I'm gonna be communicating directly with Good Arcturus. I could get lost otherwise. He makes human consciousness look like ant consciousness."

"He's not supergood at flirting, though," Jasper said.

"Or driving," I added, while KJ turned and gave us a highly indignant look.

Flora said, "Alex, you can go first. Head on the mat, please."

"Okay," Alex said. "It will probably be me, just saying. We're twins, you know? We like, shared a womb. We shared an *egg*."

"Familial connections can make powerful magic," Flora said. "But they have almost nothing to do with sharing consciousness. You gotta be able to hold another person within yourself without being subsumed, without endangering them, without losing focus. This is about strength of mind, not compatibility of mind."

So it was going to be Jasper. He was the strongest-minded individual I knew.

Alex laid back, and Flora did the same deal with the head touching and the blue chalk that she'd done to KJ before. After a few minutes, she opened her eyes, and she and Friday went over her weird runic chalk art. Then she erased the marks and gestured to me.

Alex got up. "I didn't feel anything," he said.

"I'm very quick and very quiet," Flora said. "And I'm looking, not touching. Darian, your turn."

I looked over at KJ. She had finished her strudels and was eating her way through a package of Twizzlers that she'd pulled out of her pocket.

"It is all right," KJ said. "You have nothing to fear from them."

Reassuring me about the Freys like I had reassured her earlier. When I laid back, I thought I could feel something. Like cool fingers—not on my skull but *inside* my head.

But then it was gone. Flora tapped me on the shoulder, and I got up and changed places with Jasper, who gave me an *Is this bullshit?* kind of look.

I don't know, I tried to communicate in return, with a shrug.

When they'd done the chalk procedure to all three of us, Friday and Flora went into the orange kitchen and whispered to each other for like thirty seconds before coming back.

"Okay, so describing another person's consciousness is inherently going to be an act of oversimplification," Flora said. "I just want to be clear—you all have *all* the aspects of human beings. And you'll only become more complex as you grow older."

"Some people become simpler as they grow older, more narrow-minded," Friday said. "But I don't see that for any of you."

"Alex, your soul is a doorway," Flora said. "Open to everything. That's why you love to read, I think, and why you're going to do just fine being a *real person*."

"Okay," Alex said. "Is that good?"

"It sounds like you're a big dipshit," Jasper said, and Flora turned her eyes on him.

"Your soul is a bonfire, Jasper," Flora said. "Very powerful. Being in love must be intense for you, huh?"

Jasper's eyes widened. He looked like he wanted to say something rude, but embarrassment won over, and he stared down at the carpet.

"Don't tease him," Friday said. "It's a good thing. That inner fire has kept you warm and sane in a town full of mindless people. You should be pleased."

"Yeah, you should. But it's not a hospitable environment to invite *other* people into," Flora said. "You're too emotional. There needs to be a bigger element of control—for a normal person to do this, I mean. If you were a witch it would be easier."

"Great," Jasper said.

"KJ, not that it matters for this, but your soul is a body of deep, dark water—still above, currents below," Flora said. "Nice brain. Very complex. Definitely not the place for unskilled visitors." She paused for a second, then added, "And the thing inside you has no soul—at least not like *we* do—but if it did, I think its soul would be a field of endless flowers."

"RAD," KJ said. "WE ARE AWESOME."

"Darian," Flora said. I suddenly didn't like the way that she and her hot sister were looking at me. I didn't want to be summarized like the others. I already felt scrutinized . . . and I hated it.

"Your soul is a *vault*," Flora said. "You have more control than Alex and less volatility than Jasper. Which makes you perfect for this next part."

"What next part?" I asked, even though I already knew. I was hoping to get out of it, I guess.

"You already know," Flora said. "You're going to let KJ into your mind."

CHAPTER THIRTEEN

Monday, October 30, 2000

Jasper and Alex were banished to the kitchen and told to make us all coffee. Aunt Judy went with them, but Surendra stayed to observe, looking fascinated.

"This should be interesting," Friday said. "I normally perform a spell like this on one regular person plus myself, not between *two* regular people."

"What do I need to do?" I asked. I was starting to feel really nervous.

"You both lie back," Friday said. "Facing each other. Keep the mat between you. Surendra, will you dip one of those pieces of kindling into the fire, please? Just for a second. I need it smoldering, not blazing."

"Can do," Surendra said, hustling over in his flowery bathrobe. He looked delighted to be included.

"We can simply make this mind transfer happen, if you like," KJ said. "It does not present a challenge to our abilities."

"No," Friday said. She was kneeling over both of us, and she reached out to take the smoking piece of wood from Surendra when he offered it.

"BUT WE COULD MAKE IT MUCH SIMPLER—"

"You can't interfere," Friday said. "I can't have you using your god powers, because we need to talk to Good Arcturus. Alone. He can't be occupied with a spell."

"Is it safe?" I asked. "He's . . . a pretty powerful monster. What if he hurts you guys?"

"I don't think he's going to," Flora said. "Now try to relax and let Fri do what she needs to do."

I turned my head and looked at KJ, who was laying down about two feet from me. Her red eyes were wide open, glowing with an inner light. Her eyelashes were, as always, long and dark—her high cheekbones, a worried crease to her brow—all of it so familiar and so alien at the same time. I kept my eyes locked on hers.

"DO NOT BE AFRAID," she said.

"I'm never afraid," I said, which was a big lie.

With her free hand, Friday placed the chunk of amethyst between me and KJ, directly in the center of the yoga mat.

"Each of you place your hands against that," Friday said. "You with your right, KJ, and you with your left, Darian."

We both reached out and touched the amethyst. Our fingers tangled together around it. KJ's hands were unnaturally cold, like the red sinews of Good Arcturus. And I could feel endless movement just under her skin—but not the movement of a heartbeat, or blood in the veins. The movement of *him*.

"These burnt offerings to the mind of all minds," Friday said. She shook her smoldering stick over our connected hands. Little embers rained down. One burned my arm for a second before dying. "These joined hands to the soul of all souls," she continued. "This skull to that skull. This life open to all life. This heart an abyss. In our smallness. In our nothingness. In our power, in our vastness."

Something changed in the air. I thought for a second it was just KJ's creepy ozone-buzz ramping up. But it smelled like . . . pine trees. Dead ones, the kind that are sold by the hundreds in little paved lots decked with string lights right around Christmastime. The sharp smell the air gets when it's about to snow. A trace of gasoline. It smelled like winter in New York, a smell so familiar to me that I almost couldn't register it. I heard the jingling of bells. Somehow I knew they were Salvation Army Santa bells. And car horns honking.

"Do you guys . . . hear that?" I asked. It felt like my words weren't coming out distinctly.

Then Friday reached down and pulled a strand of hair right out of my head.

"Ow," I said. But lazily. I couldn't even muster up any indignation at the pain.

"Swallow this," Friday said, and pressed one bleached strand of hair to KJ's lips. KJ opened her mouth and licked the strand of hair off Friday's fingers.

"I wish you guys would make out," I said. "That would be so cool."

Everything felt really slow. Thoughts were just tumbling out of my mouth. Approximately a million minutes after I said that, Flora laughed from the other side of the mat.

"I think she likes you, Fri," Flora said.

"How flattering," Friday said. "I'm not going to kiss a teenager, though. Sorry, kid."

"I do like you," I said. I had no filter at this point. I felt drugged, which might ordinarily have made me panic—but I was too out of it to panic. "I think you're so pretty. But I don't *like* you like you. I like KJ."

"We know that," Flora said.

"Howwww?" I asked.

"We are *psychic witches*," Flora said. "It's part of why this spell might work, even though you can't do magic. You two are compatible. You're like . . ."

"Soul mates," Friday said. "For lack of a better word."

I shook my head—or tried to. "I don't believe in that. I don't believe in soul mates."

"I know," Friday said. "Try to relax, Darian."

"Is she all right?" Surendra asked from somewhere that felt extremely distant.

"Yeah. I've just never seen someone fight a joining spell so hard in my life," Flora said. "Gotta hand it to the kid."

"When I finish this speaking part, and snap my fingers, you're going to feel a lot of power coming from the amethyst," Friday said. "And you're going to fall asleep on the wave of that sensation. Like hypnosis. Okay?"

"THAT IS . . . ACCEPTABLE," KJ said. She sounded almost as tired as I felt.

"Now listen. Darian. Your mind is like a river. Fluid. Changing. Neurons firing. But when you have a guest, everything gets more solid. There will be structures in the river. I'm going to send KJ down into the deepest parts of your mind. It's the best way to keep you from just rejecting the spell and—mentally spitting her out, so to speak. Okay?"

"Okay," I said. I thought I said it. Friday was talking again, but I couldn't figure out what she was saying. She sounded like she was really far away, high above us. The sound of the wintry city was all around me. Car horns and bells ringing and people laughing.

"Do you guys hear that?" I asked. I looked over at KJ. She was looking back at me with her red eyes slitted.

All of a sudden, my left hand felt like it was on fire. The amethyst was *burning* me. I tried to drop my fingers, tried to scream. Nothing came out. Then there was a silence—an unnatural silence. And the world got dark, so dark. I was being pushed down into an endless night.

"KJ!" I shouted. For a few terrified seconds, I thought I was back in the clearing with the black house, pounding on the doors. "KJ!"

And then I was on a street in New York. It was cold and gray, and just starting to snow. People brushed by me on the street in their scarves and gloves and winter coats.

I was facing a brick building—but before I could place it, something made me turn around, just in time to see KJ on the curb, midway through getting out of a yellow cab with a Christmas wreath on the front grille. She looked normal. Her pupils were pinpricks in the gray light. For some reason, the unremarkableness of her eyes struck me as remarkable. But I couldn't remember *why*. Everything that happened before I opened my eyes on this street was fuzzy.

KJ stood on the curb in her slouchy kind of way, exuding charm. But . . . there was something wrong. She looked *exhausted*. Big purple half circles stood out under her eyes. Her skin was dotted with little red marks, at regular intervals. A thin track of dried blood ran from her left eye to the edge of her chin.

"KJ, oh my god," I said, terribly relieved for a reason I couldn't name, and stood up on my toes. Hugged her tightly. She held still for a second, like she was surprised at my intensity, then hugged me back.

"Hey, D," she said into my hair. "I was looking for you. It's a big city."

"The biggest," I said. I kept my arms around her. It felt so good. I could feel her heart beating regularly against my chest when I hugged her.

"I actually think the *biggest* is Mexico City," KJ said. "By population. Tokyo by area, maybe?"

"Oh my god," I said again. I stepped back, but caught one of her hands with one of mine. I couldn't help smiling. She sounded *normal*. And I . . . for some reason, I had been worried about her. She had been wrong in some way.

"I had to ride for so long to find you," KJ said. "The music was good, at least. The Smashing Pumpkins on every station. I was having some trouble with the cake. Something stung me. Ma said I couldn't . . ."

"Couldn't what?" I asked.

"Leave?" KJ said. "Leave, maybe. Or smoke?"

"No smoking near the sacred cake," I said, because it was a meaningless phrase that was stuck in my mind.

"Right," KJ said. "But then I found you. Where are we?"

I turned away from her for a second to look. But I kept my hand tangled with hers. I knew that hand-holding was a thing we did now. It was allowed. And her hands were so *cold*. I wanted to warm her up.

We were in a world of repurposed factory buildings, iron foundries, sugar refineries. Cobblestones on the corners. There were people in the snowy street, and cabs going by, and outside the small grocery store was a single Salvation Army Santa, ringing his mournful bell. Above us was the blue underside of the Manhattan Bridge. "We're in DUMBO," I said.

"Dumbo?" KJ asked. "The elephant?"

"It stands for 'Down Under the Manhattan Bridge Overpass,'" I said. "It's a neighborhood. Lots of artists on a budget. Sculptors. Musicians."

In front of us was a building like all of the other warehouses, indistinguishable under a fine dusting of snow. The brick front of the building had "AIR" painted on it in big letters.

"Why does it say *AIR*?" KJ asked.

"It's something they paint on the abandoned-looking buildings so that first responders will know to look for people in them," I said. "It stands for 'Artists in Residence.'"

"We're in acronym hell," KJ said. "Why are we here, D? I was supposed to show you something."

I couldn't exactly remember why the sight of this building, so familiar, filled me with so much dread. But I knew that I had spent a great deal of time here. "I don't know," I said. "I think . . . I think I used to take piano lessons here. What were you supposed to show me?"

Down the street, a girl—no more than twelve, with long brown hair—was getting out of a dark green Lincoln Town Car. I knew the car was going to sit right where it was until the girl got inside the building . . . because . . . because it was a moderately crappy neighborhood, at that time, and Senovak had never liked it when she went there for her music lessons. He didn't *say* so—but he oozed disapproval. He was the only one, though. Everyone else thought it was *so nice, so special, what a bond they have, teaching is definitely helping him with his sobriety, she's so prodigious, his latest album is his best yet, she's going places—*

And she loved it. She loved it so much. Those lessons were the best part of her week. She told Senovak that herself, time after time.

I watched the girl walk toward the brick building without saying anything to KJ. I kept my voice very even.

"What was it you were supposed to tell me?" I asked.

"I don't remember." KJ reached into her cloak pocket. Why was she wearing a red cloak? She looked like she was dressed up for Halloween.

"What happened to my Newports?" she asked.

"I don't know," I said. Come to think of it, I hadn't seen her smoke them in a while.

"Maybe Good Arcturus doesn't smoke," I said. Things were coming back to me. Fragments. Something about a creature, made of sinewy red. I tried to remember more, but I kept getting distracted by what was happening around me.

The girl was nearer now. She was about to pass us. As she got close I saw that she had a copy of *Dandelion Wine* tucked under her arm.

Her favorite book. By Ray Bradbury. She had a favorite chapter in it, too. Something about soul mates.

"Why would the nicotine habits of a god matter to me—" KJ stopped, and literally smacked herself on the forehead.

"Rocks a-fucking-*round* us," she said. "D. D, we're like, we're like mind-melding right now. He gave me a message for you, he can't talk about it, she won't let him!"

The girl made it to the entranceway of the AIR building. She pressed a button on a beaten-up call box, then said something into the speaker.

"He said she stole his cloak. She wasn't killed. The story is a lie. What's true is that she stole his cloak. She tore it into three pieces," KJ said. "It's hidden away. The library frost and the chapel falls—"

"What?" I asked. I was still watching the girl at the door.

"The *frost* and the *falls*," KJ said and then she put her hands over my eyes.

DUMBO disappeared. The little girl with the long dark hair disappeared. The smell of winter changed into something dark and mossy.

I was in a forested place. In Kesuquosh. But a *small* Kesuquosh, like the one in the painting at the town hall. I towered above it, Godzilla-like in my enormity. The woods were tiny beneath me, the sunflower fields nonexistent. And other shapes stood at odd intervals, faceless figures, equally huge in this shrunken world.

KJ was across from me. Sinews around her head like rays of light. Her eyes were red again. She held out something shimmering and green—something difficult to look at. Her expression was scared . . . but trusting.

"That's right," I said, and my voice was not my own. It was lower, more beautiful, more adult. Infinitely more persuasive. "That's right. Give it to me. Poor creature. Poor thing. Let me help you, strange traveler."

Our hands tangled together in green silk, and I saw that this piece of otherworldly cloth was torn and damaged in many places. Crystals of frost and bits of flame on the fabric that was not fabric. I started to pull it away from KJ.

CAN YOU AID ME, MY FRIEND? JUNIE? I WOULD BE MOST GRATEFUL, KJ said.

Only in my head. KJ's lips didn't move. But I knew it was coming from her. Or from what she *represented.*

"I'll put it somewhere safe," I said in my stranger's voice. "Break it into three. Here and there and there. The frost and the falls. What a beautiful gift you are. How lucky you are that I found you. The others would not be so kind. They hate all those who are not like them."

KJ's face changed. The trust fell away. There was pain on her face, and she reached out as I pulled the green cloak away from her.

PLEASE, WAIT. I NEED THAT. I CAN NEVER LEAVE WITHOUT IT—

The scene flickered again. The woods shifted to a snowy street, back to the woods, back to the street, until the tiny village winked out of view and I was on the sidewalk, facing *regular* KJ like I had never been in that impossible forest.

She looked winded. Out of breath. Her hands had fallen from my eyes to my shoulders.

"Th-that's all I can show you," she said. "*Please.* Help him find the three pieces of the traveling cloak she's . . . hidden . . . ahhh. *Ah.* Fuck. She won't let him say anything more. D. D, are you listening to me?"

"Yeah," I said.

"*Darian*, please," KJ said. "Please listen. I need you to promise."

It was so hard to focus in there. Everything was moving and shifting. Like a river. "Okay, okay, I promise," I said, temporarily sharpening at the urgency in her tone. "I'll get the three cloak pieces. I promise. And then what?"

The little girl with the long dark hair was waiting at the door to the old brick building again, as if she'd never stopped, as if we'd never been transported to that strange autumnal town. I was losing focus again.

"Then we can all be free," KJ said.

I stepped away from KJ, looking at the girl. The door to the front of the building opened, and the girl pushed inside, leaving the snowy world.

"Hey," I said, walking toward the door. At the last second, I broke into a run. "Hey! Wait! Don't—*don't go in there!* HEY!"

I made it to the door, beating against it with my fists, and the door itself started to change. It was the door of the old factory, and then the double doors of the black house in the clearing outside of Kesuquosh, and I was equally helpless to save the people in either place.

"Darian!" KJ said, and now her voice sounded farther away. When I looked behind me, she was gone. I was alone on the silent street in the falling snow.

I was crying. I felt tears leaking out of my eyes, slower than tears should fall. The brick building–slash–black house rippled at the edges, drooped like melting wax.

"Please," I said, "Oh *please*, please give her back! Oh god. Oh god, let me in, let me in, *please*—"

The little girl was gone. KJ was gone. I was alone. I dropped my hands as the building moved and changed, and turned slowly around.

Dexter was there. Coming toward me through the snow.

He was far away, on the opposite side of the street, wearing his long coat with the fuzzy cuffs and the flowers embroidered on it, the one he called his Jimi Hendrix jacket. His glasses were covered in flakes of melting ice. And he was smiling, waving as he jogged toward me with his deck of tarot cards in one hand.

"Darian! Darian, I *missed* you—"

"No," I said. "No, no, no no no *no no no no no nonononononono*—"

Then the world pulled down to a single black point, and I was consumed by darkness.

CHAPTER FOURTEEN

Monday, October 30, 2000

I woke up screaming. The amethyst burned in my hand, and I tore my fingers away from it and sat straight up. Friday and Flora were leaning over me.

"It's okay, it's okay, you're okay," Friday said. "It's okay."

I forced myself to be quiet and still. Aunt Judy had come back into the room on her walker, and Surendra went over to her. Jasper and Alex were standing in the doorway, holding cups of coffee. They looked beyond worried. KJ was fully awake, sitting up on her elbows.

"I think we sent you both too far down," Friday said. "I'm sorry."

"Poor kid. Got some dark shit in there, huh?" Flora added.

I refused to look at them. "Did you get what you needed?" I asked.

"No," Flora said. "I mean, we talked to him. And almost got lost in there. But he can't tell us anything of substance. He's . . ."

"Being controlled by someone else," I said.

"Yes," Friday said. "You mentioned that before. How did you know?"

"He can't do the things he's supposedly *always* been able to do," Jasper said. "Darian noticed it first. He couldn't even make their mom stop calling the cops. He can't command the Kesuquoshians."

"Which is, like, his *entire* deal," Alex said.

"Well. Whoever the puppetmaster is has put a serious gag order on him," Flora said. "I have no idea who could pull that off."

"KJ gave me a message from him," I said, gesturing toward her. "In my head. She showed it to me. It was like . . . like Good Arcturus was tricked. Someone stole his green cloak and tore it into three pieces. *Junie*, he said. I think he snuck that past the things he can't say by giving KJ a memory to show me. And KJ made me promise to find all the pieces that Junie had hidden. One is in *the library frost* and one is in *the chapel falls*. Whatever that means. I don't know where the third piece would be."

"The library frost," Alex said. "That sounds familiar for some reason."

"That's a line in a bunch of our stupid songs," Jasper said. "*From frost to falls.*"

"But his cloak wasn't stolen," Alex said. "It was torn. Junie Apostle-Root didn't steal it. She tried to sew it back together and then later she got shot and died. We all know the legend."

"Evidently you don't," Friday said.

"No. The woman in my vision," I said, "she was *taking* this cloak thing from him. From Good Arcturus. I think it was supposed to be Good Arcturus. It *looked* like KJ. And I was the woman. Junie. But I was me *being* Junie. And I was fucking creepy. I acted sweet. But I was hurting him by taking it. He said he could never get home without it."

"You really think you were playing Junie Apostle-Root?" Jasper asked.

"I guess?" I said. "He said Junie. I don't know why he'd make that up."

All of us looked at KJ, like she was going to be able to articulate something, but she shook her head, her lips pressed together in a line of discomfort. She clearly could not confirm or deny, even though she was trying.

"What kind of human being could steal from a god?" Friday said.

"Maybe if they were a particularly powerful witch," Flora said.

For the second time I was forced to recontextualize the originating myth of Kesuquosh, and Junie Apostle-Root's role within it.

"Not a misguided martyrdom," I said. "A hostage situation."

"Good Arcturus comes to Kesuquosh from *somewhere else* and meets a post-Puritan witch in the woods and then she . . . traps him here," Surendra said. "Oh my. But *why?*"

"To create the current status quo?" Aunt Judy asked.

"Why would anybody *want* to live like we do, in our shitty mind-controlled town?" Jasper asked.

"I mean, *I* always wanted to live there," I said. "Not so much now, obviously."

"*You're* not being mind-controlled," Jasper said.

"Maybe she's not either," Alex volunteered. "Maybe she's the one doing all the controlling."

I inched across the floor to touch KJ's hand. She immediately sat all the way up and wrapped her fingers around mine, staring at me with a flat red intensity that made me embarrassed to have other people in the room. I looked away from her, trying to be nonchalant. But I didn't drop her hand.

"In *her* woods. In *her* little world," Jasper said. "Could it actually be Junie Apostle-Root? Could she still be *alive*, somewhere? It's been hundreds of years!"

"Regardless whether it's the woman from the legend or not, someone is keeping him bound," Flora said. "It's a thing. Personal possessions can give you control over a person. Even intangible ones, like a name."

"And that thing would need to be kept," Friday said. "Thus the hiding of the pieces. Flo . . . I'm apprehensive about *how* powerful a witch would have to be to do this. This is like *Queen of Air and Darkness*, legendary fae lord, stuff-in-fantasy-novels levels of magic. And a witch working a spell for this long . . . might not even be so human anymore. Might be . . . altered."

"That's the Quabbin for you," Flora said. "Wild as hell even before they flooded it."

"Do you want a coffee?" Alex asked me, and handed me a cup of milk and sugar with the tiniest hint of coffee. Just the way I liked it. (If there was no Diet Coke available, I mean.) I took it gratefully and drank half the mug, still holding on to KJ with my other hand.

"Do we know what happens if we get all the pieces of the cloak-door?" Jasper asked. "Do we win something, like Hungry Hungry Hippos?"

"He said . . . to free us all, I think. Or to set us all free, something along those lines," I answered. "Maybe he gets to go home or something, too."

"And then what? Kesuquosh goes back to normal?"

"I hope so," I said.

Jasper didn't ask me the next obvious question: *And what happens to KJ?*

She would be okay, then. I had to believe that.

"We need a plan," Flora said. "I think we should—"

"Wᴀɪᴛ," KJ said. She let go of me and got to her feet, craning her neck like she was trying to make out a conversation. "Wᴇ ʜᴇᴀʀ sᴏᴍᴇᴛʜɪɴɢ."

"What?" Jasper asked.

"Tʜᴇ ᴘᴇᴏᴘʟᴇ ᴏғ ᴏᴜʀ ᴠɪʟʟᴀɢᴇ. Tʜᴇʏ ᴀʀᴇ ᴄᴏᴍɪɴɢ. Tʜᴇʏ ʜᴀᴠᴇ ʙʀᴏᴜɢʜᴛ"—she paused, waving her hands in the air, clearly searching for a word—"ᴛʜᴇ *ғᴜᴢᴢ*."

"Pigs?" Jasper asked, immediately looking around. "Where are they?"

"Pᴇʀʜᴀᴘs ᴛᴇɴ ᴍɪɴᴜᴛᴇs ᴀᴡᴀʏ," KJ said. "Hᴇᴀᴅɪɴɢ ʜᴇʀᴇ. Wᴇ ᴍᴜsᴛ ɢᴏ ʙᴇғᴏʀᴇ ᴛʜᴇʏ ᴀʀʀɪᴠᴇ."

"What are they going to get us on? Kidnapping?" Jasper asked. "We can't kidnap *ourselves*."

"Surendra and Judy might get in trouble, though," I said. "For harboring us or whatever."

"Plus that pound of weed in the car," Alex said.

"We're not afraid of the Kesuquosh constables," Aunt Judy said. "They don't have a warrant. You can stay right here, cupcakes."

"Tʜᴇʏ ᴅᴏ ɴᴏᴛ ᴄᴀʀᴇ ᴀʙᴏᴜᴛ ᴛʜᴇ *ʟᴀᴡs*. Tʜᴇʏ ᴡɪʟʟ ᴛᴀᴋᴇ ᴜs ʙʏ ғᴏʀᴄᴇ," KJ said. "Aɴᴅ ʙʀɪɴɢ ᴜs ʙᴀᴄᴋ ᴛᴏ ᴛʜᴇ ʙʟᴀᴄᴋ ʜᴏᴜsᴇ. Aʟʟ ᴏғ ᴜs."

Her words scared the hell out of me. I saw Jasper's eyes widen.

"Can you stop them?" I asked.

"Wᴇ ᴄᴀɴ," KJ said, but she sounded worried. Even through her monster-voice I could hear her worry.

217

"But?" I asked.

"BUT IT MAY . . . HARM US," KJ said. **"WE ARE TRYING VERY HARD NOT TO . . . DAMAGE OUR BODY . . . IRREPARABLY."**

The hair on the back of my neck stood up. I thought about how KJ had looked inside my brain. The big slashes under her eyes. The pallor and exhaustion. And her constant eating, out in the real world. Good Arcturus was consuming her from the inside out. Even if he didn't actually *want* to.

"Okay. Then we need to go," I said, and got up.

Jasper set his black coffee down on the kitchen table and put his boots on.

"Be careful. Come back if you need to," Surendra said.

"Okay. I love you guys," Alex told them.

"Love you too," Aunt Judy said.

I caught Alex's eye. He definitely didn't want to put Judy and Surendra further into harm's way.

"Thank you for your help," I said to Friday and Flora.

"I'm sorry we couldn't do more," Flora said. "Go quick."

I grabbed KJ's hand and started tugging her toward the front door.

"Wait!" Friday said. She met me in the kitchen, and pressed a folded sheet of paper and the purple amethyst into my free hand. "Take this. You've done the spell once. You *may* be able to do it again, if you follow my instructions."

"Thank you," I said, "but I don't think we're going to need to do that again."

"You never know," Friday said. "A bit of magic can go a long way. Keep the crystal, anyway."

"I will," I said. "Thanks."

"Let's go, let's *go*!" Jasper said, holding the door open.

The four of us ran out in a line. I was at the back, holding my witch crystal.

We got into the PDA, KJ taking the driver's seat. For once I was glad that she was driving. She immediately put the pedal to the metal and tore ass out of the driveway at an insane clip.

We sped along the dirt road in complete silence. No music. Then we passed from the mouth of that street, with the mailboxes, onto the normal (if crappy) paved road, and I saw two sedans with light bars on top, followed closely by a white Range Rover. I knew it wasn't some rando cops from Cold Hollow. And as we got closer, I could see *Kesuquosh Constable* painted on the white side panels of the sedans. The Sumners. And it looked like they had more people with them, shadowed strangers in the seats. Plus whatever Kesuquoshian was driving the Range Rover.

"Fuck," Jasper said. "KJ, *go*!"

KJ sailed on by the whole clot of cars. For a second it seemed like we might make a clean getaway.

"They're following us," Jasper said from the front seat. I looked out the back window. The two cruisers had turned around. They came up behind us at an alarming rate.

But they didn't have their lights on, or their sirens, and somehow that scared me even more. Like they didn't want any witnesses when they took us in.

"They're gaining," Alex said, looking out the back window. "Maybe we should stop and try to talk to them?"

"Yeah, no fucking *way*!" Jasper said.

"WE DO NOT THINK THAT WILL BE A PRODUCTIVE CONVERSATION!" KJ yelled. We were moving so fast that it was hard to hear inside the PDA. I looked at the speedometer, and saw that we were going almost 110 miles per hour. The houses and buildings on the road disappeared into a solid ribbon of fall colors.

One of the cruisers pulled level with us, driving on the wrong side of the road.

"KJ, go!" Jasper said.

"WE ARE ALREADY DRIVING AS FAST AS POSSIBLE! THEIR CARS ARE FASTER!" KJ said. The air thrummed along with her words. My heart was beating so hard I felt it in my fingertips and throat, shaking my body.

The first cruiser pulled in front of us and then braked *hard*. KJ tried to whip around them, and keep us on the road, but she was going so fast that the car spun out when she tried to turn.

"OHHHHHHH SHIT!!!" KJ shouted. The car slid toward the side of the road, slowing down incrementally as it went.

Alex was screaming next to me. Jasper was screaming in the front seat. KJ was still fighting with the steering wheel, but it was fruitless. The PDA floated off the road and slid directly onto a small but steep incline. The grille of the car slammed down into the leafy ground so hard that my teeth clacked together in my mouth. Then the car kept falling—but falling *forward*.

Now we were *all* screaming. Alex covered his face with his hands as we turned completely upside-down. Jasper had his arms up over his head. I felt my hair brush the ceiling. My seat belt was holding me in a death grip. Twizzlers from KJ's pocket rained down over my head. The glove box opened and papers flew out.

My cell phone fell into the back of the car. My magical amethyst was clenched in my sweaty hand the entire time, doing precisely nothing magical about our slow-motion car crash.

"AHHHHHHH FUCK! WE DO NOT FUCKING LIKE THIS!" KJ yelled, and the car flipped right-side up again. My recently dropped phone hit the side of my face. We were sliding sideways down the hill, and I felt the whole car jolt as a tree ripped the passenger's-side rearview mirror completely off.

"Shit, shit, shit," Jasper chanted. But it seemed like the PDA had finally been slowed by the trees. We came to a stop at the bottom of a hill that led into deeper woods.

"Oh god. Oh god, are you guys all alive?" I asked.

"I think so," Alex said. "I can't get my seat belt off."

KJ pushed her door ajar—it opened with a decidedly unhappy popping sound—and came around to the back seat. My door wouldn't open at all. Jasper crawled out through the driver's side and came around with KJ. They both tried Alex's door together, and that one *did* open. Then KJ touched his seat belt and it just kind of . . . snapped, fraying away from his body.

"Don't do anything to our *malleable reality* unless you have to," I told her. Adrenaline made my knees weak, but there was still a good portion of my mind devoted to worrying about whatever Good Arcturus was doing to her.

"WE ARE BEING JUDICIOUS IN OUR APPLICATION, D," KJ said super-seriously.

I shoved my phone and my amethyst into my coat pockets, grabbed my purse, and climbed out on Alex's side, trying not to hyperventilate. For a second the world spun. KJ helped me out of the back seat, and I leaned heavily on her arm, still dizzy and breathing hard.

Then the four of us stood together, looking at the PDA. It was totaled. The light-up pizza slice had been torn off, just like the rearview mirror. The windshield was a spiderweb of cracked glass. The hazards were blinking irregularly. Jasper leaned back into the wreckage to retrieve the binder full of CDs.

"We *killed* the PDA," Alex said. "I can't believe it."

"Our pursuers," KJ said. She had stopped in front of the trunk. She pointed up the incline, where I could see the Constables Sumner starting down, skidding on piles of dead leaves and making tons of noise.

"The woods," Jasper said. "We can lose them in the woods."

He turned, like he was getting ready for us to run, but KJ grabbed his shoulder and turned him back around.

"We need a vehicle," she said. "We will go up as they come down. Meet them at the road."

"Are you *sure*?" Jasper asked incredulously.

"Yes," KJ said. She whipped open the back of the Tahoe and pulled out a duffel bag. As soon as she jostled it, I smelled the intense aroma of weed.

"Do you *have* to bring your pound of pot?" I asked.

"If we make it out of this alive, we will have to return it or sell it," KJ said. "Those are the rules for street-level dealers."

Then she slung the bag over her shoulder and started running up the hill as fast as she could. The three of us followed her. We ran wide to the left, so that Junior and Senior Sumner had to try to crab-walk sideways across the steep and slippery hill to get to us.

"Hey! Jasper! Get your ass back here!" the elder Sumner called gruffly as we passed him out about thirty yards to the left.

"Fuck you, you fucking pigs!" Jasper said, which seemed to enrage both the Sumners. They chased us furiously in something near slow-motion.

"*Don't* taunt them!" I said, panting from exertion as we crested the hill. "I don't want to get shot!"

They looked furious. I remembered Jasper telling me about how the Kesuquoshians were allowed to "self-police," which is why most of the town had always hated him. Now the actual police were coming after us with all their negative emotions, because we were a threat to Kesuquosh. Good Arcturus was not speaking into their minds, but *something* was.

They were coming after their own *god* with all those negative emotions.

The three of us skidded onto the pitted country lane, following KJ as closely as we could. She had moved through the woods with a preternatural swiftness.

On the road, we were met with a tableau that chilled my blood.

The two cop cars sat, quiet but running, with their doors flung open. Both of them were parked lengthwise across the street. The white Range Rover and a blue Volvo station wagon that I hadn't seen before were parked respectably along the side of the road. And all the Kesuquoshians who had been in those vehicles were standing outside them, facing KJ.

Rita was there, and so was Ken. And Lake, and KJ's traitorous ex Hunter Warren. A few other big young dudes, too. And several adult men, all of them sizable. And Birdie Plum, of fucking course, and three other councilpersons. They were all looking toward KJ.

She squared her shoulders and faced them all, like a lone cowgirl getting ready for a shoot-out.

"KJ," Rita said. "Honey. I understand that something strange is happening right now. But you have to come home, okay? You *have* to. You don't have a choice."

KJ looked at her mom.

"No," she said quietly.

"You *have* to, you stupid girl!" Birdie snapped. "You have *our god* inside you! What do you think is going to happen on October thirty-first?"

"Stop, Birdie, please," Rita said, and looked at KJ. "You have to come with us now, baby. Okay? Good Arcturus has to come home. Listen to what I'm saying to you."

KJ, to my shock, took a step toward Rita. Or maybe it wasn't that shocking. Rita was the one person here that it really hurt to be in a showdown with.

"Don't go with them," I said, and KJ looked back at me. Her red eyes were unreadable. But she paused, and shook her head.

"IN OUR SMALLNESS AND OUR NOTHINGNESS," she said quietly, kind of to herself. "IN OUR NOTHINGNESS, WE CAN SLIP BENEATH."

"GET IN THE CAR!" Birdie screamed, and then she raised her hand. The Sumners emerged from the woods at that exact moment. Everyone (except for Rita and Ken) converged on KJ. Junior Sumner pulled his gun on her, which made me gasp in horror.

"Don't!" I said, terrified. They couldn't actually *kill* us, could they? Someone would find out. Senovak would find out.

But he didn't pull the trigger, just kept it leveled at her. All of the Kesuquoshians put their hands on KJ, on her shoulders, her back. Birdie Plum touched one arm with both of her hands. They were all whispering something, and with more than a little disgust, I realized they were reciting one of their creepy songs.

Oh Lord of the Straw, who protects all we love,
and guides the hands of His Incorporations . . .

In a knot, they started to push KJ toward the nearest car, which was one of the cruisers.

"Get away from her!" Jasper said. He rushed forward . . . only to back up, with his hands raised, as Constable Sumner Senior aimed *his* gun. Right at Jasper's head.

"Interfere again," the older Sumner said with an unnerving smile on his face. "Do it, you little punk."

Alex had come up and was standing beside me. He looked stricken, and glanced over at Rita and Ken with an expression of pain and fear.

"KJ," he said, and KJ paused in the crowd of hands, her posture becoming rigid and attentive. "Don't go with them, okay? You said we needed to secure a vehicle. Whatever power they have over you—or *him*—you have to fight it. Okay?"

"Oh, Alex," Rita said. She sounded shocked at his . . . I guess at what she would consider his betrayal.

"Shut *up*," Constable Sumner Junior said. He turned to face Alex, still brandishing his gun. But Alex didn't even look at him.

"You're listening to me, right, KJ?" Alex said. "Our reality is malleable, right? You should do something about that."

"Yeah," KJ said in a scratchy, echoing whisper. "That is correct. We were distracted by her . . . power."

"Get in the car. Now. Do what I say," Birdie said again, and the whole group of them dragged KJ away from us—for a second. Then the smell of ozone got really strong. I felt the buzz of it intensifying in the air.

"Nope," KJ said. "We do not think so, actually—"

She moved her arms, shoving them outward, and it felt like the entire world moved with her. Birdie, Lake, and Hunter and the council dudes fell back, hitting the pavement. The pavement itself *rippled.* Sumner Junior, with his gun still aimed at Alex, pulled the trigger as he fell. The bullet went wide, but the sound was deafening. Jasper screamed, and Alex screamed, and then the pavement started *really* shaking, like we were in the middle of an earthquake.

I fell, too, slamming onto the road with the flats of my hands. The sirens on the police cruisers started going off. But I could hear KJ's inhuman voice over the sound.

"No guns," KJ said, holding up her hands. The red sinews of Good Arcturus had emerged from under her fingernails and beneath her skin. Her palms were dotted with strands that moved on their own. With one hand she gestured toward Sumner Senior, the only person still on his feet besides Jasper, and the threads flicked his gun away like it was a gum wrapper. He yelped.

Then she gestured with her other palm, and the red threads that spilled out from *that* hand moved with a single consciousness, picking up Junior's gun and flinging it into the treeline.

"You come here to subdue us with your weapons? Your cruel weapons? Your *small* weapons?" KJ asked. It looked like she was addressing Birdie, who was on the shaking ground, still trying to get to her feet. Rita had climbed into the Volvo, and was watching us with horror from the passenger's-side window.

"WE MAY BE CHAINED," KJ said, waving her hand, "BUT WE ARE STILL *MORE* THAN YOU. IN YOUR WEAKNESS. AND SMALLNESS. AND NOTHINGNESS. NOW, *BE STILL*."

And all of the Kesuquoshians, half-fallen on the ground as they were, knelt with their heads down, holding very still. Like they were praying. Except for Birdie. With what looked like a huge effort, she turned her head up and looked at KJ.

"You'll *have* to come back!" Birdie shrieked. "You'll have to! You know you *have* to!"

"*YOU* HAVE TO BE SILENT," KJ said, and waved her thread-covered hands again. Birdie's mouth snapped shut.

"KJ!" Jasper shouted, waving at her. "The white car!"

He pointed to the Range Rover. KJ nodded, and the car, which had nobody in it, started up. It rolled over to us on the quaking road.

KJ moved her palms again, and the threads made a gestural shape in the air. All of the Range Rover's doors opened.

I got to my feet on the shaking street, ran past the kneeling villagers, and jumped into the car. Jasper climbed in next to me. KJ threw her duffel bag of weed into the trunk, then took the passenger's seat, and Alex slammed the driver's-side door and sped away. Behind us, the people of Kesuquosh knelt on the pavement. Worshippers without a deity. I watched them until the distance swallowed them whole.

CHAPTER FIFTEEN

Monday, October 30, 2000

In a minute the sound of the sirens faded. We were alone on the bumpy street, which bled back onto a real-feeling road soon enough.

"Turn left," KJ said. "We do not think they will be able to follow us for several minutes. But we should take a circuitous path anyway."

"Will do," Alex said, and drove us farther away from the center of Cold Hollow, out onto another segment of backwoods-ish roads.

"Fuck, fuck, oh fuck, I can't believe they pulled *guns* on us, what the *fuck*?" Jasper said.

"Did you see Birdie?" I said. "She was *enraged*."

"I didn't notice," Jasper said, and lit a clove with shaking hands. "I was too busy shitting myself over being held at gunpoint."

"I've never been afraid like that before," Alex said. "I don't like it at all. It's awful, man."

Alex was driving quickly and competently—but maybe not *as* quickly as KJ would have driven. I was surprised that KJ and her lead foot had allowed Alex to drive at all—but then I looked at KJ, and I understood why.

The power she had expended during the confrontation had clearly cost her. KJ looked really bad. She leaned back against the headrest, taking shallow breaths. Her face was colorless and her skin seemed like it was stretched tightly over her bones. I thought of the way that Good Arcturus had looked in the gazebo. The thin skin of my dead aunt Blanche stretched over him as fine as paper. The husk of a corpse that had remained once he'd left her. I wondered what KJ would look like if Good Arcturus vacated her now. It made me want to fucking scream.

"WE ARE STARVING," KJ said, like she'd read my mind. "WE NEED TO EAT."

We ended up getting McDonald's—like a metric ton of McDonald's, including several Happy Meals—and then we parked behind the building. I felt like I was going to jump out of my skin every time a car pulled into the drive-thru. But nobody showed up to arrest us.

"Two pieces of Good Arcturus's cloak are in the frost and the falls," Alex said while we ate.

"Which are a library and a chapel," Jasper added, polishing off his apple pie. Weirdly enough, the apple pies at McDonald's were (incidentally) vegan. "The library *frost* and the chapel *falls*. I think 'the falls'—that has to be the chapel at Cold Falls Prep. I'm going to call Brooks and see if he can sneak us in there."

Then he took my phone and stood out in the parking lot to make the call. As usual, his voice carried without him even trying. "Yeah, I'd *love* to see you, but I need to ask a *big* favor—"

"He doesn't actually like Brooks, does he?" Alex asked, after a couple minutes of this schmoozing had gone on.

"I think your relationship is safe, Al," I said.

"I hope so. And I hope he can get us into 'the falls' chapel. But what is 'the frost'?" Alex said. "I don't get that one. I thought it sounded so familiar, but I can't place it. KJ. Can you give us, like, a hint?"

KJ shook her head no. She was eating her fourth or fifth cheeseburger and had started to look less terrifyingly drained, but she still didn't seem *healthy*.

"Okay," Jasper said into the phone, "thanks. Yeah, you too."

He hung up and climbed back into the car. "Brooks is going to bring us some school uniforms and sneak us in. The problem is that it's, like, not a big school, and the chapel is right in the middle of the grounds . . . and it's students only. They have a strict no-visitors policy for the historical buildings on campus without faculty permission, except for researchers going to the library, who need to make an appointment. Even alumni have to go on specific days only."

"That's the deal at Pelham, too," I said. "I think a lot of private schools are strict like that."

"Yeah," Jasper said. "Brooks can get us onto the grounds so that we can sneak into the chapel—I don't even know what we're gonna be looking for in there. The uniforms are insurance, but if we get seen by any faculty up close we are on our own. Okay?"

"Sounds good," I said.

Alex looked uneasy. "I've never done a *heist* before," he said.

"We're all going together," Jasper told him. "It's a bigger risk for getting caught, but we need as many eyes looking in the chapel as possible. Anything made of cloth or fabric. Green, right, Darian?"

"Yeah," I said. "Kind of. It didn't look like anything I've ever seen."

Jasper nodded. "KJ, I told Brooks we would give him a free eighth for helping us. Do you have your scale with you?"

"WE WILL HAVE TO EYEBALL IT," KJ said, and reached over me to grab her reeking duffel bag.

"I can't believe we stole a car," I said. "Dan would put me in jail himself if he knew I helped steal a car."

"*Dan*, if he knew what was happening, would be helping us root out the evil whatever-it-is," Jasper said. "And set KJ free. He'd probably just do it all himself before we even woke up and then dust off his perfect suit and make us that horribly weak coffee he likes."

Alex laughed. "I can picture that," he said.

"Milkshakes," I said, feeling wistful. I was not going to involve Senovak, for his own safety. But I could imagine it. "He'd take us to get milkshakes. But you're right."

We only had to wait a few minutes longer for Brooks Gould-Greenwood to show up.

He rolled into the McDonald's parking lot in an immaculate black Audi that matched his black Ray-Bans, and when we got out to meet him he was visibly buff even under his crisp button-down shirt and his green Cold Falls blazer, and absolutely oozing *yuppie* from every pore. Brooks jumped from his car, offered me and Alex a blindingly white smile, and grabbed Jasper's ass.

Brooks obviously thought that the "mutual handies" back in September had put him and Jasper on better terms than they actually had. Jasper gritted his teeth like he wanted to spit all over

Brooks's ironed shirt, and gingerly removed the offending hand from his butt cheek.

"Yo," Jasper said with the enthusiasm of a dead fly.

"You look *insane*," Brooks said, and pulled Jasper in for a kiss. I felt my eyes bugging out of my head. I wasn't sure if "looking insane" was, like, a compliment about Jasper being hot, or just a general statement about Jasper looking like he'd been on the run with a stolen entity in the body of his best friend and hadn't had a chance to do his hair. Either way, this was the first time I had ever seen Jasper act restrained in pursuit of something he wanted. He did *not* kill Brooks immediately. Instead, Jasper leaned back after a respectable span of seconds and smiled at him. "Thanks for coming," Jasper said evenly. His smile was scary. It was full of rage. I could *feel* him wanting to smack the shit out of Brooks for even *daring* to kiss him without some kind of explicit permission.

But Brooks was clearly oblivious to all those things. He flashed his perfect teeth again, and knocked his Ray-Bans up onto his forehead.

"You're going to need to take your nose ring out, baby," he told Jasper. I was so amused by this guy calling Jasper *baby* that I aspirated some of my Diet Coke and started choking.

"What? Why the fuck would I do that?" Jasper said, forgetting to do his coy even-keeled act for a second.

"Dress code," Brooks said. "It's super strict. You're more likely to get around without being looked at too closely if you seem like you could *actually* go there."

"Pelham is strict like that, too," I said. "No unnatural hair colors, no facial piercings, no visible tattoos. Jas, you'll probably need to wear a hat or something."

"I brought one of our beanies," Brooks said. "You go to Pelham Academy? In Manhattan?"

"Yeah," I said. "It's fine."

Brooks looked a little impressed. I wanted to tell him not to bother, that he and I were both bigger dipshits than Jasper no matter *how* expensive the schools we went to were.

"Brooks, this is my best friend Darian, my other best friend Alex, and my third best friend KJ is just getting your weed together," Jasper said. "She'll be out in one second."

"Nice to meet you," Brooks said, waving his hand at us. Al was glowering at him, but Brooks didn't notice. He looked Alex up and down and clucked his tongue in disapproval.

"Hot hippie over here poses a problem," Brooks said. Behind his head, Jasper gave him an absolute death glare when he called Alex "hot."

"What kind of problem?" I asked, before either of the boys could say something rude enough to actually piss Brooks off.

"The long hair. No long hair on dudes," Brooks said. "School policy."

"That's fucking *stupid*," Jasper said.

"Agree," Brooks said. "But there it is. You want to get a haircut, handsome?"

"No *way*," Alex said.

Then KJ climbed out of the car in her wraparound sunglasses. She was eating the rest of the French fries.

"Do you guys hear that?" Brooks asked. He was responding to the ozone smell, the buzzing in the air, the general scary-monsterness of KJ. But it was weird—he couldn't put together that it was her making him feel that way. I hadn't gotten to see anybody normal react to KJ yet, unless you counted the cashier at Martin's Quality Market, who had only briefly flinched when we checked out. Now it seemed like Brooks's own perceptions about reality were going to keep him from noticing that something was wrong.

"I don't hear anything," Jasper said. "KJ, this is Brooks."

"WE ARE PLEASED TO MEET YOU AND GAIN YOUR ASSISTANCE, DUDE," KJ said.

"Right," Brooks said, eyeballing her for a second. Then he looked back at Jasper.

"Basically no boys can have hair longer than that length," he said, indicating KJ. "My guy Jeff was doing an Axl Rose thing and had to cut it all to his chin."

"Your guy Jeff," Jasper said flatly.

"He's just a friend, baby," Brooks said. "You jealous?"

"No," Jasper said.

"He's not *jealous* of some guy called *Jeff*," Alex said. "No matter what, like, his relationship to you is."

"Uh-huh," Brooks said with a knowing little smile.

His hateability was kind of diminishing. I was actually pretty amused by Brooks, if I'm being honest, and by the appalled reactions of my friends. But I was way more used to yuppies than they were.

"HERE IS YOUR COURTESY MARIJUANA," KJ said.

"Mucho apreciado," Brooks said, and took the baggie. He threw it into his glove box, and then pulled a dry-cleaning bag from the back seat of his spotless car. "I got two girl uniforms and two guy uniforms, like you said," he told Jasper. "One petite one, for Pelham over here, I assume. Anyone ever tell you that you have a voice like Marilyn Monroe, Pelham?"

"I thought Marilyn Monroe talked like that because she was sexually abused as a child," I said. KJ's eyebrows went up so high that I could see them right over her sunglasses.

I didn't know why I said it. I had lived several years of my life *never* saying anything like that. I felt like something was happening to me, something foreign and weird and freeing. Maybe I was going insane, but, like, in a good way.

"That's debatable. The Strasbergs are still licensing her image, so we only know what we know," said Brooks. It was the first thing he'd said without a hint of douchebaggery. If he talked about music like that, I could actually understand why he and Jasper had associated with each other for long enough to get to the hand-jobs phase.

"You're never going to be able to stay in the closet long enough to get your inheritance if you keep brandishing that stupid Marilyn Monroe obsession like a big gay sword," Jasper said.

"I'm just a typical cinephile," Brooks said. "Straight guys like her too!"

"Long-dead straight guys," Jasper said. But he and Brooks traded a mutually amused look. They did have some chemistry, actually. I saw it. I saw Alex seeing it. He looked like he was being plunged into an abyss of icy sadness, which was ridiculous. It was obvious that Jasper would have literally thrown Brooks off a train to make Alex smile.

Then Brooks looked at Alex again. "But for real. What are we gonna do about your hair? I have another beanie if you want it, though I don't think all your hair is going to fit under it . . ."

KJ looked at Brooks like he was crazy. Or at least I thought she did, behind her sunglasses.

"It is strange that a uniform would have gender parame-
ters," KJ said. "We knew that, quite intimately, in fact, but we
also did not know that."

That had been a big scary thing for KJ, back when she started
wearing certain items (her hideous cargo skirts, for one) that were
considered exclusively "girl" clothing. Definitely not as big or as
scary a thing as it would have been anywhere but Kesuquosh. But
I could see the weird duality playing out on her face: familiarity
and confusion all at once. *She* got it, better than most people, but
Good Arcturus . . . might not even understand clothing? I wasn't
sure. Brooks looked pretty confused by KJ's response, anyway, so I
jumped in.

"I agree," I said. "It's kind of gross. We don't do the mandatory
skirt-pants thing at Pelham."

"Yeah, we're petitioning to change it," Brooks said. "But it's sort
of an old-fashioned school, you know? Lots of backward crap."

"We do not see an issue with swapping these absurdly
gendered clothing articles with our twin if his hair poses
a problem," KJ said. "We are largely indistinguishable from
one another at a distance, anyway."

"Right," Brooks said.

"Um," I said, "actually—"

"One minute, please," Alex said, then dragged KJ over to the
opposite side of the Range Rover. I followed them.

"Listen," I started.

"KJ," Alex said at the same time, "I'm talking to KJ, now, okay? I
get that Good Arcturus doesn't care about *absurdly gendered* human
stuff. But *KJ* cares. *KJ* is growing her hair out. *KJ* might not like to

have to wear the boy's uniform. She's had to do shit like that before, when we were younger—"

I still wasn't used to this new assertive Alex. Watching him advocate for KJ was weird. It was what I had been about to do, actually.

"WE ARE FINE," KJ said.

"I'm talking to *KJ*," Alex said again. "Okay?"

"WE ARE TALKING TO *YOU*, ALEXIOS TRISTAN JAMES JENETOPOLOUS KOBAYASHI, MOST ANNOYING BROTHER," KJ said equally firmly. "WE HAVE CONSULTED WITH OURSELVES IN A WAY YOU CANNOT UNDERSTAND. WHEN TWO BEINGS SHARE ONE BODY, THERE CAN BE VERY LITTLE IN THE WAY OF DECEPTION. OUR CONSENSUS IS THAT, FOR THE CAUSE, WE CAN TEMPORARILY SET ASIDE OUR CARGO SKIRT, AND WEAR THE LITTLE SCHOOLBOY UNIFORM WITHOUT GREAT MENTAL HARM. WE WILL STILL LOOK PRETTIER IN IT THAN YOU. LET *US* DECIDE WHAT IS ACCEPTABLE FOR OURSELVES."

Alex kind of deflated and dropped his hands. He seemed to have relaxed. "Your cargo skirts are ugly," he said. But he was smiling.

"*YOU* ARE UGLY," KJ said.

"Right back at you," Alex said.

So we all took turns in the back of the car surreptitiously changing into our—I guess our Cold Falls *costumes*—and then followed Brooks's Audi in our stolen Range Rover. The green blazer with the red school crest and the dark gray skirt and knee-high socks created a look that was not unlike something I would wear normally, actually. A little more schoolgirl and a little less Hollywood, but, like . . . I was just grateful to have a change of clothes.

Jasper was blushing. He had been blushing basically since Alex put on the girl's school uniform. Now he was blushing and looking over at Alex in the front seat, often enough that I could catch him doing it every few minutes.

"I look awesome," Alex said, for like the third time, and smiled at Jasper.

"Yeah, you do," Jasper said. "Great legs."

"You think I have great legs?" Alex asked, following Brooks around a tight turn. We were heading toward Cold Falls Prep, which also meant we were heading back in the general direction of Aunt Judy's. I was nervous about running into any of our buddies from that morning.

"Is anyone from Kesuquosh still hanging around?" I asked KJ.

"Not at this time," KJ said. "But they will continue to pursue us."

We passed a tasteful wooden sign that marked the entrance to the grounds of the school. Brooks slowed down significantly, and Alex pulled the Range Rover into a crawl behind him. We drove up a beautiful little country road with perfectly planted oak trees on either side, all of them brilliant shades of red-gold that looked even more brilliant in the sunlight.

"I've never been here before," Alex said. "Unlike *you*, Jas."

"I love it when you get all jealous," Jasper said dryly.

"I *don't* love it! It's awful," Alex said. "I don't know how people deal with this stuff. That Brooks guy is kind of full of himself, too, I think."

"I thought he was okay," I said.

"He is good at heart," KJ said, and we all looked over at her. "What?" she asked.

"Which one of you is saying that?" Alex asked.

"WE HAVE COME TO A CONSENSUS BETWEEN OURSELVES." I swear KJ was saying it to fuck with Alex, but I couldn't prove anything.

"You're being a major traitor," Alex said.

"WE ARE SORRY-NOT-SORRY," KJ said.

We followed the Audi past a series of stone buildings that looked old and regal under their ivy. Then we were in the student parking lot, which was dense with expensive cars. "Okay," Brooks said, after we were all parked, "they don't check the student lot until after sunset, so you should be safe here for now. Follow me. Jasper, you look *insane* in that uniform."

"I *feel* insane in this uniform," Jasper said.

We followed Brooks up a gentle hill that was crisscrossed by crumbling stone walls and dotted with uniformed teenagers. A group of kids playing hacky sack caught KJ's attention.

"WE ARE *VERY* GOOD AT HACKY SACK," she informed me. "WE WON A HACKY SACK CONTEST AT THE ROLLER RINK IN RABBITVILLE AND GOT THIRTY BUCKS AND A FREE PIZZA."

"Huh. You told me in August that it was a Dance Dance Revolution contest, and that you won three months of free roller-skate rentals," I said.

"PERHAPS BOTH ARE TRUE," KJ said sagely.

"Oh my god, shut *up*," I said. But KJ telling her stupid lies was good, actually. The normalcy gave me hope that things could still be fixed.

Then we passed a group of faculty members, all talking to each other as they took one of the pretty paths down the hillside. The four of us turned our faces away. I took a relieved breath when we passed by without incident.

We made it to the top of the big hill at the center of campus. Between the buildings and the trees, there was a clear view of woods stretching away below us, in a patchwork of brilliant colors, and at the edge of visibility was a thin slice of the Quabbin, glinting flat watery silver in the sunlight.

At the very top of the hill was the chapel. It was older than most of the buildings I'd seen on campus, with a big proud metal plaque talking about how it was from the 1700s and was super antique by the standards of Congregational churches. Curiously, it had the same green door as the one that hung alone in the ruins of the place that my friends called Empty Heaven.

"This chapel must have twinned with your little church," I said.

"Huh?" Brooks said. "Hey." He held the green door open for us. "I'm leaving you here. I have track. If you guys get caught, you don't know me, and you're on your own. Okay?"

"Okay," I said.

"WE THANK YOU FOR YOUR ASSISTANCE," KJ said.

Brooks checked behind us to make sure no one was watching, then leaned in like he was going to kiss Jasper again. Jasper dodged his kiss and put a hand firmly on his chest.

"Thanks for all the help," Jasper said.

Brooks, to his credit, clearly understood the rejection for what it was.

"Anytime, baby," he said, then turned and walked away.

"Now I feel bad," Alex said. "He's probably pining for you, Jas. Why do I feel bad about that? I hated him like twenty minutes ago."

"He's fine," Jasper said. "He gets around, I promise. Plus, if things don't work out with you, I can always go back for more—"

"Not cool, man," Alex said.

We slipped through the old green door and into the dim coolness of the chapel.

Inside it was all echoing white plaster walls and gleaming wooden pews. Nobody else was there.

I walked down the main aisle toward the pulpit, glancing back and forth at the walls. "I don't know what we're supposed to be looking for," I said. "KJ? Any help?"

"WE CANNOT SPEAK OF IT," KJ said, but she looked really jittery. She shook her hands restlessly, like she was jingling invisible keys.

"But do you *know* what we're looking for?" Jasper asked. "I don't know what one-third of Good Arcturus's cloak would look like. I don't see any cloaks cut into thirds around here." I didn't even see any greenish fabric.

"SHE HAS OBSCURED IT FROM OUR EYES," KJ said.

"Shhh. I thought I heard something," Jasper said, and we all froze.

"SOMEONE IS COMING," KJ said. "HIDE!"

Jasper and Alex immediately bolted for the far end of the space, where doors opened off either side of the pulpit. I grabbed KJ's icy hand and ran with her toward the stairs at the back, where a wooden balcony with more pews jutted out over the austere room.

We were halfway up the stairs when the green door at the front opened right underneath us. It sounded like an adult was talking to a group of teenagers directly below the stairwell, and we both crouched down, trying to make ourselves less visible.

"We're going to start in fifteen minutes!" a woman called out. "Miss Russell, Miss Callahan, can you go grab the new sheet music? It's in a stack on my desk."

KJ and I stayed frozen on the stairs, almost lying down. She was very cold, her arm and shoulder mashed up against my back. Her breathing was slower than a normal person's would be, and perfectly silent. I could feel the rise and fall of her chest against my side.

Then it got quiet again, and I started to crab-crawl my way up the stairs, with KJ just behind me. We reached the top and laid our stomachs on the narrow strip of floor between two pews. KJ craned her neck up to look into the main part of the church, and then carefully rolled onto her side to face me.

"The instructor is still in here," KJ whispered right into my ear. Her breath was cold enough to raise goose bumps on my neck. Her sunglasses had slipped down a few centimeters, and I could see the tops of her eyelashes and a sliver of red eyes underneath. My heart was still pounding from our near miss with the teacher and students, and it didn't slow down. I was struck by the fact that I was pressed up against a creature from another world.

But it was *also* KJ. I could see how both things were true. That didn't exactly make my heart stop pounding, though.

I started to sit up, then heard movement from the front of the chapel. A few snatches of conversation echoed their way over to us.

There was nothing to do but stay still. Nowhere to look except at KJ, filling my vision. I could see all the little details. The monstrous sinews moving under her skin. The way her jaw clenched and unclenched when she was nervous. Her schoolboy uniform, which was giving me Audrey Hepburn vibes—it was too short for her long legs, turning the charcoal-gray trousers into highwaters. My foot brushed against her shin, and her fingertips were braced on the floor so that the top of her left hand was pressed against my bare thigh. Her cold touch gave me goose bumps.

"Do you feel bad about it?" I asked, mostly to distract myself from her hand.

"Do we feel bad about what?" KJ asked quietly.

"About what you've been doing to all those people in Kesu-quosh," I said. "How you've been controlling them."

KJ looked at me for so long that I thought she wasn't going to answer. After a span of total silence, I reached out toward her face, and pushed her sunglasses up onto her forehead.

Her eyes looked like two pools of blood under candlelight. And they were full of tears. One worry line wrinkled her forehead.

"Wait. Why are you crying?" I asked.

"We are so sorry," KJ whispered. "We only came to explore. Not to harm. And we have been the instrument of such harm. Such great volumes of harm."

"Hey. It's not your fault," I said, and leaned on my elbow a little closer to her. I pressed my hand to her cheek, brushed my fingers into her thick dark hair. "I have also been hurt by someone who wielded power over me."

I was repeating back her words from the other day. But I meant it.

"Darian . . . ," KJ said. She leaned into my hand, and I drew my fingers down from her hairline and across the rise of her cheekbone.

"Yeah?" I asked. There was no sound beyond the soft movement of the a capella instructor, far away at the front of the chapel.

KJ leaned over me. One of her cold hands wrapped around me, pulling me closer, and I let myself be pulled. I couldn't look away from her eyes. They weren't flat, when you looked at them for long enough: there were slivers of movement within them, light and dark twisting like the sinews of Good Arcturus's body. Our lips were almost brushing. I wanted to touch her *so* badly. "You're still in there, right?" I asked.

"WE ARE *BOTH* IN HERE," KJ said.

"That's so fucking weird, KJ," I said. "That's so fucking weird—"

"YOU KNOW SOMETHING? BEFORE. WHEN WE COULD SOMETIMES BE . . . *OURSELF*, FOR BRIEF MOMENTS OF TIME," KJ said. I was totally nonplussed for a second. My brain had been kind of fuzzy. But I caught up, after a second of staring at her.

"You mean before?" I asked. "Before you possessed . . . yourself?"

"YES," KJ said. "BECAUSE WE CANNOT CONTROL SOMEONE WHO *LIES*. WE WERE NEVER MEANT TO BE USED FOR CONTROL, ANYWAY."

"Okay," I said. "So before this happened, when you—KJ— would have moments of clarity—"

"YES," KJ said. "LIKE JASPER."

KJ was so close to me that when she nodded, her hair brushed my cheek and forehead. She had moved the hand that had been resting against my thigh. Now it was pressed to the small of my back.

"I follow you," I said.

"THEN, IN THOSE MOMENTS, WE FELT SO MISERABLE," KJ said. "WE WOULD SEE THE BIG PICTURE. ALL ZOOMED OUT. SATELLITE VIEW. WE WOULD SEE LIKE JASPER DID. DOES."

"That must have been pretty rough," I said, and KJ dropped her gaze to my shoulder. When I leaned against her it was like I was within the eye of a storm—no ozone. No buzzing. Only perfect quiet and her slow breathing.

"WE WERE SO LONELY," KJ said. "SO LONELY, YOU COULD NEVER KNOW. NOTHING WAS REAL. NO FAMILY, NO HAPPINESS, NO DREAMS. JUST AN EMPTINESS BEHIND THE EYES OF EVERYONE. EVEN ALEX. DO YOU UNDERSTAND?"

"Yes," I said, "as much as I can. Very Schopenhauer." Very *me*, too. I didn't say that. It would sound like I thought my life was as terrible as a life lived under mind control, which I didn't. But I understood.

I'd thought about how bad everything must have been for Jasper. But KJ's situation bothered me even more. To be yourself for a *minute*—and then be pulled back down into the placid darkness—seemed like some kind of endless torture.

"AND WE SAW THE WORLD OUTSIDE OF THE PLACE WE WERE CURSED BY. THE PEOPLE IN THE WIDE WORLD HAVING THEIR HEARTS BROKEN AND MAKING MISTAKES. BUT WE WERE *IMPRISONED*. IN A SNOW GLOBE. OR UP IN A BRICK BUILDING ABOVE A SNOWY STREET IN DUMBO, WATCHING THE PEOPLE WALK BY. AND EVEN THOUGH THEY WERE IN THE SLEET, IN A QUESTIONABLE NEIGHBORHOOD, IN THE NIGHT, WE WOULD HAVE GIVEN ANYTHING TO FREEZE WITH THEM. INSTEAD OF LIVING AND DYING AS A PRISONER."

KJ's hands were trembling. Or not trembling, but moving restlessly, in a way that suggested that she was so nervous that she couldn't keep still.

"I'm going to let you have a pass on that ill-advised analogy to what you saw in my mind," I told her. "But only because you're currently half human and full dumbass."

KJ smiled. "DARIAN—"

"Keep going," I said. "You were a prisoner. In the snow globe. You could never be a part of the real world."

"AND IT MIGHT MAKE SOMEONE SAD ABOUT THE BEAUTIFUL WORLD THEY WERE MISSING," KJ said after a second. "THAT WOULD MAKE SENSE. TO BE SAD ABOUT THE WORLD YOU SAW OUT THERE, FROM WHERE YOU WERE, PRESSED UP AGAINST THE INSIDE OF THE SNOW GLOBE. BUT WE WERE SO LOCKED UP INSIDE OF OURSELVES THAT WE HATED THE WORLD. WE WERE *ANGRY* AT THE WORLD. AND WE COULD NOT EVEN EXPRESS *THAT*. WE WERE NOT *PERMITTED*. AND WE WERE SURE THAT WE WOULD HATE THE WORLD FOREVER IN THOSE FLASHES OF OURSELF, HATE EVERY LITTLE *BIT* OF THE WORLD, AND TAKE OUR CONTEMPT EVEN TO OUR GRAVE—"

Her voice, pitched low to avoid being heard by anyone below, sounded all choked up. Her hand pressed hard against the small of my back. With the other hand, she tilted my chin, until we were exactly eye to eye.

"—BUT THEN WE MET YOU," KJ whispered. "RIGHT AS WE STARTED TO GROW UP. THIS LITTLE ALMOST-RUINED KID. HAD IT EVEN WORSE THAN WE DID. AND SOMEHOW HAVING YOU AROUND MADE THINGS OKAY. YOU WERE A WINDOW INTO THE LIFE WE COULD HAVE HAD, *IF*. YOU KNOW? YOU—YOU CHANGED THINGS. FROM THE BEGINNING—"

"It's okay," I said, because KJ really was crying. Tears fell from her red eyes and landed between us. I wiped her cheeks with the sleeve of my blazer.

"AND WE ARE TERRIBLE AT TALKING, AND A VERY BAD LISTENER, AND SOMETIMES WE LIE SO MUCH WE DO NOT MAKE ANY SENSE AT ALL. BUT WE WOULD NEVER HURT YOU. WE ADMIRED YOU IN YOUR RUINS, D," KJ said. "EVEN THEN. YOUR CLEVERNESS, AND YOUR GOODNESS AND YOUR MUSIC, AND YOUR LONG SILENCES, AND YOUR *LOVE*—"

"KJ," I said.

"—AND YOUR *PAIN*, AND YOUR *DARKNESS*. WE LOVED YOU IN YOUR RUINS. AND WE WANTED TO TELL YOU THAT, BEFORE WE DIE, THAT IN A *GOOD* WORLD WE WOULD HAVE GOTTEN TO BE TOGETHER—"

"Oh stop, please," I said, and pressed my lips to hers. It shut her up. She started to kiss me back immediately. Her lips were as cold as the rest of her—it was like kissing someone who'd been outside in the snow. My skin tingled where she touched me. She kissed my bottom lip and the corners of my mouth, and every kiss made me shiver. I kissed her back, mirroring what she did—a brush of lips on her cupid's bow, her bottom lip, the edge of her mouth.

"HOLD STILL," she said, still sounding shaky. "WE ARE TRYING TO IMPRESS YOU WITH OUR TECHNIQUE."

"Why don't *you* hold still, dipshit," I said. "And let me impress *you*—"

I kissed the side of her neck and she shivered. The threads under her skin shivered, too, but I didn't even care. I couldn't think about that. I wanted to watch her face, I wanted her to put her hands all over me.

"Touch me," I said. Something about the way that KJ was holding herself gave me the vibe that, because of whatever she'd intuited about me long ago, she absolutely wasn't going to make any moves that escalated our situation without me making them first. When I said that, her hand flexed against the small of my back, and she kissed my neck the way I'd kissed hers. It felt so good that for the next second or two I couldn't think. I had to tilt my head away from her mouth.

"Wait a second," I said, and grabbed her arm, pulling her hand—the one drawing circles against my lower back—over my hip. KJ went super still when I said *wait*. She leaned back, looking at me with her big red eyes. "Everything is fine," I said. To emphasize my point, I leaned forward and kissed her mouth, bit her lip. Kept a firm hold on her hand. She still held herself back, but when I bit her lip her eyes fluttered closed for a second.

"I just wanted you to touch me like this," I whispered, and guided her hand up my leg.

KJ watched her cold hand in mine, her eyes tracing the upward progression of our arms. "LIKE WHAT," she said, her voice so low and flat that it was barely a question.

"Like this," I said. I was really scared, actually. But my desire for her was stronger than my fear. I guided her hand under my skirt and unfolded her fingers from mine. Then I pressed the palm of her hand between my legs, flat against my underwear.

"*Ah*. Just press," I said. I felt like I couldn't get a breath. KJ looked at me with her mouth slightly open. I would have teased her about her stupefying lust if I wasn't also stupefied by lust.

"OKAY," KJ said, and applied pressure. "WE CAN DO THAT."

"C-c-cool," I said, and then KJ leaned in and kissed me *hard*. I could feel my pulse between my legs. It was fast. It felt *so* good. I'd been afraid to do anything like this for so long. I looked up and saw that KJ's eyes were completely shut. Her forehead was furrowed in concentration. "I don't want to be in it alone," I said as coherently as I could manage, and dragged one hand up the inseam of her too-small gray pants. "Can I touch you?"

"PLEASE DO," she said against my lips. "*OH*—"

My heart was beating so hard that I could barely hear her whispering. KJ shifted her weight, so that she was pushing me down onto the wooden floor, with our hands trapped between our bodies, and—

"Excuse me?"

A voice rang out from underneath the balcony. KJ and I both froze.

"I was going to give you a pass on hiding up there and whispering, at least until our group started rehearsal, but if you're going to start *fooling around*, you are going to be ejected. Get down here immediately."

It was the instructor. She didn't sound like she was kidding. KJ started to sit up, and I pulled her down again. I could feel my eyes bugging out of my head.

Yes, I realize that I was literally the most brainless idiot in the entire world, instigating a heated session of groping in the church of a school we did not go to with an instructor less than a hundred feet away from us. But. It had been a really difficult few days. Preceded by a really difficult few years. And I just wanted to be with KJ so badly. And then when she was telling me about her loneliness and her love for me, I was kind of overcome.

"What do we do?" I asked in a whisper.

"WE HAVE TO VACATE THE CHAPEL," KJ said.

"She's gonna realize we don't go here!" I said.

"If you guys aren't down here in thirty seconds, you're getting detention for a week straight," the invisible teacher said. "That is a genuine promise."

"SOMETHING TELLS US THAT SHE WILL NOT BE ABLE TO MAKE GOOD ON THAT PROMISE," KJ said. She stood up despite my continued efforts to pull her back down, and slipped her sunglasses back over her inhuman eyes. Then she pulled *me* up, with such a small amount of effort that I felt as insubstantial as a sheet of paper.

"We can't get thrown out now! We need to stay and look out for one-third of the cloak," I said out of the corner of my mouth.

"Oh, D," KJ said, and looked over at me. "We do not think it is going to really work, you know?"

"What you think doesn't mean there's no point trying—" I stopped talking as the instructor became visible beneath us. She was standing with her hands on her hips. She did not look like she was a *fun* teacher.

"Who are you two?" she asked. "I haven't seen you before."

"We go here," said KJ. In her current state she was really not cut out for doing a cover story.

"We're sorry," I said. "We're going back to our dorms now."

"Wait. Who exactly *are* you?" the teacher asked. I took three quick steps toward the door, and my chunk of amethyst dropped out of my blazer pocket. I hadn't done anything to make it fall out, but I registered it falling.

I almost didn't go back for it. The teacher was walking after us, and it seemed like we were going to be in deep shit. But I had to keep the magic rock. I felt all weird about it, like I was doomed in some way if I lost it. I stepped backward, almost running into the instructor, and scooped my amethyst off the floor.

"You come here this *instant*, young lady," she said. "I don't know you at all. Are you trespassing?"

It seemed unlikely that this teacher actually knew every student out of seven hundred, but I could've been wrong. I didn't bother to answer her, just bolted toward KJ, who was waiting for me with the green door held open.

"Go go go!" I said, and met KJ at the door.

But—as I ran out the door—I felt a searing pain in my left hand. The amethyst had been at room temperature, or maybe slightly cooler, when it was in my blazer. But against my skin, it burned. I yelled in surprise when it got hot, and almost dropped it again, but—

—but then I passed all the way through the door and the burning sensation stopped. The stone was back at room temperature.

"Wait," I said.

"WHY?" KJ asked. She was already a little bit ahead of me, jogging down the hill.

"Come back," I said. "Look at this."

I held up the amethyst and stepped back into the chapel, almost crashing into the suspicious teacher, who was still following us.

The same thing happened again: the burning sensation against my palm, then an immediate drop in the temperature of the stone once I had passed through the door.

"Did you see that?" I asked KJ. "The stone. It's getting warm—"

"WE SEE IT," KJ said. "WE MISSED IT WHEN YOU PASSED THROUGH THE DOOR ON THE WAY IN."

"I wasn't holding it then," I said.

"Okay. I'm calling campus security," the teacher said, and walked angrily toward the back of the building, to the rooms where Jasper and Alex were hiding.

A group of girls, one of them holding a big stack of sheet music, came through the door. The last couple of girls stared at us curiously as we looked at the doorway. I was waving my stone around.

"It's not getting hot under the archway," I said. "Only over here. I think it's the actual *door*."

"WE CANNOT SEE ANYTHING EMANATING FROM THE DOOR. BUT IT WOULD MAKE SENSE FOR THIS PARTICULAR WORK OF MAGIC TO BE INVISIBLE TO OUR EYES."

"Because you're the one it's being hidden from," I said. "How the hell do we get the *door* off the chapel?"

"Excuse me," one of the girls who was watching us with curiosity said. "Are you new here? I've, like, never seen you. Either of you."

"WE ARE NEW TRANSFERS. THUS THE SCHOOL UNIFORMS," KJ said.

There was a commotion up by the pulpit, and I looked over and saw Jasper and Alex running toward us.

"We have to fucking go!" Jasper said. "That teacher's ratting us out to campus security!"

"We need to bring this door with us," I said, pointing at the green door. It was one single arched door, instead of a double—but it was still at least seven feet tall and made from heavy wood, with thick old metal door hinges.

"What?" Jasper said, but he trusted my judgment enough to not press for more of an explanation. He looked back over his shoulder, then at the door assessingly.

"Hi," one of the girls said to Alex. He did look very beautiful in his skirt and knee-high socks, I'll give him that.

"Hi," Alex said pleasantly, but then he turned to us, looking worried. "We can't get the door off the chapel, guys. It's probably been here for two hundred years. It's heavy."

I looked over at KJ. I *really* didn't want to ask her to do anything else that might overexert her—might lead to Good Arcturus devouring more of her being. But she was already doing it. She raised her arms. The smell of ozone cut through the air like lightning.

"You should all stand back," KJ said, to us but also to the girls who were watching us.

I heard a noise at the front of the chapel and glanced over. Angry Teacher had exited the rooms behind the pulpit and was moving toward us quickly.

"We have to *go*," Jasper said.

"Affirmative, boss," KJ said, and jolted both her arms back and up. The green door canted sideways and *ripped* off the hinges as she did it. There was a huge splintering sound. One of the girls yelped.

"Uh, what the fuck?" said the girl who was into Alex.

The door was levitating. I can't really think of a better way to put it than that. After all I'd seen, it was still surreal to see KJ start down the big hill with a floating door following her like a cloud.

The three of us followed her, too. The a cappella teacher was shouting something at us, and honestly, after the door theft, I couldn't blame her. Farther up the hill I saw campus security—a few men in full uniforms—moving to intercept us. Jasper and I ran shoulder to shoulder down the hill, going so fast that it seemed like any second one of us was going to fall and roll all the way down. Alex passed us on his long legs. His skirt flew up as he ran down the slope and I caught a glimpse of his boxers, which were covered in a print of the little dancing bears that every Grateful Dead fan is obsessed with, for some reason. Despite everything, that struck me as hilarious, so I was laughing all the way down the hill as security chased us.

We made it to the car right after KJ, but she'd already slid the huge door into the Range Rover through the back. All the seats except for the driver's seat were reclined or laid flat. I had to climb in and sit halfway on the big door. The back of the car couldn't close all the way with the door inside it, so it was open a crack. Jasper got behind me and braced himself against the door to keep it from sliding out onto the road.

KJ got into the very back and sat mashed up against the church door and the trunk door, holding the trunk shut as Alex drove us down the sedate oak-lined road at like eighty miles an hour.

"Fuck yes!" Jasper said, and gave the finger to the rapidly disappearing security guards. Then he turned back to us. "You guys think this is actually a piece of the cloak?" he asked.

"That story during the Banquet called it a cloak *and* a door," I said. "I think that's true. If my magic rock is any indication."

I was watching KJ. She hadn't turned around or said anything at all since we got in the car.

"KJ?" I said. "Are you okay?"

"WE ARE FINE," KJ said, still keeping her face turned away from me.

I crawled forward and grabbed her by the shoulder.

"Hey," I said, and then she looked halfway around at me.

Her skin had that terrifyingly taut and drawn look to it. But it was worse than that. There were narrow cracks—or *rips*—in her skin. Just a few of them: one on her cheek, two on her neck, one at her temple. But the rips didn't reveal blood or bone. They were full of moving red thread. Some of the thread ends poked out, moving in the air around her face. It was horrifying, repulsive. Something old as instinct told me that what I was seeing was wrong and bad, that it meant sickness and pain and death.

But I forced those feelings down. KJ looked so sad. So, like— *resigned*, almost.

"WE DO NOT WANT TO DESTROY OURSELVES," she said. Then she looked up at me with a ghost of a smile. "YOU KNOW?"

"I know," I said. I made myself touch her cheek on the unripped side. The cold threads arched toward me when I did it, like they were leaning into my touch. "We're going to fix it. Okay?"

"OKAY," KJ said.

I looked back at Jasper. His expression told me that he hadn't missed this new development. But then Alex braked sharply, and I saw that we'd come to a fork.

"Two roads diverged in a yellow wood, and I had no idea which one led back to the center of Cold Hollow," he said. "Guys?"

"Left," Jasper said. But Alex didn't move the car. He stayed at the fork for a second. What I could see of his profile was stone-still.

"Al?" I asked, when he still didn't start driving. "You okay?"

"I know where we have to go next," Alex said.

CHAPTER SIXTEEN

Monday, October 30, 2000

"Where?" Jasper asked as Alex started driving again.

"I can't believe I didn't think of it, or maybe I did, maybe that's what made me quote that Robert Frost poem," Alex said. "The library at Amherst College is the Robert Frost Library. The Frost. It's named after him because he taught there, I think? I've had books that we didn't stock in Kesuquosh sent through the library system a few times. Once it was from the Frost Library."

"What book was it?" I asked.

"*Dandelion Wine,*" Alex said.

But there was no way it had actually been *that* book. I had misheard him.

"What?" I asked.

"*The Wind's Twelve Quarters,*" Alex said. "It's an Ursula K. Le Guin collection. We didn't have it in town, for some reason."

"So we have to go there," Jasper said, "and find another green door?"

"I think so," I said. We stopped in the center of Cold Hollow so that Alex could go into the hardware store and buy some bungee cords to tie our recently stolen door onto the roof. KJ slumped over in the back seat, dozing. Her big skin splits had kind of healed over, but that was almost worse. Under slashes of jellylike translucent skin, I could see endless sinewy movement.

It took a half hour to get to Amherst, and we went immediately after we'd tied off our door. I sat next to KJ in the back of the Range Rover as Alex drove, and unfolded the piece of paper that Friday Frey had given me.

To travel into the mind of another, it said.

> *Hold hands around the stone.*
>
> *The person who will harbor both consciousnesses holds the stone in their left hand, the traveler in their right. Then both parties are burned. Use a small shower of sparks, to sting but not to injure. While their hands are clasped, the person conducting the spell will repeat the following words:*
>
> *"These burnt offerings to the mind of all minds,*
>
> *This skull to that skull. This life open to all life. This heart an abyss. In our smallness. In our nothingness. In our power, in our vastness."*
>
> *The joining is done when the traveler ingests a physical part of the person with the "target mind," to make it receptive to unconscious pairing. Hair, skin, fingernails, blood, semen, vaginal discharge, and saliva are all acceptable objects for consumption. If the spell has been conducted correctly, both subjects will fall into a trancelike state. The spell can be broken by a tripminder back in reality, or by the owner of the "target mind"—if they have sufficient discipline.*

"Huh," I said. That was basically exactly what had happened to us. And yet, I didn't think that this spell would just work if *anyone* tried it. You needed to be a witch—whatever that meant. I still wasn't totally clear on the qualifications. Or maybe you just needed to have a magical rock *given* to you by a hot witch.

I looked up and realized that KJ was fully awake, and watching me.

"HUMAN MAGIC IS VERY INTERESTING," KJ said, leaning over to look at my unfolded paper.

"Interesting how?" I asked.

"YOUR . . . *OUR* REALITY IS RESTRICTIVE," KJ said. "IT REQUIRES BOTH SKILL AND BELIEF TO ACT IN OPPOSITION TO IT. IN OUR SMALLNESS, AND OUR NOTHINGNESS, HUMAN BEINGS ARE ABLE TO SLIP UNDETECTED PAST THE LAWS OF OUR UNIVERSE."

"So we're good at it because we're so, like . . . beneath the notice of the mechanics of the cosmos?" I asked. "Like gnats in a forest?"

"MUCH SMALLER THAN GNATS IN A FOREST," KJ said. She was smiling, but then her smile faded, and she looked troubled. "IT IS EASY TO UNDERESTIMATE HUMAN BEINGS. WE MADE THAT MISTAKE."

"I think this is it," Alex said. "I've never actually been here before."

It was getting dark, and we had been circling the campus roads for a while, looking for the library building. Amherst College was another slice of New England autumnal heaven. It didn't quite have the isolation or the gothic vibes of Cold Falls, but overall, it looked similar.

However, the Frost Library was *not* similar to the chapel at Cold Falls. We had to get out of the car to make sure it was the right building, and as we approached, it became clear that it was not going to be easy to find a two-hundred-plus-year-old door. The building was pure mid-century modern.

"This is it," Alex said, looking at a placard on the low stone wall that encircled the building. "But it was erected in 1965, on the former site of a building called Walker Hall."

"I don't see any antique doors on this ugly bitch," Jasper said. "I wonder if that one got torn down with whatever Walker Hall was."

"It would not have been destroyed," KJ said. Even with her sunglasses on, in the dark, she looked like a reanimated corpse. The only good thing, I guess, was that we could pass off her big red wounds as Halloween makeup.

"The door? But that doesn't mean it's here," Alex said.

"It would have remained here," KJ said stubbornly. "She would want to know where it was."

"She. Can you confirm for me that it was Junie Apostle-Root who did this to you?" Jasper asked. We'd been over this already, and I wondered what his reason was for asking again. He had the same kind of crazed look that he got when he was proposing a new song idea.

KJ's slashed-up throat worked like she was desperately trying to speak. She clearly couldn't say anything—in fact, she raised one hand to her throat like she was going to choke. But all three of us stopped for a second and *looked* at her. It was clear that she was trying to convey that we were onto something. Her mouth was turned down in a grimace of pain and effort.

"It is beyond our cloakless powers," KJ said. "We are really sorry."

"It's okay," Jasper said. "We basically know it was her. What I'm curious about is who she is *now*. Because you know she's still gotta be around, right? *Watching.* Keeping everything perfect in her fucked-up utopia. Making the cogs turn so the spells hold. Making sure we participate or die. Probably . . . probably in a position of power." Then he shot me a sideways look.

"What?" I asked.

"My aunt's real first name isn't *Birdie*, did I ever tell you that? That's a nickname."

From what Jasper had told me it seemed like her first name was *bitch.* "No," I said. "What's her real first name?"

"Jane," Jasper said. "Janey. Sound like anything to you?"

"Probably someone in a position of power," I repeated. I started to see what he was getting at. "Like the First Selectwoman, for example?"

"Bingo," Jasper said grimly.

"You think *Birdie* is *Junie*?" I asked. "KJ, can you say anything? Confirm, deny, wave your hands in the air?"

KJ shook her head, one hand still at her throat.

"She'd be almost three hundred years old. Immortality," Alex said. "That's a reason someone might do this. What if all of this is so she can live forever, and always have the town just like she wants it?"

"That would be a lot of lives to ruin, just to get the life you wanted," I said. I was thinking of how Birdie had watched KJ's transformation back in the clearing of the black house—not sleepily, not like she wasn't seeing it. With a creepy avidity.

"Just a working theory," Jasper said, lighting a clove as we traced the stone path around the building that led to the main entrance.

But when we got to the double doors that led into the Frost Library, it was locked.

"Why?" Jasper said, rattling the lock. "The hours say it's open until one a.m.!"

"I don't know," I said.

"KJ," Jasper said, "can you knock the door open and take out any alarms?"

KJ looked hesitant, but nodded.

"I don't think we should make her use her powers any more right now," Alex said.

"You're right, actually," Jasper said. There was a moment of uneasy silence as we all studied KJ's deteriorated face. I had a horrible feeling that at some point soon—if it hadn't happened already—whatever made KJ into KJ was going to die without fanfare. Just disappear out of the body that was walking around with Good Arcturus inside it.

"Let's try to do this without using her powers," Alex said. "There has to be someone we can ask."

"Right," Jasper said, and then started walking down the path that led to the rest of campus.

The campus was quiet. Some of the windows on the dormitory buildings were lit up, but the vast majority weren't. It actually took a few minutes before we even saw another human being. Then we passed parallel to a blue-haired goth kid with thick glasses and the approximate physicality of Ichabod Crane, and Jasper waved him down while running over.

"Hey!"

"Hello," the goth kid said, barely slowing his stride.

"We don't go here. Do you know why the library is closed right now?" Jasper asked. "Kind of an emergency."

But the kid shook his head. "It's closed today for the faculty Halloween party."

"The faculty Halloween party," Jasper repeated.

"Yes," the kid said. "The autumn break is happening right now. It's just a long weekend, but that's why the campus is so empty."

"I need to get into that building before Halloween," Jasper said. "I was understating my case when I said it was *kind* of an emergency. It *is* an emergency."

"Well," the kid said, sparing us one super-awkward glance—he looked like he was desperate for the conversation to be over—"I'm not saying that you can't get in. I'm just saying that tonight, starting at nine, it's the faculty Halloween party. The only people there will be faculty members. In costumes."

"That doesn't *help* me," Jasper said, before realizing it actually *did* kind of help him. "Wait," he continued, looking at the goth kid. "So, theoretically, we could sneak in, right?"

"Theoretically," the goth kid said, then booked it toward the parking lot.

"Thank you!" Alex called after him, and then turned to us. "He seemed nice."

"He seemed like he was desperate to escape me," Jasper said. "But helpful. So at nine we'll sneak into the party. I fucking hope that they were getting architectural with the reclaimed doors from the old building."

"Walker Hall," Alex said. "It seems like a long shot, you know?"

"Yeahhh," I said, because it didn't sound very likely to me, either. But I didn't know what other options we had.

"We need costumes," Alex said. "That, like, cover our entire heads."

"Let's go do that, then," Jasper said, glancing over at KJ.

Our extended field trip took us to an area I wasn't familiar with: an industrial-complex-dotted road cutting through the middle of nowhere. It was kind of ugly and had warehouses, a gas station, something called Tractor Supply Co., and like three different Dunkin' Donuts. Finally, we pulled into a shopping plaza that had a giant store called Ames at the back. We parked well in view of the huge red-lettered sign.

"This is a department store, right?" I asked.

I was greeted by raised eyebrows from Alex and Jasper.

"You've . . . never been in an Ames?" Alex asked.

"I've been in department stores before," I said, feeling like I was about to be given a lot of shit. "Tons of times. Like Lord & Taylor or Tiffany's or something. Just not this one."

"Snob," KJ said, and smiled at me with her ruined face. I remembered how she had called me a snob during the Banquet. That felt like a thousand years ago.

"Well, I don't think that Ames is anything like *Tiffany's*," Jasper said. "Get ready for shopping with the middle class."

"We are going to stay here," KJ said. She hadn't gotten out of the car with us. "We need to rest. Please bring us back a large quantity of Halloween candy."

"Will do," Alex said. We were quiet as we walked into the Ames.

Once we had gone in the sliding doors, Jasper said what we were all thinking.

"She's not gonna make it," he said, and looked like he wanted to throw up. "It's too much for one body. It's destroying her."

"That—hey, that's *not* true. The Incorporations always survive for thirty-five years," Alex said. "Until the next Great Harvest Hallow."

"Yeah, but survive as *what*?" Jasper said. "As a shield made of human leather? As a shell? Because some kind of transformation happens on Halloween. And it's already happening to her."

"Guys," Alex said quietly. "What am I going to do if she dies?"

There was absolutely no answer for that. I'd never had a sibling, let alone a twin. The idea of Alex getting to experience the full spectrum of human emotion just in time to watch KJ die was horrible.

"Let's just get some fucking costumes," Jasper muttered.

Merchandise-wise, it seemed like Ames had been ransacked during some kind of Halloween apocalypse. The candy aisle was mostly empty. We picked through the dregs until we came up with enough sugary crap to satisfy the bottomless pit of KJ-slash-Good Arcturus. Then we went to a kind of sparse costume section. There was still a decent selection of kids' costumes, but the adult section was not great. There were a couple of Austin Powers outfits left and a bunch of jackets for Neo from *The Matrix*, but those did not come with a head covering.

"Okay, I'm gonna be a werewolf," Alex said. He had found a latex mask that was about what you would expect. "I'm gonna buy some clothes too, like a flannel for a wolfman look. Darian, is that okay?"

"I would challenge you to *try* to make a dent in my available credit," I said, and gave him one of my cards.

"All of this shit is *too big*," Jasper said, waving around a full-body Godzilla costume. "Who is this for? A giant?"

"I think that's just for an average-sized adult man," I said, and Jasper sighed.

"What*ever*," he said, and then went over to the kids' section.

I found a costume called Scary Scarecrow, complete with a mask that looked like a fanged, demonic version of the scarecrow in *The Wizard of Oz*, and grabbed it for KJ. Then I got myself a spooky latex clown mask, which came with a bloodstained puffy onesie that had pom-pom buttons down the front. Senovak was terrified of clowns—I think it was the only thing he was scared of. He couldn't even look at ads with Ronald McDonald in them.

And then Jasper was standing in front of me. He had pulled a Spider-Man costume over his clothes. Or, sorry—it was a knockoff costume called Spider-Kid. It fit him perfectly, even the headpiece. It was probably made for twelve-year-olds.

"Yeah, yeah, laugh it up," Jasper said.

"You look soooooo adorable," I said, and Spider-Kid flipped me off with both hands.

When we went back to the car with costumes and candy, KJ was asleep. Red tendrils waved around her face in the air like they were caught in underwater currents. But I sat close to her anyway.

"KJ?" I whispered as we took the dark back roads toward the Frost Library. Alex and Jasper were talking up front. Jasper was going through the CD case he'd rescued from the remains of the PDA.

"Yes?" KJ asked without opening her eyes.

"Are you listening?" I said, keeping my voice low.

"We are always listening to you, D," KJ said. Her eyes slitted open, but then fell shut again. Outside, the woods rolled by in blackness. The moon was covered by clouds. The streets we took were coated in a layer of brown leaves. The air smelled sharp when I cracked the window.

"I love you in your ruins," I said. KJ smiled without opening her eyes, and leaned her head against my shoulder.

"WE KNOW," she said.

"Good," I said, and stroked the hair behind her ear. But she was asleep.

I had no idea that KJ had just spoken to me for the last time. I never heard her talk again, for all the rest of that endless Halloween.

CHAPTER SEVENTEEN

Monday, October 30, 2000

We stopped to change into our Halloween costumes at a convenience store about twenty minutes from the Amherst campus, and in the bright lights of the parking lot I got a really good look at KJ. She was still in her Cold Falls uniform, red cloak draped over her shoulders, and her eyes were closed. The sinews of Good Arcturus framed her head. They moved in unison, as if a wind was blowing—but one that I couldn't feel.

"KJ? Wake up. Time to put on your second ensemble of the day," I said. I touched her shoulder while Jasper and Alex stood outside, using the side of the car as a shield while they changed. KJ's eyes flew open when I spoke, but she didn't answer me.

"You in there?" I asked. I leaned over her. "KJ?"

KJ looked up at me, and opened her mouth, like she was going to reply. But when her lips parted, the humming buzz in the air intensified. Her mouth was *filled* with red strands. They spilled over her lips and crept down her face like running ink. It looked like a forest of spiderwebs.

"Oh, okay," I said. I tried not to let my horror show on my face, though I leaned back almost against the car door without realizing it.

And far away, in the back of my head, I heard a voice. The deepest, darkest, loveliest, most soothing voice in the entire universe. It sounded like a radio dial being adjusted in my head: faint, staticky, but *there*.

WE ARE HERE, D.

"That's good," I said. "I thought I lost you."

I scooted back toward her. To show her that I wasn't afraid. After a second, she leaned her head against my shoulder, and red strings brushed against my right temple. The whole moment felt weirdly fragile. I could definitely start crying any second.

"Are you ready to party?" I asked. KJ looked at me. I could feel her head tilt toward the side of my face, anyway.

"The party at Amherst College," I clarified. "I got you the Scary Scarecrow costume."

How ... APT ...

Alex and Jasper climbed back in, fully werewolfed and Spider-Kidded.

"Looking great," I said. "Especially you, Mister Werewolf Lumberjack."

"Awoooooo," Alex said behind his mask. Then he pulled it off. "I kinda can't wear it to drive."

I guided KJ out with me onto the hidden swath of pavement behind the car like she was an invalid. But once we were out there she started getting into her Scary Scarecrow outfit right away. A light rain began to fall, emphasizing the bitter late-October cold.

Finally, KJ pulled her mask over her face and turned around. I examined her.

"You look very creepy," I said.

There was that voice again in my head.

THANK YOU, it said.

"How are you—" I started to ask her how the hell she was doing that, but then my cell phone started ringing. I picked it up. "Hey, Dan," I said.

"Darian. How are you?"

"Half in a clown suit," I said. "We're going to a Halloween party."

"Ugh," Senovak said, his voice rife with clown-hatred. "Glad I'm not there to see it. Where is this Halloween party?"

"Cold Falls Prep," I said.

"Fine. Do not do anything stupid," Senovak said. "Make good choices."

"I always do," I said. We just both kind of let the absurdity of that claim hang in the air for a second.

"Right. So I'll be back tomorrow," Senovak said. "Tuesday morning."

"Okay," I said. "How are you holding up?"

"I'm okay," Senovak said. There was a tiny pause, then he added: "Lonely. The funeral was today. Ironically, Linus would have been able to make this whole situation much easier to deal with."

"I'm sorry," I said. If anything but what was happening had been happening, I would have gone and kept him company. He sounded like he could use it.

"Have to run," Senovak said. "But you *will* call me if anything goes awry at this party, right?"

"Yes, I promise. See you tomorrow," I said, and hung up. I climbed into the car feeling about as miserable as it was possible to feel in a clown suit.

The rain intensified minute by minute, and the car sliced through icy sheets of water all the way to Amherst. Leaves tumbled down in the storm, coating the streets. The drumming of the rain was loud on the car, and Spider-Kid cranked the radio up. He left it on an alternative station and started rifling through the album of CDs.

"I can't believe none of these broke. Where's my Swell Maps CD? I swear I put it in here," Jasper said.

"What album is it?" Alex asked.

"*A Trip to Marineville*," Jasper said.

"I think that's one of the ones I took out and left at the house to make room," Alex admitted.

"Oh, you *fucker*," Jasper said.

"I think I put *Tidal* in there over the summer," I said.

"Fiona Apple? No fucking *way*," Jasper said.

On the radio, the DJ started doing her between-sets bit.

"*Got some great things coming up for you this Mischief Night, during our indie movie soundtrack appreciation episode, here on 104.1, central New England's home for alternative rock. Kicking it off with 'Empty Heaven,' the breakout track from 1997's surprise Best Picture winner,* Still Life with Bleach. *Dex Coffin got a posthumous Oscar nom with this one, but it lost out on Best Original Song to 'You Must Love Me,' from* Evita. *Bad call, Academy Awards dudes—*"

"Oh, keep it," Alex said, and Jasper nodded and cranked up the volume.

The thing about Dexter was that *of course* they all liked his music. He was a mash of influences in the same way that Army of Dolly was, only executed a million times more brilliantly: the driving, staticky industrial *I made this in my basement sound* of Skinny

270

Puppy or Nine Inch Nails, sad singer-songwriter lyrics that spoke to universal truths in the vein of Joni Mitchell, and the willingness to stretch his weird, amazing voice out to do anything it needed to do a la Bowie or Nina Simone. Sprinkle in some grunge aesthetics and they were all hooked, just like the enthused reviewers from *Spin* and *Rolling Stone* and everyone's cool older siblings.

And me. I remembered how exciting it had been to meet one of my musical idols, someone whose dad was a friend of *my* dad. Because Dex Coffin actually came from money, even though the narrative of his life that had been popularized after he died spoke a lot about him being a poor couch-surfing drug addict like Kurt Cobain or something.

Actually, I want to take part of that back. Dexter's lyrics didn't *actually* speak to universal truths. They just pretended to, and people put their own interpretations on that.

The intro, with the drum machine beat and the heavily modified sample of Dexter's own piano playing, started. He'd worked on that piano composition in front of me for *hours*. I could play the original piece myself, by heart. I could picture the lights on the two Akai S1000 samplers he'd used for mixing. My palms were sweaty inside my clown gloves. I had somehow always avoided listening to his music with my friends, in all our years of listening to music together. Then Dexter started singing:

> *I hope we die at the same time*
> *And we're born again*
> *(Again again again)*
> *But only if it means something*
> *Otherwise I'll take the static—*

I could stand it, I decided. No matter how nauseous it made me. I'd heard it enough fucking times to stand it. My piano playing was probably even *in* there somewhere, layered in with the innumerable other recordings that gave the track its messy, miserable, otherworldly, driving, night-clubby, weepy, angry sound.

But then Jasper turned the volume up even *more*, so that he could sing along without drowning it out and ruining our experience. He was polite about music-listening like that, unfortunately for me.

> *And I love you you you you you*
> *And everything else in this poor universe*

"*This poor universe, even when I sleepwalk*," Dexter sang. Jasper sang along with him.

> *And your billion years of silence,*
> *   your entropy, your tired talk*
> *Your pearly gates,*
> *(Oh, this poor universe)*
> *I hope we never leave it—*

I was *not* going to throw up. If I was quiet enough and small enough and still enough, they wouldn't notice anything. We were almost at the college. I curled my hands in my lap.

STOP PLAYING THAT, came a voice in my head. I looked up sharply. I saw Jasper and Alex look around, too, like someone had whispered in their ears.

"What?" Jasper yelled over the music.

"Stop playing that song?" Alex asked. "What?"

"No way! Eat my entire ass!" Jasper said, and went to turn it up louder.

KJ reached out with one hand. A few threads emerged from under her fingernails. The radio got deafeningly loud for a second and then *exploded* into a wall of static that made us all flinch and cover our ears while she sat there calmly in her scarecrow costume.

Then the dial twisted and the music turned off completely.

"Ahhhh!" Alex said, and swerved the car a little before recovering.

"Uh, what the *fuck*?!" Jasper said, whirling around in his seat.

"I guess KJ didn't want to hear that song?" Alex said.

"Listen, fuck *you*, you stupid straw man," Jasper said. "I want you out of KJ's *body*, dipshit! *My* best friend loves this album, you bitch—"

The voice in our heads was loud now. I saw Jasper register it.

SHE DOES NOT. IT WAS MADE BY SOMEONE WHO CAUSED HER GRIEVOUS HARM.

"How can I *hear* her right now? Guys? And what are you *talking* about?" Jasper said—but then, he glanced over at me.

And I must've been giving something away with my expression. Something pretty significant. Because Jasper shut his mouth super fast and looked at me like he'd been smacked hard across the face with a dead fish.

"I don't know what she's talking about—" I started to deny everything, but it was too little too late.

"What . . . Dex Coffin? You knew *Dex Coffin*?" Jasper asked.

"No," I said immediately.

Yes, said the voice in our heads.

"Yes," I amended. "Just for a few years. He was my . . . my instructor."

"Your instructor," Jasper repeated. "Darian. When did you meet him?"

"When I was almost eleven," I said. Couldn't meet his piercing eyes. I still felt like puking.

"Rocks around us," Jasper said, in a tone of detached horror. "What the *fuck*. What the *fuck*, Darian, what the *fuck*!"

"Oh my god. *Stop*," I said.

"What are we inferring right now?" Alex asked.

"I think Dex Coffin is a pedophile," Jasper said in that same horrified voice, "a fucking child molester."

"Isn't he dead?" Alex asked.

"Yeah," I said.

"That's disgusting," Alex said. "I always liked his tunes. Guess he's another one for the trash compactor of history."

"I can't fucking believe it," Jasper said. "Darian—"

"Jas," Alex said mildly, "why don't we leave Darian alone for a few minutes, okay?"

Jasper snapped his mouth shut.

"Good," Alex said. "Here we are, guys."

He pulled into the Frost Library parking lot. It was packed full of cars. Outside, I could see a bunch of costumed adults smoking, taking shelter from the rain under an overhang near the door. Alex guided the car around to the back, where we (and the big door bungeed onto our car) would be less visible.

I was kind of at a loss for what to do. I looked through my bag, rifling my crap, and pulled out a lip balm. My hands were stupidly shaking, and I dropped the cap.

"Shit," I said. I felt like I was going to cry over a dropped lip balm cap.

KJ leaned forward and grabbed the cap. She placed it neatly back on the lip balm.

"Thanks," I said. "For the cap. Not for outing me about the Dexter thing."

KJ just regarded me silently. If she was making an expression, I couldn't tell.

Then we had to get inside. For all of my fear that the members of the faculty would be super on guard against Amherst students trying to sneak in, the front doors to the library were unchaperoned. One of the cigarette-smoking professors, someone dressed as a ladybug, waved at KJ as we walked in, trying to look inconspicuous.

"Lydia! Come out here after you get a drink!" she said, and KJ nodded silently in her scarecrow mask.

The inside of the library was probably mid-century boring, normally, but tonight it was beautiful. The reception desk was covered by a solid wall of orange balloons. Fake jack-o'-lantern lights with glowing faces grinned at us from the stairway and a huge line of costumed adults flowed outward from the bar. I thought of stopping off to get a vodka cranberry, but being buzzed would not help me now.

Music was blasting loud enough to cover any weird buzzing sounds emanating from KJ: as I listened, "Human Fly" by The Cramps bled into Siouxsie and the Banshees' "Spellbound." People were dancing—I saw a cowboy dancing with Ghostface from *Scream*—and faculty members sat on the sofas and chairs that were pushed against the walls. Orange bulbs threw streamers of light across bookshelves.

"We'll start at the top," Jasper said. "Check every door. Work our way down."

We went up the stairs in a line, the thump of the music and the laughter of drunk people following us. On the mezzanine there were more people, but they were lodged deep into party conversations, and nobody asked us any questions or even gave us lingering looks.

We climbed all the way to the fourth floor, then skirted the perimeter of a dark and endless world of silent computer labs and faculty offices. The sounds of the party vanished behind dense concrete walls. I didn't know if security patrolled up here, but it felt like we were miles away from everyone.

There was a locked special archives area, but it looked like it had only one door, and it was not our door. I took off one clown glove and held my amethyst, waiting for any hint of a burn.

"Let's go down," Jasper said, and we descended to floor three, where the stacks were. Now I could hear the party a little, but it was so soft that it became a phantom whisper just slightly resembling music and laughter. Rain pelted against the narrow windows, and emergency exit lights lit up aisle after narrow aisle. It smelled like books and carpet.

"This is an amazing library," Alex whispered, his voice coming out really muffled through the mask. "Look at that! A *map* room? A periodicals room?"

"That door looks pretty old," Jasper said. There *were* lots of antique architectural flares mixed in with the boring concrete of it all—windows and doors and stained glass and even light fixtures. Reclaimed from the old hall that had once stood there, I hoped.

I waved my amethyst in front of the door, but nothing happened. I was looking for a green one—I was almost certain the door was going to be green, like the one on the chapel at Cold Falls . . . and the one hanging off the ruins of Empty Heaven.

"There!" Jasper said, and I saw a room at the extreme end of the huge floor. A room with an old archway worked into new concrete. A room with a very old-looking green door. A room with a big computer-paper note tacked on the wall next to it:

Temporary home of the Holloway Classics Library thru 11/19

While Grosvenor House undergoes repairs.

Classics/Greek/Latin Majors who wish to access the collection may contact Dept. Chair (Prof. Youssef Attia) during office hours. Thanks!

The amethyst burned my hand when I waved it over the door. This time I didn't drop it.

"It's this one," I said. "Ow."

KJ nodded and lifted her Scary Scarecrow head. She raised her arms. The ozone smell filled the library air around us.

The door made a horrible *creeeeeaking* sound, snapped off its hinges, then hovered in the air like it was awaiting further instruction.

We all looked at each other.

"How the hell do we get out with an entire door?" I asked, thinking of the sea of people below us.

Follow us. We will make sure the path is clear, said the voice in our heads. It sounded a little bit like KJ . . . but not as much as it had when she'd still been able to speak. Her stolen door followed behind her like a giant green butterfly.

"I don't know how I can be hearing that," Jasper said. "I haven't heard a voice in my head since I fell out of the attic."

"How can *I* be hearing that?" I asked as we started back down the stairwell we'd come up. I was whistling in the dark, nervous about getting out of this crowded building. And more nervous as we descended. "I thought you couldn't hear it unless you were born in Kesuquosh."

"I think you can technically assimilate. It just takes longer than you've ever stayed in town," Alex said. "But that's not the voice of Good Arcturus. Jasper, remember what it sounded like when you were little?"

Jasper was quiet for a second. He followed close behind the floating green door as we descended. KJ was silent in front of us as the noise of the Halloween party got louder and louder.

"You're right," Jasper said. "It doesn't sound anything like the voice I always heard in my head until my concussion. That's not the *You are safe, my child* voice."

"Yeah," Alex said.

"I mean, KJ called the voice in everyone's heads 'the voice of Kesuquosh,' which is a different thing than what you guys have always been led to believe," I said. A thin thread of laughter floated up to us.

"It's Birdie," Jasper said. "Or Jane. Or Junie. Whatever her real name is. That fucking bitch. I fucking *know* it. We've been fucking bamboozled this whole time. She's been using him to control us like he's a *battery*, or something."

"And keeping him in the black house, where she . . . does something with him," Alex said. "But keeping him prisoner. Essentially."

We hit the mezzanine. There were still faculty members up there talking to each other, and absolutely every single one of them went silent when KJ walked into their midst. Or not so much when KJ walked into their midst as when the floating door followed her.

"Do you see that?" a pirate said, pointing to the door.

"Crazy, huh?" Jasper asked. KJ started moving faster. I didn't make eye contact with anybody as we descended the final set of stairs, my heart pounding.

We reached the bottom level of the stairwell, and the costumed adults spread out before us like a sea. "Dead Man's Party" by Oingo Boingo was blasting. More people were dancing, probably because they were getting progressively drunker.

I took a deep breath. But KJ just strode confidently into the middle of the crowd, the door following in her wake. STAY CLOSE TO US, the voice in my head commanded.

The party was big enough that not *everyone* noticed a girl in a Scary Scarecrow costume being followed by a levitating antique door, but as KJ cut across the center of the room, a lot of people *did* notice. If we had been outed as non-adults, I think they might have tried to stop us. But the people surrounding us as I followed in KJ's wake were just . . . staring. Probably wondering if it was a trick done with wires, or a costume, or something.

"Excuse me! Pardon us!" Jasper yelled, and it actually *worked*. People backed away from the front door of the library so that we could get out. One Queen of Hearts looked particularly suspicious as we went by—even reached out to touch the door—but nobody stopped us.

We made it outside. My heart didn't stop racing. I kept expecting some kind of faceless authority to call out and make us return the door.

The night had gotten windier. We passed Austin Powers kissing Catwoman against a car, both of them totally soaking wet, so wrapped up in each other that they didn't notice our hovering door.

Alex bungeed the door to the top of the car.

"I can't believe we're getting away with this," I said.

"Thank fuck for booze," Jasper said. "All these dipshits don't even keep us from stealing pieces of their literal *building*."

"They just didn't know what the hell was up," I said, glad for the inaction of the partygoers. "No clear reason to stop us."

"Sheep. Sometimes *everybody* acts like they're from Kesuquosh," Jasper said.

"People might hesitate in weird situations," I said. "But at least it's *them* not doing anything. Not someone else telling them what to do."

"Okay," Alex said. "That should be secure."

Then we all got in the car and pulled our masks off. Outside, the world was filled with rain and darkness.

"What now?" Alex asked. But I knew what we had to do next.

"I don't know how these doors become a *cloak*, any more than I understand how a person is a *shield*," I said. "But I know the third piece . . . has to be the doorway to Empty Heaven. It's identical to these. He asked us to find all the pieces for him. We need to go back to Kesuquosh."

"Rocks. It *is* identical," Alex said. Jasper looked like he'd been slapped when I said "Empty Heaven."

"You're right," he muttered. "But also, I can't believe we called it that. How did you not lose your fucking mind?"

"It wasn't that bad," I said. "Hearing it on the radio is the worst thing."

"It's about you, isn't it," Alex said. "And that other single that was really big. 'Later, Adrian.' That's about you, too, isn't it? Darian. Adrian. The name is an anagram. A pretty obvious one."

I nodded.

"How . . . did no one ever catch him?" Alex asked. He was trying to be delicate, I think, but I could see how much it disturbed him. And hear it in his voice.

"I covered for him," I said. "You know?"

I didn't want Alex to worry about me right now. He had so much to worry about already.

Plus . . . well. I could take them all knowing about this. But I couldn't stand too many more questions. I was scared, even then, that they would find out about the horrible thing I had done. The thing I never thought about. The reason Dexter still followed me. And then the only people who knew who I really was would know that I was a bad person.

I could see Jasper mouthing the first chorus of "Later, Adrian" to himself in the front seat, silently. I even clocked what part he was at, in his soundless recitation:

> *Oh Adrian, time is so strange*
> *Oh Adrian, why did we meet?*
> *Oh Adrian, your hair hangs down*
> *A night-black velvet sheet*

Then he stopped, and grimaced, and wiped the back of his mouth with one web-slinging hand like he had tasted something terrible.

Next to me, KJ slipped her hand out of the faux burlap of the Scary Scarecrow glove. She wrapped her cold fingers around mine. Red sinews poked out from under her fingernails and brushed my skin. *I could probably even love her like this*, I thought. Maybe she heard me, from wherever she was inside of Good Arcturus. Or maybe Good Arcturus just appreciated the sentiment. KJ's hand squeezed mine. I squeezed back.

We held hands all the way to Kesuquosh.

CHAPTER EIGHTEEN

Monday, October 30 & Tuesday, October 31, 2000

On the residential streets before Route 202 there were lights and jack-o'-lanterns and general signs of Halloween decor, but as soon as we turned onto the road that led into Kesuquosh, everything was dark.

It was weird how dark everything was. The fields were dark, which was normal, but so was Jasper's place—when we passed the farmhouse on the hill overlooking the orchards, no lights shone in the windows. And when we got to Good Earth Way, all the streetlights were out. The buildings were unlit. The only source of illumination was the neon pizza sign at K-Family, cutting through the rain as we drove by. And even that was flickering, like it was about to burn out.

"Where is everybody?" I asked.

Bunches of chrysanthemums and braided calico corn that had fallen from fences and streetlamps littered the empty road, mixing with the brown leaves that had been knocked down by the storm.

Jasper was craning his head around, looking to the left and right as we rolled around the town green.

"I don't see *anybody*," he said. "And . . . everything looks—"

"Abandoned," Alex said. "This place looks like it's been abandoned for years."

It did. It was harder to tell in the dark and the rain. The Fieldstone Inn's gate was closed, but behind it I could see that the big old Colonial house had peeling paint. I never remembered it having peeling paint before. There were cracks in the pavement, too—our stolen Range Rover thumped over potholes every few seconds.

"Anyone hearing Good—I mean, the voice of Kesuquosh?" I asked. "Anyone being a safe little child with the sweet baby world?"

Jasper laughed and shook his head. "Nooope."

"Me either," Alex said. "Probably because they didn't have KJ. I feel like she—or Good Arcturus, I mean—is the engine that keeps this place running."

"Why does everything look like ass, though, that's the real question," Jasper said.

"Maybe this is how it really looks," Alex said. We drove down by the houses that got older and older and were spaced farther and farther apart, and down Deep River Road until it turned into what had once been Church Street. Alex slowed the car to a crawl, but kept going as the cobblestones gave way to dirt and the woods crowded around the path. Until we saw the ruins of Empty Heaven, with the door hanging all alone.

Alex parked the car. Rain drummed down on the windshield.

"Okay. Now we get the three doors together and . . ." Alex looked over at us.

"Hope like fuck something happens," Jasper said.

"Something is going to happen," I said. We all looked at KJ.

"Do *you* think this will work?" I asked her.

She didn't open her mouth, but she looked at the door, and I swear I could almost *feel* her emotions. Or Good Arcturus's emotions, actually. In my mind, I heard one word:

...Home... It was so full of longing that it made my throat tight.

"Let's go," Jasper said, and got out. He reached up onto the roof, unhooking the bungee cords that secured our two giant doors. I got up on the running board in the back and did the same thing.

Alex turned the car off and came to help us.

KJ got out and walked through the wind and rain toward the hanging door and the old foundation of the church. Then she stopped. I saw her looking left and right before whirling around and coming back.

I watched KJ as she started to run toward us, and then I heard the voice in my mind, louder and more distinct than it had been so far:

Hiding from us. Blocking us. SHE IS HERE! RUN RUN RUN RUN RUN RUN!

I whipped my head around and saw Jasper and Alex hearing what I was hearing.

"Get in the car!" Alex said.

KJ made it back to us, and threw herself into the front passenger's side.

I swung myself off the running board and into the back seat, and then I heard a sound so loud it made me recoil, made my ears ring: a loud, low popping from across the clearing. A gunshot.

Then another one. Jasper reached up and slapped Alex on the shoulder. "*Drive!*" Alex slammed on the gas, and for a second we were moving, turning around on the dirt path so that we could get back to town and away. But then there was a huge *POP*, and the car started to pull to one side, so dramatically that we were rolling into the woods. I heard another sharp *POP* from across the clearing.

"No, no, no, oh man," Alex said. "I think they just shot out our tires—"

"Fuck! Stop the car, we need to run for it! Oh fuck!" Jasper said.

Alex stopped the car. I threw open my door and started to sprint down the wet path toward the sunflower fields, Jasper right next to me and Alex on my other side.

"KJ, come *on!*" Jasper shouted. KJ was following us, but slower, looking around.

I couldn't see anyone either. I had no idea where the gunshots had come from, where the constables could be hiding.

And then, like the worst fucking magic trick of all time, I saw them.

Two red-robed Kesuquoshians stepped out onto the path to block us. The Sumners, both of them holding guns. They had been crouched behind the dark trees around us, I think, but by some trick "she" had kept us from seeing them.

"No," I said. "We were so close, come *on*—"

"Please don't shoot," Alex said, holding his hands up.

"Move your ass," Sumner Senior said. We backed away from him and his gun, pushed back up toward the middle of the clearing. I was pressed up against KJ, who stood still and silent, with Alex crowded against my arm and Jasper in front of me.

"Please," Alex said again. "Good Arcturus just wants to fix his cloak! Please, guys, help us! We need to put those doors together, I think. You all should understand, right? He's helped us for so long. We need to help him with this—"

"You are a *liar*," came a sweet voice, and then I turned as much as I dared and saw Birdie, perched on the crumbling edge of the low wall that marked out the old church.

She was sitting with her legs crossed, her red cloak still jaunty, one foot swinging slightly. And six figures stood behind her in a semicircle, all of them within the foundation of Empty Heaven. My eyes passed over Birdie. In my fear, I took in every detail. Adrenaline made me feel hyperaware. The six rain-shrouded figures behind her were not like regular people. Their red robes were threaded through with a black *something* that looked like tree roots. That blackness flowed up their robes almost organically, gleaming like oil in the intermittent beams of light. And then, at the top of their robes, the black material covered each one of their faces like gauze. They were completely masked. Their heights varied from very, very tall to child-sized. I thought I saw the gleam of teeth and eyes behind the black gauzelike stuff that covered each face. Little glints of light in the darkness.

For a second, I wondered if anybody else could even see them—or if they were a product of my imagination.

It made me think of Dexter. Nocturnal eyes. Animal eyes and gnashing teeth.

"These children have been corrupted by some outside force," Birdie went on. "Stolen our Incorporation. Perverted the will of our Lord to their own ends. Led, of course, by the one citizen among us who has been cut off from His voice for years. Our town is dying without Good Arcturus. Which is exactly what Jasper wants."

"Who are you *talking* to? You sound fucking insane! We're the only ones even doing what he wants!" Jasper said, waving his hand at the immovable Sumners. "You're all being tricked by *her*!"

He tried to dart over toward Birdie, but was stopped by the broad arm of Sumner Junior. I was glad, actually. I hated the idea of Jasper anywhere near the six silent figures who were standing behind the First Selectwoman. Something about them filled me with a terror *beyond* terror. Facing the gun-toting constables was preferable.

"I'm talking to your *mothers*, Jasper," Birdie said, and pointed with one elegant hand toward the far side of the clearing, where we'd parked our car. "In honor of the great mother of Kesuquosh, Elisabel Apostle-Root, it is always the mother of a transgressor who must cast the deciding vote for censure."

I saw them, standing under one umbrella together: Mrs. Plum and Rita. Rita was holding a flashlight canted upward toward her face, like a kid telling a horror story at a bonfire. She was crying.

"Rita! Rita! Please listen to me," Jasper said. He pointed at Birdie. "She's been around for centuries! She changed her name, but she's the same old fucking *witch*—"

"I don't want to hear this madness anymore," Birdie said. "It has been almost a century since Kesuquosh has had to take a measure like this. It brings me absolutely no happiness. Rita. Constance. Will you please step forward?"

The two women walked together as one under the umbrella. Rita's flashlight-holding hand was shaking all over the place, splashing the trees with white stripes of light through the rain.

"For your sons," Birdie said, "who have absconded with the newest shield of Good Arcturus, and attempted to prevent the culmination of the Great Harvest Hallow, the council—with myself representing them—recommends censure by Incorporation. But we require you, as the ones who gave them life, to cast the deciding vote. Rita. What say you for Alex?"

"What the fuck is *censure by Incorporation*?" I asked, but nobody answered me.

I saw Rita hesitate. She let go of the umbrella, leaving it in Mrs. Plum's hands, and stepped out into the rain, holding her flashlight like a candle.

"I can't," Rita said. "I'm sorry. I can't. I don't think he *meant* to do this. I see his heart. His heart is full of love. I just can't. Not now."

"Why not?" Alex said suddenly. He tried to get around the constables, but they blocked him. "Why not, huh? Everything we do here is so *great*, why not this?"

Rita looked back at Alex, her face blotchy, her beautiful black curls plastered to her face.

"Baby," she said, "Alex. Honey. Please stop fighting us. You have to understand that this is the only way for us. I can't stand the idea of losing *two* children."

Alex looked back at his mom with a combination of fear and disgust.

"Rocks around us, Mom," he said. Sarcastically. Coldly. It was amazing to hear him talk that way. Rita looked shocked. "Why on earth do you think we're *losing* KJ? This is supposed to be beautiful, right? Beautiful and necessary?"

That just made Rita start crying again. Birdie cleared her throat, barely audible under the sound of the rain.

"Very well. Censure will not be enacted for Alex Kobayashi. As for Jasper, arguably the ringleader of this little . . . insurrection. What say you, Constance?"

Mrs. Plum pressed her thin lips together and nodded tersely. "Yes. We must."

"*Mom.* Don't you get it? I'm trying to help *you*, too—" Jasper said, sounding frightened for a second. Frightened and wounded. Confessing his failed hopes after the Banquet of the Needle: *I want to save all of them.*

It was the first time he had addressed his mother. But then he cut himself off, angrily shaking his head, and looked defiantly at Mrs. Plum and then around at Birdie, rainwater dripping off his face.

"Fine. If you actually mean censure," Jasper said, "I will happily take your condemnation. If you mean some other creepy thing you're *calling* censure, then fuck you all."

"It is done," Birdie said, ignoring him. "Incorporations, come forward!"

I felt someone grab me from behind. Sumner Junior had holstered his gun and was holding firmly on to both of my arms.

"Get the fuck *off* me," I said, trying to pull away from him.

"Be quiet, kid," the man said. "You're gonna watch this."

Sumner Senior grabbed Alex. Now nobody was encircling KJ. But she wasn't trying to escape. She stood extremely still, red threads twirling out from underneath her fingernails, watching Birdie and the six figures behind her.

Alex was next to me, also trying to extricate himself from the constable holding him, also with no success.

Jasper faced Birdie, totally unrestrained. And then Birdie stepped to the side, and the six masked people came forward.

They didn't walk so much as *drag* against the earth, leaving trails of burnt organic blackness in their wake, so distinct that I could see it even in the dark.

"What the fuck is *this* now?" I asked, trying to look over at Alex.

"The six former Incorporations," Alex said. "From our stories. I've . . . never . . . seen them. I thought they were, like, a beautiful concept. I didn't think they were *real*—"

"But they put her in the fire!" I said. "I *saw* them! Birdie put my aunt's *body* in the fire!"

Alex shook his head. "I don't know," he said, and Sumner Senior grabbed his hair and *moved* his face.

"Shut up and watch," he said.

"Your mind is full of unhappiness, Jasper," Birdie said. "And I know what you think of me. But I've never actually wanted you to be unhappy."

"Liar, fucking *liar*," Jasper said.

"None of us have ever wanted you to be unhappy," Birdie said, ignoring him. "But there is a thing inside of you—a darkness eating at your heart—that separates you from happiness."

"I'm the only one of you who even knows what happiness *is*!" Jasper said.

"We are going to take the darkness *out* of you," Birdie said.

Then the six shrouded figures with their hidden eyes and their trails of burnt blackness were surrounding him. Jasper tried to step back, but they were too quick. Deceptively quick.

The smallest figure reached out one hand—and I realized that it wasn't gloved at all. It was *charred*. Like this child-sized thing had been thrown into a bonfire.

Jasper was pinned between the other five Incorporations and the little charred girl with the reaching hand. She stood on her tiptoes and touched her fingertips to Jasper's face.

And he *shrieked*. It was a sound I'd never heard Jasper make. The second he started to scream, I saw Alex straining against the man who held his arms. I had never wanted KJ to use the powers that were devouring her, but at that second I couldn't help it. I opened my mouth and screamed:

"*Help* him, KJ—help him. *MAKE THEM STOP!*"

I guess KJ . . . or Good Arcturus . . . had been doing something already. Because she nodded at me, just slightly.

The low staticky sound came, louder than the rain dripping down around us. The air smelled like striking lightning.

The ground started to shake. More even than during our roadway conflict with Birdie and the constables. *That* made the constables let us go. I saw Rita stumble, Mrs. Plum stagger to the side and catch herself against our stolen Range Rover. Even the little burnt girl and her five phantom cohorts slithered backward.

The voice inside my head spoke:

YOU WILL NOT TOUCH THIS ONE.

And I saw everyone else around me hearing it, too. Birdie and the constables, braced against the shaking earth, looking around. In *confusion*. It was clearly not the voice they had been hearing all their lives—the voice they had been told was Good Arcturus.

KJ's single remaining Scary Scarecrow glove slipped off her hand for the last time. The sinews of Good Arcturus wound out from underneath her fingernails, forming a protective circle around Jasper.

YOU WILL ALL DISPERSE, the voice said.

KJ's palms split open. I saw her skin rip apart, only a few little rivulets of blood running from the wounds. Red threads poured out of her hands like water. The threads began to make ropelike walls, a barrier—cutting Jasper off from the six horrible Incorporations.

"Aughhhhhh, *stop*, STOP—"

I could hear Birdie screaming. Mrs. Plum and Rita were shoved toward the perimeter of the clearing by a million advancing threads. The woods were vibrating. The *rain* was vibrating before it even reached the earth. The constables were backing away, tripping on the quaking ground. I saw Birdie stumble back, brace herself against the door of Empty Heaven.

I fell completely to the ground and moved forward on my hands and knees, made it to the wall of sinews, and pressed my hands against them as they moved. It felt like touching a pillar of snow. For me, the sinews parted. I crawled into the eye of the storm, where KJ and Jasper were. Alex stumbled in behind me, barely staying on his feet, and pulled me up.

For two seconds, maybe less, I made eye contact with KJ. I couldn't see that she was looking at me . . . but I could *feel* it.

She stood, a nightmare rendering of a Virgin Mary statue, in her scarecrow costume with her arms slightly extended and all the red force of Good Arcturus pouring from her palms like the world's biggest version of the stigmata.

And then, as the earth shook and the people shouted, she winked. Just for me. Smiled a little without opening her mouth.

I reached out for her split hand with mine.

And I heard another one of those incredibly loud *POPs*—this one close enough that it made my left ear ring, blocking out all other sound. A gunshot.

One of the Sumners—whichever one shot out the tires on the Rover, I guess—was actually a marksman. A red hole appeared in KJ's forehead.

"*KJ!*" I screamed.

KJ staggered back in slow motion, thread and blood emerging from the bullet wound and flowing into the air in a line, in defiance of gravity.

"No! *No!*" someone cried out. Birdie. They definitely weren't supposed to shoot the newest Incorporation of their god, no matter *what* KJ was getting up to.

But Alex was screaming, too, screaming his sister's name. Together, the two of us grabbed KJ before she could fall. Jasper was kneeling on the ground in front of us, holding his face where the burnt girl had caressed him. He didn't even look up when KJ was shot. It seemed like time was moving too slowly. I grabbed the front of KJ's scarecrow costume, attempting to help her stand straight. Blood drifted out from the bullet hole between her eyes, floating in the air without falling. *WE ARE ALL RIGHT*, said the voice in my head, even though KJ still felt unsteady in my arms.

"I'm going to *kill* that fucking guy," Alex said, the only time I'd ever heard him make a violent threat in my entire life, and then he looked down with a fearful expression, and dropped to the ground next to Jasper.

"Jas?" he said, trying to pull Jasper's hand away from his face. "Hey. Jasper?"

Jasper didn't move his hand at all. Or even respond.

"Shoot her again!" one of the Sumners cried to the other, and KJ, still bleeding from the hole above her eyes, whirled around.

YOU. WILL. DISPERSE, came the voice, and it was *loud*. KJ raised her arms.

The healed-over splits on her face opened up. Sinews rushed out of her cheeks, her throat, her arms—from underneath the clown costume—and then from her left eye, leaving a bloody streak of tears to match the one on her forehead.

The threads did not fuck around with building a protective wall this time. Or driving people back. Sinews simply reached out and *threw* everyone away from us in a wide radius. Birdie was tossed against the tree trunks and Mrs. Plum hurled into the wet leaves that littered the ground. The constables started to flee. The former Incorporations were pressed back toward the woods. I saw Rita— already shunted to the periphery of the clearing—escape into the trees, her expression totally blank with shock.

The ground was still shaking. I tried to call out for KJ to stop, that it was enough now, that we had a minute to get away, but my voice was lost under the endless drone of Good Arcturus's power.

Finished with their mission of driving away our attackers, the threads came back. And back and back and back, wrapping around KJ's hands and face. More and more and more. The mass of sinew, too much to be believed, rushed all around KJ's body, obscuring it for a moment.

So sorry, said the voice in my head. *Too late.*

"Wait!" I screamed. "Stop!"

Alex seemed to realize what was happening and joined in, yelling.

"They're all leaving! They're all leaving! Back off on the powers," he shouted, "you're going to *kill her!*"

But there was no stopping it. KJ disappeared into a moving world. Sinews surrounded us, blotting out my vision. And then, all at once, the thread retracted. Vanished.

Everything was quiet. The clearing was empty.

Jasper looked up just as the world stilled, his eyes wide, his hand still pressed to his cheek.

"Oh no," he whispered.

KJ was gone. Her face was gone. Nothing human remained. Just a scarecrow, made of red sinew, draped in a faceless shroud. Good Arcturus stood stiffly, bound in human skin that looked like gauze. And I understood what it was, then. Not a shield. Not a shield made from a human being to *protect* him. Nothing of the kind.

A binding spell, put in place by the witch Junie Apostle-Root, who had tricked him and stolen his only means of escape. A spell refreshed every thirty-five years. A thing to keep him chained.

A straitjacket.

"No," Alex said. He actually *touched* Good Arcturus, running his hands up the scarecrow's massive frame like a blind man. "Put it back. Put her back. Please—"

OUR TIME IS UP, AND I AM CONSTRAINED AGAIN, came the voice in my head. I CAN NO LONGER PROTECT YOU, MY FRIENDS. SHE HAS ME TRAPPED. SHE IS IN MY MIND WITH HER NEEDLE, WITH HER INEXORABLE VOICE. SHE BINDS MY LIMBS. SHE WILL USE MY POWER AGAINST YOU ALL. YOU MUST GO. NOW.

Alex dropped his hands. Nodded.

I couldn't even think. I was caught, horribly, on the fact that Good Arcturus had said *I* instead of *We*.

"Okay," Alex said hoarsely. "Guys. Jas. Can you walk?"

"I don't want to leave her," Jasper said. He did manage to get up, when I grabbed his hand and pulled. He had a black mark across one cheek that looked like spilled ink and smelled like cooked meat.

"We have to go," Alex said.

"But the doors—" Jasper said. There was something terrifyingly vague about the way he was speaking. Like he wasn't really aware.

Go, commanded the voice. *SHE KNOWS SHE CAN CONTROL ME ONCE MORE. THEY WILL RETURN VERY SOON.*

Alex started pulling us toward the sunflowers. I slipped down the wooded hill with him, Jasper between us, walking like a man in a dream.

I turned back. Good Arcturus was standing still. Trapped in his cloak. The first flashlight of one of the returning Kesuquoshians had nearly reached him. We had been so close, I thought. All three doors were *right there.*

"Come on, Dare," Alex said. He put one guiding hand on Jasper's shoulder, and disappeared into the sunflowers.

I turned away from all that remained of the girl I had loved, and ran into the darkness.

CHAPTER NINETEEN

Tuesday, October 31, 2000

It might have been that final push of magic that turned KJ into an empty shell, or it might have just been the timing: by the time we got into the sunflower fields, it was after midnight. At least according to the phone in my clown pocket. I would never know if it had been exactly twelve o'clock when KJ had disappeared and Good Arcturus had been re-chained. But I thought it might have been.

We were staying very quiet, moving with our heads low. And Alex and I had Jasper between us, kind of herding him along. He seemed really out of it—he kept touching his own face.

"We're going straight over to the Quabbin," Alex said. "Directly east. From there we can go south along the shore until we get to Rabbitville."

"Can you find your way?" I asked.

"I've done this a thousand times," Alex said, but he sounded worried. It was *so* dark, and the rain dripping down into the endless span of dead sunflowers made it feel shuttered like a room, made it seem like we were walking blindly through a field of people looking quietly down at the earth. My amethyst was in my other pocket. But it wasn't doing anything.

Some fucking magic, I thought. *Not even a little bit of help*.

"There has to be something we can do to get her back," Jasper said slowly. He had his hand to his face again.

"Right now we just have to get out," Alex said. I nodded behind them.

"There *has* to be something," Jasper said loudly. There was a dreamlike, slurry quality to his speech. He clearly wasn't all there mentally. "It can't go like this!"

"Shhh!" I said, and Alex clamped his hand over Jasper's mouth.

There were voices in the distance. I could hear them, shouting to each other. Moving through the field behind us. Making the stalks of the flowers rustle. Jasper made a noise of pain when Alex's hand pressed against his wound, and Alex took his hand away quickly. "I'm sorry," he said, and touched Jasper's unmarred cheek. "But be quiet."

I wanted to take a look at his injury, but there was no time. There were adults off to our left, shouting to each other in the dark. I didn't know if they were . . . somehow using Good Arcturus to come and find us.

Then a voice said "Maybe over here?" close enough that I could have touched them. I froze, half bent over. Alex froze too, holding Jasper still with hands to his shoulders. Jasper turned his face to me, and even in the dark I could see that his injury was spreading.

I stayed like that—fear making my heart race, my body screaming at me from being held in such an awkward way for so long—until the person moved off to the left. Away from us.

"Okay," Alex whispered. "This way."

We crept through the flowers. The smell of them, combined with the wet earth from the day of rain, was thick and cloying.

The cold had kept the dying scent muffled, but the damp brought it out, so that everything smelled like rot and moldy bouquets in vases with yellowing water, and dark soil.

Finally we came to a patch of clearing. The sound of the Kesuquoshians was far away, and I imagined that I could feel the Quabbin close to us.

"Let me see that," I said to Jasper. He tilted his face up immediately, toward the nonexistent starlight, and let me get really close to him. My hands were shaking. It was scary how pliable he was, how silent.

"Does that hurt?" I asked, and pressed lightly on his cheek. My eyes had adjusted to the dark, and I could see that the bloom of blackness had spread all the way down his cheek. And up to his eye. It felt hot to the touch.

But I couldn't make out anything more.

"Jas. Does that hurt?" I asked again, prodding his jawline.

"Yeahhh," Jasper said, sleepily and without a hint of emotion.

I looked at Alex, behind him. We both shared a silent look: we had to get the fuck out *now*. Get *him* out. Before the touch of a former Incorporation ate him alive.

"This way," Alex said. "Shouldn't be too much farther now."

We kept walking. The rain, which had already slowed to a sludgy drizzle, almost gave up the ghost. I couldn't hear anyone else in the fields.

But after a while—a really *long* while—it became clear that something was very wrong. I mean, more than the fact that everything in the entire universe was wrong. We weren't reaching the Quabbin. Even at the slowest pace with the most zigzags, it shouldn't have taken more than an hour to make it to the reservoir's edge. In fact, we weren't getting to *any*where. There was no end to the field, no border, no variation.

"Okay," I said. "This isn't working. I'm calling 911—"

"They won't *do* anything," Alex said.

"—and telling them we're *lost* in the woods around the Quabbin Reservoir," I said. "Nothing about Good Arcturus. I think they'll come for a standard lost hiker call, right?"

"Maybe," Alex said. "I hope?"

I dialed 911. The call took a long minute to connect, ringing through on a staticky line. Then the phone picked up.

"*I'll be reborn, me and my lying tongue. My weeping eyes, my bleeding hands, my awful fate,*" Dexter sang. I could hear the famous riff from "Later, Adrian" playing in the background. But this time I was not deterred.

"I CAN'T HEAR ON THIS SIDE, BAD CONNECTION, BUT I NEED SOMEONE TO SEND POLICE," I talk-shouted. "WE ARE LOST ON THE WESTERN SIDE OF THE QUABBIN NEAR ROUTE 202, THREE TEENAGERS. PLEASE SEND HELP. WE NEED A SEARCH PARTY, WE CAN'T FIND THE ROAD!"

Alex was looking at me like I was off my fucking gourd. He held one finger to his mouth in a *keep it down* gesture, and I thrust the phone at him.

"*You* talk to them," I said.

Alex took the phone. "Hey, um, we need help?" he said. "Hello?"

Then he held the phone away from his ear and looked at me. "It's just ringing forever. There's nobody there—"

"Fuck, fuck, shit! Oh my fucking god!" I said. "I hate this fucking place!"

"Told you," Jasper said absently.

Then there was a *new* sound.

A really quiet sound. It was so quiet that it almost didn't register. I looked over at Alex, who started to walk backward slowly. I followed him, pushing Jasper along as I went.

Then, when I was starting to think I had imagined it, the sound came again.

It wasn't the sound of the villagers hunting us through the sunflower stalks. It was a little, tiny, thick, wet sound: a drop of heavy water hitting pavement. It stopped again immediately when we stilled.

Like whatever was making the sound wanted to hide the fact that it was there.

Alex looked at me and then grabbed Jasper's hand.

"Run!" he said.

I did, following him as he dragged Jasper along. We were full-on sprinting away from the sound of the thing that was hiding from us, crashing through the bent leaves and downed stalks and high weeds, and on that fresh wave of adrenaline I felt like I could go for *hours*—

And then we ran out into the clearing with the black house.

It was lit up from inside. The windows shone with a crimson light so bright that it almost hurt to look at. The clearing literally glowed with the house's inner illumination. The sky above us was clouded and flat with rain, so it looked like the black house took up the entire length from the earth to the heavens.

"We shouldn't be here," Jasper murmured. "We shouldn't *be* here, shouldn't *be* here—"

There were no villagers. There was no sign at all of Good Arcturus. But the double front doors of the house, at the end of the slate walkway, were open. Just a crack.

Then, as we turned in the center of the clearing, they came through the sunflowers, bringing their soft wet sounds and the smell of burning. The six previous Incorporations.

They moved toward us with their masked faces and the glint of teeth and eyes behind the masks, making no sound with their invisible mouths.

Jasper screamed as they got closer, and I saw the black wound on his face actually *moving*, spreading like octopus arms down his throat and over his eye, leaving the smell of hot flesh as it went.

They were surrounding us from all sides. Backing us up against the house. And through the slit in the doors I saw Good Arcturus, bent down in the doorframe, perfectly still, with no face at all.

"Make them *stop*!" I screamed—but the scarecrow couldn't help me then like he'd helped us before. He didn't move even a single sinew. He might as well have been a doll—he was powerless to stop this. In fact his own power was probably *facilitating* it.

The tallest of the Incorporations reached us, and held its blackened hands out to Jasper, who backed up until he was flat against one red-lit front window.

And then I had an idea. I reached into my pocket and pulled out my amethyst. It was just a pretty rock, but it could be more. If I needed it to be. I held it up in my left hand and shouted what little I could remember of Friday and Flora's spell at the things that had once been people.

"In our smallness," I said, waving the crystal back and forth, "in our *nothingness*! In our power, in our vastness, oh my god, this heart an abyss, *please*, help me, someone—"

An Incorporation in the middle of the group—it had maybe been a young woman, once, but now it was just a shape—knocked into my wrist with one hand. The touch of its fingers burned instantly, the worst pain I had ever experienced, and I screamed. My wrist felt like it was full of hot knives. The amethyst fell from my grip and skittered into the cracked-open door, tumbling past the body of Good Arcturus into the red void.

Then the Incorporation turned away from me. All six of the figures surrounded Jasper, who tried to fend them off with both hands. I could see his palms blistering as he struck out at them. Slowly, like he was too exhausted to keep fighting.

None of the Incorporations spoke. None of them said a single word. But the air was filled with vibration, coming from inside the black house—and their veiled teeth clacked together, like the six of them were communicating something with their chattering.

"Please help me—" Jasper said weakly, and Alex and I both tried to shove the burning creatures away from him.

"GET OFF, GET OFF HIM!" Alex said, snatching at their hands until his own hands started to turn red and bubble with heat.

But the silent group of Incorporations was inexorable. They surrounded Jasper, pushing him toward the slitted doors where the scarecrow watched. Every place one of the Incorporations touched him left behind a black mark, burning his costume and his skin alike.

I reached through the forest of red-hot limbs and grabbed on to Jasper's right hand.

Alex grabbed Jasper's other hand. I watched him thread their fingers together.

"PULL!" I shouted, and we both pulled on Jasper's arms until he screamed, while the things dragged him in the opposite direction.

The Incorporations didn't care that two people were trying to wrench their victim away from them. They didn't even acknowledge us after the one knocked my amethyst away. We reached the doors, and they started to pull Jasper through. I was dragged along, holding his hand. "Jasper," I shouted, over the buzz in the air, "you have to try! *Fight them!*"

It was like my words woke Jasper up from whatever spell the touch of the Incorporations had placed him under. He looked at me from his half-burnt face, his eyes sharp for the first time in hours. Then he glanced down, at where Alex and I held his hands. The mass of figures had him almost inside the house. I was halfway in too, along for the ride.

"Guys," Jasper said. "Guys!"

"Come on, *pull!*" Alex said.

"I love you both, okay?" Jasper said. "I love you so much. And KJ. More than anything."

Alex realized what that meant before I did.

"No," he shouted. "No, *don't—*"

Jasper let go of both our hands.

"Wait!" I screamed, and for the second time in five days someone I loved was dragged inside the black house. I saw one final glimpse of Good Arcturus, leaning against the frame, as Jasper was spirited into the red beyond.

CHAPTER TWENTY

Tuesday, October 31, 2000

The doors slammed shut, a second too late for Alex, who threw himself against them, rattling the handles, pounding on the wood until it shook. It shook, but it didn't give.

And then the buzzing got so loud that we both fell back, with our hands over our ears, crawling away from the deafening vibration and the house that seemed to produce it. Tears leaked from my eyes. The red light from inside the house spilled out, growing brighter and brighter, until it was absolutely blinding, stripped of all color. The whole world was lit up like daylight. Everything was reduced to a wall of brightness and sound. I was screaming against the sound. I felt Alex's hand touch my wrist, feeling for me in the dirt of the clearing. I took my hand away from one ear and grabbed his fingers. I was going to go deaf, blind, and I didn't care if only it would make the pain of the light and sound stop.

And then it did stop. All at once.

Or *actually* what happened was that I lost consciousness. For a while, I'm not sure how long, I laid there in the dirt.

By the time I woke up it was almost morning. I opened my eyes, and for a scary second everything was blurry.

Then my vision adjusted. I looked around. Alex was next to me on the ground, and I shook his shoulder, afraid he was dead. But his eyes fluttered open.

Where the black house had been was just an ancient shell. Stripped to the foundations. Maybe it had once been a house, but now it was only an old skeleton of wood and stone. The sky had cleared up from the rain, and there was a gray glow to the world that heralded a not-too-distant sunrise. In that gray light, I could see clear from one side of the ruined house to the other. No rooms, no doors, no second floor. No windows. Just the suggestion of a wall and an old stone foundation.

It looked a lot like the ruins of Empty Heaven, actually.

"Where . . . ?" Alex said. He got to his knees, slowly, and then stood up with a stagger. I saw that a little blood had leaked from one of his ears. I felt like both my eardrums had been seconds away from rupturing. When I touched my face, there was flaky dried blood around my nose.

The force of the house disappearing—or the culmination of the Great Harvest Hallow—had probably come close to claiming my life, and Alex's.

Then all *four* of us would be dead.

Alex helped me up with arms that seemed to have very little strength in them. We walked around the foundation together, silently. Alex had tears in his eyes. He scrubbed at his face with the back of one dirt-covered, blistered hand.

"You won't find them," came a voice. "The black house will not reveal itself again. Not to you, certainly. And not for another thirty-five years."

Alex and I both turned, and saw Birdie standing at the edge of the clearing, holding a basket of chrysanthemums, watching us. Putting out the flowers for the dead. She looked a little wary.

The constables were not there. Only Rita, Birdie, and Mrs. Plum. And for a second, beneath her pinched expression and her dilated eyes, I swore that Mrs. Plum looked . . . sad.

Then it was gone. Maybe I'd only imagined it.

The earliest part of the morning shrouded the ground in a low layer of mist. I stepped through the fog with my hands out, ready to run or fight if I had to.

Alex stood just next to me. He was still crying, but he balled his hands into fists instead of wiping his tears. His expression, when he looked at the adults who faced us, was as close to hatred as I could imagine it ever being.

"You—you killed them! You fucking *killed* them!" Alex said. "You're all *monsters*—"

"We didn't kill anyone, Alex," Birdie said.

I chose to ignore that bullshit statement.

"So now what happens? Do you feed us to the house, too? Maybe to those burning *things*?" I asked.

"Nothing happens," Mrs. Plum said, softly. "It was awful, what's been going on. We can all go back to our good lives now."

"Oh, awesome," I said faintly. I pictured KJ's empty skin, wrapped around a scarecrow, and Jasper, sinking forever into the red darkness of the house. Alone except for the burnt things. I wanted to run. But Alex approached them, his face twisted into contempt so sharp that it cut to look at.

"Is this worth it?" he asked. "For your precious town? Your utopia, where everyone is trapped in their own mind? Is it worth people dying? Is it worth protecting?"

He was asking Birdie, I think. But it was Rita who answered.

"Baby," she said. "Alex. If there was any way to choose, you know I never would have let the needle choose Kahie. I don't want to lose you, too."

"KJ," I said. "She didn't like that name. That was a guy's name. Her girl name was KJ."

"Alex," Rita said, ignoring me, "it's *one* person's life against the happiness and health of *every single person* in Kesuquosh. Not even a life being ended—just being altered for the greater good. Please—"

"Don't talk to me, Mom," Alex said. "I think I'm done with you."

"You're all . . . you're all monsters," I said.

Alex nodded. His lean face dropped some of its anger. A little bit of horror crept into his expression, a little bit of despair. "Darian's right. You're monsters. You don't even know you are. I can't live with any of it. And you—you're all making him into a slave, into a *slave*, on top of everything! He doesn't even *belong* here!"

"Do you mean Good Arcturus?" Birdie asked, incredulity all over her sweet little face. "*Really?* He is our guardian. He loves us—"

"He's not *your guardian*. He's a traveler," I said. "He tried to help us. Even after what all of you did to him."

"We haven't done anything to Him," Mrs. Plum said. "He chose us. To protect, to watch over. It's always been this way. None of you can seem to understand—"

"Shut up," I said in the tone I'd always wanted to take with Jasper's mom, but never been able to, because before, things like "manners" had seemed to matter. Now, of course, it was all out the window. "Shut up, you stupid asshole, you killed your fucking *kid*. Shut up."

"And now you either kill us, too, or you let us go," Alex said. He put one arm around my shoulders. "I'm not staying here until I go back to how I was before."

"We're not going to *kill* you," Birdie said. She sounded appalled. Like they hadn't literally murdered Jasper.

"Okay," Alex said. "Then you let us go."

"*Will* you let us go?" I asked. My voice only shook a tiny bit.

"Of course," Birdie said. She looked at me. Scrutinized me, a little, like she had during the Banquet of the Needle. "Of course you may go. I don't . . . believe you should come back."

"Come on," Alex said. "They're never going to understand. Let's go."

"Can you just tell me one thing?" I asked as we started to walk away.

"If we can," Birdie said. But her tone—it was like she'd already dismissed our conversation and was irritated that I was bringing it up again. Like it was all so forgettable.

"Why did KJ manage to run away with Good Arcturus?" I asked. "The Incorporation never did that before, right?"

"I don't—"

"Because she was my baby," Rita said. "She was special." She looked at me, her pretty face etched with sorrow.

I didn't know what to say to that.

KJ *was* special. I loved her so, so much. And now she was gone.

Gone. I felt something crushing me, keeping me from speaking. Unshed tears, maybe, or unvoiced screaming. Begging. I wanted her back. I wanted Jasper back. I wanted to undo everything. I wanted to fight these blank people, to make them sorry, tear them all limb from limb. I hated them. I couldn't believe any of this was *real*.

But I couldn't talk. And Rita just shook her head, and went to scatter chrysanthemums with the others.

So Alex and I walked back through the dead and dying fields as the sun rose and the low mist burned away. It was easy to find our way out now. We got to the Range Rover with no problem.

"The doors are gone," I said. Someone had untied them from the roof and taken them away. Now we would never find them. Except for the door to the church. That was still hanging there.

The car was obviously undriveable. I took my bag out of it, and my jacket. On the seat was KJ's red cloak, which I left there, and peeking out of one pocket were her Newports, which she hadn't touched since Good Arcturus had moved into her brain . . . and her purple Soundgarden beanie. I reached out, picked it up. Started crying. Put the beanie on my head, and choked back my tears as much as I could.

"Why didn't he want me to go with him?" Alex asked suddenly.

"What?" I said, slamming the car door. We started walking toward Deep River Road.

"He let me go. I would have gone into the darkness with him," Alex said. "Or the *redness*. Whatever. I would've done it. I was *ready* to do it. But he let go of my hand. I thought he . . . I thought we . . ."

I don't want to die without you, Dexter said in my head.

"If someone *really* loves you, they don't want you to die with them," I said. "They want you to live."

"Oh," Alex said, and the flatness of his acknowledgment broke me out of myself a little.

I looked at him. My thoughts were slow. Sticky with shock. My head hurt. But I recognized the look on his face. No—not the look, exactly. But the feeling. Not just because I was feeling it. Because I was *remembering*. Remembering a December day in New York when I was forever changed. Seeing a change in him now.

Maybe it would have been better for him if KJ had never set him free. He had been happy during the Banquet of the Needle. It had been false. But he'd felt no pain.

Don't you dare say you love Big Brother, Jasper murmured in my memory.

"Al," I said. "Hey. Alex. Alex. Are you—"

Okay, I was going to ask. But that was stupid. He was never going to be okay.

I took his hand and he let me. Squeezed it, even though it hurt my blistered palms. He didn't squeeze back, but he didn't let go, either. We walked down the road together, and I waited for him to fall apart. But he just looked up above me at the trees, his expression muted and distant.

When we reached the common, everything was beautiful again. Restored in the new sunlight. Leaves were vibrant and perfect, yards and houses immaculate. The town slept peacefully as the dawn broke.

At the turn onto my road, Alex dropped my hand.

"This is where I leave you," he said, like he was reciting a line in a play. His mouth was a flat line. Dark circles under his dry eyes.

I reached out and grabbed the sleeve of his grime-encrusted flannel shirt.

"No. I think you're still in shock, Al."

"That's probably for the best," he said, and offered me a scary and unconvincing smile. Like a corpse with lips drawn back in a rictus of death. "I can think about my exit strategy. Gotta bail on this place. You dig?"

"No. Uh-uh. Come with me," I said. "Dan and I will take you away with us. We can go to the cops . . . we can try to mount a case, anyway. Even with Good Arcturus's protection, there are still two kids missing. That has to count for something."

But Alex shook his head. "That's really nice. I'm grateful. But I'm not coming with you."

"Al, *please*—"

"No, Darian," Alex said. Finality in his tone. "I need to be alone. I know you . . . I know you must know what that's like."

It's not so good to be alone, actually, I thought. *Trust me. I have experience.*

But I couldn't imagine what he was going through. Not *really*. I still had Senovak. And Ed. And he had nothing. Except me . . . and he didn't want me around.

"Where are you going to go?" I asked.

"I don't know," Alex said. He wouldn't look me in the eyes. "Maybe to Judy and Surendra. Make sure they're all right. And then away. I just have to get away."

"But then you'll call me, right?" I asked. I started to cry again, I couldn't help it. "You'll call me. And we can come and get you. You can come to New York. We can . . . be there together."

I wished badly that he would come with me. Alex looked like he was a million miles from everything.

"Sure, of course," Alex said, with a ghost of his old smile. "That sounds good. I just have to figure out who I am for a little bit."

When he noticed my tears, he hesitated for a second. Then added, "I'll call you. Next week. Okay?"

Needless to say, that never happened.

"You're going to have to come back," I said, wiping my face. "For the next—"

"Harvest Hallow, yeah, I know," Alex said. "And the next one. Like, forever."

"You're really not going to come with me?" I asked.

"I just need to be alone for a while," Alex said. I still believed, in my heart, that after losing your sister and your best friend (true love?) in one day, all while feeling *real* feelings for the first time, the last thing in the world that you should do was *be alone*. But I could tell that Alex wasn't going to listen.

"At least take some money with you," I said, and dug around in my bag until I found the wad of emergency cash Senovak had left with me. I handed it to him.

"I can take money out of the restaurant," Alex said, but I shook my head.

"*Please* take it. I feel . . . I feel so fucked up about you leaving."

He nodded, stuffed the money in his pocket. "I'm going to go home and pack some stuff. Then head out."

"Dan should be back to get me soon," I said. "Are you sure—"

"I'm sure. Goodbye, Dare," Alex said, and bent down to hug me really tightly.

I hugged him back. I felt hollowed out inside.

"I love you," he said, into my shoulder.

"I love you more," I said.

"Not possible, my dude," Alex said.

Then he straightened up and walked away.

"Alex?" I said when he was a few paces from me. He turned around, hands in his pockets.

"Yeah?" he asked.

"I'm sorry we couldn't save them," I said.

Alex nodded. "It wasn't your fault, Darian," he said. "Don't carry this around with you. Okay?"

"Oh yeah, no problem," I said. Alex ignored my flagrant sarcasm. He turned away.

With his back to me, he seemed like a stranger. And I guess he was, in a way. I'd never really known him until Saturday.

I watched him go until he disappeared around a bend in Good Earth Way and out of my view. Then I walked back to Number 19. Alone.

Alone in the one place where I *hadn't* been alone. For a little while.

I took a shower. Packed my stuff. Put bandages over my worst blisters. Washed out the chipped Garfield mug that Jasper had ashed his Djarums into approximately a thousand years earlier.

Outside, Dexter leaned against the porch railing and smiled at me through the windows. He was shuffling his favorite deck of tarot cards. Picking cards out one by one. When I looked at him, he turned his wrist and showed me The Lovers, his smile growing so wide it almost split his face.

I had believed, for a few summers, that I wasn't actually alone with Dexter. I'd made myself believe it. Or maybe they had.

KJ and Jasper and Alex.

My friends.

But Dexter had known. I saw it in his face as he watched me from the porch. He'd known that we were always going to end up alone together.

Told you, that smile said. *You should've come with me when you had the chance. Into the darkness. I mean the redness.*

When Senovak came back, I was ready to go. Normally I bitched about having to leave Kesuquosh. But this time, I was good. I knew I was never coming back. And Senovak was too emotionally drained from burying his boyfriend to look into my mood closely.

How could I tell him about my Halloween?

I would have tried, for Alex's sake, if he had stayed with me. But I was afraid. Still afraid of the Kesuquoshians. Afraid of *Junie*, whether she was Birdie or not, orchestrating some further punishment. If I didn't tell Senovak anything, then he was safe. If we left and never came back, this place couldn't hurt me anymore. Everything had been taken from Alex. I couldn't lose Senovak.

On our way out, as it was getting dark, I leaned against the passenger's-side window and watched Good Earth Way go by. K-Family Pizza, with the lit-up neon slice. The Plum farmhouse. The sunflower fields. And finally the two signs: the official one, and KESUQUOSH: HOME OF SQUASH!

"Did you say goodbye to your friends?" Senovak asked me as we crossed the town line.

"Yeah," I said. "I said goodbye to them."

PART THREE

THE HANGED MAN

CHAPTER TWENTY-ONE

Wednesday, September 12, 2001

When Alex—this *new* Alex, who was gaunt and covered in track marks and somehow, even with all of that, still more real than the smiling, placid, dark-eyed kid I'd spent all my most formative summers with—showed me the gun in his bag and said he was "going to kill *her*," I still didn't understand his plan.

The stress of being in the middle of the city when the Twin Towers fell—combined immediately with the stress of going back to the place where KJ and Jasper had died—compounded *further* by the shock of seeing Alex again—had made me a little slow to comprehend.

"Kill *her*?" I asked, chasing him along.

"Yeah," Alex said, not looking at me. Still heading toward the town hall building, which was just as gorgeous and immaculate as it had been on that horrible Halloween morning eleven months earlier. "Like I said. I still love them all, even if I hate them for what they were complicit in. And I had this idea that killing her might set them all free. Even Good Arcturus."

"Her? Do you mean *Birdie*?" I asked. We were almost at the double staircase that led up to the quaint town hall building.

"I mean Junie Apostle-Root," Alex said. "But yes. I hate the idea of killing anyone, you know? Even her. But the opportunity to steal a gun from this dealer—this guy Chris P., Crispy—like, presented itself. So I took it. I thought about it. And I prayed for a sign, a sign so big and so clear that I couldn't mistake it for anything else. And then, well, you know. Yesterday."

"You prayed? To *what*?" I asked. I got in front of him again, making him stop with his forward march.

"The god all the rest of the world believes in," Alex said. He glared at the ground, not meeting my eyes.

"Okay. There isn't one single god that everyone in the world besides Kesuquoshians believe in. And I don't believe in *any* god," I said.

"Well, why not?" Alex asked stubbornly. "Everything might be true."

He tried to step around me, and I stepped with him, blocking his path.

"Think about this, Al, okay? I wouldn't pray to a god that would kill hundreds of people in a city just to give me a sign that it was okay to shoot *one* woman. That would be an *evil* god. I—"

"This is why I didn't want you here with me!" Alex raked one hand over his skull like he'd been expecting to find his long hair still there. "I don't need you making me feel all bad by being—"

"By being reasonable?" I asked. Alex deflated then, and I took the opportunity to grab the arm that wasn't steadying his drawstring backpack.

"I know it's been so bad for you, I know," I said, trying to get him to look at me. "I shouldn't have let you leave last year. I would never have let you go if I'd been thinking more clearly. But we're together now and we can get through it without killing any-body. Okay?"

"I don't want to kill anyone," Alex whispered. He was looking down at the sidewalk again. "But I can't *stand* it. Every day Jasper and KJ are the first thing I think about when I wake up and the last thing I think about before I go to sleep. Even drugs can't really take it away."

"If Birdie really *is* Junie Apostle-Root," I said, "we can talk about what to do then. But murderous revenge isn't going to bring them back. The only thing that will happen is you'll lose yourself."

Alex finally met my eyes, and to my *endless* relief, I saw that he was giving in. "Okay," he said. "Fine. Okay. Why are you so good at being reasonable?"

"I've always been the reasonable one," I said. "That's why—"

"Alex? Rocks around us . . . Alex!" We both turned around. The oldest of the Kobayashi-Jenetopolous kids, Isabella, was hustling toward us as quickly as she could. Which wasn't super quickly—she looked like she was eight months pregnant.

"Hey. Izzy," Alex said, and he looked emotional at the sight of her . . . and fully distracted, for the moment. Isabella reached him and threw herself into his arms, while Alex lightly patted her back.

"We missed you so much!" Isabella said. "Mom is gonna freak, I can't wait for her to see you, and I got *married*, and—"

"Wow," Alex said. "You're *really* pregnant, huh?"

Isabella laughed, and hugged him tighter, and I used their reunion to my advantage.

"I'll go check out that thing in the town hall," I said, and lifted Alex's bag away from his arm. I didn't want him carrying a gun through the village. I mean, I don't want anyone carrying a gun, but someone like Senovak having one seemed less likely to end in the unnecessary loss of human life than Alex, completely unstable, toting a firearm around in his backpack. I didn't even know if it was loaded, and I was too afraid of touching it to check.

Alex made a gesture like he was going to grab the drawstring bag out of my hands, but Isabella was in his way. And he was at least with it enough to not have a tug-of-war over the bag with the gun in it in front of his heavily pregnant sister.

"Wait," Alex said.

"Go say hi to your family," I told him. "I'll talk to Birdie. I'll meet you at your house when I'm done."

Isabella glanced over at me like she had legitimately just noticed I was there. Her dilated eyes kind of looked me up and down and then dismissed me.

"Oh. Hi, Darian," she said, with less than zero enthusiasm.

"Buongiorno," I said.

"Are you sure?" Alex asked.

"I'm *sure*," I said. Then I walked away before he could try anything crazy, and paused at the double stairs into the town hall building. I didn't want to go in there. I was scared to see Birdie. I turned back and saw Alex getting led down the street. "Okay," I said, and pushed the door open.

Inside the town hall was small and quaint, of course, with old plaster walls and the enormous folk art painting of Junie Apostle-Root and Good Arcturus dominating the space. Hunter Warren was sitting at the receptionist's desk chatting with Councilman Grandpa, the guy who'd retold the (patently untrue) origin myth at the Banquet of the Needle. They both fell silent when I walked over. I guess I had been expecting hostility, but they just looked at me like I was kind of impolitely showing up where I shouldn't be: a wedding crasher, maybe, or a loud drunk guy at a movie theater.

"I need to speak to Birdie Plum," I said, pretending like I had never met either of them before. I had no idea *what* I was going to say to Birdie when I did see her—or how I would even get her to admit to being Junie, when she hadn't so far—but I'd told Alex I would do it.

"With Birdie?" Hunter asked.

"I'm sure she's busy with the, like, fallout from the attack, but I need to see her," I said. "We have big stuff to discuss."

"The *attack*?" Councilman Grandpa asked. He looked at me like I might be a little insane.

I *felt* a little insane. "Um. Yes? The World Trade Center just got blown up? Shouldn't the town government be, uh, concerned?"

"Oh yeah, that thing in New York," Hunter said. "Or was it DC?"

"It was both," I said. The two of them stared at me with their dark eyes. They did not give one single fuck about what had happened yesterday. And why should they? It didn't matter here.

"I remember you, little miss," Councilman Grandpa said. "I thought Birdie said you weren't supposed to come back to our village."

"Yeahhh. You can take that up with Daniel Senovak," I said. "Or better yet, Ed Arden. I need to speak to the First Selectwoman."

"Birdie has stepped down," Gramps said, looking at me. "A few months ago, after her accident. *I* am the First Selectman now. You can find her at home if you need to speak to her so badly."

"Her accident?" I asked. "What happened?"

"She fell," the First Selectman said, "and hit her head."

CHAPTER TWENTY-TWO

Wednesday, September 12, 2001

Birdie lived in a small but well-appointed old house a few hundred yards down Good Earth Way, painted a rich dark blue with white trim. The plaque said it was built in 1801. The flower boxes were full of dark red chrysanthemums. All the curtains were drawn. I went up and knocked on the front door. *What the fuck am I doing here?* I thought.

It occurred to me that it was no longer about going along with Alex until he got over his weird murder impulse psychosis. I needed to know what was going on.

It took a long time for Birdie to answer the door. When she did, we looked at each other assessingly. She looked the same—except for her eyes. When she opened the door against the bright afternoon sun, her pupils constricted into tight little dots.

"Miss Sabine," she said. "I didn't think you would ever come back here."

"Yeah, well, I'm still a minor, so I'm required to do what the big people say," I said. "I need to talk to you."

Birdie looked left and right down the street and then let me in.

Inside, she had the television on in the kitchen—it was tuned to coverage about the terrorist attacks. I would have bet anything that she was the only person in all of Kesuquosh who was watching the news for updates.

She stood at one end of the kitchen, leaning against the counter with her arms crossed.

"What was it you wanted?" Birdie was trying to be everything she actually *had* been the year before: brisk, cool, adult, in charge. But I could see the emotion under the facade. She was *freaked*— and I didn't think it was because of me.

"Alex Kobayashi came home today," I said. "Not with me. On his own. I just had to talk him out of *assassinating* you. Because he believes that you're Junie, from the old story about Good Arcturus, and that you've been holding this whole town hostage to your whims for like, centuries." I paused, looking at her face. Birdie looked back at me with a carefully blank expression.

"But I don't think you're Junie, not anymore," I said. "How did you hit your head?"

Birdie looked away from me, out the window over the sink. "I don't know. It was odd. I was at the top of my stairs and I just missed a step. That was a few months ago. I had to go to the hospital. But sometimes I think that maybe I did it on purpose. After serving her for so long . . ."

"Her. Yeah. Who *is* she?" I asked.

Birdie looked over at me. "How did your little group come to know so much, anyway?" she asked.

"Jasper tried to tell you last year. It was because of Good Arcturus," I said. "We believed that he was the monster, at first. But he was being controlled. By *her*. And we figured, like because of the stuff he said, that this woman who was his jailer had been around for a long time. So we ended up thinking it was Junie Apostle-Root, from the stories."

Birdie nodded.

"We were right?" I asked. We had fucked up literally every-thing we'd tried to do so spectacularly that I was surprised we'd been right about *anything*.

"Yes," Birdie said.

"You want to elaborate on that?" I asked, and Birdie paused for a second. Thinking about it.

"I was her—her helper, I guess you could say. And her watch-dog. She always has someone around to run the town, do the prac-tical things," Birdie said. "And she took me under her wing when I was just a girl. She loves children, always adopting them as her own. She's very maternal that way. Family-oriented. Hates being alone. But now that I can't hear his voice, she's gotten a new helper."

"It's not *his* voice," I said. "That's just propaganda. Listen, we all talked about this . . . this voice of Kesuquosh. Which is not the voice of Good Arcturus. Good Arcturus is just amplifying what his jailer wants to say. *She*, KJ kept saying. She—*Junie*, I guess—what you all hear is *her* voice, her desires. She uses Good Arcturus's power to keep everyone complacent."

"And to live forever," Birdie said. "I'm fifty-six. She's never been a day older than she was when I was born. But nobody ever notices."

"Birdie . . ." I stared at her, this woman I had despised, trying to figure out if she could be trusted. With her pale blue eyes look-ing normal and her hair a little mussed, it was easier to see how she and Jasper were related. "I have a gun. I mean, Alex does. It's in this bag. Where can we find Junie? Is she out in the sunflower fields? Is she in the black house?"

Birdie laughed. Her voice still had that girlish lilt to it.

"You can't kill her with a *gun*," she said. "You can't kill her at *all*. Don't you think other people have tried? My nephew wasn't the first to ever understand the situation wasn't as rosy as it all seemed."

"Now you know it too," I said.

"Yes. If I'd known then what I know now, I would have helped him."

The way Birdie said that made me believe her.

"Where can we find Junie?" I asked again. "Where is she?"

"Don't you know?" Birdie asked, looking honestly surprised. "I thought you were a smart girl."

"Well, I'm a stupid girl, actually, so explain it to me," I said. "Please."

"It's so obvious," Birdie said. "She never *acts* like the rest of us, even though she hides her eyes. Makes them look like everyone else. But she gives it away in a million places. Even her current name. It's a joke. An anagram of her *original* name. Junie Apostle-Root."

"What *is* the anagram?" I asked.

"Rita Jenetopolous," Birdie said. "Of course."

CHAPTER TWENTY-THREE

Wednesday, September 12, 2001

"No," I said. I honestly didn't believe her *at all* for a second. "Wait. No. Rita's like the only decent person in this whole town!"

"One might even say she's the only *person* in the whole town," Birdie said. "I adored her, you know. For decades. She was like a mother to me. But sometimes I would have this awful feeling that what we were doing was *wrong* . . . just for a moment. Then the voice would whisk that doubt away again."

"No. She runs a *pizza place*," I said. "She's not an immortal witch. She runs a pizza place!"

"She has the belonging she always wanted," Birdie said. "No big dreams of power or incredible wealth. She doesn't even want to run *Kesuquosh*. She has a community that accepts her, with no conflicts, no disruptions—save what you and your friends did—no exile, no isolation. Forever. And she likes to cook. Always has."

"No, no, no *way*," I said. I felt like the room had gone wobbly. "If that were true, like, she would never have picked her own kid to be the next Incorporation!"

"You're right, she never would have," Birdie said. "In fact I think she was devastated. Even people who do evil can be devastated.

328

But when the magic required to do the binding ritual is so power-ful, you pay the price of chance. There is a loss of control. It has to be conducted in a specific way, to chain a being with so much more power than we have. That's why everyone has to be there. That's why all the pomp and circumstance. That's why the towns-people are rewarded with death if they don't participate. It makes the whole thing *run*. Once the Needle had been passed to a new Incorporation, not even the creator of the spell could go against it."

"But KJ," I said. "KJ managed to work around the rules. For a little bit. She and Good Arcturus escaped with us."

"Yes," Birdie agreed. "I don't know how. Something made her different from the others. Different enough to keep her *self* about her."

In our smallness and our nothingness, we can slip beneath, KJ had said to me last year.

"It's a prison for him," I said. "You know that, right? The Incor-poration doesn't protect Good Arcturus from our world. The shield, the flesh . . . I think it chains him *to* our world. So he can't get back to his . . . traveling cloak, or whatever, and escape."

"I never thought that before. I thought we were saving him the way he saved us," Birdie said. "But now I understand. We are . . . monsters."

"If it's really *Rita* behind this," I said, "she's the actual monster. The rest of you are victims."

Birdie looked at me. She seemed almost nice at that moment, and sad. Scared. I saw another person, like Alex, not used to being a whole person.

"I can't believe I'm talking to you about this," she admitted, and then she sat down on one of the stools at her tasteful kitchen island. Put her head in her hands. Her narrow shoulders collapsed inward. I was about to go over to her when she started talking again, through her hands. Her voice was strained.

"My entire life was turned into something different when I . . . when I fell. Even speaking about her in this way feels—almost sacrilegious."

I was still numb. Disbelieving. And yet it—it made sense. I mean, it didn't make sense, but I could see it.

"Alex is with her now," I said. "Oh no. Oh shit. Is he safe?"

"I don't think he can be put back, after he's been . . . you know," Birdie said, lifting her head.

"Un-brainwashed?" I said.

Birdie nodded uncomfortably and wiped her eyes. "Or else she would have surely done it to me. And Jasper. And a few others, down the years, who came back to themselves."

"Like my mom," I said.

"Yes," Birdie said, with a weight to her voice that made her sound like a real person who understood real pain. "There's no going back. Unless she chooses to *censure* Alex, but I don't think she will. She couldn't bring herself to do it last year, even at the council's recommendation—"

"Why would they even try to make her do that?" I asked. "Their leader?"

"She *isn't* their leader. Or. Well. She doesn't want to be. Only her helper ever knows what her role in all of this is."

"But she thinks she's special. That's why she let Jasper get censured but not Alex."

"It wasn't her choice to make. Usually she doesn't interfere with town business. I think Jasper's censure actually bothered her, at first. It's a drastic measure. You have to call on all the Incorporations that have ever been. I'd never seen it done before. And I felt that it was justified, then. That he really was threatening Good Arcturus, and the happiness we'd built."

I thought of the possibility, however slim, of Alex being dragged away by those burning creatures into the redness. "I have to go," I said. "I can't leave him with her."

"I don't know what you're thinking you can do, but do *not* attempt it," Birdie said. "If Alex smiles and nods and attends the next Harvest Hallow, he should be fine. She's had other families over the centuries, and I believe she has honestly mourned them when she's outlived them. Rita loves her children. She wouldn't hurt him unless she felt he was a threat to her life."

"Can you hide this, please?" I asked, and thrust the backpack with the gun in it at her. "Be careful. I don't know if it's loaded."

Birdie took the bag from my hand, and I booked it out into the road, leaving behind the darkness of her closed-off home. I ran down the street in the brilliant sunshine. I was going toward the Kobayashi-Jenetopolous house, but then I passed K-Family Pizza—or *almost* passed it—and skidded to a stop in front of the big plate-glass windows.

Senovak was *sitting* in there. Like, waiting for a pizza. In a booth.

"Oh my fucking god, Dan," I said, under my breath.

I walked in. My heart was pounding.

"Didn't I just get rid of you?" I asked, trying to make my voice lighthearted and playful.

Senovak looked at me so nonchalantly that I knew it was bullshit. It made me want to fucking scream. He was spying on me.

He knew something was up, even if he didn't know what. "I was peckish," he said. "Dropped off the bags and thought I'd grab a bite to eat."

"We ate in Rabbitville like *two hours ago*," I said.

Senovak met my glare with a look of placid innocence. "I was still hungry."

"Right," I said.

"Where were you, anyway?" he asked, his voice deceptively mild.

"Just taking a little walk in the sunshine," I said.

"You missed the big reunion," Senovak said. "Alex and Ken and the little sister and the oldest sister. It was very touching."

"Where are they?" I asked.

"They went out back to talk," Senovak said.

"They're out back?" I asked. "Where's *Rita*?"

"They said she'd be here soon," Senovak said. "She's out doing a delivery. Where's the girl? Where is my dear old Professor Plum?"

"I don't know," I said. The more dire the situation became, the more I wanted to let Senovak in on everything, even if it *did* make him think I was crazy. At the same time, the more dire the situation became, the more I wanted to keep him safe by keeping him out of it. "I don't talk to them anymore, remember?"

Then I went around the counter and through the kitchen. A few of the guys working there recognized me and waved. I slipped past all of them, past the storeroom, and out the back door onto the green strip of lawn that ran behind the businesses on Good Earth Way, broken up by neat gravel driveways. Down the street, I could see the backyard of the Kobayashi-Jenetopolous family home. Alex and Ken were coming out the back door. Ken had his arm over Alex's shoulders, smiling gently, talking to him. I went to meet them at an almost-jog.

"Oh my! Darian!" Ken said, and hugged me. He had his usual absent smile on his face, like it was just a lovely day. Not even a hint that he was upset about his obviously fucked-up runaway son, or surprised by his sudden reappearance.

"Hey, Mr. K," I said, looking only at Alex. Alex looked back at me. His face was pale. He looked . . . not hostile and crazed, like he had when he was thinking about killing Birdie. Not tender and distracted, like when he'd hugged Isabella. He looked *scared*.

"What's up?" I asked quietly. Had he somehow also found out about Rita? How? She wasn't even around at the moment.

Alex pulled me off to the side, leaving Ken to walk back into the K-Family kitchen by himself. "I'll be there in one minute, Dad," he said.

"What's going on?" I asked.

"I went into the studio," Alex said. "I ducked in there, I wanted to look at, like, our old setup for Army of Dolly and make myself miserable, I guess. And in the corner, I pulled down a tarp and they were in the corner."

"In the corner?" I said. "Al. What is it?"

"The other doors," Alex said. "The two green doors. His cloak pieces. *Why* are they in my studio?"

The green doors. They were so close. "Because," I said. Now I was fully buying into Birdie Plum's accusation. "Your *mom* is Junie."

It sounded absurd. But . . . I believed it. I didn't want to believe it. I knew all about being betrayed by adults who you thought wanted what was best for you. I just didn't think Rita was ever going to be on that list.

Alex snorted. His laughter was fragile but genuine. He didn't think I was serious. "My mom is not the centuries-old witch. She's the main reason I came back. I mean, besides revenge."

"Yeah, about that revenge," I said. "I found Birdie. She's gone into early retirement. She's also joined you in the no-longer-brainwashed club. And she told me it was Rita who she'd been doing stuff for all along."

"You—you like, don't actually *trust* her, right?" Alex looked at me. "You can't actually think that my *mom*—"

"The name is an anagram," I said.

"Huh?" Alex said.

"Rita Jenetopolous. Junie Apostle-Root. Your mom likes word games, right? Isn't she the other big reader in the family besides you?"

"I . . ." Alex paused. Then he shook his head. "No. That's *insane*, I can't—"

We both stopped at the sound of crunching gravel under tires. I stepped toward the rear door, pulling Alex with me, as a car backed up into the driveway and parked alongside the restaurant. A *new* PDA, a nice shiny car from last year with a pizza-slice topper on it, to replace the one we'd stolen and totaled.

Alex and I both got quiet immediately. At our angle, you could only see the corner of the car. And then from the passenger side, Rita got out. She came around the corner and looked at us, every part of her pretty face communicating surprise. A few dark curls had worked themselves loose from her low ponytail and brushed her face. How old did she really look, I wondered. I had never wondered about it before. Did she look old enough to realistically have a twenty-two-year-old? Isabella was twenty-two. Did she look like she'd aged a day since the first time I'd ever talked to her, when I was thirteen-almost-fourteen?

"*Alex?*" Rita said. Then she looked at me. "*Darian?* What are you—oh my god—"

"Hi, Mom," Alex said, and Rita threw her arms around him.

She sometimes said *oh my god*. A phrase that I'd never heard another Kesuquoshian utter. The god of the Christians was not part of their culture.

I probably could have debated for days whether or not what Birdie had claimed about Rita was true, racked by indecision, not wanting to believe it. Even with the green doors from the Frost and the Falls resting in her garage like an accusation. But that question was solved for me.

The driver's-side door of the PDA, invisible from where I stood, opened and shut. I heard someone coming lightly over the gravel driveway.

"Baby, oh baby, I didn't think I would ever see you again," Rita was saying. Alex was hugging her back. His eyes looked bright and teary.

"I'm sorry, Mom," he said. "But I couldn't stand to be here anymore, without KJ and Jasper. I couldn't stand it."

"Without Jasper?" Rita said. "You don't have to be without Jasper. He's right here."

The crunching of the gravel terminated as the person driving the PDA came around the corner and stopped. Alex dropped his arms from his mother's shoulders.

It *was* Jasper. He had a gentle smile on his face. And his eyes were so black that all the blue was gone.

CHAPTER TWENTY-FOUR

Wednesday, September 12, 2001

"Alex," Jasper said, looking us both up and down. "Darian. How absolutely wonderful to see you guys!"

Jasper's hair was trimmed neatly, grown out into the dirty blond I'd always seen at his roots. The purple was almost gone, except at the tips. And his eyes. His eyes were far beyond how anyone else in the town had ever looked. They were black holes, so dark and big that he hardly looked human at all. His smile was white, even, and somehow *uncanny*, like he was a puppet and not an actual human being.

Alex stopped dead in the middle of leaning forward like he was going to embrace him.

"Jasper?" he asked in a very small voice. "Are you . . . what's wrong with you?"

I caught the *tiniest* look of distress or displeasure on Rita's face. She clearly hadn't expected us to show up. Explaining Jasper might be a little hard for her to do.

"Nothing's wrong with me!" Jasper said, and smiled again. "I'm absolutely bowled over at the fact that you two are here. How wonderful! We should celebrate our reunion!"

His golden voice, which I'd always found so beautiful, was different now. It sounded like it was bouncing off metal walls inside of an empty room. I thought, involuntarily, of the sound it might make if you spoke inside a closed mortuary cabinet.

"You—you—" Alex was totally lost for words. For a second, so was I. But I knew Rita was watching. I tried to come up with something to say to this smiling thing that had once been my best friend.

"Hi, Jas," I said. I wanted to vomit.

"Darian, hello," Jasper said.

"Honey, why don't you go in and set us a table," Rita said. "We can all have coffee and catch up."

"Will do!" Jasper said, and turned his blank-eyed face toward the door. As soon as he went inside the restaurant, Rita turned to us with a look of slight sadness on her face.

"I've been having Jasper work here since the censure," she said. "It's been hard . . . he's different from before. But I wanted to keep him close. He needs someone to take care of him."

It was good. Convincing. It might have even *worked*, if I hadn't talked to Birdie. It certainly would have worked on Alex. I could see it now:

Jasper needs someone to take care of him. He's still in there, just a little lost. A bit changed. Why don't you stay, Alex. Keep an eye on him. Help him find his way back.

And Alex *would*, because love makes you do shit like that, and Alex didn't have anything else to love. And the years would run by, and maybe eventually Al would get used to waking up next to this doll-eyed thing that had once been the most wonderfully intransigent person ever.

Maybe they could get married, out in the fields, Alex and the thing that used to be Jasper. Flower crowns and all.

I realized that I'd given myself goose bumps.

"But I . . . I thought he died," Alex said. He looked blankly shocked. "I . . . Mom . . . he got dragged into the black house. I saw it. They were burning him."

"The former Incorporations eat bad thoughts, honey," Rita said. "That's why. They were burning the bad thoughts out of him. He came back three days later. He's different, but he's still in there."

"Sounds great," I said. I didn't mean to say *anything*, but it came crashing over me all at once. That gross slimy feeling, when you know someone is crafting a narrative to manipulate you.

Dexter in my head, holding a copy of *Dandelion Wine*, reading aloud about the doomed love of Bill and Miss Helen Loomis, from Chapter 28: *"Time is so strange, and life is twice as strange. The cogs miss, the wheels turn, and lives interlace too early or too late."*

Looking at me from behind his glasses. *It's the greatest love story. They're soul mates. Separated by age. But their souls, Darian. Their souls know each other.* The first chorus to "Later, Adrian" quoting that chapter, just for me.

Oh, Adrian, time is so strange . . .

I had been fooled then. But I was not fooled now.

And when I looked at Alex, I saw that he wasn't fooled, either. I think maybe he *wanted* to be. But he couldn't convince himself.

"It was awful," Rita said. "I wish they hadn't done it."

"Do you?" I asked.

"Of course I do, honey," Rita said.

There was that expression again on her face: a tiny look of displeasure. I snapped my mouth shut.

"Let's go inside," Alex said quickly. "I want to talk to Jasper."

We went into the kitchen. Alex reached out and squeezed my wrist, briefly, but it communicated everything I needed to know: He got it. He knew what was going on.

Rita was right behind us. *She's going to move those doors as soon as she can*, I thought.

I didn't know if anything could be done, now, to fix the ruins of Jasper. KJ was definitely lost forever. But I still wanted to get those doors together.

If it worked like we'd hoped, it would set the town free. Fuck up Rita's little dystopia. And help Good Arcturus.

My friends, he'd called us. If being held prisoner for centuries in a strange world didn't make you into a hateful asshole, you were probably a pretty good guy. Or creature. Whatever.

But as soon as we walked into the restaurant, I realized we had another problem.

"I don't understand what's wrong with you," Senovak was saying. He sounded about as distressed as he *ever* sounded. "Your eyes—and your *affect*—"

"I'm fine, Daniel. Thank you so much for your concern," Jasper answered. He turned and smiled as Alex and I walked into the dining area.

Jasper was standing in front of the booth that Senovak had been sitting in, but Senovak was on his feet now. Standing with a look of alarm on his face and one hand on Jasper's shoulder. A couple people who were there eating were watching the situation go down.

Senovak getting caught in the cross fire was the last thing I needed. I walked over to him quickly, grabbed his arm.

"Can we talk outside for a second?" I asked him. I was giving him my *it's really important* look, the one that meant he absolutely needed to listen to me.

Sometimes Senovak would ignore that look, if he decided he knew better. But this time he didn't.

"I'll be right back," he said to Jasper.

"Great!" Jasper said cheerily.

Senovak followed me outside. As soon as we were on the sidewalk, he whirled back toward the window and jabbed one finger at it illustratively. "*What* is going on in there? What's wrong with him?"

"Jasper's just been going through a lot," I said. "He's been doing drugs—"

"Sometimes I swear, Darian, I swear you think I am the biggest fool alive," Senovak said. "*Alex* has been doing drugs, poor fucked-up kid. *That's* what someone looks like when they've been doing drugs. *Jasper* doesn't look like anything I've ever seen in my entire *life*. He looks like someone took a pen and scribbled out his eyes. And why is he acting like that?"

"He's just been through a lot," I repeated. "If you would just give me some time to myself, to, like, handle it, please—"

"No, goddamn it," Senovak said, and I saw that he was mad, like *really* mad, and scared. "I have given you *time to handle things* when I should not have. You asking me to give you time is you asking me to let you drown. I did it with the aftermath of that absolute fucking *creep*, and don't say anything, I *know* what you say and I know what your damned father says, and I also know that he was an absolute creep, I wish I'd shot him years before he got around to killing himself—"

"Can you stop FREAKING OUT?" I said, raising my voice to almost a shout. But that just made *Senovak* raise his voice. Now we were yelling at each other on the sidewalk, attracting attention.

"WHAT is going *on*?" Senovak asked. "What am I missing? And *where* is KJ?"

"I think *maybe* you're taking some of your stress about the planes crashing out on me," I said, trying to make less of a scene.

"I am not, and stop deflecting, you are so infuriating sometimes," Senovak said. "I was concerned, after a few months. I had the police do a welfare check on your little friends, but they said everyone was fine. Obviously a lie—Alex wasn't even *in town*—"

"You had the *cops* come?" I asked. Senovak ignored my indignation, though. He just kept going.

"And KJ isn't anywhere to be seen, is she? Where is she, Darian? What happened last October? Did these people—did someone *do* something to her? I knew when she started to wear her girly things it was a bit of a risk, but everyone here is so woo-woo love and acceptance that I thought she would be fine. It seemed like it was going well for *years*. Did someone *hurt* her for being—"

"Nobody hurt her for being transgender," I said. I felt like crying. I guess I'd felt like crying for almost a year. "She's just not around anymore. I don't even know why you care. You don't even like her."

"Of course I don't like her," Senovak said. "She has the personality of a weasel. *What happened to her?*"

"You wouldn't believe me if I told you," I said.

"Try me," Senovak said.

"Fine," I said. Through the window I could see Alex and Jasper. Alex was watching us. Jasper was, too, but with a blank little smile on his face. Rita had been back in the kitchens when I walked outside, and I kept looking over at the building, acutely aware that I couldn't afford for her to overhear us. "Good Arcturus is real. Two hundred and fifty-ish years ago, a witch who was exiled from the village here found him. She kept him from returning to his home with her . . . witch magic, or something . . . and she used his power to fuck up Kesuquosh in revenge for what they'd done to her and her mom. Every thirty-five years there's a lottery and they pick one innocent citizen to sacrifice. They use that person's skin to, like, refresh the binding spell on him."

I could see by Senovak's expression that he was completely bewildered. I just kept going, though.

"That same witch—who is *immortal*, I have to add—imprisons Good Arcturus out in a black house in the fields with his former skin-sacrifices," I said. "I think they suck up all the bad vibes or something. And Good Arcturus keeps the town happy and prosperous and everyone is always chill. Always. But he's just as much of a slave as everyone else here. And last October, the lottery winner was KJ. And we . . . tried to stop it from happening to her. But we lost anyway. And then Jasper was punished for leading our little uprising. He got like, brain-sucked by the things that eat the bad thoughts. Are you following me?"

"I . . ." Senovak clearly thought I had gone completely insane. Which made me angry, in addition to the almost-crying, because he'd forced me into this pointless explanation.

"Are you *following* me?" I asked. "Because here's all the honesty you wanted! It ruined Alex's life. It ruined *my* life, because I was finally, *finally* starting to think the world could be okay after Dexter, and then the only person I ever wanted to be in a relationship with got turned into a skin suit by an unwilling but very large *scarecrow*! It ruined KJ's life most of all, obviously, because it killed her! And the punch line is that we spent the whole time thinking the immortal witch was Birdie Plum."

"Who—"

"The First Selectwoman, Jasper's aunt, the little lady with the short hair, but then I found out like an hour ago that the evil witch is"—I looked around and lowered my voice to an urgent whisper—"*Rita!* Okay? Is that good? Does that clear up all your confusion?"

"What kind of bullshit are you saying right now?" Senovak asked. His eyes were narrowing in classic Senovak-suspicion.

"I'm not bullshitting you," I said. "I have never been more honest in my entire life."

"Right," Senovak said, looking pissed, and baffled. "Well. If you're just going to fucking *lie*—"

"You were right about Dexter," I said. "It was going on for almost the entire two years. He did everything you could imagine to me. I covered it up because he convinced me I wanted it. And I am so glad he's dead."

Senovak stopped in the middle of a word, I don't know what. The anger dropped off his face. The sharpness that was always around his features slipped away into the same kind of look he'd had when he told me that Linus was gone.

"Does that *prove* my honesty? Do you believe me *now*?" I asked, wiping one hand across my stupidly watering eyes. "I would never say that unless I was telling you the truth. I'm telling you the *truth*, Dan, I—I—"

I couldn't even talk anymore. I was crying. I felt grossly *embarrassed*, as strange as that sounds—to be so vulnerable and unhinged. Even in front of Senovak. Maybe especially in front of Senovak. Sometimes I felt like my careful and constant act of holding myself together was *for* him, in some way. To convince him that I was all right. If I could convince him, I could convince myself.

Senovak put his arms around my shoulders and pulled me to his chest.

"Okay, okay, okay," he said. "I'm here. It's okay. I'm listening to you."

I cried into his immaculate shirt, trying to stop myself before I really started sobbing and got snot on him, something that he would deem unforgivable. Though I probably had a momentary pass.

"I'm sorry," I said. "I'm sorry, Dan, I'm sorry I didn't tell you. Please don't be mad at me—"

"Oh Christ, Darian, I would never be mad at you," Senovak said. He hugged me very tightly.

"You get mad at me all the time," I said through my tears.

"I would never be mad at you about *this*," he amended.

"Daniel? Darian? Are you two quite well?"

I stepped back and wiped my face. Jasper was in the doorway of K-Family, looking at us with something that I thought was supposed to resemble concern.

"We're fine," Senovak said. "Just a little emotional today."

Jasper nodded. We were using the attack in New York as cover for our big moment of scarecrow-cult-witch-monster-molestation truth, I guess.

"We'll be back in, like, one minute," I said.

"Sounds good!" Jasper said, and ducked back into the restaurant.

It was quiet on the street, except for a pair of women chatting to each other on the sidewalk opposite us. Senovak and I stood in silence while they strolled into the microscopic bagel shop. A breeze moved the flowers in the window boxes all up and down Good Earth Way.

"Kesuquosh has always been strange. But I'm struggling to believe you about the magical cult thing," Senovak said, "led by *Rita*? Rita, of all people. She runs a *pizza place*."

"Shhh. Don't say her name too loud," I said. "Even if you don't believe me, will you help me?"

Senovak looked me over. He sighed deeply.

I've mentioned how I always felt a little weird about the fact that he was paid to be there. But I saw in that moment, very clearly, how much he loved me. It had nothing to do with his job. "What, exactly, would I be helping you *with*?" Senovak asked.

"I need you to steal two doors," I said.

CHAPTER TWENTY-FIVE

Wednesday, September 12, 2001

Somehow I managed to choke down exactly one-point-five pieces of pizza. Rita and Ken brought our food out themselves—Rita kissed Alex on the top of the head several times and he managed to look okay about it—and Jasper smiled at us and took a big bite of a pepperoni slice.

Alex and I both stared at Jasper, the person who had given us shit about our ethical choices regarding food *forever*, as he chowed down on meat and cheese with his blank black eyes looking out at us.

"Are you—are you not a vegan anymore?" I asked.

"Me? Oh no," Jasper said. "I gave that up! It was too inconvenient, you know?"

"And it can be hard to get enough protein," Rita said. "Probably for the best."

That protein comment was a *berserk* button for Jasper. Jasper pre-brain-suck would have been ranting at Rita about how she should know all about soybeans, plant-derived proteins, complex carbohydrates, the links between animal consumption and various cancers, Asenath Nicholson and the history of vegan feminism, etc. But this strange new Jasper just smiled and had another bite of pizza.

When we were done eating, Senovak got up and dusted imaginary crumbs off his pants. "I think I'm going to head back to the cottage," he announced. "Air the place out a little."

Then he gave me money and I went up to the counter. But Rita waved me off when I tried to pay.

"On us, on us," Rita said. "For bringing back my prodigal son."

"Thanks," I said, and Rita looked across the counter at me. So pretty. So sweet.

"Will you be staying long, Adrian?" she asked.

"W-w-what?" I stammered. Rita was still looking at me. In my head I heard the low and lovely voice that had come from my lips when KJ and I had mind-melded, all those months before. When I had been Junie. Reenacting something from long ago.

Poor creature. Poor thing. Let me help you, strange traveler.

It was *her* voice. And she repeated herself now, with that same false sweetness.

"I said, will you be staying long?" Rita said, and smiled. "Darian?"

"Um. Not sure yet," I said, and tried to sound normal.

"It depends on when Edward can join us," Senovak said, having missed the earlier part of our exchange. "And when it's safe to go back to the city, of course."

"Of course," Rita said, with a look of concern. *Bullshit, bullshit, bullshit,* I thought. She wanted us fucking *gone.*

"I'll come with you and unpack my stuff," I told Senovak. Then I made myself smile. "Al. Jas. You guys want to hang out tomorrow?"

Alex looked bewildered as to why I was abandoning him. I leaned down and grabbed his hand under the table. Nodded once when he met my eyes.

"That sounds great! I should head home," Jasper said. "Got some chores to take care of for Mom and Dad."

"Awesome," I said. "I'll call you both later. We can plan something excellent for tomorrow."

"And you can spend some time with us and your sisters," Rita said, and came over to hug Alex again.

I guess un-brainwashed Alex wasn't *actually* a stranger to me. I really did know him on a deep level. Because I saw the exact moment when he almost said "But not *all* my sisters, right?" or something equally snarky, and then decided against it. "Sure," he said instead. "That sounds cool."

Then we left.

"Do you have bungee cords?" I asked Senovak as soon as we were in the car.

"Hmm. Maybe in the garage," Senovak said. Obviously I had to give him a longer version of what had happened last Halloween. We sat in the kitchen and I talked until I couldn't think of anything else to add.

He didn't seem like he actually believed me, but he was being weirdly diplomatic. I guessed he thought I'd had a full break from reality. He listened while I told him the rough outlines of my plan. They were *very* rough, since I'd just started coming up with a plan during our fight on the sidewalk.

"After this, after I do this for you, you are going back to therapy," Senovak said.

"Deal," I said. If we made it through the night, I would enter psychoanalysis, go to a vow-of-silence retreat, and eat an all-hemp-seed diet to satisfy Senovak. Whatever he wanted.

Senovak nodded. He drummed his fingers against the side of his coffee cup.

"But you do think there's a chance I'm right," I said, watching the rhythmic movements of his hands.

"I don't know," Senovak said. "Something. There's something. His eyes . . ."

"Let me just call Alex and fill him in," I said.

Then I called the Kobayashi-Jenetopolous household. A thing I'd done a zillion times that was now really scary. I hoped that Rita wouldn't pick up, but it was actually the youngest Kobayashi kid who answered.

"Hi, Darian," she said.

"Hey, Athena," I said. "Is Alex there?"

There was a pause and a bunch of laughter and talking in the background, and then Alex picked up.

"One sec," he said. "I'm on the portable phone. *I don't know if she can hear me.* I'm going to call you back in five minutes, okay?"

I hung up and waited anxiously until he called me back.

"Hey," I said. "Are you okay?"

"Yeah. I'm at the pay phone by the post office. Feeling pretty paranoid. Maybe she can even hear me from across the street, who knows."

He sounded so scared. For a second I wanted to tell him to forget it all. It was too much for him to have to deal with an evil mom on top of all his other losses. I would tell him I had been mistaken, then handle it myself.

But it felt unfair. Patronizing, after all he'd lost. Alex deserved to be . . . in on this.

"How is it going?" I asked.

"She hasn't, like, done anything. It's going weird, without KJ here. But they're all acting normal. I mean, yeah, as much as like, you know," Alex said. "I . . . I told them I was going for a walk earlier and I went to talk to Birdie."

"You left the house?" I asked, feeling a spike of anxiety. I thought for sure Rita would move those doors as soon as Alex wasn't there to notice.

"Just for a little while," Alex said.

"The doors," I said.

"They're still there. She has no idea I've been in the studio," Alex said. "The doors were under a tarp. I don't even know what made me *look* under there. I'm sure she's gonna make them disappear really soon. But I needed to talk to Birdie."

"You didn't shoot her, did you?" I asked, which made Senovak, who was washing our mugs, turn around and give me a look.

"No, of course not!" Alex said.

"Well, you wanted to *kill* her earlier, Al," I said.

"I think I was having some kind of breakdown, then," Alex said. "I think I've been having a breakdown for a long time. But I feel okay now."

"Good," I said. "I mean, not *good*, but better. Did you talk to her?"

"Yeah. I believe her," Alex said. "About Mom. I didn't want to believe her. I *love* my mom, you know? But I believe her."

"Me too," I said.

"I let her keep the gun," Alex added. "Living here like . . . a normal person . . . seems pretty dangerous. And I'm scared to have it. I don't know what was going through my head."

"Good," I said. "I don't want you to have it. Now listen. I have a plan."

CHAPTER TWENTY-SIX

Thursday, September 13, 2001

The last thing I did while I was waiting to get "the signal" from Alex was call Aunt Judy and Surendra. I'd gotten their number from Alex. It was well after midnight and the bungee cords were already in the back seat of the Lincoln when I dialed their number. Senovak and I had been sitting together in the kitchen, both reading, not talking much. Only I don't think either of us were successfully reading at all. The words in my Oprah-endorsed copy of *White Oleander* kept blurring together.

Despite the lateness, Surendra answered on the second ring.

"Hello?" Surendra said, and I felt startlingly happy to hear him.

"Surendra?" I asked.

"Darian," he said immediately. "Judith said she saw you and Alex. What is happening? Are you safe?"

"We're going to try to set Good Arcturus free. Tonight. We figured out who *she* was, the she who'd been keeping him prisoner. In case things go really bad, I wanted *someone* to know that it was—"

"Rita Jenetopolous!" I heard Aunt Judy say from behind Surendra.

"You guys figured it out already?" I asked. "Am I an idiot?"

"Of course not, darling," Surendra said "Alex visited us before he disappeared, last year, and told us what had happened. We talked it all over with the Freys . . . even discussed trying to take on the monster of Kesuquosh ourselves, just the four of us, though Friday was fairly certain that even together we were no match for the power behind the creature, as it were. And then when Judith saw Rita going around with—with what remained of Jasper—we began to have suspicions."

Senovak had come up next to me during the course of the conversation and was listening in with all of his might. I saw a kind of troubled expression move across his face. I felt troubled, too. If Friday and Flora didn't like *their* odds against Rita, how low were *ours*?

"We're going to that old abandoned church tonight. We're going to try to put those doors back together and set Good Arcturus free. And the town. I just wanted you to know. In case we don't . . . make it," I said. "Thanks for everything."

"Tell her that they're absolutely *not* trying anything without us," Judy said, loudly enough that I could pick up all the separate scratchy tones of her voice. "Darian! We're coming there right now."

"No," I said. "Please don't, guys. We're good. I have my . . . Dan here and he's going to help. I don't want you, like, in danger."

"Friday and Flora are out of town," Surendra said. Clearly repeating something Judy was saying to him. "But if you wait until tomorrow, I think they would be willing to help."

"We don't have time. She's going to move the doors and then—" I stopped, feeling a little shaky. We really did have to do it *now*. "It has to happen tonight. I'm sorry," I said.

"We're coming," Surendra said firmly. Aunt Judy was talking behind him again.

"No," I said. On the kitchen table, my cell phone started ringing. "Gotta go."

"Darian—"

I hung the corded phone back up on the wall while Surendra was still talking, and grabbed my cell phone. Alex's house number appeared on the screen; the phone rang twice and then disconnected. Which was the sign we had agreed upon. "Time to go?" Senovak asked.

"Yes," I said. Before we got in the car, I went to my bedroom and pulled KJ's purple Soundgarden beanie out of my suitcase. And I put it on. For luck.

On the short drive into town, Senovak kept glancing over at me.

"What?" I asked.

"It's troubling to hear presumably sane adults corroborating your insane story," Senovak said.

"Worried it might be true?" I asked.

He glared at me when he saw me raising an *I told you so* eyebrow at him. But he switched off the headlights on the Lincoln as soon as we turned onto Good Earth Way.

The Kobayashi-Jenetopolous house, like back in the days when Army of Dolly had practiced there, wasn't blocked in by any cars. The family always parked a few hundred feet away, in the K-Family restaurant driveway. That was good. Senovak pulled all the way down the empty driveway and turned the engine off.

No lights suddenly came on from inside. I crept over to the double doors of the studio without making any sound.

Alex was there, waiting to meet me.

He opened the doors all the way. Senovak was right behind me.

"Darian and I will drag the doors out," Senovak whispered. "You take the keys. The second I've got them tied on, you drive us to this church place. Yes?"

"Okay," Alex said.

Alex disappeared, and Senovak flicked the light switch and surveyed the cluttered studio. Other projects and pursuits had edged out the Army of Dolly stuff over the last year. I could just barely see the old yellow love seat and the makeshift stage and the amp underneath a bunch of boxes, completed paintings, and dollhouse parts. And there, in the corner (thankfully), tarp pulled down and bunched around them, were the two big green doors.

I saw Senovak pause for the *tiniest* second.

"Just like I said," I said.

"Hmm," Senovak said, and walked over to them. He touched one door, testing its weight, and then turned around.

"Very heavy. Not quite as bad as I feared, though," he said. "*How* did you do this last time?"

I had gone over the minutiae with him, and I hadn't made it any less fantastical and insane than it actually was. "I told you. KJ levitated them with her magic powers."

"Right. We're going to grab this one and turn it on its side," Senovak said. "This one. Are you ready?"

"Yes," I said. I followed Senovak in an awkward run-walk, holding the first huge door sideways. It hurt my hands, and I dropped the end of it once we reached the driveway, where it made a horrible sound as it scraped on the pavement.

"Shit!" I said.

"Alex," Senovak said. "Leave the car running and the door open. Darian. Turn it upright with me. We're going to push from the bottom and slide it up onto the roof. Alex will secure it with the cords. While he does that, we go grab the next one."

I crouched down with Senovak and pushed the door up onto the trunk of the car and then the roof of the car. It made a horrible sound as it scraped the roof of the Lincoln, taking a bunch of paint with it.

"Fuck *me*," Senovak said.

"It's fine, we'll fix it," I said. Then we ran back to the studio as Alex was tying off the first door.

We were pushing the second door up onto the roof when the lights inside came on.

"Tie it, tie it, tie it!" I said. Alex nodded silently, working without looking up at the house.

Senovak got into the passenger's side and I crawled into the back.

"Alex, let's *go*!" I said, and he slid into the driver's seat and slammed the door shut.

The door swung open as we pulled away, and I saw Rita silhouetted there, her long hair loose and wild. Something about her looked different in that brief glimpse. Frightening.

"I am going to be arrested," Senovak said. He raised one hand to Rita as we pulled away.

"Way to be conspicuous," I said. My heart was pounding. I felt alive with triumph, and I tried to squash that down. It was definitely premature.

"Maybe she'll think the two of you have taken me hostage," Senovak said.

"I hope this makes something *happen*. I have really, like, had enough of driving around with these stupid doors to last an entire life," Alex said.

"Ditto," I said.

I felt a terrible, dreamlike sensation of déjà vu as we pulled up at the clearing that held the door to Empty Heaven. I had this awful thought that I was doomed to keep coming back to this place with a singular goal until everyone I loved had died here.

"What do we do now?" Senovak asked. But the second the car was turned off he was already out and unhooking the bungee cords.

"Line them up so they're touching?" I said. "I think?"

"I'm glad you have such a coherent plan. Stay clear of that side," Senovak said, and one door fell to the ground with a crash, taking part of the rearview mirror as it went.

"Goddamn it!" Senovak said. Alex and I dragged the fallen door away from the increasingly battered Lincoln and toward the old church foundation.

"His cloak was torn in three pieces," Alex said. "Here we go. I really hope getting all the doors together *does* something."

We leaned the second door against the first one.

Behind us, the last door crashed to the ground. Senovak got down and dragged it with the two of us.

Together, we pushed the third door up. It seemed to almost *click* with the other two doors, like it was magnetized. All in a cluster like that, the doors made an odd peaked shape: the silhouette of a standing, hooded figure.

"Now what?" Senovak asked.

The woods were quiet . . . but I thought I could hear a car approaching in the distance. Somewhere way up Deep River Road.

The doors stood still, the left and right ones canted out at a sloping angle. For a second nothing happened.

"Oh, man," Alex said. "Please do something."

Then I smelled ozone.

It was really faint at first. Just a tiny little whisper. But it got stronger and stronger, until it smelled like a lightning storm all around us.

Then the ground started to buzz. The air vibrated so hard that I felt my back teeth clattering. Senovak put a protective arm over each of our shoulders, even though he had to reach up to sling an arm around Alex.

"What the hell is that?!" he asked, raising his voice over the increasingly loud buzzing sound.

"That's the sound of Good Arcturus!" I said. "It's working. It's *working*!"

The noise of the approaching car was lost under the vibration that was coming from the three green doors. But I saw headlights—getting nearer, cutting through the dense trees that lined the side of the rutted old path.

"Someone's there!" I shouted, pointing. My voice was lost in the buzzing. But Senovak followed my hand with his eyes. Alex turned and mouthed something to me—I couldn't understand him—and then came a vibration so deafening that I threw my hands over my ears. It was like the sound the black house had made before it vanished into ruins last Halloween.

whump whump whump whump WHUMP WHUMP WHUMP WHUMP WHUMP

I thought I could hear Alex yelling, maybe, buried under the pulsing sound. Another vibration shook the earth so hard that

Alex and I fell to the ground. Senovak fell with us, trying to cover both of us with his body.

The voices and sounds, the ground under my feet—every aspect of reality was stretched, rubber band–like, around my limited perception. Then the light that had been too bright to look at dimmed, all at once. The buzzing stopped.

I heard something new. It was almost like the ringing of bells. And as the bell sound came, the world seemed to snap back. I snapped back with it, feeling like I'd been struck. The ground had stopped shaking.

I opened my eyes as the sound of the phantom bells faded. The only noise in the forest was the wailing of two different car alarms going off: the Lincoln's, and the one on the car that had been approaching us through the woods. *That* car seemed to have been knocked off the path by the shock waves emanating from the three doors. It was lodged on the far side of the street, a hundred or more yards from us, headlights shining into the bushes.

Actually, there was another sound. A low humming. It was like the sound of Good Arcturus, but made into something soft and melodic. And the forest was lit with an eerie green light—or at least I *thought* it was green. I would have described it as green. But it was unlike any green I'd ever seen before. It seemed like the visible light spectrum had expanded to allow an entirely new color.

The light was emanating from the place where we'd set the three old doors together.

But they weren't three doors, not anymore. Instead, there was an opening in the air. In the *world*. A peaked shape, brilliant with that impossible color, shimmering as it sat in the air and on the earth. Shimmering like the fabric in my vision from last year.

A wind was blowing out of the opening in the world. It smelled like grapes and rich earth and the coppery tang of blood; and pine needles, and fresh water in a stream, and a million things that called up a million ideas. But those were only tiny things, impressions. The overall smell of the wind was just like the color of the light. Impossible. Incomprehensible.

There was a view through the fabric—or the door. Or the traveling cloak. Maybe all those things meant the same thing to Good Arcturus. Something dense, like a jungle. Or a field. Maybe like sunflowers, if sunflowers were conceived of in another dimension, by a creator who'd only had sunflowers described to them.

Senovak got up. His face showed absolute astonishment. He walked toward the portal in the earth, then behind it, around the now doorless ruins of the old church.

"Dan," I said. "Be careful!"

But Senovak emerged unscathed from behind the green threshold.

"Darian," he said, and his tone held a simple kind of wonder that I had never heard from him in my entire life. "There's another world. There's another world through there."

"I told you," I said. "I *told* you. Do I still have to go to therapy?"

"Don't doubt it for a second," Senovak said. He offered me and Alex each a hand up. "Look."

I stood next to Alex and looked into the moving green world. It was frightening, and alien, and beautiful. For a second I felt a wild impulse to just walk through the gateway and see what happened. And I saw that same fascination written all over Senovak and Alex.

"Wow," Alex said. That pretty much summed it up.

Then I heard a noise behind us. Bodies crashing through the bushes. Senovak whirled around just as I did.

"They're coming," Alex said.

"What do we *do*?" I asked. My plan had basically ended here.

"Where's your big fucking scarecrow?" Senovak asked.

"In the black house!" I said.

"Yes," Alex said. "We have to get him! Come on!"

For the second time in less than a year, I sprinted toward the sunflower fields.

This time the flowers were almost all still in bloom. They grew close together in the dark, and once we hit the field we had to run in a tight single file.

"What—if—it—isn't *there*?" I said, through gasping *I'm running really fast* breaths. "What if we can't *find* it? Or it's just ruins again?"

"It's gonna be there! It's gonna be there!" Alex said. "We put his *cloak* back together, it's gonna *be* there—"

And even before he finished his sentence, the sunflowers were parting. We were in the clearing. I *knew* the house was farther into the fields than this. It had moved closer for us.

Senovak emerged last from the flowers, swiping cobwebs out of his hair. He looked up at the black house with the same expression he'd given to the green doorway.

No, actually. This time he looked more trepidatious.

"If we survive this, I'll go to therapy *with* you," Senovak said.

"I would never allow you in my therapy sessions," I said. Then I heard a sound in the field, somewhere behind us.

"Think, like, really good thoughts, guys," Alex said. "We *can* open these doors."

We ran across the clearing to the front of the house. Alex paused with one hand on each of the old iron handles, and then pulled. The doors opened like they had been waiting to open, revealing nothing but the red glow I'd seen in my nightmares for almost a year.

I looked at Alex. "Into the redness," I said. "Dan, maybe you should stay out here?"

"Like hell," Senovak said.

The three of us walked into the house together.

CHAPTER TWENTY-SEVEN

Thursday, September 13, 2001

At first we were blind. I grabbed Senovak and Alex's hands as we walked in, and it was a good thing I did—the dull red glow of the house interior blotted out *everything*. We were in a void, moving forward as best we could with zero markers. I could barely feel the ground under my feet. For a second I was totally disoriented, like gravity didn't exist at all.

And then, after a terrible few moments, my vision cleared. I saw Senovak to my right and Alex to my left, blinking like they'd come out of a long sleep.

We were in the entranceway of a very old house, low-ceilinged and made entirely of wood. I could almost touch the beams above me, and Alex had to duck as he passed through the doorway.

A single oil lamp burned on a side table. The flame in it was an unnatural red.

"The room goes farther back than should be possible," Senovak said. "See?"

Alex grabbed the oil lamp, making all the shadows rearrange themselves. The room seemed like it went on for far too long, incredibly larger than what the black house could possibly contain.

And as we walked, Alex holding the lamp aloft, I saw strange shapes in the redness. *Trees.*

Senovak stopped to touch one. In the red light it looked like a young dogwood. He craned his head up and so did I. The top of the tree disappeared into the darkness near what should have been the ceiling. I saw chips of light far above us, impossible stars.

Then came the sharp smell of dying leaves. Too early in the year for that smell to be so strong. But we were walking in the woods *inside* a house, so anything was possible. The floor under my feet was scattered with moss and crunching leaves, and Senovak suddenly stopped and put his arms out to block us from going any farther. We had reached a line of actual *forest*, dense trees creating an edge to the inside-outside.

I had a sudden memory of KJ, pushing in front of me to go up the steps of the gazebo. *Stop being a human shield*, I'd said. How funny that was now. How terrible.

I missed her. It was a stupid time to miss her as much as I did, but I missed her so much. I wished she was there.

Senovak dropped his arms, glanced back at us as he reached the treeline, and then walked through. I followed him, and Alex came last with his oil lamp, pulling all the light with us.

Then we were in the forest. But something about it felt false, unreal in the red glow. Not just because it was inside of a house. There were no animal sounds. No breeze, gentle or otherwise. It felt artificial, like contained air inside the world's biggest amusement park attraction.

"We're going to get lost in here," Alex said nervously, but Senovak shook his head and pointed. Up ahead of us, the trees thinned out. And a faint glow emanated from the clearing.

I stepped out into the clearing with my heart racing. No idea what I was going to see. And it took me a moment to understand what I *was* seeing.

"What . . . ?" Alex said, looking over at me in bewilderment.

It was *Kesuquosh*. But smaller.

Dollhouses spread out before me, some covered in ivy and moss, all of them old, in the process of becoming one with the forest. They were large—the smallest of the little structures reached to my thighs, and others were even higher, occupying a liminal area between a child's toy and a child's playhouse. In all directions the small houses spread away, filling up the wide clearing, all of them lit from within by illumination with no visible source. And then I saw those . . . those trails of organic burnt blackness that the Incorporations dragged in their wake the night they pursued us. Black veins spreading across the earth. Across the houses. Wrapped up into the very nature of things in this false Kesuquosh. Polluting everything.

"What the hell is this?" Senovak asked. There were little divots carved into the moss between the homes, tiny arterial roads, and Senovak put foot in front of foot and walked next to one of the roads from the edge of the clearing until it ran up against . . . what I thought must be a facsimile of Good Earth Way.

It wasn't an exact representation of the town. Too old-fashioned. Not enough houses. It looked like the little village that Junie and Good Arcturus marched through forever in the painting at the town hall.

Alex and I walked into the clearing. It was light enough there that the red glow of the lantern became indistinct. A few normal-sized trees grew in between the houses like unearthly megaflora, throwing everything out of perspective. I touched the roof of a dollhouse situated right around where I thought Birdie lived, marveling at the detail of the little mossy shingles.

"I think my mom . . . these look like she made them," Alex said. "She normally doesn't work *this* big, but . . . it looks like her pieces, doesn't it?"

This was where Rita moved the world. Kept the spells going. Crushed everyone to her will. The whole village was her plaything.

"Yeah," I agreed. "In her woods. In her little world." And then I flinched. Near the edge of the model village—close, in fact, to where I thought Number 19, my family's cottage, would be in the real-world equivalent—stood the smallest of the previous Incorporations, the roofline of the house almost to its chest. That was the Incorporation I believed had once been Blanche Sabine. Perfectly still. Head bowed and covered with its hood and gauzy mask. Its black, charred hands rested on the roof of the nearest house like it was mid prayer. Nothing moved. I came to a sharp standstill when I saw the Incorporation, but it was like it was frozen.

"Dare," Alex said, and I looked over. He was pointing to the opposite end of the town. At the other side of the large clearing, I could make out a different color. More red light. The black house. Senovak was already almost to it. And over that house stood Good Arcturus, bound in skin.

His head was inclined downward, his body illuminated by the red light spilling out of the little windows of the black dollhouse. He was enormous, maybe bigger than I had ever imagined, but even he was dwarfed by the forest around us. His arms were clamped on the edges of the dollhouse. They terminated in thousands of red threads instead of hands or fingers, and the threads spread rootlike all over, spilling onto the mossy earth, making everything they touched look like it was shot through with veins.

As I ran toward the end of the clearing, catching up with Senovak, I passed the other Incorporations. All six of their heads were similarly bowed. All of them hidden within the false Kesuquosh like a Magic Eye. When you saw them, traced their oily roots with your eyes, you realized they had been there all along. But none of them moved. It seemed like they were sleeping.

"Is that your man?" Senovak asked, gesturing at Good Arcturus with one hand. His eyes were wide.

"Yes," I said.

"I think we should try to wake him up," Alex said.

"Don't touch it," Senovak said, holding an arm over Alex's chest. "I'll do it."

"*Dan,*" I said. "He doesn't even *know you.*"

"I'm not letting either of you anywhere near that thing," Senovak said. I rolled my eyes, wondering what his reaction would be if I told him I'd let *that thing* (mostly KJ, granted, but Good Arcturus had undeniably been there) get to third base with me in a chapel. Senovak stepped forward, and I followed him as he cautiously approached the black dollhouse. As we got closer, I saw a glint of something. Against the carved double-doorway of the dollhouse, resting like it was waiting to be found, was my lost amethyst. Given to me by the beautiful Friday Frey. I used my sleeve to scoop it into my pocket.

"Okay," Senovak said. He reached out one hand. "Let me just—"

"Here they are, Rita!" came a hollow, chipper voice.

I turned and saw Jasper, smiling widely as he emerged from the trees around the clearing.

"Guys," he said, and waved a finger at us. "I rolled up to help Rita move some heavy furniture just as you were leaving. Crazy timing! But you really shouldn't be in here. This stuff is delicate!"

We had evaded Rita's door-moving plan by minutes.

"Fuck," Senovak said, and reached way up. He briskly backhanded Good Arcturus across his skin-shrouded face. "Wake up!"

"Wake up," I said. "Please!"

Good Arcturus did not move. Nothing moved except Jasper, who turned his black eyes toward the edge of the clearing just as Rita stepped into it.

She was beautiful, her hair streaming down her shoulders in a mass of wild curls, her lovely face solemn and her nightgown billowing around her as she moved. I could almost imagine her, centuries in the past, leveling the church as payback for the small-minded people who had exiled her mother, damned Elisabel and Junie to lonely lives and lonely deaths.

Or maybe they'd just been regular people, and she'd been a narcissist with magic powers.

"How could you do this?" Rita said, walking crossways over the tiny streets, cutting through the clearing toward us on bare feet. "*Why* would you do this?"

"Mom, please," Alex said, putting his hands up. "You don't have to control everything anymore. We can live our lives like *real* people—"

"It was *Him*, you know, who punished me," Rita said, and pointed to Good Arcturus's still form with one hand. "By choosing one of *my* children. And then taking you away from me, from our home. I wish that this had never been done to you, baby. I wish you could have kept on being yourself."

"I wasn't *myself*! I'm only myself *now*!" Alex said.

"You've all been wronged. Darian, you should have never been brought into this by Jasper," Rita said. "And Daniel, Darian should have known better than to involve you."

Up close, she appeared . . . *different*. The startling beauty I had seen before revealed itself to be an illusion. There was something wrong. Rita's nails were longer, more clawed. Her feet gripped the earth with unnatural dexterity. Strange leaves clung to her wild hair. Her eyes no longer looked dilated at all. They threw back circles of blank light. And the worst part of all of it was that her features . . . *moved*.

Her face and arms rippled. Her finely-wrought features seemed to shift and vibrate. Her limbs were too long, and they moved with an eerie fluidity. Like she was shot through with sinews under her skin, or a holographic projection moving in space. Or a ghost. As if all of her years, all of her long life, had made her somehow . . . unfixed. Outside of reality.

"I'm sorry they let your mother die," I said. I don't know what made me speak. My voice shook. I was terrified. But I had adored this woman for a good chunk of my adolescence, wanted her to be my mom. Even now, I couldn't truly believe she was *this* selfish, this cruel. She seemed like a monster. More and more by the moment. But maybe . . . maybe she was just lonely. Afraid of loneliness.

Rita actually stopped and looked at me. I tried to meet her blank animal eyes bravely. Tried to imagine Junie as a little child, growing up alone except for her mom, in primitive exile.

"I'm sorry too," Rita said. "Sorry to have found myself on the wrong side of them."

For a tiny second she looked faraway. And sad.

"It, um, it wasn't fair what they did to you guys," I said, words tripping out of my mouth in a frantic rush. "But it won't be like that now. You have people who love you. You can just let us *go*—"

Rita laughed. Her eyes were flat as death, her laugh went high-low-high like the howling of wild winds. "Oh, honey. You're so little, still. You think that human beings are mostly good and only sometimes bad, don't you? Don't you?"

I nodded.

"Well," Rita said, taking a step closer to me, "you're wrong, Darian. Human beings are monsters. Disgusting, untrustworthy, selfish, wicked. Even you, whether you know it or not. Fearful cowards screaming at the dark, stabbing at shadows. I learned that long ago. And I have been able . . . with help, of course . . . to correct them."

"They're not corrected!" I said. "They're *empty*."

"Empty of evil," Rita said. "Made to accept one another by force. But give them even an *inch* of free will and they will *cut* and *tear* and *claw* at each other like the animals they are. War and blood and hate. Neglect of people who need them and *exile* and *death*. Only here are they good. Only here are they worthy of love."

Her flat eyes narrowed. A small smile appeared on her face. "Kesuquosh is the only good place, the only place where people are actually deserving of their brief lives. Of any existence at all. All we need is one sacrifice to make a perfect world. If I could do it to all of humankind, I would. In a *heartbeat*."

Her voice held nothing but absolute conviction. If she'd ever thought anything else, the centuries had made her firm in her hatred. And I realized what, exactly, her changing features and moving skin and long limbs made me think of.

It almost seemed like there was something *else* inside her.

Like her body was a too-small vessel that some other shape was threatening to tear apart, so the real thing beneath could be revealed.

"Rita," Senovak said, and approached her, coming slightly down from the place where the black dollhouse stood. His voice was perfectly calm, reasonable. "Let's just leave this place and discuss this rationally, how does—"

But when he was within arm's length of Rita, she reached out one hand and slashed his cheek with her nails. I saw Senovak's cheek split open like Rita's nails were razor-tipped. He staggered back as if she had applied more force than possible, blood pouring out of his face from under his hand. The highest slash had gotten his left eye. I couldn't see if his eye itself was damaged, but blood dripped from his eyelid between his clutching fingers.

"Don't *touch* him! DAN!" I yelled, and grabbed his side as he staggered back, stumbling into another of the dollhouses and nearly falling. It was like she'd shoved him away with ten times the strength she could possibly have.

"You aren't going to subdue me, monster," Rita said. Her voice rippled like her features rippled. Low and soothing, then high and wailing. A comforting whisper in a nursery and then a rushing wind. I saw Alex flinch. I wondered if *this*, at long last, was the voice of Kesuquosh.

Rita came closer. Her eyes flickered. Something crawled restlessly under her face like many veins. Her skin was the color of flesh but the texture of moss. "I won't be subdued. I don't allow that. I've never asked for anything grand. My ambitions are small. But firm. I've made a heaven on earth, and I won't have you threatening it. No matter who you are."

"You didn't make a heaven," I said. "This is dystopian Thought Police *hell*. You have to know that, right? You have to know that!"

"You need to run. Get out of here," Senovak said to me quietly. Blood was running all over his hand. She'd given him some kind of fucked-up magic wound.

"Nobody is getting out of here. You can't move," Rita said. She lifted her arms up like a puppeteer moving invisible strings.

And I couldn't move. I saw Alex struggling too—but his movements were so slight, hardly betraying the enormous fight he must have been putting up inside. I tried to lift my foot so hard that I felt like I was going to have an aneurysm, and absolutely nothing happened.

Rita walked by the three of us, close enough that I could smell Crème de la Mer on her skin, while we stayed still as statues. "Time to wake up," she said. Then there was a soft rustling from around us. I could move my eyes, but not enough to see what she was doing. Just enough to see Alex, looking at me with unmoving horror, as Jasper looped one arm around him, rested his head against Alex's still shoulder, and pulled the red-flamed oil lamp from Alex's rigid hand.

"We're going to be *so* happy together," Jasper crooned. "This is the best part!"

I had a visceral memory of KJ, lying to me to keep her mind straight, on the night of the Banquet of the Needle:

This is the best part. I've been waiting for my whole life to do this. I'm so glad you're here—

There was a smell of burning behind me. Soft little sounds, like the sounds I'd heard when the Incorporations were following us quietly through the cornfield.

"Censure. For the three of them. Do as I say," Rita said. "Now, Darian, you'll see what I mean. I'm going to make all of you worthy of love. Fix you right up."

We're all getting brain-sucked, I thought. The Incorporations were moving through the model town toward the black dollhouse, where we were all frozen. I could hear them coming. When I looked past Alex, past Jasper, all the way over to the far side of the clearing, I could see Dexter sitting on the limb of one of the trees that disappeared into the overhead space, his legs dangling in the air.

I thought of how KJ had called Kesuquosh a snow globe. I tried to fix her face—her smiling face, her *real* eyes—in my mind, so that she was the last thing I pictured.

I felt a burning hand touch my shoulder. It was the worst pain I'd ever felt—my memory of the hot little knives slicing through my skin didn't do it justice—but I couldn't scream.

"It only hurts for a minute," Rita said, and laughed her high-low laugh again.

"Less than that!" Jasper said.

Then something happened. Another sensation. Very cold, in counterpoint to the burning. Something—many delicate *somethings*—were wrapping around me.

I was yanked backward through the air so quickly that I felt my stomach bottom out. I skidded along the table, grazing the black dollhouse with my feet, and landed on the earth at the edge of the clearing. The air was knocked out of me. But I could move again.

The false village was being crisscrossed by Good Arcturus's sinews. I saw them wrapping around Senovak, hauling him away from the two Incorporations that had been preparing to do *whatever* it was that made people like Jasper. He was lifted in the air and thrown toward the opposite side of the town, blood falling from the cuts on his face as he went. Jasper was knocked back by a clutch of threads thicker than an adult man's arm. The oil lamp he held smashed against a blue house with a peaked roof, the flame inside it winking out. The air was vibrating again. The Incorporations were held in place by strands.

"Ahhhhhhhhhh!" Alex screamed as he was pushed back, stumbling over the houses at the edge of the common that were painted to look like stone, knocking against two of them as he fell. The whole village was strung with moving red, connected by string. It threaded through the trees around us, looking like the inside of a spiderweb. The earth was shaking so hard that my vision started to blur. Through all of this, Good Arcturus himself did not move at all. He remained totally shrouded, face cast down, in motionless contemplation of the black dollhouse.

None of the threads touched Rita. But she reached out and *tore* at them, long rippling limbs crawling over the sinews, screaming until her strange voice broke apart into echoes, her face twisted with anger—

"*No!* You may *not* interfere! You will return to your rest!"

And Good Arcturus had to listen to her. I knew he had to listen to her. He and KJ had tried hard to rebel against the centuries of control. But I thought that what had just happened was the last of his ability to defy her. She was in his mind. There was no way to get him free from something that was in his mind. The same as it was for everyone in Kesuquosh.

The red sinews started to retreat. And then I had an idea. But I had to do it *now*. Right now, while we were all still connected by the red threads. Even the burning Incorporations. They were an ingredient.

Between the vibration and my shaking legs, I couldn't stand. I crawled forward, and leaned against a white dollhouse—and pulled out my amethyst.

It burned my hand so badly that I screamed. But I didn't drop it. This time I knew the entire spell. I'd read it so many times in the eleven months after I failed to save my one true love and my best and dearest friend.

I held the amethyst in my left hand. In my right hand, I reached out and grasped one of Good Arcturus's red strands. I looked out at the shaking village. Each of the six Incorporations, rising to stand. Jasper at the far treeline, his eyes black and fathomless. Senovak on his feet, one hand over his bloody face. Alex against the houses that lined the miniature town common.

Rita advancing toward me through a mist of sinews.

Every single one of us connected by Good Arcturus.

"These burnt offerings to the mind of all minds," I said.

"This skull to that skull.

This life open to all life.

This heart an abyss—"

"Put that *down*," Rita said. She got to the house I was crouched against and started to come around it, her face twisted, hands hooked into wicked claws still wet with Senovak's blood. A bad witch could recognize the magic of a good witch, I guess, even if Friday and Flora were miles from here. I crawled backward, keeping my fingers around one red thread.

"In our smallness," I said.

"*STOP!*" Rita screamed. She was right *there*, almost touching me, her arms out.

"In our nothingness," I said.

"In our power, in our vastness—"

I took my hand and pressed Good Arcturus's red thread between my lips like a strand of hair, looking at every single person who was touched by his sinews. We were all connected. I swallowed the thread until I choked, spinning the spell into a stable loop with myself as the center.

The woods disappeared.

I was falling through a dark and endless space. Far above me, I could feel Rita's words, like a rope, pulling me back. Pulling us all back. Pulling *herself* back to the world where she had control. She was so strong.

"Baby, please don't *do* this," she said. And it was so compelling. I *wanted* to go to her.

I fell past the sidewalk outside of K-Family Pizza where Senovak and I had argued the day before. I fell past the car ride where I told KJ I loved her in her ruins.

I fell past the nights I'd lain awake over the past almost-year, while Dexter watched me from the dark. I fell past the snowy street in DUMBO where a little girl with long hair was buzzed into a building that had AIR painted on it.

It still wasn't deep enough. I could still feel Rita far above me, reaching down to pull me out of my mind.

I hoped I could drag her down with me. Otherwise this was all for nothing.

I fell past Dexter, reading from my battered copy of *Dandelion Wine*.

Chapter 28. The story of the two soul mates who had been separated by a large span of years, one on her ancient deathbed and the other one barely thirty, doomed to keep meeting each other too soon or too late. I'd loved that story so much. I had wanted to *believe* in it.

But that still wasn't deep enough.

"Come back, honey," Rita said. "You don't want to be alone in this darkness."

"I'm not alone!" I screamed up into the ether.

And I was right. I saw other things, other flickers of memories that didn't belong to me. Senovak, impossibly young, surrounded by greenery and vines, in his Army uniform, standing with his forehead pressed against the forehead of Linus Hekekia. There and gone.

KJ sitting cross-legged on the yellow couch in her garage, smoking, wearing a pale blue dress that I'd never seen, with "The Way Things Are" by Fiona Apple—courtesy of one of my carefully crafted mix CDs—playing at top volume. Shuffling through a bunch of Polaroids she and I had taken together the summer before, her eyes undilated for the briefest second, her face tracked with tears.

I thought I would hate the world forever, she said in my head.

Jasper, a tiny little-kid Jasper, sitting up in a hospital bed in a quiet room, looking around with a bewildered expression on his face.

Alex in a dark and abandoned place, wrapped in a blanket, taking a syringe that someone handed to him.

Two little girls who had a familial resemblance to me walking toward Good Earth Way in their child-sized red robes, holding hands.

A minister in the kind of old-fashioned clothing I'd only ever seen crudely replicated in movies, standing in a primitive town center, holding a rifle, pleading with a beautiful dark-haired woman while behind her the scarecrow she'd captured loomed and loomed . . .

And it still wasn't deep enough.

"Come back to the world," Rita said. Her hand reached down into the bottom of the universe in my head. I wanted to take it. I missed my mom.

But I didn't. I had been trying not to go to the place I knew I had to go.

The worst thing I ever did.

"Come with me," I said, to everyone inside my head but mostly to Rita. "Let me take you down."

I grabbed her hand and sank. I felt her coming with me. Falling out of the world and into my mind, unable to guard the prisoners she kept.

Please let this work, I thought. *Please let this set Good Arcturus free, because this is everything I have.*

It was Christmastime in New York when we stopped falling.

CHAPTER TWENTY-EIGHT

Friday, December 13, 1996

We met on Friday that week, just twelve days shy of my thirteenth birthday, and Dexter was in a very dark place. He had been talking about our suicide pact again.

Dexter had been getting worse for weeks, as the days grew shorter and darker, and he was frightening me a little more every time we saw each other. He'd relapsed sometime earlier in the year, and his addiction burned like a conflagration made of everything else in his life, consuming him while the months turned toward winter. Most days I had to give myself my own lessons on his beautiful upright piano, a one-hundred-and-three-year-old Heintzman that I was a little bit in love with.

Sometimes Dexter wouldn't even come into the recording studio at all. He would just stay holed up in the bedroom at the far end of his labyrinthine warehouse apartment until I went and found him, lying there under his down comforter with his current musical obsession on the record player, tarot cards scattered all over the bed, vintage clothes in piles, the Victorian box (lined in purple satin) that he kept his syringes in thrown carelessly to the side.

But today he was manic, and that kind of darkness was just as frightening to me as his sad moods were. Pacing. Talking about the suicide pact. He had given me a heavily embroidered silk piano shawl as an early birthday present. I stood in front of the mirror in his room while he draped it over me just so, his glasses glinting in the low light like a larger pair of eyes.

"Very cool. Very Janis Joplin," he said.

"It's so pretty. But I can't take it home," I said. "Dan will say something."

"Fucking *Dan*," Dexter said, his usually soft voice full of contempt. "That stupid prick. I want to get away from all of the Dans of this world, you know?"

I nodded. I did know. He had been talking about it a lot lately. *Getting away*, of course, being code for killing ourselves together.

Behind the walls of the snow globe, out in the space of our shared minds, I could feel people watching. I had pulled everyone from the black house down here—they were my captive and unwilling audience. No freedom of movement now, not like when KJ had hailed a cab inside my consciousness. They were all in too deep with me. I couldn't exactly see them, any more than I could exactly remember why we were here. Everything was blurred and indistinct in the snow globe except for this one moment in time. But I knew that I couldn't reach them . . . that they couldn't stop what happened next.

"I think we should do it now," Dexter said, after a thousand beats of silence. I knew him well enough to know that he was referring to suicide, not sex. I think that was the only tiny bit of mercy in the whole situation, the fact that we hadn't, on that last day. I knew that Senovak was there somewhere. I didn't want to make any of them witness a graphic act of child rape. But him least of all. I thought it just might kill him.

"Now?" I asked. I turned away from the mirror to look at Dexter directly, stepping over the Ten of Wands card, which had been carelessly thrown on the floor.

Dexter nodded, pressing his lips together. His gaze looked haunted and tired and sad behind his glasses, and I tried—in a way that was still pretty clumsy, pretty childlike—to emotionally prepare myself for another one of his attempts at persuasion.

"It's only going to get harder," Dexter said. "To be together. I'm supposed to go to LA to do some work. The world will pull us apart, apart, apart. Time, babe. Time is against us. If we do it now, we can reset the clock. It can always be just like this. Our souls can be born into a new life together. Like Bill and Helen in *Dandelion Wine*."

I wish I could explain to you how many times, how many *ways* I had already talked him out of this double-suicide plan. I was an expert at it.

Everything will be okay. We'll be together. When I'm older. When I'm free.

Nothing can stop us then.

We don't know if death would really give us another chance.

Stay with me, Dex, I love you so much.

I'm not ready to go yet.

And on and on and on.

But that day, at that moment in time, something was different.

I felt something give way inside me. For a moment it was like I was a stranger to myself. I felt my *real* feelings, the ones I always held back.

The revulsion and pain. The fear of being found out, of being touched again, of being dragged down with Dexter into a place where nobody would ever be able to find me. The self-loathing. And the thin strand of something within me that hadn't been destroyed: a desire to survive.

To escape. To be free.

"Okay," I said, and turned around. Gave Dexter a look.

"Really?" Dexter asked, and I nodded.

"I think . . . I think I'm ready," I said.

"So brave. So brave, baby," Dexter said. His face was a mask of wistful pain and pleasure. He kissed me, and I kissed him back. Putting everything into it. Making it convincing.

"But you have to let me do it *my* way," I said. I was using my most grown-up voice, the one that had the best success rate when it came to Dexter giving me what I wanted. The voice of reason. "I don't want to do drugs with you, okay? I want like—like pills or something."

"You're such a square," Dexter said, like it was an adorable quirk, instead of just me being a frightened kid. He hadn't ever been able to get me to shoot up with him. Honestly he hadn't tried *that* hard. Maybe he thought Senovak would sniff that out. Dexter got up and put his single of "Collapsing New People" by Fad Gadget on the record player. He said that the bridge in that track was, to him, the perfect sound for dying to.

The last thing I want to hear, he'd murmur. *What about you?*

And I would come up with some new answer every time. "Rhapsody on a Theme of Paganini" by Rachmaninoff. Or Natalie Merchant's "Carnival," which I thought was incredibly sophisticated, then. But no Debussy, no Chopin, not a whisper of Samuel

Coleridge-Taylor's *Valse Suite*, none of Tori Amos's luminous pieces with the brilliant piano playing, the level of genius that I aspired to. Nothing that really mattered to me, not one of the songs that changed my life. Because I didn't actually *want* to die, so I couldn't actually pick the ideal music to score my death. No matter what I said, he would call it an "immature choice," anyway.

"Come here, babe."

Dexter was smiling. Holding his arms out. Probably thinking we would rock back and forth and have a nice long heartfelt cry before we killed ourselves. But in my strange new mood, I wanted to get it over with.

"I'll be right back," I said, and went into the bathroom. I knew where he kept everything, after two years.

I opened the medicine cabinet and pulled out one of Dexter's many pill bottles from his library of intensely abused prescriptions. I read the label. My audience watched me through the snow globe. Inside I felt nothing but absolute calm, a bright void.

When I went back, Dexter had finished cooking up his heroin.

"I've never done this much before," he said.

He sat on the edge of the bed, his legs facing toward the head-board, and I sat next to him.

"You will follow me, baby," Dexter said, "won't you? I don't want to die without you."

For a second, behind his glasses, he looked afraid. If there had been anything left in me, I would have talked him out of it then.

But I didn't. I gazed at him with an innocence that wouldn't have been studied, too many years before. But now it was an act.

"Of course I will," I said, and smiled. Shook my bottle of pills.

Dexter nodded. Kissed me. I was usually very still and compliant when he kissed me. But now, in my moment of crystalline clarity, it was difficult not to flinch when his lips brushed my cheek.

He took his syringe, tapped out the air bubbles. Drew back the needle until he saw one dark and shining drop of blood.

And stopped.

Something came over his face, something . . . something *sly*. I had seen that expression before, and it always frightened me.

In the moments when Dexter looked like that, I had the uneasy thought that he was something else, wearing the face of a human being.

"Wait," he said. "It's not right unless we both do it at the same time. Show me those," Dexter said, and took the pill bottle out of my hands.

The sly look was still on his face. He didn't trust me. I waited without hardly taking a breath until he read the label, opened the bottle, and handed it back to me. He looked at me in a way that made me feel like I was going to crawl right out of my skin. Little half smile on his face. His eyes hidden by the way the light reflected off his glasses.

"You're really ready?" Dexter asked. He touched my cheek.

"I'm ready," I said. My voice broke a little on the lie. But Dexter smiled.

"Then take them," he said.

"Okay," I said.

I knew I wasn't going to get out of it.

I swallowed several of the pills with a big swig of sparkling water while he watched me closely. Then another handful.

Then Dexter, satisfied, kissed me on the head.

"Good girl," he said. "I love you so much, Darian."

"I love you too, Dex," I said. The room was starting to spin. I felt the effects of the pills stealing over me, making it hard to focus.

I watched as Dexter overdosed. His body relaxed. He laid back, dangling off the edge of the bed until his upper body met the floor, one leg bent and folded under the other, his shaggy gold hair spread around him in a crown. He faced me and the ceiling, his pupils constricted into pinpoints and his eyelids drooping. He looked like his favorite tarot card.

The Hanged Man. The card of sacrifice.

It had probably taken a long time, all of this, from the moment I had agreed to go along with it until this moment. The big suicide thing. But it felt like minutes. Nothing happened inside me. Not even a whisper.

"Darian . . . Adrian . . . ," Dexter whispered, looking up at me. His glasses were askew. He was on the verge of nodding off. "You're . . . coming? Coming with me? . . . Right . . . right, baby. Right . . . ?"

"Yeah. I promise," I said. My words sounded a little slurry.

Then I got up—I staggered, trying to get to my feet—and walked around him. The room was tilting like it was going to tumble over. When I reached the bathroom, I had to hold on to the doorframe so I didn't fall.

"Darian," Dexter said from behind me. "Wait. Wait . . ."

It seemed like he was trying to get up. But he didn't have the strength. For a few seconds I watched him struggle before he gave up. Drifting. His eyes falling shut.

Then I calmly walked into his bathroom with the snowy windows and the glass block wall, knelt in front of the toilet, shoved my finger down my throat, and threw up until there was absolutely nothing left in my stomach. Pills and bile poured into the toilet.

When I was done vomiting, I sat against the wall. I rocked back and forth for a while while "Collapsing New People" played over and over and over again.

I sat there for a long time, until it was almost dark and I was running out of time before Senovak came to get me.

Then I got up and walked back into the bedroom. Dexter's face was utterly pale, his lips blue.

I went into the living room and called the police.

Yes, I'd found my piano instructor. I thought he was dead. Could they please come quickly?

My voice shook, and that was okay. I was crying by the end of the phone call, and that was okay too.

But I wasn't crying because he was gone.

I was crying because he was sitting in the living room, smiling at me, his eyes invisible behind his glasses.

You promised, Darian, he said. *You promised. You promised.*

In my memory I hadn't said anything to his shade, the first time it ever appeared to me. I'd hidden behind the couch in a ball until the police arrived.

But this time I turned toward him. He stood in his Jimi Hendrix jacket and his shining glasses, his back against the huge wall of lattice windows, the snow blowing around behind him.

"You promised, Darian," Dexter said. "You lied to me. You killed me."

"I didn't," I said. My voice was pathetic and broken. "I didn't."

"I needed your help," Dexter said. His face was sad.

"I—"

"I needed your help and you *killed me*," Dexter continued, and he reached one arm out—it was too long, a spider's arm, and it burned like the hands of the Incorporations. He pulled me across the entire room to him, until we were pressed together. I tried to scream, but I choked on my words.

"That was unforgivable," Dexter said solemnly. "Now they all know who you really are. You liked it when I died. You *delighted* in the death of a troubled man. You *pushed* me."

He leaned in, his teeth too sharp, kissed my neck as I struggled. But he was so much stronger than I was. So much.

"But now," Dexter said, pressing another kiss to my neck. "We can finally be alone."

And I was alone.

Alone alone alone.

Alone with Dexter forever.

I closed my eyes, tears slipping down my face, and waited for it to be over.

And then I felt something. Something very slight and very cold, on my ankle bone.

I looked down, Dexter's breath hot at my throat, and saw a single strand of shining red.

One tiny piece of Good Arcturus, reaching out to touch me from another world.

MY FRIEND, it said. *YOU ARE NOT ALONE.*

I took a step back. Dexter reached for me again.

"I'm not alone," I said.

"Come here, baby," Dexter said, showing me the inside of his sharp smile. "You owe me."

"No," I said. "I'm not alone. And I don't owe you anything."

"You owe me. You *killed* me," Dexter said. "You KILLED ME, Darian, you *killed* me—"

"I DIDN'T KILL YOU," I said. Actually, I was screaming, screaming so loud that it felt like my voice was going to break. "BUT I WISH I HAD, DEXTER, OH MY GOD, I WISH I HAD, YOU FUCKING MONSTER—"

I reached out with both arms, and Dexter reached out at the same time. His hands curled in my long, dark hair. He dragged me close to him. His teeth were razors, so sharp they cut his lips open when he spoke.

"Stay with me," he said.

"*No!*" I screamed, and twisted my head until I felt hair tearing from my scalp. I smacked Dexter in the chest with both hands, pushing him impossibly hard, and the leaded windowpanes behind him shattered like strands in a spiderweb.

We fell backward into the snowy night.

I laughed as we fell, giddy with the stomach-dropping feeling of it.

"My hair is short and blonde!" I said, keeping my hands on the lapels of Dexter's coat as the wind made a void around us. "I'm going to be an adult in December! And I'm not alone! I'm free!"

"Darian," Dexter said. He reached for me one last time as the earth rushed up to meet us.

"No more," I said.

Dexter's face cracked. *Cracked*, like a china doll dropped from a great height. His glasses cracked, too. Each lens fragmented to shards.

I saw his face twist in hatred for a single second—my hands were still on his jacket—and the next moment he was disintegrating into atoms. His ghost became one with the snowflakes. I landed gently on the cold ground.

KJ was there. She was looking down at me as I sat, unmoving, in my shock. She seemed completely fine.

"D," she said, and sat down next to me when I didn't immediately get up.

"Hey," she said. "D. You in there?"

"I'm okay," I said. "I think I just—"

"Had a WWE SmackDown with your own post-traumatic stress disorder?" KJ asked.

"Oh my god, fuck *off*," I said. "I think I just saved everyone's ass at the cost of my own sanity, you fucking hick."

"Snob, such a huge snob," KJ said. "Such a snob that even your abuser won a Grammy."

I laughed. I couldn't help it. I missed her *so* much.

"I must look like a complete psycho," I said. "I made him kill himself. I . . ."

"Sincerely? It was the most badass thing I have ever seen in my entire life," KJ said. She leaned against me for a second. Never asking for too much. Not even in my head.

"Put your arms around me," I said.

KJ shuffled over a little more and wrapped her arms around my shoulders. *That* was when I really started crying again.

"I wish you were actually here," I said, brushing snowflakes away as they settled on her hair. "Oh shit. I wish it so bad."

"Uh, D," KJ said. "I *am* actually here."

"I mean *alive*," I said.

"I mean alive, too," KJ said. "But we'll have to go back and find out for sure."

"Let's just sit like this for a little while," I said.

"No way. You don't get to do all that work and then just stay in the dark," KJ said.

She got up. In the streetlights, in the snow, she was the most beautiful girl I had ever seen. But she would have been that beautiful anywhere.

She offered me her hand, and I took it.

"Brilliantly executed spell," KJ said. "Now let's go back and defeat my mom."

CHAPTER TWENTY-NINE

Thursday, September 13, 2001

I opened my eyes and my hand was on fire.

I screamed, dropped my burning crystal, and looked around at the suddenly quiet village. All of the threads of Good Arcturus had retracted. He stood against the black dollhouse with his head bowed and his face covered, like he'd never intervened to begin with.

Senovak was getting up from the far side of the clearing. His face was still wounded, but it wasn't gushing blood, and he seemed like he was moving okay. One of his eyes was rapidly puffing shut.

Against the treeline, Jasper opened his eyes. They were *normal*. He stood up unsteadily, holding on to a tree trunk.

"Dan!" I said. "Jasper!"

I went to run to them—but I was stopped. In front of me was the town common, and *on* the common was Rita, splayed across the square of grass like she was asleep. Her hair covered her face almost entirely. Her clawed hands and feet were covered in flesh-colored moss. I saw shapes like eyes growing in the moss that spread up one of her wrists. Her skin moved even as she lay still.

I turned right and circled around the head of the common, running past Good Arcturus, dodging around two perfectly still Incorporations.

On the ground in front of me Alex climbed to his feet, looking dazed.

"Come on, kids," Senovak said. "We need to go!"

It was too late, though. As the four of us reached each other, I heard a gentle noise. Rita sitting up, standing up. Walking along the tiny version of Good Earth Way in her bare feet.

"Wait," Rita said. Her voice—the shuddering voice of Kesuquosh—sounded like the insidious promise of the voice I had heard in my mind-meld last year. An undercurrent of sharpness. Cruelty.

"Fuck you, Rita, you fucking *bitch*!" Jasper shouted. "I trusted you! Fuck you! The *biggest* fuck you to you in the whole fucking *universe*!"

Even if we were completely screwed, I couldn't ever express to you the relief I felt when I heard Jasper say *fuck*.

"That's great, honey," Rita said. "Now everybody stop moving."

I guess her power wasn't in a wand or a piece of chalk or rock, but in her *voice*. Her words had always been able to convince me. Maybe every witch was different that way.

We stopped. For the second time, I was held still by the power of her voice. We all were.

"Daniel," Rita said. "You've killed people during active duty, haven't you?" She turned around us, her mouth hanging open and showing only darkness within, skin wriggling like maggots. Did a delicate little spin on her clawed toes, sending a few dead leaves scattering, light-footed as a cat. She moved like she had all the time in the world.

Senovak watched her approach with his eyes only. With his *one* good eye. The other one had swollen fully shut above the slashes on his face. I saw the cords of muscle in his neck standing out as he tried to fight off the stillness she'd imposed on us.

"I think you know I've always loved children," Rita said. "Even your child. Or, I should say, your employer's child. She's been so dear to me."

Rita stroked one hand through my hair as she walked around me, her clawed fingers grazing my scalp almost hard enough to draw blood. One mossy arm touched my cheek. I could feel *things* moving in the moss, opening like lidded eyes. I tried to moan, to cringe away in revulsion. But I was held utterly still.

"Didn't do a very good job looking out for her, though, did you?" Rita said. Then she leaned right toward me, her soft breath against my cheek. Her eyes had perfect moons of white light in their center. Inhuman eyes.

"It was very smart, what you did," she said. "For someone who isn't a natural witch. But it didn't work, honey. I'm so sorry."

Then she turned away from me. "Daniel," she said, almost conversationally. "There's a straight razor in Jasper's pocket—I gave it to him in case this little conflict went terribly awry, which of course it has. It's my husband's. A previous husband. It's so *sad* when I outlive them. And this is a hand-me-down. I want you to kill Darian and Jasper with it. Then yourself. Okay?"

Then she stepped away from us, and took Alex's face between her clawed hands. His eyes were wide and horrified. One tear ran out of the corner of his eye and dripped off his chin.

"You I can still fix," Rita said. "My baby."

"You can move now, Daniel," she said, still looking at Alex.

Senovak took a breath. His hand extended, shaking. He reached into Jasper's pocket.

No, please don't make him do this, I thought. *No, please, no, please.*

Senovak pulled the straight razor out and unfolded it. It was old, but the blade glinted, perfectly sharp. He turned it slowly in his hand. I could see him shuddering with effort, trying to turn the blade back on himself. Kill himself before he had to hurt us.

Then I smelled ozone.

Heard the vibrations start, like a generator powering up.

whump whump whump whump WHUMP WHUMP WHUMP WHUMP

Rita whirled around, and in that one moment of broken concentration, Senovak threw the razor across the clearing so hard that it smacked against a tree trunk and brought down a little fall of bark.

"What was that?" Rita said, and then Good Arcturus stepped over the black dollhouse on his many sinews.

He was massive.

It had worked. My spell had broken Rita's hold for long enough. Freed him. It had *worked.* He was waking up.

"No!" Rita said. "Return to your rest! You *must* stop—"

No, said a voice that I could hear only in my head.

I found that I could move again, and took one staggering step, almost falling against the shuddering of the ground. I caught Alex's elbow with my arm and Dan's shoulder bumped mine, and Jasper tumbled back into us, all four of us leaning against a clutch of dollhouses in a knot, trying to stay on our feet.

Rita stood beneath Good Arcturus, screaming at him.

"*You will return to your rest!*" she commanded, raising both arms.

But the sinews of Good Arcturus batted them down.

She shrieked in rage, and ran *at* him, raising her arms again. But she was cut off by a wall of moving red string.

Good Arcturus bent in half, his sinew arms working, and pulled the swath of skin away from his body like he was taking a dress off over his head. Then he set it down on the tiled ground. Carefully. Gently.

And it wasn't a shield at all, and it wasn't a sheet of skin, and it wasn't a straitjacket.

It was KJ. She was lying on the leaf-strewn ground, her face dirty and pale, wearing the tattered remnants of her Scary Scarecrow costume.

She had a bullet hole in her forehead, right between the eyes. A thin stream of dried blood ran out of it.

Poor child, said the voice in my head. One sinew reached out and touched KJ's cheek.

"KJ!" I yelled. Alex and Jasper and I all tried to run to her, and we all skidded along the moving ground, unable to cross the clearing. Rita alone stayed on her feet, screaming. Behind her, the motionless Incorporations started to come back to life, jerking around like puppets on long strings.

Rita didn't even *look* at KJ. She darted to the side, jumping onto the roof of one of the dollhouses in an elegant movement, and she ran straight across it toward Good Arcturus. Her hands tangled in the mass of his sinews, trying to drag him down, back toward his spot behind the black dollhouse.

She still had power, even if it was not power *over* Good Arcturus. When she pulled at his threads, her mouth open in a snarl of hatred, the whole giant glowing space of the false village pulled *with* her, flexing like a soap bubble. Tree branches rained down over us, hitting the ground and the houses. Jasper and I were the ones closest to the middle of the clearing, and we both threw our arms over our heads, trying to shield ourselves.

"You are *mine* to command! *Mine! This place is mine!*" Rita screamed. She made another pulling motion with her arms, and when she threw her hands to the side, the entire forest tilted. I felt like I had at Dexter's apartment, all those years ago, when the pills started to take effect. Only this time the world was *actually* tilting.

The mossy ground cracked in a hundred places, one line directly under the spot where I'd fallen trying to get to KJ. I rolled away as a thin chasm opened up beneath me, scrabbling to an unbroken piece of earth. Dollhouses started to fall into the fresh fault lines, bits of them shearing away.

The house that I thought was Birdie Plum's cracked in half and slid into a hole that had opened up along the common. A chasm devoured most of Good Earth Way.

The black veins that shot through the village flowed *backward* into the Incorporations like film played in reverse. And Rita stayed on her feet through it all, screaming at the scarecrow, trying to command him—

"You have to *do as I say!*"

And Good Arcturus, amid the silt and branches and crashing chaos of the crumbling world, leaned forward and down until he was eye level with the witch screaming up at him.

YOU HAVE KEPT ME FOR A WHILE IN YOUR SNARE, LITTLE JUNIE, came Good Arcturus's voice in my thoughts. *YOUR LUCK, PERHAPS, THAT I AM NOT A SEASONED TRAVELER.*

I found that I couldn't look directly at his bare face. Whenever I tried, my eyes seemed to move away from it, or else it was turned away from me.

Then, more elegantly than I could have imagined such a creature moving, he formed a bunch of sinews into the rough shape of a hand.

In the center of this makeshift hand lay a very large needle.

Rita's mouth opened. Her face was white. Inhuman, with her crawling skin and her fleshy veins of moss and her shining eyes.

I BELIEVE THIS BELONGS TO YOU, Good Arcturus said.

He dropped the needle on the ground, and Rita bent to snatch it up.

MY FRIENDS, Good Arcturus said, and I could feel him focusing on us, even though I couldn't look at his face.

Jasper was weaving his way toward KJ's body, staggering every time a shock wave rolled through the model town.

I tried to get up again. This time I made it to my feet, following Jasper. A falling branch from one of the shaking trees almost knocked me to the ground, but I managed to dodge it.

Good Arcturus moved his sinews over KJ's head.

For a second she was hidden. Then his threadlike appendages fell away from her face, revealing unscathed skin where the bullet hole had been.

KJ sat up. She was on the ground between Rita and Good Arcturus.

Jasper reached her first, grabbing her arms with his hands. He tried to pull her up and she ended up pulling him down. Behind them the black dollhouse split in half, spilling out red light like a bloody wound.

It is time for an end to your dominion over this place, Good Arcturus's voice said.

"No!" Rita screamed. "No! I won't have you destroy *everything I have made*—"

Her arms reached for him. She stretched out over KJ, paying her no mind. Her face roiled, caving in on itself. Her skin was more moss than skin, and I saw dark fissures underneath the moss. Something inside her threatening to come out. And she spread herself out like a spider, snatching at Good Arcturus, trying to tangle her hands inside his threads, trying to pull his limbs away from everything they touched.

Underneath the crashing and smashing and vibration of forest collapsing in on itself, I could hear KJ's voice, her *real* voice, not doubled:

"You didn't make anything but a prison, Ma," KJ said. "Stop fooling yourself."

Then I reached KJ and Jasper, grabbed for her as she tried to get up and just slid back down onto her elbows. Working together, Jasper and I managed to pull her up.

"*KJ*, oh, *oh* my god, are you all right?" I asked, and she stumbled into my arms, folded herself around me. Hugged me tighter than she ever had. It was part unsteadiness and part emotion.

"You're alive," I said, arms clutching her shoulders. I felt like if I let go she would die again, or disappear. She was bent over like a willow tree, her face against my neck. "You're alive, you're alive—"

"I told you, D," KJ said. She leaned back, smiled at me kind of woozily. "I told you in your freaky mind fortress. I . . . um . . . I w-w-wanted to help you in there but I—"

"You did help me," I said. I had tears in my eyes. "You always help me. KJ. KJ. We all saw you *die*—"

"I think you helped yourself," KJ said, and dropped her head into the crook of my shoulder, exhausted, her face drawn and still crusted in dried blood from her vanished bullet wound, lips barely touching my skin.

Then the ground shuddered again, moving under us like a raft on choppy seas, and she staggered. I wasn't strong enough to hold her up myself. Jasper put his hands against both of us.

Senovak reached us, and helped steady KJ, the four of us struggling to stay upright on the shaking ground.

I CANNOT BRING MYSELF TO JUDGE YOU, Good Arcturus said to Rita. *BUT I DO BELIEVE THEY HAVE THE RIGHT.*

I turned around. Behind Rita, five of the six previous Incorporations were lined up in a semicircle.

AND I DO NOT THINK THAT THEY WILL JUDGE YOU KINDLY, Good Arcturus said.

"Wait," Rita said. "No, no, *wait*—"

She backed away. Only then did she seem to remember that there were other people in the woods with her. Her gaze slid over me and Senovak, KJ and Jasper, and stopped on Alex.

The tallest of the burnt things—the one I thought was maybe the *first* one, the minister from the original story—reached out and touched her mossy shoulder. Rita screamed in agony, and stabbed the needle she held into the shoulder of the Incorporation, and pulled away from him.

"Alex!" she cried in her ancient and inhuman voice. "Baby! Please help me! Don't let them do this to me!"

Alex, who had almost reached us, looked at his mom. His face showed real pain.

But then he took a breath. I couldn't hear it, with the noise of the village breaking apart around us, but I *saw* it. The inhale, the resolve in his posture.

"Mom," Alex said. "It's *one* person's life against the happiness and health of *every single person* in Kesuquosh."

He was quoting her own words back to her. What she'd said to him last Halloween morning.

Rita's eyes widened.

A huge oak tree limb broke off and hit the ground. A flying fragment grazed Rita's shoulder, and she cried out. She stumbled forward, into the hands of the tallest Incorporation.

The thing dragged her into the waiting arms of the others.

I saw Senovak grab Alex's shoulder and turn him away.

"Go now," Senovak said. I saw his look. *You don't need to see this*, it said.

He steered Alex and Jasper toward the treeline, sliding every time a tremor rocked the little town. He left them at the edge of the forest, then made his way back to us.

The miniature Kesuquosh was in a thousand pieces. Wind howled through the previously still world. Leaves and branches dropped like snow. I had to hold my arms over my head.

Senovak steadied KJ with both arms, and started guiding her out.

"Come on, Darian," he said.

I started to follow him, and something pulled me back. I turned in a panic, expecting to see one of Rita's clawed hands—*knew I wouldn't make it*, I thought, in a flash of terror—and saw the sixth Incorporation behind me. The small one.

It reached out with one burnt hand, and offered me my fallen amethyst.

I took it. It hurt to touch, but I dropped it into my pocket without crying out.

"Thank you," I said. "Blanche."

The little Incorporation stood there silently.

"Can you come with us?" I asked.

But it shook its head, once. *She* shook her head. I could see the glint of eyes way back behind the gauze mask.

"I'm sorry for what happened to you," I said, and felt like I was going to cry.

The Incorporation made no acknowledgment of my words. It only stood facing me for a second longer. Then it turned away to join the others.

The forest was filled with dust and ash. The Incorporations were pulling Rita toward the largest chasm that had opened up in the center of the town common. The clearing tilted inward like a melting candle. It was *hell* in there.

And Good Arcturus towered over it all, his many sinews overlapping in ceaseless motion.

There was a tremendous crash, and debris filled my vision, blocking off any view I had of the caverns opening underneath the town. It was collapsing in on itself.

"Come along *now*!" Senovak shouted.

Then I turned and ran, and followed the others through the dark woods and out into the world.

CHAPTER THIRTY

Thursday, September 13, 2001

We stepped out of the black house at sunrise. In the forest I'd caught hold of KJ's hand, wrapped my fingers around hers, making sure she was okay, that she could walk. Senovak was basically holding her up on the other side, but when we got back out into *reality*, he left her leaning against me and turned toward the house.

KJ immediately shifted so that we were facing each other. Her big dark eyes were ringed with sleepless purple, but she was real and touching me and *alive*.

I felt my face crumpling as I looked at her. It was so much to look at her that I couldn't even cry at all. Like the feeling of it was too big to come out. But then she brushed one thumb over my cheek and I realized that I *was* crying.

"I thought you were gone," I said. Put one hand to her head, touched the side of her face, tracing my fingers against the silky hair above her ear. "Gone. The only one—"

"D. Thank you for coming back. We would still be prisoners without you," KJ said, and I startled a little.

"W-w-we?" I asked.

"Yeah. Me, myself. And Good Arcturus. Us," KJ said, and hooked one thumb over her shoulder like she was hitchhiking. Behind her the black house loomed.

"Oh. When you said *we* I thought for a second he was back in there with you," I said, and KJ shook her head. Then she carefully turned around, looked at the building.

"Nope. Not in here. He's in *there*," KJ said, and the entire house *juddered*, like a boat at sea.

"Should we run?" Jasper asked.

"Not yet," Senovak said. "Give it a moment."

I glanced over at him. For a second we caught each other's eyes. And I knew what Senovak was thinking: that he wanted to make sure only the people (beings, creatures, whatever) who *should* make it out *did* make it out.

Alex was shaking. He came up next to me and hugged KJ hard around the neck—a thing she looked way too weak for—and then he started crying.

"I can't believe you're alive," he said through his tears. "Rocks, oh rocks, oh KJ, I thought you were dead. I thought you were dead."

"I'm not dead, dipshit," KJ said, hugging him back as tightly as she was able.

"KJ. Oh man, I—I let them kill Mom," Alex said, like he was sharing some huge secret with the side of KJ's head.

"You couldn't have saved her, even if you wanted to," Senovak said diplomatically. "She clearly had her own debts to pay."

Jasper was less diplomatic. He spit right on the ground and wiped his lips with a look of disgust.

"He's fucking traumatized now, just like *your* ass. I'm going to be hearing about this for years," Jasper said to me. "Maybe I should've dated Brooks instead."

"I'm so glad you're back, so I can remember how awful you are," I said. Then Jasper hugged me, like a *real* hug, and it was so surprising that I stopped talking. I wanted to ask him what his time as the black-eyed chipper creature from my nightmares had been like, but I thought I should wait. He was probably traumatized too, even if he was refusing to acknowledge it.

"Those Incorporations," Alex said, still looking a little glassy-eyed. "They killed her."

"Al," KJ said, still staring straight at the black house, "as much as it hurts me to say this, Ma kind of had it coming. You know?"

"I *know*," Alex said, like that was the worst part, and he started crying more, and holding her really tightly again.

"Go easy on your sister," Senovak said, guiding Alex away. "Maybe less aggressive with the squeezing."

"Were you really going to kill us, Dan?" Jasper asked. "Your will had to be stronger than hers, right?"

"I was going to dispatch you quite painlessly," Senovak said. "But just you. For fun."

Jasper laughed, and then the front door of the black house swung open, and the world started buzzing as Good Arcturus emerged from it, bending nearly in half to fit out the doorway. He *was* bigger than I'd thought. And I still couldn't look at his face.

As he crossed the clearing toward us, there was a tremendous *crack*. It echoed through the fields, seeming to cut into the actual morning itself. I looked left and right, trying to discern the source of the noise . . . and when I looked back, the black house was gone.

Only the ruined house remained, a rough frame where an ancient house had once stood. The ruin Alex and I had seen last Halloween.

But I had a feeling that this time it would stay ruined for good.

"What happened?" KJ asked as Good Arcturus approached. "What happened to the other Incorporations?"

I COULD NOT SAVE THEM, Good Arcturus said. *THEY WERE BEYOND EVEN MY ABILITIES. KEPT ALIVE ONLY BY JUNIE AND HER WILL. THEY WILL BE ASHES NOW. BUT HOPEFULLY AT PEACE.*

His voice in my head sounded sad, like truly sad. Like he was sorry he couldn't help them. It made sense, actually. He'd lived with each one of them for a while. Maybe not a *long* while, for him. But still.

"Our mom . . . is gone, isn't she?" Alex asked.

YES. IF IT IS ANY CONSOLATION, HER NATURAL LIFE WAS AS BRIEF AS ANY OF YOURS, Good Arcturus's voice said. *SHE WOULD HAVE DIED LONG AGO, IN A WORLD WHERE SHE WAS KINDER.*

Alex nodded, wiping his eyes. But KJ looked over at me and smirked.

It was a shitty attempt at a smirk—she was so tired and pale and fucked-up that she kind of looked like she was having a stroke, or a spasm. But it was legit.

"Big A just took a page out of Darian's book and talked Rita into killing herself. Isn't that right, boss?" KJ said.

That sent Jasper off into *big* laughter. I elbowed him right in the side, because KJ was too weak for me to elbow her.

"You guys fucking suck," I said. I carefully avoided looking at Senovak. "I literally saved *all* of you."

"You shouldn't joke about that," Alex said. "That was awful. And I'm, like, crying about our horrible mom, oh man. Dare, are you okay?"

"Yes. I'm the only one. I'm the one who's magically okay," I said, drizzling a ton of sarcasm over my words.

"We were all there with you, though," Jasper said. "For real."

In my head. They'd all seen . . . everything.

"I know," I said. "I felt you watching. Looking in from outside the snow globe."

"There was no snow globe," KJ said, and touched my forearm. I glanced up into her eyes.

"Yeah," Jasper agreed. "We weren't watching you from outside. We were *with* you. You were never alone."

Then Jasper and Alex and KJ and I were all looking at each other. And for a second I could . . . I could *feel* their love, like a palpable, tangible thing. And Alex said something that perfectly echoed that feeling.

"If it was any other four people," he said, like he was really thinking about it, "if it was any other four people, I don't think they would have made it."

"Four people and Dan," Jasper said.

"It's because we're all—even though we're all kind of fucked-up—" *Even in our ruins. We are strong. We have a bond,* I tried to say. But I couldn't finish the sentence. I felt my stupid throat get all stupidly tight and choked up again.

I was not okay. But at the same time, I was better than I had been in . . . well, than I ever had been. And KJ somehow knew what I felt, or maybe what I was trying to articulate. As she looked at me her expression got soft. In front of Senovak and Good Arcturus and the sky and everything, she leaned down and kissed me on the cheek before turning to face the creature that waited patiently for our attention.

Good Arcturus inclined his head to us, his imperceptible face dipping down and then up in the light. The sunrise touched the world with pink and gold.

THANK YOU FOR REPAIRING MY TRAVELING CLOAK, he said inside all of our brains. *I WILL TAKE MY LEAVE NOW.*

"Hey," KJ said, "let us walk you to the door. It's a human tradition when you're saying goodbye."

"How do *you* know there's a door?" Alex asked.

"I was living with him in the same body and consciousness, dipshit," KJ said. "I know *everything*."

THAT IS MOST KIND OF YOU, KATHERINE JEAN, Good Arcturus said. *I WOULD BE HONORED TO HAVE YOU "WALK ME TO THE DOOR."*

"Katherine Jean?" Jasper asked.

"I'm still gonna go by KJ," KJ said quickly. "But I've, uh, I've been thinking about that for a while."

She went to push her sunglasses up in the exact way that she sometimes did when she was embarrassed, but of course she wasn't wearing sunglasses. "He agreed with me that it was good."

"Rad new name," Alex said.

"I wouldn't call it 'rad,'" Senovak said. "More like pleasant and dignified."

"See? Dan likes it too," Alex said.

"Do you like *me* now, Dan?" KJ asked.

"I'm thinking about it," Senovak said.

"I love it," I said, standing on my toes to say it right next to KJ's ear. Just to see her get kind of red.

We walked through the field in the wake of Good Arcturus's sinews. The dead sunflowers started to bloom again, and the already living sunflowers stood straighter as he passed, opening their faces like he was as much a star as his namesake.

We reached the end of the field, the slight incline that led to Empty Heaven, and Senovak grabbed me by my shoulder and tugged me back.

"Darian," he said. "What we saw, in there . . ."

The worst thing I'd ever done.

I knew this was coming. I knew it was coming. I couldn't look at him. I couldn't be judged by him. I looked at the ground, instead.

So Senovak bent down, and tilted his head up, until he was making eye contact with me (with his one open eye) whether I wanted him to or not.

"I am in awe of you," Senovak said. He put his hands on my shoulders. "Do you hear me? I am in *awe* of you."

"Oh my god. Stop," I said, and gently pushed him away—feeling weird and raw and embarrassed—though I was flooded with the deepest and most profound relief at the fact that he wasn't saying I was a crazy monster, or a murderer. He kept one hand on my shoulder when he straightened up, and we started walking toward the others together.

"You hate talking about serious things, I know. Since you were little you've tried to appear invulnerable," Senovak said. "You get that from me. But what you did, it was very brave. Are you listening?"

"I'm listening," I said. Senovak had a little half smile on his face. I didn't say anything about the technical impossibility of the "you get that from me" statement. I knew what he meant.

"Good. Moving forward, you should try following this *current* approach. Involving me when you need help. Okay?"

"I hope I don't have to deal with any more, um, pedophiles . . . or like. . . . whatever *this* is . . . ever again. But if I do, I promise to let you in on it," I said. And I meant it.

"Thank you. And, Darian? I love you. More than anything."

"Okay, chill with the feelings," I said, feeling embarrassed all over again at his sincerity. "Like, god."

We caught up to the others then, thankfully. They were moving slowly. Good Arcturus was moving slowly too, but I think that was out of politeness. KJ looked kind of winded, even from the gentle walk.

"Do you think the town will be all fucked-up and dilapidated once he leaves?" Jasper asked. "Remember last year?"

"Everyone's going to be a real person again," Alex said. "No more Thought Police."

"No more Big Brother. Wait. Big *Mother*," Jasper said.

"Oh man. I think I liked you better when you were a zombie," Alex said. But then he leaned over and kissed the top of Jasper's head. And Jasper took his hand.

I caught up to KJ. She looked over at me, then reached out and pulled her beanie off my head to put it on her own.

"Rude," I said.

"*Pfft.* Thanks for keeping my hat warm," KJ said. She still looked fucked-up. But beautiful.

"You know you're beautiful, right?" I said. "I don't know if I've ever actually told you that. I think it all the time."

"D," KJ said. "Three things. Really quick. I figure I can get some leeway now that I, you know, came back from the dead."

"You definitely can," I said. I felt a weird cosmic echo of that day in the long-ago August of the year 2000 when she'd handed me a mix CD and pushed her sunglasses up onto her head to show me the pained sincerity in her face. The longing.

"One. *You* are beautiful. You are the most beautiful girl I've ever met. I hope you don't mind me saying so."

"I don't," I said. Now it was my turn to get kind of red. I could feel my cheeks burning.

"Two. I'm sorry I called you a 'sad girl' and said you were *in ruins* when I was possessed by the big guy over there. I still think both of those things are *true*," she added, when I started to say something, "but it was rude. We should have talked about everything a long time ago."

"I wasn't ready then," I said, and the simple truth of it surprised me. I didn't really know I could be so forthright about my shit. But it had been . . . an intense twenty-four hours. "I am now."

"Okay," KJ said, and then she stopped walking entirely. I did, too, and when I turned toward her she took each of my hands in hers.

I looked up at her and she looked down at me. And then she moved—really slowly, never asking for too much—until she'd telegraphed exactly what she was going to do. My heart started pounding like I was running for my life again even before she kissed me. When she *did* kiss me, I reached up and put my hands in her hair and kissed her back. It was even better than it had been in the chapel at Cold Falls. After a second she leaned away a little, so that our lips were just barely brushing.

"KJ," I said against her lips. "In your ruins. But also in everything else . . . I love you. I love you *so much*."

"Same, D. For a while now," KJ said.

Then she pulled away, dropped one of my hands but kept the other. Started walking again, following in the wake of Good Arcturus.

"I would really like to do more," she said, glancing at me sideways. "But Dan is right there and he doesn't look like he wants a show. And also I feel like fucking garbage."

"You were shot in the head in addition to being a skin suit," I said, trying to sound normal. I felt giddy and a little tingly where her mouth had met mine. "If you had a brain you'd probably never have been able to recover."

"So true. And if *you* have a brain you're not gonna agree to the third thing. But I hope you don't, so you do. Or something."

"Hit me with the third thing," I said, swinging our clasped hands.

KJ looked at me and grinned her stupid grin. It looked even better with her eyes all normal. "Do you want to go on a date with me sometime?"

"No," I said immediately. "That whole thing in the school chapel was a big smoke screen. I'm actually interested in Good Arcturus."

"Aw, shit," KJ said. "Maybe I can get him to crawl back in here for long enough to catch a movie with you."

For the first time in a really long time, I felt like playing the piano. Ravel. Debussy. Or even one of Army of Dolly's more melodious songs. *Maybe that would be a good first date,* I thought. *We could make music together.*

Behind us Jasper had been saying something to Senovak, and Senovak was answering him.

"We're going to get in the Lincoln," Senovak said. "The Lincoln that is fucked. One of you will have to drive, because I have no depth perception right now."

"Apparently I got my license when I was all brainwashed," Jasper said.

"I love driving," KJ volunteered.

"Alex will drive," Senovak amended after a pause. "Then we are going to roll into town. We can pick up that pitiable First Select-woman, if you want. And Ken, if he's up for it. I know he's single now. And—"

"Fuck," Jasper said, laughing again.

"Ken is a very handsome man," Senovak said primly. "As I was saying. We can also bring your sisters, if you two are so inclined. And then, with our very full car, we are going to go find a place to get a goddamn milkshake."

"You're going for *milkshakes*? What am I going to eat?" Jasper asked.

"I will get you a premium cup filled with ice," Senovak said. "Then I am buying a pack of cigarettes. Then I am going to an urgent care center to get my face stitched up."

"I just remembered Djarum Blacks, rocks around us," Jasper said. "I think I accidentally quit smoking."

"Same," KJ said, feeling around in the pockets of her scarecrow costume with her free hand like she was going to find her New-ports in there.

We all reached the clearing. Then I heard a car coming down the road, and I tensed up as it pulled even with the Lincoln on one side and the PDA on the other. But it was Aunt Judy's blue van.

"Oh my god, I told them not to come," I said.

"Hey, you guys! Hey!" Alex called. Through the windshield, I saw Judy and Surendra looking straight out at Good Arcturus. Their eyes were *huge*. KJ gave them a thumbs-up.

"Those people can come with us to get milkshakes as well," Senovak said. Good Arcturus stopped in front of the shimmering doorway, with his back to us.

My traveling cloak, he thought inside my head. *My home*.

He turned around. I still couldn't look at his face. I *really* tried, knowing that I would never have another chance. But all I could make out, even when I stared with all my might, was an overpowering brightness.

It has been most wonderful to meet you all, Good Arcturus said. The grass turned greener in the church ruins where his tendrils passed over it. *Thank you for helping me.*

He reached out with his many cold sinews, and I touched one in simple acknowledgment. But KJ dropped my hand and stepped forward. In the green light of the other universe, she hugged Good Arcturus tightly, with her eyes shut. She could not have hoped to get her arms around him. But he bowed way down, until he was embracing her in kind.

"I'll miss you," KJ said. She stepped back, wiping at her eyes.

I will miss you always, Katherine Jean. And if your people should ever come traveling . . .

"You'll be more hospitable than we were?" I asked.

Yes, Good Arcturus answered. *But it is immaterial. If your people should ever come traveling, they will find that we have always been waiting for them, because we are always together.*

No matter how many worlds stand betwixt us, we are all one. You are not alone.

Then he turned around for the last time, and stepped into the glowing green doorway. He drew it around himself as if it were a cloak, and it shimmered in the air, slipping away, disappearing with a ringing of bells, until nothing remained but the faint scent of that alien wind, and the miraculous blooms on the sunflowers behind us.

ACKNOWLEDGMENTS

I wish for other words to express my gratitude—some new turn of phrase that would really hammer home how much I mean it, without sounding cliché—but I don't have the secret language that shows my sincerity. Probably because writing is a joint effort, and these people made my work so much better with their own work, so I would need them all to workshop the acknowledgments with me to make them really good.

To Abby Ranger and Sarah Levison, my wonderful and clever editors, my agents Martha Perotto-Wills and Molly Ker Hawn, who are as talented as they are interesting (and they are VERY interesting)—and Tess Hamilton, Liam Donnelly, Amelia Mack, Stefanie Chin, Diane João, Castle Yurán, Chad O'Connell, Paul Benincasa, Amy E. Chace, and Sam Nardone: thank you so much for everything.

Tip of the hat to the Swift River Valley Historical Society (you guys don't know me and will never read this book, but my wife and I sat in on one of your presentations and listened to you all squabble about who was who and which island used to be what hill before the Quabbin was made, and it was amazing).

Allie: everything is for you. Thanks for loving me in my ruins ♥

ABOUT THE AUTHOR

Freddie Kölsch is a connoisseur and crafter of frightful fiction (with a dash of hope) for teens and former teens, and the author of *Now, Conjurers*. She lives in Salem, Massachusetts, with her high school sweetheart-turned-wife, a handful of cats, a houseful of art, and a mind's eye full of ghosts.